I0626598

The Sean O'Rourke Series

Book 3

O'Rourke's Revenge

by

Michael E. Cook

TELEMACHUS PRESS

The Sean O'Rourke Series, Book 3, O'Rourke's Revenge

The publisher does not have any control over and does not assume any responsibility for author or third-party websites or their content.

Cover art and design by Telemachus Press, LLC with assistance from Beatrice Gallaugher

Published by Telemachus Press, LLC
http://www.telemachuspress.com

Contact the author at mailto:cookorourkeseries@gmail.com

ISBN: 978-1-942899-51-8 (eBook)
ISBN: 978-1-942899-52-5 (Paperback)

Version 2015.11.16

10 9 8 7 6 5 4 3 2 1

Table of Contents

The Sean O'Rourke Series

Book 3

O'Rourke's Revenge

CHAPTER ONE

After the five men left for Ft. Worth, Sean went to the bunkhouse to take a count of the twelve dead men's weapons. He had told Flying Eagle that the Kiowa could have all the weapons. It was still pretty messy in the bunkhouse. Besides all the blood, there were pieces of skull and brain all over the place. Sean rounded up every weapon and all the ammunition and took it outside. There were ten rifles total not counting Anderson's Henry. Eight of them were Henrys and the other two were Spencers. Of the eight Henrys, six of them were damaged so badly that they couldn't be used. Four of those had their stocks shot off next to the receivers, plus their magazines shot off. Two of them had been hit on the receiver and were bent so much that the action wouldn't work. The other two just had the magazines bent a little, and holes in their stocks, but could probably still be used. One of the Spencers was missing a hammer. The other one had been hit two times on the receiver and the action wouldn't work. There were twelve pistols, and only two of them were conversions. One of the conversions was missing a hammer, and one of the other pistols had its loading rod missing. There was not as much ammunition as Sean had expected. He figured that anyone working for Anderson would be well supplied. Maybe there was more ammunition in the house, but he wouldn't worry about that now.

The Kiowa picked out the weapons they wanted and with the extra horses, were on their way. Sean could tell that the Kiowa were disappointed about the weapons, but they were glad to get what they could. Sean told them that he and his men would be staying at the place for a week. Then they would go to Ft. Worth. He told the Kiowa that it would be all right with him if they burned the place down after he left.

Sean and his men were pretty shot up, and he needed someone to take care of their horses, so he went to the cook shack to ask the cook if he would stay for a week. "We need someone to look after the horses for us," said Sean. "Would you be willing to stay? I'll pay you for your time. I'll also give you a month's pay like I did those other men."

"Sure, I'll do that for you," he said. "I got nowheres to be right now anyhow. I can help with the cookin' too if that woman needs help. By the way, name's Joe, Joe Taylor."

"Pleased to know you Joe," said Sean. "You got a cook wagon, don't you?"

"Sure do. We can use it to help take you and your boys outta here when you're ready to go," said Joe. "Don't reckon you all will be up ta ridin' for a spell."

"You're right there, Joe," said Sean. "That big geldin' a mine is a smooth ride, but a wagon'll be a might easier on me and the boys. Well I'm gonna go see how the boys are doin'. See you later."

When Sean went back to the house, Michael and Jon were asleep in some big fancy chairs in the entertaining room. Miss Sanchez was in the kitchen preparing the next meal. Sean went into the kitchen to talk with her. "Miss Sanchez, have you got any relatives around or anywhere to go after we leave here?" Sean asked her.

"My husband and I didn't have any children," she began. "My husband was Mexican, and he got himself killed fighting the French. My parents are long gone, and I have no idea where any of his family would be. I have been taking cooking jobs wherever I could get them. I should be able to find something. And would you please call me Barbara?"

"Sure, I'll call you Barbara," responded Sean. "I was thinkin' that maybe you would come to Kansas with us. Abilene is gonna grow soon, and I'm sure you could find work there. I got a lotta influence there, too. I can help you with a place to live while you're lookin' for work. As good as you are with bullet wounds, you could probably be a nurse anywhere. You're a handsome woman too. Could be you might find yourself a new husband."

"You are embarrassing me, Mr. O'Rourke," Barbara said. "I haven't thought about a man for some time. I suppose if a good one would come along, I could make myself available. I'll think about Kansas. We have plenty of time. I hope you and your men like my cooking."

"I'm sure we will," said Sean. "Now you can call me Sean. I have something to ask you."

"What can I do for you?" she asked.

"Michael was shot in the leg, and it might be too much for him to sleep upstairs," said Sean. "Would you mind letting him sleep in your room and you can have your pick of the rooms upstairs?"

"That will be all right with me," Barbara answered. "I'll get my things out of the room right after we eat."

Michael was awake now, and Sean could hear him saying something and went to the other room to see what he wanted. "Is there anything to drink around here?" Michael asked Sean.

"I'll see what our former host has in the house," said Sean. "I would say that Anderson had only the best." Sean looked around the entertaining room and didn't see evidence of any liquor. Then he went into the study. Sean came back out carrying two bottles and four glasses. "We're well supplied," said Sean. "There's a big cabinet in that room that is just clear full. I brought a bottle of Irish Whiskey and some good bourbon. What'll you have, my friend?"

"I'll have some of that Irish Whiskey," said Michael. "I haven't had any of that for years. You should try some too, my friend. The smoothness of it will amaze you."

"All right, my friend, I'll give it a try," said Sean. "Barbara, would you like a glass of whiskey too?"

"I'll try some of that Irish Whiskey too," she said. "I have heard that it's very smooth."

Jon was still asleep so Sean filled three glasses. "Oh my, that stuff is amazing." said Sean after he took a sip. "A fella could get himself drunk pretty quick drinkin' that stuff. It would go down so quick. How in the hell can they make that stuff so smooth?"

"I don't know," answered Michael. "Sure is good, isn't it? What do you think, Barbara?"

"I think a person could get hooked on this stuff very easily," she answered. "I've never had anything like this before."

Jon was starting to wake up now. "So you all are drinkin' without me," said Jon. "Somebody get me a glass." Sean poured Jon a glass of the Irish Whiskey. "Whoa, this is some good stuff," said Jon after he took a sip. "Let's make sure we take this stuff with us when we leave if there's any left."

"There's a liquor cabinet in the next room and it's clear full," said Sean. "We'll take all of it with us when we go. We'll try some of this bourbon next. I'm gonna go ask Joe if he would like a drink. Don't wanna be selfish." Sean left the house and returned in a few minutes with Joe. "Try some a this Irish Whiskey," said Sean. "You'll like it for sure." Sean went to the study and got a glass for Joe.

"I never had nothin' like this before," said Joe. "It goes down too good. Are you sure it's whiskey?"

"Yes, I'm sure," said Sean. "We'll have some bourbon next and you can decide which one you like the best."

When everyone was finished with the Irish Whiskey, Sean got everyone a fresh glass and poured the bourbon. "This is some damn good bourbon," said Sean. "Anderson musta liked good liquor." Everyone enjoyed the bourbon, but no one could decide which of the two whiskeys they liked better. "I could drink either one of them any time," said Sean.

"Same for me," said Jon and Michael.

When mealtime came, they all sat at the kitchen table. Barbara had made a stew because it would be easier for the men to eat. Everyone thought the food was great. Joe was asking her what she used for seasonings and such. After the meal, Joe helped Barbara with the dishes. "How bout I hang around and help with the next meal," said Joe. "Mebbe I can learn somethin' from ya. When yer out on a drive, it sure helps if the men are happy about what they're eatin'."

"Sounds good," said Barbara. "After breakfast in the morning, you and I can look around and see what's here, and figure out what we'll have for supper tomorrow."

The next morning after breakfast, Sean had a talk with Jon and Michael in the big room. "I told the Kiowa we'd only be here for a week," started Sean. "Joe's gonna take us outta here in his wagon. We'll use a buckboard too if needed. I figure we'll go to Ft. Worth and catch a stage that can get us to the closest train station. We should be able to take a train all the way to Kansas City and then take a stage to Abilene. Does that sound all right to you men?"

"What about the horses?" asked Jon. "I'd kinda like to keep my horse."

"We'll take'm with us," said Sean. "I intend to keep that big red a mine too. The railroad should be able to come up with a stock car for us. What about you, Michael? Are you wantin' to keep your horse?"

"I've spent half my life in the cavalry, so I'm used to havin' different horses," said Michael. "Makes no difference to me."

"All right then, we'll take the horses with us," said Sean. "You men keep gettin' your rest. I'm gonna look around this house and see what I can find. I bet Anderson's got a bunch of ammunition stashed somewhere in here."

Sean started his search upstairs with Anderson's bedroom. There were two big closets and a chest of drawers. One of the closets was full of fancy clothes and shoes and boots. The other closet was full of ammunition. Sean figured there must have been 10,000 rounds of Henry ammunition, and another 2000 rounds of Sharps ammunition. There was also a few hundred rounds of .44 pistol ammunition and 1000 rounds of Spencer ammunition. The bottom drawer of the chest of drawers was full of shotgun shells. "Me'n the boys won't hafta buy any ammunition for quite a while," Sean said to himself. "It's a good thing we're usin' Joe's wagon." No more ammunition was found anywhere. The pistol that Anderson had used to shoot Bob was laying on the bed, and his LeMat was under the chest of drawers. The LeMat was loaded, but Sean could not find any other caps or balls for it.

The days went by quickly, and the men tried to rest as much as they could. Sean felt sorry for Jon. He and Michael both had slings for their left arms, but Jon had a sling for each arm. Barbara checked them every day to make sure they were healing well and there was no infection. Sean was impressed with the care she gave them. During this time, Jeb decided that Sean was going to be his new master. Sean didn't mind.

When it was time to leave, they needed the wagon and a buckboard to haul everything. The ammunition and the liquor took up a lot of space. Joe drove his wagon and Michael and Jon rode in the back. Barbara drove the buckboard and Sean sat beside her. Jeb and Dog followed. It was winter, but it was not cold yet. They took some canvas with them so they could build shelters if necessary. It took them three days to get to Ft. Worth and they had no problems on the journey.

Upon their arrival in Ft. Worth, Sean went straight to the Marshal's office. When he walked in the front door, the Marshal was half asleep at his desk. Sean let out a short whistle to wake him. "Sorry to wake you, Marshal," began Sean. "Name's O'Rourke, Federal Marshal O'Rourke. Got a bit a news for you."

"So yer really him. Yer really that man that shoots so good." said the Marshal. "Pleased to meet you," he said as he extended his hand to Sean. "Name's Mark Sims. What can I do fer you?"

"First off, George Anderson is dead. Me and my deputies killed him and a buncha his men," began Sean. "The fella you knew as Thomas Sanderson was really George Anderson."

"Are you fer real, mister?" Mark said. "He seemed like a nice fella to everone here."

"Well he was not a nice fella," replied Sean. "I knew him from when we were kids back in Tennessee. He was Anderson all right. Now I hear he had beef contracts with a buncha army posts around here. If he did, I'd take it kindly if you'd send a telegram to the army and tell them they better get their beef somewhere else."

"I can do that fer ya," said Mark. "Looks like you and yer boys been shot up some. We got us a good doctor here."

"We got a good nurse with us," said Sean. "Now I need to know when the next stage is leavin'. We need to get a stage that'll get us to the nearest train station so we can get back to Kansas."

"Next stage should be leavin' in bout four hours," said Mark. "That clerk'll know about the closest train station."

"I thank you." said Sean. "Is there a freight office in this town in case our stuff won't all fit on the stage?"

"The stage depot is just down the street and there's a freight office right beside it," said Mark. "Can't miss it."

"I thank you again," said Sean. "Now I got a favor to ask of you, Mark."

"Sure Marshal, what do you need?" Mark asked.

"I'd really appreciate it if you wouldn't tell anyone that me and my boys killed Anderson and some a his bunch till we're outta town," said Sean. "Might cause some gunplay. Me and the boys are shot up some, but we'll hit what we shoot at if we have to."

"I understand," said Mark. "Won't say a word and I won't send that telegram till yer gone."

They all went to the stage depot and Sean showed the clerk everything that they intended to take with them. "All of that stuff will not fit on the stage," the clerk said. "If I was you, I'd talk to the freight office. They do a good job."

"Thank you very much," said Sean. "I'll do that. Now we're gonna need four tickets that'll get us to the closest train station so we can get to Kansas."

"That'll be no problem. You four are the only customers I got for the next stage," the clerk said. "That'll be $16, and the stage should be leavin' in just under four hours." Sean paid the clerk, thanked him, and then went next door to the freight office.

"I got some stuff I need shipped up to Abilene Kansas," said Sean. "It'll need crated up too."

"We can do it for you," the freight clerk said. "Show me what you got, and we'll get started cratin' it up." Sean showed the man what they needed shipped. He could tell that the clerk was astonished by all the ammunition and the liquor.

"Are you a drinkin' man?" Sean asked him.

"I appreciate good whiskey just like any man should," the clerk answered.

"Well we got plenty," said Sean. "You pick yourself out two bottles. Consider it a gift since my men and I can't help you much with the unloadin'."

"I got a man out back," the clerk said. "I'll get him, and we'll get it done. I'll guarantee that no bottles will get broken during shipment unless there would be a natural disaster like a flood or a cyclone or somethin'. By the way, my name is George Claybourne. Pleasure to do business with you."

"I'm Sean O'Rourke," said Sean as he extended his hand. "Pleasure to meet you."

"I've heard that name O'Rourke," said George. "Are you that Marshal that everyone's talkin' about?"

"Yes I am," said Sean. "Could you keep that to yourself till we get outta town shortly."

"I will," said George. "It's an honor to meet you. Hope you get that Anderson son of a bitch soon. He killed some a my kin back in Missouri."

"We'll get him," said Sean. "He's number one on the hangin' list."

After Joe's wagon was unloaded, he said his goodbyes and took off heading south. He was hoping to get hired on at a ranch or whatever he could find. He learned a few things from Barbara and was hoping to try them out soon. Sean found the livery and sold the buckboard and the extra horses. They found a small eatery and had a meal while they waited on the stage.

The stage left on schedule, and they were still the only passengers. There would be four horse changes before they got to the nearest train station. On the third change, they picked up another passenger. He looked like a gambler to Sean, but he never said one word after he first boarded the stage. He gave a second look when he saw that all the other men were wearing slings but didn't speak. He slept all the way to the next stop. Their horses were tied to the stage, so every stop, Sean got out and made sure the horses got a drink and a little feed.

The train ride worked out well. They would only change trains once before getting to Kansas City. The train wasn't crowded so they could stretch out and sleep all they wanted. On the train ride, Jon told Sean that he wanted to take some time off and decide what he wanted to do. "I got a baby comin' and I wanna be around to see him grow up," said Jon. "I need to make up my mind about this job. I been shot five times in the last three to four years. That's enough for a while."

"You take all the time you need," said Sean. "I'll go along with whatever you decide."

"Thanks Sean," said Jon. "Me and Dog'll get off somewhere before we get to Kansas City. It'll be closer to Cherokee Territory for us. I'll send you a telegram now and again."

When it came time for Jon to leave, Sean and Michael gave him a hug and a handshake as best they could. "You take it easy on horseback," said Sean. "You're gonna be sore for a while yet. Stay in touch so I can get your money to you. Dog, you make sure he does all right and keep him outta trouble."

When they got to Kansas City, Sean sent a telegram to Maggie and told her when they should be in Abilene. They would spend the night in Kansas City and leave the next morning. Barbara was amazed in Kansas City. She had never been to a city that was that big. Sean found a livery for the horses, then got each of them a hotel room. Michael went to his room and went to sleep. Sean took Barbara downtown and let her do a little shopping. Sean went to the bank and withdrew some money. There was a saloon downstairs at the hotel that also served food, so when they got back, they got Michael and went downstairs for a meal. Jeb went with them. They took a table, and the bartender came over and asked what they needed. "Bring us a glass of your best whiskey," said Sean. "And what do you have in the way of food in here?"

"We got a good cook here," the bartender said. "I'll bring you a menu when I bring your drinks over. I'll get that dog a pan of water. That dog sure looks familiar. There was a lawman in here a while back that had a dog that looked just like this one."

"Probly same dog," said Sean. "My deputy was here sometime back when he drove a herd here."

"Where's your deputy?" asked the bartender.

"He's dead," answered Sean. "His dog claimed me now."

"I'm sorry for your loss," the bartender said. "He seemed like a good man."

"He was a good man," said Sean. "I'll miss him."

"I'll get those drinks and menus," the bartender said. "How bout I get that dog a steak, uncooked of course?"

"That'll be just fine," said Sean.

They ate their meal, had another drink, and went to their rooms. Sean had a hard time getting to sleep thinking of Maggie. Michael had the same problem with Betty. Barbara couldn't sleep either. She was going to a new place and would meet new people. Hopefully, she would be accepted.

When the stage pulled into Abeline, Maggie, Betty, and Lolita were there waiting. Maggie ran to Sean and they hugged and kissed till they were out of breath. Betty did the same to Michael. Lolita introduced Barbara to Maggie and Betty and then gave Barbara a good hug. Sean instructed Lolita to show Barbara to a room upstairs, or outback if she preferred, and then he and Maggie headed to their room. No one saw them till late the next day. When they got to their room, Sean told her, "I been shot again. Take it a little easy on me."

"I can do easy," said Maggie. "I have missed you, my lover. I can do easy for a long time."

No one saw Michael and Betty till late the next day also. "We gotta get you healed up, you big Irish hunk," said Betty. "We gotta get married soon."

"I'll heal as fast as I can," said Michael. "Don't wanna be limpin' when it's time to dance. Now let's have some more of that healin' you've been givin' me."

The next evening, both couples were at their regular table for the evening meal. "I have some sad news, darlin'," started Maggie. "Right after you left, Cookie's wife caught pneumonia. She hung on for two weeks, but Doc Rawlins couldn't save her. Cookie's not sure what he wants to do now. Lolita's been doing all the cooking. Jug's been helping out wherever he was needed."

"I feel for him," said Sean. "I hope he figures out what he wants to do. Was there any other trouble while we were gone?"

"Nothing serious happened," said Maggie. "One evening, some man saw Lolita and said something out of line and Jug broke his jaw."

"That's how it should be," said Sean. "A man should stand up for his woman. That Barbara Sanchez is a good cook. She was Anderson's cook at his ranch, and she cooked for us for a week while we were healing up some. Her and Lolita can work together in the kitchen till we see what Cookie's gonna do."

"She's already in the kitchen with Lolita," said Maggie.

"That's good," replied Sean. "Once I give Jug his reward money for Anderson, he and Lolita might decide to move on. I was gonna give him the whole $2000. I got plenty of money to give Jon and Michael. Bob left all his money to me. He made a bunch from that cattle drive. We got us a dog now too. Jeb here decided I'm his now . Hope you don't mind."

"I like that dog too," said Maggie. "He can't sleep in the bed with us though."

"No, he won't be in bed with us, but he can sleep at the foot of the bed if that's all right with you," said Sean. "That dog's like you, darlin'. Neither one a you is gonna let anything bad happen to us. Now if it's all right with you, I'd like to get some real sleep now. Didn't sleep much on the stage or the train. "

The next morning when Sean woke up, he felt really good. His wounds weren't hurting at all. "You go ahead and sleep, dar-lin'," he said to Maggie. "I'm goin' down and get some coffee." Sean and Jeb went downstairs and Jug was setting at the usual table drinking coffee. "Just the man I wanna see," said Sean. "Got somethin' very important to tell you."

"I'll get you some coffee," said Jug as he got up and headed to the kitchen. He brought back a full pot and another cup for Sean. "Now what you got that's so important?" asked Jug.

"I'm gonna give you all the reward money for Anderson, $2000," said Sean.

"What about your men?" said Jug. "They deserve some of it."

"I got plenty of money for them," said Sean. "They'll be fine. Now just what would you do with that kinda money?"

"That gets a man ta thinkin'," said Jug. "I always wanted my own ranch. That might get us a good start."

"Well if all them longhorns in Texas are free for the takin', all you need is a place and some good men," said Sean. "Tell you what. If you're serious about ranchin', I'll stake you. You can pay me back on your first drive. Maybe it'll be to Abilene."

"I know ranches are sellin' for just back taxes," said Jug. "That's how Anderson got his. I'll talk to Lolita and see if she wants to do this. Ranchin' can be lonely for a woman. Reckon we'll hafta have a buncha kids too. You're a good man, Sean O'Rourke. I'm proud to call you my friend. If I do good, I'll pay you back with interest."

Sean and Jug were enjoying their coffee when three men came into the saloon. All three of them were wearing cavalry hats and one of them had something long and black hanging from his belt. They sat at a table at the other end of the saloon. Tom went over and asked what they needed, and they ordered a bottle of whiskey and three glasses. Sean wasn't too concerned about them, but he still kept an eye on them. Jug could tell that Sean was watching the three men. "Are we gonna expect trouble from those three?" asked Jug.

"I'm not sure," answered Sean. "I'm just keepin' an eye on them. I think one of those fellas has a scalp hangin' from his belt. Let's see how they act when that whiskey bottle is about empty."

Sean and Jug sipped their coffee and talked about ranching and such while still keeping an eye on the three men. As the bottle got emptier, the three men's conversation got louder and louder. One of them sounded like a big braggart. He said something about riding with Chivington and being at Sand Creek. Jug saw a change come over Sean when they heard the man say Sand Creek. The only time he had ever seen a look on a man's face like that was during the war. Jug knew something was going to happen.

Sean had two pistols on him and he checked them to make sure they were fully loaded. Then he got up and walked over to the table where the three men were sitting. Jeb went with him. "Did I hear one a you say somethin' about Sand Creek?" Sean said.

"I did," said the braggart. "I rode with Chivington and proud of it. We killed us a buncha redsticks that day. Got me a scalp here ta prove it."

Sean was able to see the scalp now. Something shiny with a long chain was hanging from the man's belt with the scalp. Sean knew right away that this was the necklace that he had bought for Katie and gave to Blue Swan when he had left the Cheyenne. Rage was overtaking him. Jeb had a low growl going. "Where did you get that scalp and that necklace?" Sean asked him.

"It's from a redstick bitch I kilt," he said. "She was older, but she was a looker."

Sean pulled a pistol and stuck the muzzle of it right in the man's left eye. "You're gonna die mister," said Sean. "I'll give you your choice on how . There's three choices. One, I'll put my pistol back in my holster, and you can try to pull your pistol and kill me. Two, I can beat you to death with my fists. Three, I can take you out to Indian territory and give you to some Cheyenne Dog Soldiers. You got one minute to think about it."

"Mister, you git yer damn pistol outta my eye and we'll see who's gonna kill who," the braggart said. "I know who you are. Yer that damn Marshal that everone is so scared of. Well I'm not a scared a you. I think I'll scalp you too after I shoot you dead. I hear yer worth a lotta money and I could sure use that bounty money."

Sean was having a very hard time controlling himself. He wanted so badly to blow this man's head off, but he got control of his anger. "All right, you piece a scum," said Sean, "I'm gonna take this pistol and put it back in my holster. Then I'm gonna back up a couple steps and you're gonna stand up and try to pull your pistol. You other two fellas will put your hands on the table and leave them there or I'll kill you too." Sean started backing up as soon as the two men had their hands on the table. As soon as Sean started his second step, the braggart started to stand. As he was starting to stand, he was also reaching for his pistol. Before he was completely standing and before he had even touched his pistol, he was falling backwards. The back of his head exploded and blood went flying everywhere. Sean stood there with the smoking pistol in his hand watching the man fall. Then he turned the pistol on the other two men. "Am I gonna hafta kill you fellas too?" asked Sean.

The two men were shaking from fear. One of them had an accident in his pants. "Please don't kill us Marshal," one of them pleaded. "Neither one a us killed no Injuns at Sand Creek. I swear on my momma's grave. Let us live and I'll tell you all about us."

Sean put his pistol back in his holster and stood there staring at the two men. "Go ahead and tell me all about yourself," said Sean. "I'm pretty good at spottin' a liar too."

"My name is Josh Sims and this other fella is Wayne Collins," Josh began. "We was both in the 1st Colorado Cavalry. I was at Sand Creek, but I never shot no Injuns. My Company Commander was a fella by the name of Captain Silas Soule. I was in Company D. When the orders came down for us to start firin' and such, Captain Soule give us orders to stay put and not shoot. He said we was not gonna kill no women and kids. All the other companies commenced to killin'. Wayne here was in the same company, but he was back in the hospital with a bad case of the "screamers." He damn near died. After the massacre, they had some investigations cause they heard about the women and kids and what was done to 'em. Captain Soule testified against Chivington. A few weeks after he testified, the Captain was murdered. Never found out who done it. Me and Wayne got mustered out not long after that."

"I heard they had some investigations after the massacre, but I never heard about your Captain," said Sean. "Sounds like he was a good man. So why are you with this other piece a scum and why are you around here?"

"That other fella's name was Dave Woods," said Josh. "He got mustered out bout same time we did. He was a loud mouth braggart, but we hung around together figurin' it would be safer on our way down to Texas. We was over around Ft. Wallace and we heard stories about this beautiful redhead in Abilene, so we had to come and have a look-see. That paintin' bout takes my breath away."

"That gorgeous woman is my wife, and that's her coming down the stairs now," said Sean. "She came down to see who's dead now." Maggie walked over to Sean and gave him a hug and then saw the dead man on the floor. Sean could see that Josh and Wayne were mesmerized by Maggie's beauty.

"Pardon me ma'am if I don't stand up," said Wayne to Maggie. "I done had an accident and it would be embarrassin' for me to stand up and greet you proper. Yer the most beautiful creature I ever did see. I can tell Josh here thinks the same. My name is Wayne."

"Why thank you Wayne, and you can call me Maggie," said Maggie. "I'm sorry if my husband caused you to have an accident. He can have that affect on some folks." Then Maggie looked down at the dead man.

"You shot his eyes out," exclaimed Maggie. "I only heard one shot and both of his eyes have been shot out. How did you do that?"

"I fired twice, darlin'," answered Sean. "They was so close together it sounded like one."

"Why'd you shoot his eyes out?" asked Wayne.

"It's got to do with the afterlife," answered Sean. "Some Indians believe that if you have no eyes, you wonder around in the afterlife and will never be able to see where you're goin'."

"Do you believe that, Sean?" asked Maggie.

"Don't matter if I do or not," answered Sean. "Blue Swan believed it and that fella killed her so that's why I shot his eyes out."

"So that's why some tribes mutilate bodies after they kill'em?" asked Josh. "Like if they cut off your hands, you won't have no hands to use in the afterlife."

"Yep, that's what they believe," answered Sean. "I 'spect most folks think they do it outta just plain meanness." Sean looked to his left across the room and saw Jug standing there with a shotgun in his hands. "You can put that thing away now Jug," said Sean. "These fellas won't be no trouble. Thanks for bein' there. How bout you two fellas help get this body over to the barber shop.? You can check his pockets and keep whatever you find. Be a good place for a person to change his pants after havin' an accident seein' as how they got a bath house there too. The livery'll buy his horse and saddle, and the general store'll probably buy his pistol. After you do all that, then you give a few dollars to the barber to pay for buryin' him. The rest is yours. Just why are you two goin' to Texas anyhow?"

"We both spent some time workin' cows and we figured we could get a job on a ranch if there's any of'em still workin' now that the war's over," said Josh.

"Jug here might start himself up a ranch before too long," said Sean. "He just came up from Texas not long ago. You oughta talk to him some."

"I thank you," said Josh. "Now me and Wayne'll git this body outta here and take care of the other business."

"Leave that scalp and necklace boys," said Sean. "I'm not sure what I'll do with them, but leave'em lay. Maggie, would you get me a shoe box or somethin'? I'll keep'em in that till I decide what to do with'em. I wish Braddock was here. He might have somethin' special in mind."

"Don't some Indians use burial platforms?" asked Maggie.

"Yes they do," answered Sean. "I'll probably do that or just have a burial. I'll think on it for a while."

Maggie found a box and Sean placed the scalp and necklace inside and took it upstairs to their room. He put the box under the bed and came back downstairs.

Just as the body was being dragged out, Michael showed up. "I heard the shootin' so I figured I better come and see who's dead now," said Michael. "Was it anybody that we know?"

"That fella was at Sand Creek, and he killed and scalped Blue Swan," said Sean. "He won't hurt no more women or kids ever again."

"Are you sure it was him, young Sean?" asked Michael.

"Yes I am." answered Sean. "He had that necklace that I had bought for Katie and gave to Blue Swan when I left the Cheyenne."

"Who were those men taking out his body?" asked Michael.

"They was ridin' with that fella on their way to Texas," said Sean. "They was both in the Colorado Cavalry, but they never killed no one. I believed the story they told me. If I didn't, they'd be dead too. I'm hungry now. Jeb, how bout you and me and Maggie go see what Lolita's fixin' up for breakfast?"

CHAPTER TWO

Sean and Maggie sat at their regular table eating their breakfast. Jeb was right beside Maggie and Michael was at the table drinking coffee. "Me and Betty are gonna get ourselves married next week if Jason can do the honors," said Michael. "I'm healin' up good and I should be able to dance all I want after the weddin'."

"That's great Michael," said Maggie. "We'll have Lolita make us a good feast and we'll get the blacksmith to play his fiddle. We'll have a great time. Are you two going on a honeymoon right away?"

"Betty wants to go someplace big back east, so we might go to Chicago or even as far as Philadelphia or Washington D.C.," said Michael. "With all the trains they have now, it doesn't take too long to get anywhere over east. That is, if young Sean can spare me to be gone that long."

"You two go anywhere you want for as long as you want," said Sean. "We'll still be here when you get back. Stay in one a them real fancy hotels where they wait on you hand and foot. Have breakfast in bed. Drink some champagne. Eat some food that has funny names that you never heard of before. You're a good man, Michael O'Connor. You and Betty deserve the best."

"I believe we'll do just that," said Michael. "Now I'm gonna go talk with Jason and see what day is good for him next week."

~~~~

Sean and Maggie stayed at their table and drank some more coffee. "I'll talk with Lolita and Barbara and let them know about the wedding," said Maggie. "I bet they can come up with something special."

"I'll need to talk to Jug and see if he's made any decision about goin' back down to Texas," said Sean. "With Michael leavin' soon, I'd like it if Jug would stick around till Michael and Betty get back. Have you heard anything from Cookie recently?"

"I heard he's going back east to visit some of his wife's relatives. Then he intends to come back to work," said Maggie. "If Jug and Lolita go back to Texas, I just know that Cookie and Barbara will get along great."

"Cookie and Barbara are both easy goin' people and get along with everyone," said Sean. "Who knows what might happen if them two work together."

"Sean, you should be ashamed of yourself," said Maggie. "The man's wife just died and you're getting him married off already. Shame on you."

"Yep, shame on me," said Sean. "But you gotta admit, Barbara is one fine woman and Cookie is a darn fine man. Some folks don't need as long to grieve as other folks."

"You are right darlin'," said Maggie. "Now I better get that mess that you made cleaned up some. Maybe we should have a rule about shootings. They need to be outside."

"That would make sense darlin'," replied Sean. "I'll try to remember that from now on. Now I'll get Jug and find out what he's gonna do."

~~~~

Jug was over behind the bar helping get ready for the day's business. Sean motioned for him to come over to his table. "Have a seat Jug," said Sean. "I need to know if you have given much thought about what you'll be doin' with all that money."

"Me and Lolita decided we'll be goin' back down to Texas and startin' our own ranch," said Jug. "We was gonna wait till spring before we headed out."

"That's good that you're waitin' till spring," said Sean. "We still got a little winter left. It hasn't been too cold yet, but you never know when it could be. I was hoping you'd stick around till Michael and Betty got back from their honeymoon. You not leavin' till spring will work out good. Is Lolita sure she wants to be a rancher's wife? It can be pretty lonely for a woman."

"She knows it could be lonely," said Jug. "But we're not gonna be like other ranch folks. She can ride and she's gonna be right out there with me movin' cows and such. I'll have her ropin' and brandin' in no time. When we make our first drive, she'll be right there with me."

"That sounds good Jug," replied Sean. "But she won't be able to do all those things if she's got a baby on the way."

"We decided we would wait a year and a half to two years before we had any kids," said Jug. "That'll give us some time to get set up and such without worryin' bout kids. Lolita says she knows about times when she's fertile and times when she isn't. I don't know such things. If kids come before we're ready, I reckon we'll love'm just the same."

"You got a good woman Jug," said Sean. "You two will do good. Those two fellas that were at that table when I shot that other fella will be wantin' to talk to you. They say they spent some time workin' cows and was goin' down to Texas lookin' for ranch work."

"I'll talk to 'em," said Jug. "There's an awful lotta men lookin' for work but there's not that many men who know how to work longhorns. They can be downright mean and dangerous at times. I'm gonna go help Tom now if you don't need me for anything else. We got a whole wagon of whiskey due in today."

"Go ahead and help Tom," said Sean. "I think me and Jeb'll take a stroll around town and talk to folks. I'll let'em know about the weddin' next week too."

~~~~

Sean went to the leather goods store first to see Jason. Jason and his son were in the back room putting away their last delivery. "Michael just left here," said Jason. "We'll be doin' the wedding next Wednesday."

"That's what I came to hear," said Sean. "Now I can go spread the word to everyone."

"What was that shootin' we heard earlier?" asked Jason. "It wasn't another fool lookin' to collect that bounty that was on you, was it?"

"No, it was the man who killed my mother-in-law at Sand Creek," said Sean. "He won't be killin' any women or kids again. Now I'll be on my way. See you at the weddin'."

"Pa, did he say that man killed his mother-in- law?" Jason's son asked.

"Yes he did," answered Jason. "Sean was married a while back to a woman whose mother was a Cheyenne and her father was a mountain man. Sean lived with them when he was with the Cheyenne. His wife and child died of the cholera, and then Sean left the Cheyenne and ended up in the Union Army. Sean's folks were at Sand Creek when that idiot Chivington massacred the women and children. I heard his father-in-law got away and went back to the mountains."

"How did Sean know that was the man who killed her?" asked Greg.

"I don't know son," answered Jason. "But he knew. Sean is not the kind of man who would kill for no reason."

"I s'pose you're right Pa," said Greg. "I sure hope I never have to kill someone."

"I hope so too," said Jason. "It's not something you ever forget. No matter what, it's always there in your head somewhere."

Sean made his rounds and let everyone in town know about Michael and Betty's wedding. The blacksmith said that he had been practicing some new tunes and was ready to try them out. While he was making his way around town, Sean decided to send a telegram to the Judge. It went as follows:

Judge David Simmons
Federal Court House, St. Louis

would like to take some time off << stop >> one deputy getting married and will be gone for month or more<<

stop>> other deputy not sure if will stay a deputy<<
stop>> notify me if needed

O'Rourke

Sean made his way back to the saloon. Maggie was straight-
ening up some tables and chairs. Jeb was beside her. Sean went to
Maggie, wrapped his arms around her, and kissed her very passionately. "How would you feel about takin' a bath right now?"
Sean asked Maggie.

"How about we go upstairs first, then take a bath after," said
Maggie. Before Maggie had finished talking, Sean had her arm
and was leading her upstairs to their room. Clothes went flying
everywhere. After what seemed like hours, they laid there in each
other's arms.

"Maggie darlin', I will love you forever," said Sean. "I can't
wait till tomorrow because I love you more each day."

"I will love you forever, too," said Maggie. "Now what brought
that on? You read that last line in a book or heard it somewhere,
didn't you??

"I heard it somewhere once," answered Sean. "Can't remember when or where, but it sure sounds good, don't it."

"Yes it does, darlin', especially when you say it to me," said
Maggie.

"I sent a telegram to the Judge and told him I wanted to take
some time off," said Sean. "I reckon he won't mind unless somethin' serious happens somewhere. Do you reckon you can stand
havin' me around for a spell?"

"I can always stand having you near me," said Maggie. "I miss you and worry about you more than I can say when you're gone. " Then Maggie pulled him to her and they were again making love.

"If this keeps up, we may never make it to the tub," Sean said when they were done. "Not that I mind though."

"Let's get to the tub," said Maggie. "I want to get in that nice hot water and soak with you. I might even have my way with you again."

"I'll get down there and start heatin' up some water," said Sean. "You just stay here for a while and look beautiful."

"You always have the right thing to say, darlin'," said Maggie. "I'll be down shortly."

~~~~

The water was heated in no time. They spent a full two hours enjoying the tub. "I just love this tub," said Maggie. "I never did ask you how you got it."

"I had my friend Sam Draper get it for me," said Sean. "If you remember, I told you about him. He owns "The Palace" in St. Louis. I told him to find me the biggest, best, and most beautiful tub he could find. He surely did."

"Yes, he surely did," said Maggie. "Let's see if we can decide what the animals mean."

"Well I know what the female lions mean," began Sean. "The female lion takes care of the business for lions. They do the huntin' and raise the cubs. The males only show up when they want to mate. So basicly, the woman are the bosses."

"How do you know that?" asked Maggie.

"I read it in a school book one time," said Sean. "Now I got no idea what these buffalo mean. Maybe it means they are majestic creatures. What do you think, darlin'?"

"I'll go along with that," answered Maggie. "I'm sure the doves stand for purity and innocence and such, but I'm not sure about the eagles."

"Well eagles are probly the biggest birds around here, and they are good lookin' birds," said Sean. "Maybe they stand for the beauty of the country."

"That sounds reasonable," said Maggie. "Now you know all these naked ladies were put there to get you excited, don't you?"

"I'm always excited when I'm around you," said Sean as he pulled her to him and began kissing her passionately.

~~~~

It was another hour before they were dressed and setting at their regular table downstairs. "I need to eat," said Sean. "I gotta keep my strength up."

"I need some food too," said Maggie. "I'll get us a bottle and see what Lolita and Barbara have fixed for today."

~~~~

A few hours later, Josh and Wayne came back to the saloon. Both of them were wearing new clothes. "That fella at the livery musta thought that horse was somethin' special cause he give us $25 fer it and another $5 fer the saddle," said Josh as he and Wayne walked up to the bar. "We got $10 fer the pistol. With all that money, we decided it was time fer some new clothes. I'd like to buy everone a drink." Maggie, Sean, Michael, Jug, and Tom were the only ones in the saloon.

"That's not necessary," said Sean. "We own the place. How bout we buy you two a drink?"

"Sounds good ta us," said Josh. "I'll have a whiskey and a beer. I reckon Wayne'll have the same."

"Yep, that'll do fer me," replied Wayne. "So Jug, Sean says yer gonna start a ranch down Texas come spring."

"Yes, I am boys. Me'n Lolita'll be leavin' come spring," said Jug. "We'll be lookin' to buy a place south a Ft. Worth, but not too close to Comanche land. If you boys know cows, look me up when you get down there. Right now, there's not too many workin' ranches. Damn war bankrupted'em all. Should be able to get a place fer back taxes, and there's longhorns everwhere. Should be able to put a herd together in no time if I can get good help."

"Well me'n Josh know how to work longhorns, and we'll do ya right if ya take us on," said Wayne. "We'll be headin' that way come mornin'. We can look around and see what there is, and if'n we find a good place, we can send ya a telegram."

"You do that fer me, and I'll take ya on," said Jug. "I'll give ya some money fer the telegram before ya leave."

"Don't worry bout that," said Wayne. "Thanks to ole Dave, we got 'nough money fer that and to get by fer a spell."

"My last name is Carter," said Jug. "I'll be hopin' ta hear from you boys. You have a safe trip goin' down there. There's lotsa bad men and plenty a Comanche and Kiowa down there."

"We're gonna go down through Missouri and Arkansas and then over into Texas," said Josh. "Be a lot safer goin' that way.

We'll do our best ta find ya a place."The next morning, Josh and Wayne were on their way before daylight.

~~~~

Almost everyone in town was there for Michael and Betty's wedding. Sean was best man and Maggie was the Maid of Honor. Jug gave Betty away. The blacksmith played his fiddle and everyone danced and danced. Lolita and Barbara prepared a great feast. No one recognized some of the food, but they sure enjoyed it. For most of the people, it was the first time they had ever tasted Mexican food. There were several toasts too. The freight company had made a delivery to town the day before the wedding, and the liquor from Anderson's place was now at the saloon. Several bottles of the Irish Whiskey were consumed that day.

Michael and Betty were taking the morning stage heading east. Michael got very drunk at the wedding, and Sean was worried he would not be able to get up in time, but when the stage was ready, Michael and Betty were there. Michael looked like he hadn't been drunk the night before at all. As he was getting on the stage, Sean told him. "You have a great time, but don't get careless. A lot of people know you are my deputy. Keep yourself armed. Now you two enjoy yourselves."

"I'll keep my wits about me," said Michael. "Besides my revolver, I keep a knife in one a my pockets. We intend to have a good time, but we'll be careful too. Now I'll be back in a month or so. Hope things are quiet while we're gone."

~~~~

Just as the stage pulled out, the telegraph operator ran to Sean with a telegram. "This just came in for you, Marshal," he said as he handed the telegram to Sean. "I didn't know if it was real important or not, so I got it right to you."

"I appreciate that," said Sean.

The telegram read as follows:

Marshal Sean O'Rourke
Abilene, Kansas

Man named Braddock was here asking about you<< stop >> said he was your father in law << stop >> told him you were in Abilene<< stop>> headed your way two days ago

Captain Edward Maxwell
Ft. Wallace

Sean went back to the saloon to tell Maggie the news. "Maggie darlin', do you remember me tellin' you about Braddock?" asked Sean.

"Yes, I remember," answered Maggie. "You said you wished he was here the other day when you shot that man who killed Blue Swan."

"Well he's gonna be here in a few days," said Sean. "Captain Maxwell sent me a telegram from Ft. Wallace. I guess Braddock was there and was asking about me. It'll sure be good to see him after all these years. I'll let him decide what to do about Blue Swan's service."

"I knew that Captain was a gentleman," said Maggie.

CHAPTER THREE

One week later, Braddock rode into Abilene. Captain Maxwell had told him where to find Sean, so he went straight to the saloon. He was tying his horse to a hitching rail when Sean came out of the saloon and spotted him. Sean ran straight to him and gave him a huge bear hug. "I never thought I'd see you again," said Sean. "No, I never did. I don't know what to say." Then he hugged Braddock again.

"It's been lotsa years," said Braddock. "Just let me look at you." Braddock stood back and just looked at Sean. "You was always a good lookin' man," said Braddock. "I bet the women'r always after ya."

"I got me a good beautiful wife now," said Sean. "This saloon is ours. C'mon in and we'll have some drinks and talk, and you can meet Maggie."

"You say her name is Maggie?" said Braddock. "Well what do ya know about that. Just like you and Katie's child." When they entered the saloon, Braddock's eyes went straight to Maggie's painting. "Would that be Maggie there on the wall?" asked Braddock.

"Yep, that's her," answered Sean. "Her first husband was an artist. He painted that when they were first married several years ago. When you meet her shortly, you'll see that the painting doesn't do her justice."

"I don't know," said Braddock. "I can't figure any woman could look better than that." As soon as Braddock finished his words, Maggie came down the stairs to the saloon. Braddock's eyes were glued to her. "I take that back," said Braddock. "She is better'n that picture."

"Maggie, I got someone I want you to meet," said Sean. "This is Braddock. He was Katie's father."

"It's a great honor to finally meet you," said Maggie. "Sean has told me all about you and Blue Swan and Katie, and little Maggie too. Please take a seat and I'll bring you and Sean some of our best bourbon."

"Maggie, you are truly the most beautiful woman these old eyes have ever seen," said Braddock. "You and Sean look so good together."

"Thank you for your kindness," said Maggie. "I'll get the drinks now.'

~~~~

Sean took Braddock to his usual table. "I see why you sit back here," said Braddock. "You can see everything in here and no one can get behind you."

"Yep. that's why I sit here," said Sean. "Can't afford to get careless in my line a work. Now let's have a drink, and I want you to tell me about everything from when I left till right now."

~~~~

Maggie brought everything to the table and then excused herself. "You two need to be alone so you can talk," said Maggie. "I'll come back later when you've had a chance to catch up."

Sean thanked her then filled the glasses. "Here's to us," said Sean. "May the bad times be behind us. They both took a drink and then Sean asked Braddock if he would start filling him in on all those years.

"After you left, our band took up with another band cause we was so small after the cholera," started Braddock. " Black Wolf ended up bein' the Chief of our new clan. We followed the herds as always, but more and more, we run inta white folks. Black Kettle didn't want no trouble, but he couldn't always control some a the young warriors. Them Dog Soldiers went out raidin' whenever they wanted. Can't say as I blame'em. Everytime we turned around, them blue soldiers was havin' Black Kettle sign some treaty, and it was always broke in no time. This went on till we ended up at Sand Creek. I was out huntin' when them soldier boys came. Most of the other men were out huntin' too. Black Kettle had an American flag flyin' in front of his lodge. There was a white flag right below it. I was on my way back when I heard the shootin'. I darn near run my horse to death getting back. I got up on a high rise where I could see. The stuff them soldier boys was doin' would make most folks sick. I was mebbe three hunnerd yards away, but I spotted Blue Swan. She was on the ground tryin' ta fight off a soldier. I seen blood all over her. I got down and was taking aim on that fella. Just as I squeezed the trigger, another fella got in the way. That slug darn near took his head off. I tried to get another shot at that fella who was on Blue Swan, but there was too much confusion. I sighted in on another soldier and dropped him. Then I got back to my horse and got outta there. I knew Blue Swan was already dead. Them soldier boys was rapin' the women, and scalpin' them. They cut off arms and legs and breasts and was dancin' around with'em stuck on their sabers. They shot kids and when they was outta bullets, they smashed their heads with rifle butts. There musta been five ta six hunnerd soldier boys there."

"Well you don't hafta worry about that fella that killed Blue Swan," said Sean. "I killed him not long ago."

"Just how did you end up killin' him?" asked Braddock.

"Three fellas came into the saloon one day," started Sean. "As they got ta drinkin' they got louder and louder. I heard one of'em say somethin' about Sand Creek, so I went over to ask about it. One was a braggart. He had a scalp hangin' from his belt. He also had a necklace hangin' from his belt. It was that necklace I bought for Katie and give to Blue Swan when I left. I asked him where he got it, and he said he rode with Chivington and was proud of it. He said he got the scalp from some red stick bitch he kilt. I killed'em. I shot his eyes out. I got the scalp and necklace upstairs. I was still thinkin' about havin' some type a service or somethin'. Now that you're here, you can decide what to do."

"We'll have a buryin' tomorrow," said Braddock. "If we built a burial platform or put her scalp up in a tree, some dern fool might grab it. Some white folks think it's good business to sell scalps."

"So you went back to the mountains?" asked Sean. "How was that bein' alone after all that time with the Cheyenne?"

"It was good for about the first six months," said Braddock. "After that, things got bad. I didn't know it at the time, but after I shot them two soldier boys, someone saw me ridin' away. I don't know how they found out who I was, but that first soldier boy I shot had a big famly. One day I was settin' by the fire keepin' warm, and someone started shootin' at me. I shot back and hit'em good. Before he died, he told me that was his youngest brother I shot at Sand Creek. There was nine brothers and their Pa was a Hell Fire preacher back in Denver and he wanted an eye fer an eye. His name was Mose Crandall, the Reverend Mose Crandall. He told his boys if they didn't get me killed, he'd kill them. They been callin' me a "Renegade" and put up a bounty of $1000 on me. When I was in Ft. Wallace talkin' to that Captain Maxwell, he asked me all about it. He said he wasn't too happy about what happened at Sand Creek. Said he'd try to protect his famly too. He said if any a them Crandalls or bounty hunters showed up there lookin' fer me, he'd tell'em he hadn't seen nothin'."

"That Captain Maxwell is a good man," said Sean. "I hope he don't git himself killed. That bounty money will attract a lotta fools lookin' for some fast money. I know all about that."

"Well that's all about me," said Braddock. "Now tell me about you."

"After I left the Cheyenne, I wandered a little bit," said Sean. "I was gonna go to Texas cause I never been there. I made friends with some Kiowa on the way. Then I ran into an army patrol and I made friends with a Sergeant. He's a deputy a mine now. He just got married and is on his honeymoon. Be back in a month or so. Anyway, when that unit got ordered back east for the war, their Commander asked me to scout for 'em through Indian territory. I joined the army along the way. Before our first fight, I joined a group of sharpshooters."

"I never did see anyone that could shoot better'n you," said Braddock. "What was that war really like? I heard stories."

"It's just hard to even imagine," said Sean. "Can you imagine maybe thirty to fifty thousand people tryin' ta kill each other?

Just plain slaughter. Artillery blowin' the hell outta everything. Men and horses gettin' ripped ta pieces. I got wounded at Shiloh. That Sergeant, Michael is his name. Well he got wounded there too. We was at the same hospital. We started drinkin' our toast, "here's to not getting killed." We've used that toast many times, even after the war. While we was fightin' in Tennessee, I come across my old childhood sweetheart. Later on I got a furlough, and we fell in love and was gonna get married. She was killed by some Union deserters. I killed'em. That's when I met my boss, Judge Simmons. He was a Colonel then. He asked me to be a Federal Marshal after the war. I got wounded again around Atlanta and after I was healed up, I spent the last few month of the war doin' nothin'."

"Sounds like you was bein' looked out for," said Braddock.

"Maybe so, but soon as Lee surrendered , I got outta there and went to St. Louis," said Sean. "While I was there waitin' for Judge Simmons to get back from the war, I worked at a fancy saloon called "The Palace." Me and Michael decided we was gonna own a saloon after the war, so I was workin' there to learn the business. "

"I bet they had some good lookin' women at that place too, didn't they?" asked Braddock.

"They surely did," said Sean. "There was ten of'em."

"Well you was young," said Braddock. "I got no doubt you could handle em."

"Didn't last too long," replied Sean. "The Judge got back from the war and swore me in and I been all over Kansas, the Nations, and Texas after outlaws. I've had two deputies killed and the rest of us been shot up some. I met Maggie when I first come here. We been together ever since. We got married a while back. Me'n her'n

Michael are partners in this saloon. It's been a little quiet since we got Anderson killed a while back. I been takin' a little time off to enjoy the quiet."

"I remember you tellin' me about an Anderson sometime back," said Braddock. "Was he any relation to that outlaw?"

"He was that outlaw," said Sean. "It took us a while to get him killed, but we got it done. Sometime when we got a lot of time, there's a lot more stuff I can tell you. How bout for now, we just enjoy this good bourbon."

"Sounds good," replied Braddock. "If we keep reminiscin', we might end up cryin' in our liquor. Don't wanna do that."

"Let's have a couple more, then we'll get your horse over to the livery," said Sean. "I'll show you around the town, and then we'll get somethin' ta eat. We got us some really good cooks here. I got a room for you too."

~~~~

After they had their drinks, they took Braddock's horse to the livery. Braddock grabbed his bag of possibles and took his Sharps from the scabbard. "That Sharps looks like it's been took care of," said Sean."

"I took care a it and it took care a me," said Braddock. "It sure shoots true."

"The Sharps and that Walker I had got blowed up at Atlanta," replied Sean. "The Sharps I got now uses those new metallic cartridges. You'll be amazed when you see one of them cartridges. My pistols have been converted to metallic cartridges too. It sure is nice not havin' ta worry bout gettin' the powder wet."

"I heard a them cartridges, but never did see any yet," said Braddock. "It sure would be nice not worryin' bout wet powder."

"Well I'll see if I can get you fixed up with a new sharps," said Sean. "I got a gunsmith in St. Louis that does all kinds a work for me. I'll send'm a telegram and see what he says. We can stop by the telegraph office while I'm showin' you the town."

"I still got most a that money you give me when you and Katie got married," said Braddock. "I spent that little bit that time we went ta that town, and I bought a little whiskey ever once in a while after that. Buyin' a new Sharps won't be no financial burden."

~~~~

Sean took Braddock to every business in town, and then they went to the telegraph office. He sent the following telegram.

Walter Black Gunsmith
St. Louis

Need another Sharps same as before<< stop>> two hundred rounds ammo<< stop >> will send bank draft

Marshal O'Rourke
Abilene

After the telegram was sent , Sean and Braddock went back to the saloon. "We'll get us somethin' ta eat, then we'll have some Irish Whiskey," said Sean. "You'll be amazed at how smooth it is."

Braddock really enjoyed the meal. "I haven't et like that for who knows how long," he said. "I don't know what it was, but it sure et good."

"We got us some good cooks here," said Sean. "Both of'em do a lotta Mexican stuff. I never had that kinda stuff before, but I sure do like it myself. Now I'll go get us a bottle a that Irish Whiskey. Sean went to the bar and returned with everything. "Now remember, I told you this stuff was real smooth," said Sean.

"Are you sure this is whiskey?" asked Braddock after he took a sip. "It's got no kick to it. It tastes good, but I'd probly drink too much a it. I'll have a few more fore I pass judgement." After his fourth drink, Braddock started changing his mind about the whiskey. "This stuff does it's job," said Braddock. "I'm startin' ta feel darn good."

Sean could tell that Braddock was starting to notice the women. "How bout I introduce you to one a the girls," said Sean. "We got some real nice girls here."

"I've not been with a women since Blue Swan," said Braddock. "I'd feel guilty."

"Blue Swan wouldn't want you to turn into no priest," said Sean. "Now you just sit there and I'll bring one a the girls over." Sean was gone a few minutes, then he came back with Martha. Braddock got up and pulled out a chair for Martha. Sean was surpised by Braddock's manners. "Martha, this is Braddock. He was my father-in-law," said Sean. "Would you mind spending some time with him."

"I wouldn't mind spending the whole night with him if that's what he would like," said Martha.

"Well you have a drink now and tell me your life story before we get down to business," said Braddock. "I wanna tell you right now, lovely lady. I've not been with a women for a spell and I might have some rough edges."

"Soon as I finish this drink, I'll go take care of any rough edges you got," said Martha.

~~~~

They finished their drinks and Braddock led Martha to his room. Martha spent the whole night with him. The next morning when Braddock woke up, she was on top of him ready to go again. When they were finished and dressed, Braddock went to pay her. "That's already taken care of," said Martha. "I may just give Sean his money back. You didn't have any rough edges that I could find. I greatly enjoyed being with you. You made me feel needed, and a person in this line a work doesn't get that too often. Now if you need me anytime, I'll be available."

"If I was a younger man, I'd be available a lot," said Braddock.

"Them young boys got nothin' on you," said Martha as she was leaving. "Now remember what I said."

~~~~

Braddock made his way into the saloon. Sean was already there at the ususal table drinking some coffee. "You sure got a nice girl there with Martha," said Braddock. "If I was a young fella. Well anyway, let's get some breakfast and then have that service for Blue Swan."

CHAPTER FOUR

The Reverend Mose Crandall was born in Michigan in 1808. His given name was Moses Alexander Crandall, but when he went to school, the other children just called him Mose and the name stuck. His parents were killed during the War of 1812 by some Indians who were allied with the British. No one was sure, but most folks assumed that they were Shawnee. After his parents were killed, Mose went to live with his uncle. He was a Presbyterian Minister and usually preached from the New Testament about love and forgiveness and such. After his brother was killed, he preached more and more from the Old Testament. By the time he died when Mose was eighteen, he was all Hell fire and brimstone. There was no one to take his uncle's place, so Mose began doing the services. He had no formal training, but the people really liked his sermons and the congregation got larger and larger. The larger it got, the more Mose preached about an eye for an eye and how the red menace should be eradicated.

After several years, the people finally got tired of Mose and asked him to move on. He moved all over from state to state. It was always the same. They liked him at first but after a while he got too radical and was asked to move on. Finally he ended up in Missouri. He decided to start his own church. The place he picked was perfect. There had been a lot of Indian trouble there in the past so he fit right in. Every Sunday there was a young girl who always sat right in the front row during the service and appeared to be hanging on to every word Mose spoke. Her name was Mary Hall. One Sunday after the service, the girl's father invited the Reverend over for supper. When the meal was finished, the father asked everyone to leave the room so he could have some private words with the preacher.

"If you haven't noticed, my daughter is in love with you," he began. "She is only fourteen. When she turns fifteen, I will give you her hand in marriage if you will have her."

Mose was kind of surprised. He had not thought about taking a wife since before he could remember. He was twenty nine now. He would be thirty and Mary would be fifteen. She would be young enough to give him plenty of sons. "I would be priviledged to give your daughter my name," said Mose. "It's about time I started having some sons to carry on my work."

~~~~

They were married the day after Mary's fifteenth birthday. They did not waste any time. A son Noah was born the next year. The next year came Abraham and Isaac the next year. After that came Jacob, Aaron, Joshua, Caleb, Gideon, and then David. The day after David was born, Mary died. The doctor told Mose that she was just worn out. He accepted her death as God's will. David became Mose's favorite son. They did everything together.

The next year, Mose took another wife. Her name was also Mary. She was a young woman of twenty two and she gave him two daughters, Ruth and Sarah. She was worried that Mose would not be happy because she didn't give him more sons, but he assured her that he was happy. "If nobody had any daughters, there would never be more sons," he would tell her.

~~~~

When gold was discovered in California, Mose lost almost his whole congregation. It seemed as though everyone had gotten gold fever and was hoping to strike it rich. Finally in the summer of 1849, Mose decided to move his family to California. They were not going for the gold, but were going to look after the souls of the ones who had been overtaken by greed. They had to take two wagons with them because there were thirteen of them.

One week after the wagon train started, there was an Indian attack. Mose lost his left eye when an arrow went by his head so close that it clipped his left eye. No one knew for sure what tribe had attacked them. They were just a bunch of dirty rotten red devils. A month later, there was another Indian attack. Mose was hit by an arrow just below his left knee. When the arrow struck him, he fell from the wagon. The rear wheel of the wagon ran over his leg, crushing his left ankle. After the fight was over, his left leg was amputated just below the knee. They were now in Colorado, so Mose decided they would stay there while he healed. There was a small settlement close by, so that's where they went. He healed well, and it wasn't long before he was holding services in the settlement. Almost everyone in the area had lost a friend or a relative due to Indian attacks and they just loved Mose's sermons, especially when he told them that God had given the whites this land and it was up to them to rid the land of the red menace. He was always referring to stories in the Old Testament where God gave the Hebrews some land. All they had to do was go in and kill every man, woman, and child. The settlement grew and grew and Mose's congregation grew right along with it. As his son's got bigger and bigger, he would let them take turns giving the sermon. Mose was not going to continue to California. This place was just fine.

Mose was a very strong believer in the tithe and every service he would always slip in a line or two about the tithe. His sons were always the ones who passed the plate during services, and anyone who did not give a proper offering was paid a visit. If there was no money to be had, then food or animals were given. No one was actually beaten or hurt, but they were surely intimidated at times. One man had nothing to give at all, so he made Mose a wooden leg.

~~~~

When the boys got older and there was any Indian trouble, they were always the first to join the local militia. When the Civil War broke out, they all spent some time in the Union Army. In late 1864, young David found himself in the Colorado Cavalry. Their Commander was a man named Chivington. He hated Indians as much or more than Mose did. When they left for their campaign against the Cheyenne, young David told his father he would make him proud.

When Mose heard that David had been killed at Sand Creek by a renegade, he went crazy for almost a week. Then he sent his oldest and most experienced son Noah, out to get David's killer. "You will avenge your brother's death," Mose told Noah. "It is God's will."

When Noah was killed, he sent out Abraham, Isaac, and Joseph. "You will avenge your brother's death, or you will die trying," he said as they left. "God will be with you."

~~~~

The brothers searched and searched and were having no luck. At Fort Wallace, they asked Captain Maxwell if they had seen or even knew the renegade. He assured them that he had not seen or ever heard of the man. Just outside of Fort Wallace, they ran into some Pawnee. These Pawnee spoke perfect English and it didn't take the boys long to find out that these Pawnee had scouted for the Army. When the boys asked them if they knew about a renegade, the Pawnee told them about a man named Braddock who was married to a Cheyenne woman. They said that this was probably the man who killed their brother. They also told them that this man had a son-in-law who was the "one who kills with the long gun and the big pistol." This son-in-law was now a lawman and could be found around Abilene. The boys decided that they would go to Abilene and hope that Braddock would show up some time to visit his son-in-law. Several days later, they were a few hours from Abilene and decided they would stop for the night and go into town the next morning.

After a breakfast of coffee, bacon, and biscuits, they headed to town. Young Billy was out in front of the livery scooping manure when the brothers entered town. "You men need your horses took care of?" Billy asked them. "We do a real good job here."

"Mebbe we'll need some feed later boy," answered Isaac. "We're lookin' for that Federal Marshal. Do you know where he might be?"

"You're not a buncha bounty hunters after that money them outlaws put up on the Marshal, are you?" asked Billy.

"Don't know nothin' bout no bounty," said Isaac. "We just got some business with the Marshal."

"You can find him over at the saloon," said Billy. "If he's not there, someone'll know his whereabouts."

"Thank you son," said Isaac. Then all three of them dismounted and started walking their horses. As they got closer to the saloon, they each pulled a double barreled shotgun that they had tied to their saddles.

~~~~

Braddock and Sean had just returned to the saloon from Blue Swan's service. Braddock had decided that he had enough of being in town and was heading back to the mountains. He had just told everyone goodbye. He had his Sharps rifle in his right hand and his possibles bag over his left shoulder. When he came out the door, the Crandall brothers all saw him at the same time and raised their shotguns. They had never seen Braddock before and this man was dressed in buckskins so Isaac yelled to him. "Braddock, is that you?" They were just a little to Braddock's left no more than fifty feet away. When Braddock heard his name, he turned toward them and began raising his rifle. Before he could fire, all three of the brothers cut loose with their shotguns. Braddock was thrown through the doors and back into the saloon.

Sean pulled a pistol and ran outside. The three men were trying to mount their horses. Sean dropped two of them, but the third one got mounted and was moving out fast. Sean yelled for Jeb. "Go get'm boy," Sean said. Jeb was at a dead run when he jumped up and knocked the man off his horse. Jeb stood over him growling. The man did not move. Sean went inside to see if there was any chance Braddock could still be alive. Maggie was next to him crying. He had taken three loads of 00 buck in the chest. Sean held his tears back and went back into the street. He went to check on the man that Jeb had knocked from his horse. The man was dead. His neck had been broken. Then Sean went to the other two men. One was dead, but the other was still barely alive. Jug came outside.

"Can I do anything?" he asked.

"Go get the Doc," Sean said. "One of'em is still alive." Jug returned in just a few minutes with the Doc.

"This man'll be dead in fifteen minutes or less," the Doc said. "Only thing I can do is slow the bleeding some but I can't stop it."

"Well let's just leave'm here while I ask him a few questions," said Sean. "Now I figure you boys are some a the Crandalls, right?"

"Yes we are. I'm Joseph, and those other two are Abraham and Isaac," he answered.

"How did you know this was the man that killed your brother?" asked Sean. "You never seen him before."

"We ran into some Pawnee around Fort Wallace that used to scout for the Army," Joseph started. "They told us about a mountain man who had a Cheyenne wife and his name was Braddock. They figured it was him that killed our brother. They also told us about his son-in-law. You were the "one who kills with the long gun and the big pistol" and you were now a Marshal and could be found around Abilene. When we heard that, we decided we'd take a chance and come here."

"Since you got yourself killed too, do you reckon your Pa will send more brothers to find out how you got killed?" asked Sean.

"My Pa is an eye for an eye man," gasped Joseph. "Don't know for sure what he'll do. There's still four more of us boys. I just don't know."

"Is there a telegraph where yer from?" asked Sean. "I'll let'em know you all got killed."

"Denver is only a day's ride away," said Joseph. "If you send it there, they'll make sure he gets it. Just tell him that David's killer is dead and we got killed doing it." Then Joseph got a big smile on his face. "Leave me be now," he said. "I feel the Lord taking me." Then he died.

"That man must be sure he's goin' to heaven to be smilin' like that," said Sean. "Jug, get some help and get these bodies over to the barber shop. Then Sean went back inside the saloon. Maggie was still there with Braddock. Together they cried for another five minutes.

Then Sean went and got a piece of canvas and wrapped Braddock's body. He put the body over his shoulder and he and Maggie went to where they had placed Blue Swan's remains. There were no words spoken the whole time while the grave was being dug and for five minutes after. Then Maggie and Sean went back to the saloon. "I think we could both use a nice smooth drink," Maggie said. "I'll go get us some Irish Whiskey."

"Sounds good darlin'," said Sean. "That's just what I was thinkin'." Maggie returned with the bottle and glasses and poured each of them a drink which they sipped slowly."

"Let's get somethin' ta eat then I'll get over to the telegraph office and tell them boys' Pa that they got themselves killed," said Sean.

"What are you going to tell him?" asked Maggie.

"The one named Joseph said just to tell him that David's killer got killed and they got killed doin' it," answered Sean. "If I say more than that he's liable to send some more a his boys after me. Hope he's got more sense than that. If I don't tell him everything, that would be lyin'. I'm a terrible liar."

"It wouldn't be lying if you tell him just what Joseph wanted," said Maggie. "You just wouldn't be telling him everything."

"Well he might wanna know just what happened," replied Sean. "I reckon we'll find out soon enough after I send the telegram. I'll just tell him what Joseph said."

As soon as Sean finished speaking, Jug came back to the saloon and walked over to the table. "We got them boys over to the barber shop," Jug said. "While we were there, the telegraph operator give me this telegram. It's from Josh and Wayne. They already found me a ranch in Texas. It's just south a where Anderson's ranch was and I can get it for back taxes. The boys'r gonna go ahead and get some help and start roundin' up a herd."

"Sounds like you got a good crew to start with and you'll be leavin' shortly," said Sean. "I'll just bet we'll see you up here next spring."

"I hope to have one of the first herds up here," said Jug. "I'll damn sure make sure my men behave while they're in your place. Any man don't'll get his head broke and then he'll be lookin' fer work somewhere's else."

"That Lolita'll be doin' the cookin' on that drive I 'spect," said Sean. "That crew a yers'll be well fed. She's one hell of a cook."

"I hate ta leave ya when Michael's not here," said Jug.

"Me and Maggie can handle just about anything," said Sean. "Michael'll be back soon. Things'r quiet for now anyway."

"I'm gonna go tell Lolita the good news," said Jug. "Then I'll be helpin' Tom."

~~~~

Maggie and Sean ate their meal, then Sean told Maggie he was heading to the telegraph office. As he was leaving, Maggie stopped him and asked him a question. "Darlin', would you have hanged that man if he hadn't died?" she asked.

"Yes I would have," answered Sean. "Murder is a hangin' offence and he sure as hell done murder." Then Sean turned and left. At the telegraph office, he sent the following.

Reverend Mose Crandall
Denver

Three sons killed while killing other sons killer

Federal Marshal O'Rourke Abilene

CHAPTER FIVE

Michael and Betty were now on their way back from their honeymoon. They had been to New York City, Philadelphia, and were now in Chicago. They had stayed in the best hotels and had eaten the best food, but the both of them decided that big city life was not for them. While they were in Chicago, Michael purchased a piano. It wasn't the most expensive one, but Michael thought it would look good at the saloon. The sales clerk assured Michael that it would be delivered in a month. After they left Chicago, they wanted to spend a couple of days in St. Louis and meet Sam Draper, the owner of "The Palace."

After they checked into their hotel, they went to find the saloon. When they found it, they were both amazed. It was beautiful. They went inside and took a table, and Michael walked up to the bar and talked to the bartender. "My name is Michael O'Connor and that is my wife Betty," Michael began. "Sean O'Rourke and I are best friends and I am here to meet Sam Draper if he is available." Just as Michael finished his words, Sam came out of the back room. He extended his hand as he approached Michael.

"I'm Sam Draper and I'm very pleased to meet you," Sam said. "Sean has told me about you. May I have the priviledge of meeting your lovely wife?"

"Yes you may," said Michael. "Sam, this is my wife Betty."

"I am so pleased to meet you," said Sam. "I am honored that you came here to meet me. I hate to do this to you, but I have an appointment at the bank in five minutes. I'm thinking about expanding some. Please stay and have some drinks on the house. We can get together this evening and have a great time."

~~~~

Michael and Betty stayed and had a few drinks. Michael could tell that Betty was totally amazed at everything about this place. The furniture, the bar, the windows, and just everything was excellent. "I bet he has the most beautiful women working here," said Betty.

"I imagine he does," said Michael. "We'll find out this evening. Now let's go take a stroll around town."

~~~~

Betty was amazed at how many shops were in St. Louis, but she did not want to stop in every one they saw. She had done enough of that in the other big cities. When they came to a place with a Gunsmith sign, Michael decided to stop in. "I'll bet this is the man who does all the work for Sean," said Michael.

When they went inside, a tall middle aged man was standing behind a counter. "I'm Walter Black and this is my place," he said. "What can I help you with today?"

Michael extended his hand to Walter. "My name is Michael O'Connor, and this is my wife Betty," Michael said. "I'm one of Sean O'Rourke's deputies, and I believe you made this pistol I'm wearin'."

"I believe you're right," said Walter as he shook Michael's hand. "I hope you haven't had to use that pistol too much."

"All the pistols you made for Sean have been busy," said Michael. "There's just too many bad people out there."

"Well I got something brand new that I think Sean would really like," said Walter. "It's a brand new rifle that just came out. It's called a Winchester and it's gonna replace the Henry. I'll get one and show you. Walter went to the back room and came back with a brand new Winchester. "It has a wooden forearm so if you shoot a lot you won't have to worry about a hot barrel," said Walter. "It loads through this side port on the receiver. The magazine is fully enclosed. Holds the same amount of rounds as the Henry and shoots the same cartridge." Then he handed it to Michael. Michael shouldered the weapon and worked the action.

"That's very smooth action," said Michael. "Feels good on your shoulder. I bet Sean would want one a these. Have you got two of them?"

"Yes I do," answered Walter. "We can take them out to where I test fire my weapons if you'd like. We can be there in a few minutes and I guarantee that you won't get your good clothes dirty."

"Betty, would you mind goin'?" asked Michael.

"No, I would not mind at all," answered Betty. "This would be a good time to teach me how to shoot. If I'm going to be a lawman's wife, I should learn how to shoot."

"I got a buckboard out back and we'll be on our way in no time," said Walter.

~~~~

They arrived at Walter's target range in no time. Walter set out a couple of targets about fifty yards away. Michael took one of the Winchesters and showed Betty how to hold it properly, sight it in, and work the action. He then gave Betty a quick safety lesson. "Never point a rifle at anyone unless you're going to shoot them," started Michael. "Keep the rifle pointed at the ground or away from you at all times. Do not have the hammer cocked until you're going to shoot. Do not touch the trigger till you're ready to shoot. Then he showed Betty how to release the hammer after it had been cocked. He took five shells and showed her how to load properly. "Now we have shells in the magazine but none in the chamber," said Michael. "Soon as I work the lever, a round will be in the chamber, the hammer will be cocked, and it will be ready to fire. Squeeze the trigger. Do not pull it." Michael chambered a round and began to fire. All five rounds hit their mark. Then he took five rounds and gave the Winchester and the rounds to Betty and told her to load up. When she had the last round in the magazine, Michael told her to face the target, chamber a round, and begin firing. All of Betty's rounds found their mark. "Fine job Betty," said Michael. "That's very good for your first time. Now we'll fire a few rounds through the other rifle just to make sure it's all right." Michael let Betty shoot the other Winchester, and she did very well again.

"Now show me how to use that pistol of yours," said Betty.

Walter took the Winchesters and put them in the buckboard. Michael took out his pistol, unloaded it and began with safety lessons. "These pistols can be very touchy, darlin'," Michael began. "It doesn't take much to set one off. When you're shooting, the hammer needs to be fully cocked, but if you are not shooting and the hammer got bumped or the pistol was dropped, it could fire if there was a round under the hammer. That's why most people don't put a round under the hammer until they're ready to shoot. Always hold the pistol pointing away from yourself and others. Now this is the half cocked position. You lightly pull the hammer back until you hear it click. This will allow the cylinder to turn freely. Then you open the loading gate and insert the shells into the cylinder. Then you close the gate and then release the hammer. Do this by keeping your thumb on the hammer and very gently squeezing the trigger. This will release the hammer. Now you are ready to shoot. When you cock the hammer you will see the rear sight. It's on the hammer. You should shoot with two hands. Hold the pistol with your right hand and extend your arm. Then take your left hand and place it under the butt of the pistol against your other hand. this will help steady the pistol." Michael handed the pistol to Betty and had her practice with it empty before he gave her some bullets. "Are you comfortable with it now darlin'?" asked Michael.

"I'm ready," Betty answered. "Gimme some shells." Michael handed Betty the shells and she safely loaded them and got ready to fire. She began firing. At first she was not comfortable with the recoil, but she did well and hit the target. "I didn't expect it to kick that much," said Betty. "Maybe you'll buy me a smaller pistol sometime."

"That would be a good idea darlin'," said Michael. "Now let's get back to town."

"When we get back, I'll clean these up for you and have them ready to go," said Walter. "I'll box them up so it won't look like you're going down the road looking for trouble. Sean ordered another Sharps too. I don't know when you two are leaving, but it can be ready in the morning."

"Our train leaves late morning," said Michael. "I'll pick them up before we leave."

"That'll be good." Said Walter. "When we get back to the store, I'll give that pistol of yours a real quick cleanin' too. Won't take but a few minutes."

"That's another thing to learn about Betty darlin'," said Michael. "When you shoot guns, they need to be cleaned soon. That gunpowder will corrode them quickly. I'll give you a lesson when we get home."

~~~~

After they left the Gunsmith shop, they went back to their hotel. Betty was feeling a little amorous and wanted to have her way with Michael. Michael did not mind. After they were finished, they took a bath, put on some fresh clothes and went to a nice restaurant for a meal. Michael had a steak, and Betty had something that Michael had never heard of, but Betty said it was good. When they finished, they made their way to "The Palace." Sam saw them coming and motioned them to come to a table that he had been saving for them. "This is the best table in the house," Sam said. "You can see the whole place from here. Now what would you two like to drink?"

"I think I'd like to try some champagne," said Betty. "I've never had it before. I don't know why I didn't try it when we were back east."

"I'll just have some bourbon," said Michael. "I've never had champagne either, but I'll just try a sip of Betty's if she doesn't mind."

"Of course I don't mind," said Betty. "Maybe you'll decide you like it."

"Comin' right up," said Sam.

~~~~

While Sam was getting the drinks, more people started coming into the saloon. Betty and Michael both noticed how beautiful the girls were. "I bet Sean had a good time while he was here," said Betty. "They would be hard for a young man to resist."

"I think it was mutual between the girls and Sean," said Michael. "Anyway, just look at this place. It sure is grand. Sam must be a very good business man."

Sam was back now and Betty took a sip of the champagne. "I don't know," she said. "I think I'll stick to beer and whiskey. You take a sip Michael." Michael took a sip and was not impressed.

"I'll be stickin' with my bourbon," said Michael. "Hope we haven't offended you because of the champagne."

"I don't drink that stuff either," said Sam. "I like my beer and whiskey too. I'll go get you some beer and a glass of whiskey Betty. I'll bring you a beer back too Michael."

~~~~

Sam got back to the table and they began talking about anything and everything. Sam wanted to know all about what had been going on with Sean and his friends. He told them about how Sean had saved his life that night. They talked well into the night. Betty was finally getting tired so they decided to get back to their hotel. They were just outside the front doors of the saloon saying their goodbyes when two men started running towards them. Sam and Michael both saw them at the same time and pulled their pistols. The two men had their pistols out and were about to fire when Sam and Michael both fired. The two men fell and as they were falling, their pistols fired. The bullets struck the sidewalk between Michael and Sam. The two men fell onto the sidewalk and did not move. Michael walked to them and checked to make sure they were dead.

"Just what in the hell was that?" screamed Betty. "Do you know those men, Michael?"

"I've never seen them before," answered Michael. "How bout you Sam?"

"I've never seen them either," answered Sam. "I'll send someone to get the Marshal. I wonder who they were after. Maybe it was someone I kicked out of the place sometime back and they were out for some revenge."

"Maybe they were after me because I'm Sean's deputy," said Michael.

"We may never know," said Sam. "I'm glad none of us were hurt. I hope you are not too shaken by this Betty."

"I'll be all right," said Betty. "We've had our share of shootings in Abilene. This is just the first time I was very close to it."

The Marshal had heard the shots and was already on his way to the saloon. "What happened here?" he asked Sam. "Do you know these men?"

"Michael, this is Mike Kiley, the town Marshal," started Sam. "Mike, this is Michael O'Connor and his lovely wife Betty. Michael is one of Sean O'Rourke's deputies." Michael and Mike shook hands. "I have never seen these two men before. Michael and I were saying goodbye out here and these two men came running at us with their pistols pulled and we shot them."

"They coulda been after either one a you," said Mike. "I have heard all about O'Rourke and his deputies. They've made a lot of enemies. You have probably made some yourself there Sam. I'll check around and see what I can find out. I'll get some boys and get these bodies off your sidewalk. I'd sleep lightly if I was you two."

~~~~

The two bodies were removed, and Sam and Michael and Betty said their goodbyes again. Michael and Betty went to their hotel, and Sam went back to work. On the way back to the hotel, Betty asked Michael if he would go ahead and get her that small pistol tomorrow at the gunsmith shop when they picked up the Winchesters and the Sharps. "We'll see what he's got darlin'," said Michael. "If he doesn't have one on hand, we'll have him order one. If he has to order one, you can carry this newer pistol and I'll carry the old one till your pistol comes in after we get home."

~~~~

The next morning after breakfast, Michael and Betty took another quick stroll around town and then went to the gunsmith shop. Walter had everything ready for them. "Got you all fixed up," said Walter. "Glad to do business with you. Tell Sean that maybe when Abilene does grow, I might move my business there. If those Texas boys do come to Abilene, I just bet some of 'em will be wantin' some new hardware. That is if they got any money left after they spend it on liquor and women."

"That might just be a good move for you Walter," said Michael. "Now we need a small revolver for Betty. We had us a shootin' last night in front of "The Palace". We think it would be a good idea if Betty was armed at times."

"I heard about that shooting," said Walter. "Glad you weren't hurt. Now I've got just the thing for Betty. It's really small and it'll fit in the smallest purse or pocket. It's a .32 and up close it'll take care of business. It's a little loud for as small as it because of the short barrel, but it'll do the job. It's not new but it's in good condition. I bought it from a gambler who decided to get outta that line a work. He carried it in his coat pocket." Walter checked the pistol to show that it was empty and handed it to Betty.

"I believe this'll do me just fine," said Betty. "I can hide this thing anywhere. We'll take it and a box of shells."

"I test fired it several times last week so I know it's in good working order," said Walter. "Would you like me to box it up with the rifles?"

"No, I believe I'll load it right now and stick it in my purse," said Betty. "That is if you don't mind me loading it in your store."

"I do not mind one bit," said Walter. "I watched Michael give you safety lessons and I know that you can handle a weapon properly. I hope you two have a safe trip home and make sure you tell Sean what I said."

Michael paid Walter and shook his hand again, and then Betty and he went back to the hotel to get their luggage. The hotel had a buggy that took them to the train station. They would take the train to Kansas City, spend the night there, and the rest of the trip would be by stagecoach. When they got to Kansas City, Michael sent a telegram to Sean telling him that they would be home soon. They would spend the night in the same hotel that they had stayed on their way home after the fight with Anderson. They checked into the hotel in the early afternoon. They were just about worn out from all the traveling so they decided to take an afternoon nap. It wasn't much of a nap. As soon as they laid down, Betty got a little amorous and the nap was delayed by an hour or so. They got up around 6pm and went downstairs for the evening meal.

The bartender recognized Michael from his last visit there. "I remember you," he said to Michael. "You were here with that lady and the Marshal who had that big dog. I hope the Marshal and that dog are doing well. As I recall, he said that the previous owner of the dog was dead."

"That's right," replied Michael. "That deputy was killed while we were getting Anderson. We lost another deputy that day too. Anyway, Anderson is dead. Hope no one comes along and takes his place."

"Me and you both," added the bartender. "Now what can I get you and your lovely wife to drink and would you like a menu?"

"I'll just have a beer," said Betty. "You can bring this big Irishman a beer and a glass of some good bourbon. We'll take a menu too."

"Comin' right up," said the bartender.

"They got a pretty good cook here," said Michael to Betty. "Can't hold a candle to what we got back home, but he's good."

"I hope so. I'm starting to get pretty hungry," said Betty.

~~~~

The bartender was back in no time with the drinks and the menus. "I'll be back in a few minutes for your order," he said. Just as he finished speaking, two well dressed men walked into the place and went straight to the bar. Michael thought they looked like trouble. They were too well dressed for their mannerisms. They were loud and impolite and talked down to the bartender. Then Michael heard them say that they wanted to talk to the owner. Michael tried to not pay them any mind, but it seemed they were getting loud and rude.

Betty and Michael ordered their food and after another drink, the food arrived. When the bartender brought the food to the table, Michael asked him if those two men needed escorted out the door. "I don't know who they are," said the bartender. "They come in here about every five days and try to talk the owner into selling. He keeps telling them he will not sell and to tell whoever their boss is to leave him alone. The Town Marshal says he can't do anything to them because there is no law against trying to get someone to sell to you. I still think something bad is going to happen."

Just about that time, Michael had had enough. They were getting loud and obnoxious. It was obvious that the owner wanted nothing to do with the two. They had been asked to leave but would not.

"Excuse me," Michael said to Betty. "Those fools over there need some help leaving. I'll be back shortly." Michael walked over to the two at the bar and tapped one of them on the shoulder. When the man turned to see who it was, Michael spoke. "My wife and I are trying to have a nice quiet meal and you are ruining it for us," said Michael. "I heard the owner ask you to leave so you will be leaving. You can leave on your own, or you can be carried out."

The one he had tapped on the shoulder didn't say a word. He rared back to take a swing at Michael with his right hand. Michael reached up with his left hand and caught the man's fist just inches from his face. The man tried but couldn't get it free. Then he swung with his left hand. Michael caught the man's fist with his right hand. Michael held to the man's fists and forced the man down on his knees. When the man was down to his knees, Michael brought his right knee into the man's face. Blood went flying. At first the other man was amazed at what Michael had done to his partner. He regained his composure and then took a swing at Michael. He was on Michael's right side, and the blow caught Michael on his right jaw. Michael was shaken a little by the blow, but he just shook his head and looked in the man's eyes. "Is that the best you got mister?" asked Michael. Michael turned to face him and gave him a crushing right hand that sent him flying backwards and onto a table. The legs of the table broke, and the man and the table fell to the floor. The other man was wiping the blood from his face. His nose had apparently been broken by Michael's knee. Michael was facing the man who had landed on the table. He wasn't moving.

Betty knew that her man could easily handle the two men, but something about them worried her. When Michael struck the second man, she had reached into her purse and pulled out her

.32. She had it down under the table so it couldn't be seen. As Michael was watching the second man, the first man was reaching into his jacket and pulling a pistol. As soon as Betty saw the pistol, she stood, aimed, and fired. The bullet struck the man in the head, killing him instantly. "Oh my God," screamed Betty. "I've just killed a man."

"Yes you did darlin'," said Michael. "If you hadn't killed him, he surely would've killed me. Now I think someone should get the Town Marshal." The owner himself went to get the Marshal. The Marshal was out of town transporting a prisoner, so Deputy George Watkins came. The owner had already explained to the deputy what had happened.

"I am George Watkins. I'm a deputy here," he said to Michael. "Who might you be?"

"My name is Michael O'Connor and this is my wife Betty," answered Michael. "I'm a Federal deputy for Marshal Sean O'Connor."

"So you're another one of O"Rourke's deputies," George said. "I met another one of his deputies a while back. Believe his name was Bob Wallace. There was a shootin' when he was here. How's he these days anyway?"

"He was killed when we got Anderson a little while back," said Michael. "So do you know who these two are?"

"I've seen them around town, but I don't know who they are or who they work for," answered George. Maybe when that other ones comes to, we can find out somethin'. How bout I throw him in jail now for disturbin' the peace.? Maybe someone'll come to bail him out. That might give us an idea."

"Well I bet if you go around to some of the other businesses in town, you'll find out that these two, or others have been trying to convince people to sell out," said the owner. "Someone's gotta be their boss. These two aren't smart enough for that."

"Well I'll get that body outta here and get the other one locked up," said George. "Then I'll be askin' some other places about this."

~~~~

The owner of the place walked over to Michael and shook his hand. "I want to thank you for what you did," he said. "I am sorry that your wife had to shoot that man, deeply sorry." Your stay here and your meal and drinks will be on the house."

"Thank you," said Michael. "I was glad to help. I can't abide rudeness. I just hope Betty is not too shaken."

"I was at first, darlin'," said Betty. "Now I do realize that what I did had to be done or I'd be a widow. Now let's eat this fine meal. I am hungry." They finished their meal and had a few drinks and decided to go ahead and get to bed. Michael went right to sleep, but Betty was wide awake. She thought that maybe she was upset about the shooting. Then she decided that she was just too tired to get to sleep. With a little coaxing, Michael was awake and they were making love. They finally collapsed in each other's arms.

Their stage was leaving at 9am so when they woke up at daylight, they had plenty of time to be frisky again and then have a good breakfast. George met them at the stage depot as they were getting ready to leave. "Can't get one word outta that fella," George said. "No one's come up with bail money either. Just thought I'd let you know. Now you two have a safe trip to Abilene."

~~~~

Several days later, the stage pulled into Abilene. Maggie and Sean were at the depot to meet them. "Welcome back," said Maggie. "I hope you had a great time. We have missed you."

"We missed you too," said Betty. "We did have a good time, but that was too much traveling. Michael and I decided that we are not big city folks. We did stay in the best places and eat some really good food. Some of it, I couldn't tell you what it was. Anyway, it's good to be home."

"How bout you Michael?" asked Sean. "Did you have a good time?"

"I always have a good time when Betty's with me," said Michael. "It doesn't matter where we are or what we do. If she's with me, it's a very good time."

"He's learning the right things to say to a woman," said Betty. "I believe he's been learning from you, Sean."

"You'll have to ask Maggie if I say the right things or not," said Sean.

"You're getting better all the time," said Maggie. "I have no complaints."

"Well let's get you two home and unloaded," said Maggie. "You've got to be tired after spending the last several days on a stagecoach."

"When we get unpacked, I've got something to show you Sean," said Michael. "I know you'll like it. And Maggie, I have a piano comin'. It should be here in a couple more weeks or so."

~~~~

After they helped Betty and Michael get home and unloaded, Sean and Maggie headed back to the saloon. "I'm glad they're back,"

Sean said to Maggie. "Jug and Lolita'll be leavin' any day now. It's been quiet for a while, but it won't last. Michael's a good man to have around." Just as they were about to enter the saloon, the telegraph operator shouted that he had a telegraph for Sean. Sean thanked him and read it. It went as follows:

Federal Marshal O'Rourke
Abilene

Mose Crandall sending four sons to find out how other sons died

Mary Crandall
Denver

"Just what in the hell is this all about?" said Sean. "Is this the old man's wife or daughter? And just why would she let me know that they're coming here?"

"Maybe she's warning you," said Maggie. "Maybe she knows that Mose is crazy. I bet that if this is the wife, she got tired of him getting the boys killed and left him. I suppose we'll find out when they get here. So how long do you think it'll be before they get here?"

"If they ride hard and keep at it, they could be here in two or three weeks," said Sean. "That man must be crazy. He's already got five sons dead. If these four are as crazy as him, I'll hafta kill'em."

~~~~

The next morning when Jug found out about the telegram from Mary Crandall, he asked Sean if he wanted him to stay a while longer. He figured two or three more weeks wouldn't matter. Josh and Wayne would have that much more time to get things set up. Sean assured him that it was all right for him to leave. "Michael and me will be all right," said Sean. "We been through at lot of different things. Them boys won't be anything we can't handle. You and Lolita go get your new life started. We'll look for you next spring or summer. You and Lolita have been good friends. We will miss you. Now I gotta see what Michael's got for me to see." Michael was in the back room of the saloon opening some packages when he heard Sean in the saloon.

"Just stay at the bar," said Michael. "I'll bring one a these out."

"What have you got there?" Sean asked. "Looks like a fancy Henry."

"That's just about what it is," answered Michael. "It's called a Winchester and it'll be replacin' the Henry. It's got this wooden forearm, and the magazine is fully enclosed. It loads on this side port here, and it shoots the same cartridge as the Henry. Holds the same amount a shells too. Me and Betty have already fired it. I like it." Then he handed it to Sean.

"I like it too," said Sean. "It's much stronger than the Henry."

"Glad you like it," said Michael. "I got one for both of us. I didn't tell you when we first got back, but we had some trouble in St. Louis and Kansas City."

"You and Betty didn't get hurt, did you?" asked Sean.

"No, we didn't, but I had to kill a man in St. Louis," said Michael. "Me and Sam Draper and Betty were out front of his saloon saying our goodbyes when these two fellas came at us with their pistols out. Sam and me killed'em. Sam and me never knew either one of'em. The law there never knew them either. So Sam and me don't know if they was after him or me or both of us."

"What happened in Kansas City?" asked Sean.

"We were in that same hotel that we stayed in after we got Anderson," started Michael. "We were about to have our evening meal when these two fellas came to the bar and were gettin' loud and rude. They were tryin' to get the owner to sell his place. I was tired of their rudeness, so I went to have some words with them. It turned into a fight. Wasn't much of a fight. I put'em down pretty quick, but after I put down the first one and had just finished the second one, the first one pulled a pistol and was gonna shoot me in the back. Betty pulled her pistol and killed'em."

"Since when did Betty start carryin' a pistol?" asked Sean.

"When we were in St. Louis, we got these Winchesters from Walter Black," Michael began. "When we went out to test fire them, Betty decided she wanted to learn how to shoot. She fired the Winchesters first, then she fired my pistol. She decided my pistol was too much gun for her and asked if we could get something smaller. Walter had a .32 so we got it for her. It's a good thing we did."

"I hope Betty was not too shaken by that," said Sean.

"She was a little at first, but then she realized that I'd be dead if she hadn't shot that man," said Michael. "The other man was still in jail when we left. He wasn't talkin' and no one came forward to bail him out. And before I forget it, Walter said that he might be bringin' his business to Abilene. He said if they bring the herds here, it'd be a good business opportunity."

"Well I'm glad you two are both all right," said Sean. "Havin' Walter here would be good. He could make a lotta money off the

Texas boys. Now I think we are about due for a toast. I'll get a bottle and some glasses. Sean produced a bottle of bourbon and two glasses. "Here's to not getting killed," toasted Sean. Michael repeated the toast.

"I almost forgot," said Michael. " I also brought that Sharps that you ordered. Walter had it done."

"I ordered that Sharps for Braddock," began Sean. "He was here for a visit and got killed. I'll tell you all about that another time. I don't wanna cry in my liquor right now."

CHAPTER SIX

When Mose Crandall received the telegram from Marshal O'Rourke, he went into a very depressed state of mind for a few days. He spent that whole time reading parts of the Old Testament over and over. He didn't sleep either. He finally called his remaining four sons together. "You boys are going to Kansas and find out what really happened to your brothers," Mose began. "There is just no way that one renegade could kill my sons without help. You will find this Federal Marshal, and you will find out what happened. If he will not tell you, but you think he knows, you will kill him. When you find out what did happen, you will kill anyone who had anything to do with killing my sons. You will kill them, their families, and their friends. Anyone that gets in your way will be killed. Do you all understand?"

"Yes, we do Pa," answered Aaron. "We know that God will be with us, and we will smite these Philistines. I know I speak for all of us."

~~~~

Mary Crandall was in the next room and heard everything. That evening when she was alone with Mose, she finally spoke her mind. "Mose Crandall, I will not have you sending your sons out to kill or be killed," Mary began. "You have lost five sons already. Nothing you can do will bring any of them back. If you are set on sending your remaining sons out, I will take the girls and leave you. We are tired of all this death. I have been a good and faithful wife, and have stood by you all these years, but you are killing this family."

"The boys will be leaving in the morning, woman," said Mose. "They are doing God's work. If you can't see that, then take the girls and go. I'll not have a woman who goes against me. Now leave me alone. I must pray now."

"Go ahead and pray you old fool," said Mary. "Pray that God doesn't strike you dead for what you're doing."

~~~~

The next morning, Mary played the dutiful wife and mother. She made the boys a big breakfast and helped them pack extra food. Then she gave each of them a goodbye kiss on the cheek. Mose made sure they were well armed and had plenty of ammunition. They took two pack horses and three extra horses with them. When they were finally out of sight, Mary and the girls packed up a wagon and headed out. "I'll probably see you in Hell, Mose Crandall," Mary said as she was leaving. Mose did not even look her way as she was leaving.

It was about a day's ride to Denver. When they got there, Mary went straight to the telegraph office, but they were closed till the next morning. After breakfast the next morning, Mary sent the telegram to Marshal O'Rourke. She wasn't quite sure why she sent it. Maybe it would do some good. Maybe it wouldn't. Maybe the renegade did kill the three boys and nothing would happen.

It was almost spring now and Mary hoped that they could join a wagon train that was headed to California. She had enough money to get by for a few months. This was money that she had basicly stolen from Mose because he never gave any money to her or the girls. Their duty was to take care of the house and everything around the house. They had no need for money.

Mary was now 41 years old, but she was still a very handsome woman. Having the two girls had not affected her figure one bit. She did not go unnoticed. They set up camp at the edge of town and it wasn't long before a lot men were stopping by offering their services for any needs they might have. Ruth and Sarah were 18 and 17 respectively, and they had their mother's looks. They had never been away from Mose and his strictness before, and now a whole new world was open to them. The young men came courting.

In less than a month, both girls were married to respectable men. Mary had also met a good man. Mark Wagner had been a lawyer in St. Louis for several years and was offered a position in San Francisco. He was on his way there when he met Mary. He was a widower. His wife had died from influenza five years before. There were no children. He treated Mary like a lady, and she loved him for it. He did not have a religious bone in his body, but he was a kind, gentle man. She went with him to San Francisco right after the girls were married. She made sure the girls knew where to reach her before she left.

~~~~

Jacob was the oldest of the remaining four brothers so he was in charge, but when they had been on the trail for just under a week, they ran into some Cheyenne Dog Soldiers. Jacob took an arrow in the throat and Aaron took one in his right thigh. Jacob died quickly as the arrow had cut his jugular. During the fight, the boys managed to kill two Cheyenne, but the Cheyenne had managed to steal one of their pack horses and two of the spare horses. When the fight was over and the Cheyenne had left, Caleb tried to get the arrow out of Aaron's leg, but the tip of the head was stuck in the bone. They made it all the way to Fort Wallace, but it was too late for the army surgeon to save him even if he took off his leg. The blood poisoning had gone too far. They sent a telegram to Mose telling him what had happened to Jacob and Aaron. They did not stay at the fort to wait for a reply.

Caleb and Gideon decided that it was still their duty to get to Abilene and find out what had happened to their brothers. They still had one pack horse and four riding horses. The second day after they left Fort Wallace, one of the riding horses stepped in a hole and broke a leg. The horse was put down. Gideon was on the horse when it went down and when it fell, he dislocated his left shoulder. Caleb gave it good yank and put it back in place, but it hurt like hell, so the boys decided to find a good spot and lay up for a few days.

They came to a fair sized stream with good clear water and plenty of shade on both banks and set up camp. Caleb made a rope corral so the horses could graze and he built a small leanto for shelter. There was plenty of fish in the stream and the first evening, Caleb made himself a spear with two prongs on the end, and the boys had catfish for supper. The next morning they were awakened by what they thought was thunder. It kept getting closer and closer. Caleb wasn't quite sure what it was yet, but he quickly tied the horses and best as he could and grabbed Gideon and got as close to some trees as they could get. Then they saw this huge thundering herd of buffalo coming their way. Caleb and Gideon both climbed a tree and got up as high as they could. The buffalo were almost upon them now, but for some reason, they changed direction. The buffalo were within fifty yards of the boys when this happened. Two of the horses broke free and fled, but the others stayed tied. It took a full fifteen minutes for the whole herd to get by them.

They waited a few more minutes before getting out of the trees to make sure all the buffalo were past them. After they got down, Caleb made a check of their camp. Everything was all right except for the loss of two horses. Now they were down to two riding horses and a pack horse. They built a fire and were getting ready to make some coffee and breakfast when they both heard a horse whinny. To the north about three hundred yards out was an Indian on horseback. They could see that he had his face painted and was holding a war lance. Caleb got his Sharps and gave Gideon his Henry. They sat there and watched the Indian for maybe fifteen minutes. Another Indian joined the first one. He also was painted but he had a rifle in his left hand. The boys couldn't tell what it was.

The Indians had not moved one bit, so Caleb decided to go ahead and make the coffee. When the coffee was done and Caleb had poured each of them a cup, two shots rang out. Both of the Indians were thrown from their horses. "Where did that come from?" Gideon asked Caleb. "I didn't see anyone or their smoke."

"I didn't see anything either," said Caleb. "We'll just sit tight. I figure that whoever shot them two'll be along shortly." Caleb was right. Two riders rode up to the dead Indians and proceeded to scalp them. After they had finished, they rode into the boys' camp."

"Just what in the hell'r you fellers doin' out here?" one of them asked. "How come ya still got yer hair?"

"I reckon we're just lucky," said Caleb. "I'm Caleb Crandall and this is my brother Gideon. Now who might you be and what'r you doin' out here?"

"I'm Frank Miller and that other feller is Al Sharp," Frank said. "We're huntin' buffalo. There's two more of us follerin'. We got two wagons almost filled with hides. We was doin' purty good till them Kiowa came by and started'em stampedin'."

"So them was Kiowas, huh," said Caleb. "We had some trouble with some Cheyenne Dog Soldiers a ways back. Lost two a our brothers and some horses."

"You don't wanna tangle with them Dog Soldiers," said Frank. "They're as mean and as tough as they come. I'm surprised you two'r still breathin'."

"I'm kinda surprised myself," said Caleb. "Would you two wanna get down and have some coffee and breakfast?"

"We done et this mornin' but some coffee sure sounds good," said Frank. "I'm obliged."

Caleb got the men some coffee and then thought for a second. "Why did you scalp them Kiowas?" Caleb asked.

"Them scalps is worth money," answered Frank. "City folks buy'em for decoration. Sometimes there's a bounty for'em. A scalp might bring more'n a buffalo hide. Them Kiowas woulda scalped us if they'd a kilt us. Don't you boys know nothin' bout Injuns?"

"We know bout Injuns," answered Caleb. "We just want'em dead. We don't worry bout scalpin'em."

"That's good. So why'r you boys out here now?" asked Frank.

Caleb proceeded to tell them the whole story about David's death and then Noah's, and why they were going to Abilene to find out how the other three brothers were killed.

"I don't know as I would go to Abilene if I was you," spoke Al. "I never been there, but some a my friends been there. That Federal Marshal lives there somewhere. They say he's the best with a long gun and a pistol. Friend a mine said he killed two men at over eight hunnerd yards with one shot with his Sharps. They was ridin' away at a full gallop. They say he was a sharpshooter in the war and kilt hunnerds a rebs. I hear he only shot Sergeants and Corporals. He's kilt plenty a men with them pistols a his too. I hear he wears three of'em and he's as good with his left hand as he is with his right. They say not ta blink when he draws cause if ya do, ya won't see it. If'n ya do talk with that man, I'd be awful polite if I was you. Mebbe he would know somethin' bout yer brothers. Mebbe he's the one who kilt'em. Don't seem likely that renegade could kill all three a yer brothers before they kilt him. Anyway, I'd go lightly if I was you."

"I thank you for the information," said Caleb. "We'll be stayin' right here for a few more days then we'll be headin' east."

Frank and Al finished their coffee and then mounted up. "You fellers keep your wits about you," said Frank. "Ya still got a good ways ta go, and there's plenty more Injuns over that way. Could even run into a Comanche war party. They been raidin' up this way some. Thanks fer the coffee."

"We hope you men do good on the rest a your hunt," said Caleb. "I reckon the more buffalo you kill, that'll be some that won't feed no Injuns."

~~~~

Caleb and Gideon watched the buffalo hunters till they were out of sight, then proceeded on with their breakfast. While they were eating, Gideon started wondering about this Federal Marshal the buffalo hunter had told them about. "Are you worried about that Marshal?" Caleb asked Gideon. "He sounds like one tough customer ta me," answered Gideon.

"If he's a Federal Marshal, he's gotta be tough," said Caleb. "If he wasn't, he'd be dead. If he's a good lawman, he'd do what was right. I'm not worried about him. What I am worried about is those two dead Kiowa over there. We should either bury'em or get outta here. If some more Kiowa find them and we're here, I'd say they'd kill us without so much as a by your leave. I think we better pack up after breakfast and make a new camp. I'd say them Kiowa'll be after them buffalo hunters anyway. If they got two wagons like Frank said, they'll be easy to track."

~~~~

The boys finished breakfast, loaded up, and headed east. They ate jerky on the way and only stopped to rest and water the horses. They didn't stop till it was completely dark. They wanted to get away from the dead Kiowa as far as they could that day. The next day they did the same. When they finally stopped, it was near another small stream and there was some small trees on the banks for shade. Caleb took care of the horses and then built the leanto. That evening after the meal, Gideon was doing some more thinking. "It seems that what we're doin' is dern foolish," said Gideon. "Seven of us'r dead now. We might be dead before this is over with. Why are we doin' this?"

"How can you even ask that?" said Caleb. "Pa said to do it, and that's what we'll do."

"Maybe Pa's just a little crazy," said Gideon. "Would you do the same thing if seven of your boys were already dead?"

"If you weren't stove up right now, I'd give you a whoopin' you'd never ferget," said Caleb.

"If I wasn't stove up, I'd git on my horse and take off for someplace besides Abilene or Denver," said Gideon. "If we did git to Abilene and find out that someone besides that renegade killed our brothers and we killed them, it won't bring our brothers back. I won't be part a no murder. Have you ever thought about doin' somethin' that you wanted to do and not somethin' Pa wanted you to do? Well I have. I'd like to maybe get married one day and have my own family. We won't be a bunch a Bible thumpers neither."

"I'm bout tired a yer whinin'," said Caleb. "Anyway, it won't be murder if we kill our brothers' killer or killers. An eye for an eye by God, and that's what we'll be doin'," added Caleb. "Now you get to sleep and git your head on straight cause we'll be in Abilene before too long. No woman with any sense would have you anyway."

~~~~

It was a Friday morning when the telegram got to Mose Crandall. When he read that Jacob and Aaron were dead, he must have had a heart attack right on the spot. The telegram had been delivered right to his house. No one missed him till it was time for Sunday service. When he had been about an hour late, someone from the congregation went looking for him. He lay dead just inside the front door with the telegram still in his hand. The local doctor said his heart had probably given out.

The two daughters, Ruth and Sarah still lived in the area, and they were notified. Ruth remembered that her mother had sent a telegram to a Federal Marshal in Abilene stating that the brothers were going there. She decided to send a telegram to that Marshal so the brothers could be told of their father's death. It went as follows:

Federal Marshal O'Rourke
Abilene

Tell Crandall brother's their father has died<<stop>>
Doctor said it was his heart<< stop >> two more brothers
killed by Indians

Ruth Russel formerly Ruth Crandall sister

Sean was at the saloon eating dinner when the telegram arrived. Maggie and Michael were at the table with him. "Well now when them Crandall boys get here, I gotta tell them that their Pa is dead," said Sean. "Wonder how they'll take that. Mebbe they'll turn around and go back home and not worry bout anything that happened here."

"I hope so too," added Maggie. "They should remember that seven of them are already dead. That should be enough. Now let's talk about other things. I hear that Bill Thomspon is going to start building a couple of saloons and maybe a couple of hotels in a few weeks. I also heard that some fella is going to come here and start a newspaper."

"Well the railroad has started this way," said Sean. "If they don't get here before winter, they'll be here come next spring. It's a good thing we got most a our stuff done. All those people doin' all that work'll need a place to get a drink and such. Speakin' a such, we'll need ta get us some more girls."

"I'll take care of that," said Maggie. "We've got plenty of time before then so I should be able to find some good girls."

"Do you think maybe we should build us a hotel too?" asked Michael. "Might be a wise investment."

"How bout we wait till after several herds come and see how things are?" said Sean. "If things are boomin', maybe we should build us a hotel."

"I agree with Sean," said Maggie. "I think we should wait and see how things are."

"Maggie and you are probably right, Sean," said Michael. "Maggie's got a better head for business than I ever will. Let's have a toast to whatever comes. May it always be good." Michael went to the bar and got a bottle and three glasses. Just as he had finished filling the glasses, a familiar voice came from across the room.

"So yer drinkin' without me again," the man said. They all looked at the same time. It was Jon O'Brien. Dog was beside him. Jeb went over to Dog and they got reacquainted.

"Sean and Michael got up and shook his hand and gave him a hug. "Just what are you doin' here now?" asked Sean. "I never sent you a telegram sayin' I needed you here." Maggie went over and gave Jon a big hug too.

"Pull up a chair," said Maggie. "I'll go get you a glass." Jon sat down and when Maggie filled his glass, he slammed it down hard.

"I've never seen you do that before," said Maggie. "Have you got troubles?"

"I came to be with my friends," said Jon. "I'll try not to cry when I tell you what happened. We had an outbreak a smallpox at our village. We lost about half of the people. My wife was one a the last ones to die. Our baby was due this summer. Her father was one a the first ones ta die. I don't know why I didn't get taken. I been around the pox before and never got it. Mebbe I'm just one a those people who can't get it. When I left, nobody else was gettin' sick, and the ones that were sick were gettin' better. I burned all my clothes and such and started over with new stuff. I even got rid of my old saddle and got a different one. I didn't want be responsible fer spreadin' the pox. I heard that even if you don't get it, you can still spread it if ya been round them that had it."

"I'm truly sorry for your loss my friend," said Sean. "I know that if I was to lose Maggie, my life would just as well be over. I'm not very good at this sort a thing, but you're our friend and we'll help you anyway we can."

"I've been doin' pretty good," said Jon. "It's been a month now since Leah died. I'll be all right. It'll just take a little more time. I'll keep myself busy and time will pass."

"There's gonna be a whole lotta buildin' goin' on shortly," said Michael. "I'll bet you'll be able to find some work then. Plus, you are still a deputy."

"That's right," said Sean. "Yer still one a my deputies. It's quiet right now, but you never know around this place. One a these days we might find out that Anderson did have a boss, and we'll go find him and his gang and hang all of 'em."

"Well I sure hope that Anderson didn't have a boss," replied Jon. "But if he does, we will get him and hang'em." Just as Jon finished speaking, Jug came over to the table.

"How are you doin'?" Jug asked Jon as he extended his hand. "Good to see you again. I see you healed all right after that shoot-out in Texas."

"Yep, I healed good," said Jon. "How's that good lookin' woman a yers?"

"She's doin' good," answered Jug. "She cookin' in the kitchen. We'll be leavin' fer Texas any day now. Got us a ranch lined up and we hope to bring a herd up here next summer."

"If she's cookin', I believe I'll have whatever she made today," said Jon. "Been a long time since I et."

"I'll go get you a plate," said Jug. "You'll like what she fixed today. Don't know what she calls it, but it eats good." Jug brought several plates to Jon. "These things here are called tortillas. You take that meat there and them beans and all that other stuff and put it on a tortilla. Then ya roll it up in the tortilla and start eatin'. Kinda like a sandwich."

Jon followed Jug's instruction and took a bite. "Damn, that is good," exclaimed Jon. "It's a little spicey but it is really good. You are gonna be one well fed man."

"I don't figure on losin' any weight in the next forty or fifty years," said Jug. "Nice seein' you again Jon. I better go help Tom now."

"Has much else happened since we last saw each other?" asked Jon.

"Do you remember me tellin' you about Braddock?" asked Sean.

"Yep, he was your father-in-law wasn't he?" answered Jon.

"Yes he was," replied Sean. "Well he got killed here a while back. When them idiots did that massacre at Sand Creek, Braddock was there with the Cheyenne. Most a the men were out huntin' when the soldiers attacked. Anyway, Braddock was on his way back when the shootin' started. He got back too late to do any good, but he killed a couple a them idiots before he took off. One a them soldier boys saw him and somehow they found out who he was. One a the boys he shot had eight more brothers and a crazy Pa. The Pa sent the boys out after'em. He killed one in the mountains and when Braddock came here for a visit, three more showed up. They killed Braddock, and I killed two a them. Jeb knocked the other one off a horse and broke his neck. Now there were four more brothers comin' here ta find out what really happened, but two of'em got killed by Indians. The two that's left could be here in a week'r so."

"Two fellas won't be no problem," said Jon. "Let's just hope they got enough sense to not start any trouble."

"Michael got married to Betty and they just got back from their honeymoon," said Sean. "He had to shoot a man in St. Louis, and Betty shot a man in Kansas City to keep him from shootin' Michael in the back."

"I'll tell you all about that another time," said Michael. "Tomorrow I'll show you one a these new Winchester rifles I picked up in St. Louis. I bet you'll like'm too."

"I still got my Henry," said Jon. "It's been good ta me. Now I think I'll have me a few more drinks."

"You can have your old room back," said Sean. "Hasn't been used for a bit, but it's got clean sheets and blankets. There's plenty a wood for the stove if ya get cold."

"I'll have them drinks then get on ta bed," said Jon. "I rode hard gettin' here. I could use me a bed."

~~~~

Gideon's shoulder was feeling a lot better and he figured it was now time to have it out with Caleb. They were maybe four days from Abilene now and as they were riding along, Gideon stopped his horse and dismounted. "If you wanna try and give me that whoopin' you were talkin' bout, git down off yer horse and do it," said Gideon. "I am not goin' to Abiliene with you. You can't whoop me anyhow."

"You asked for it, big brother," said Caleb. He got off his horse and the fight began. Both boys were about the same size and weight. Caleb would get in a few good punches, and then Gideon would get some in. This went on for a good while. When they had finally just about beat each other senseless, they both decided that they had had enough. "Yer goin' to Abilene," said Caleb.

"No I am not," replied Gideon. "We can whoop on each other some more if ya want, but I am not goin'."

"Yer just a coward," said Caleb.

"You got no right to call me that," replied Gideon. "I fought in that damn war and had my share a fightin' Injuns. I'm no coward and you know it. I'll be leavin' in the mornin'."

The next morning after coffee and biscuits, the boys went their separate ways. "I reckon I'll never see you again," said Caleb.

"I reckon not," said Gideon as he was leaving.

~~~~

A few days later, Caleb rode into Abilene. He went straight to the livery and boarded his horse. Billy was there was there with his dogs. Susie and Sam were now the proud parents of six. There were three males and three females. All of them were healthy and there wasn't a runt in the bunch. "Those'r some nice lookin' dogs boy," said Caleb. "I reckon you'll be goin' inta business soon. I just bet them dogs are good stock dogs."

"They sure are mister," said Billy. "Susie and Sam there been on cattle drives and I use'm to help move the horses around. I just tell'em what I want and they do it. The horses don't mind'em at all. I reckon these pups'll learn good too."

"I'd say they will," said Caleb. "Now I got me some business with that Federal Marshal. Could you tell me where he might be?"

"Last time someone asked me where ta find the Marshal, some men got killed," said Billy. "Mebbe I shouldn't tell ya."

"Well I'm here to find out about some men that got killed here a while back," said Caleb. "They was my brothers."

"I reckon I won't be tellin' you anything," said Billy.

"Suit yerself boy," said Caleb. "Town's not big. I'll find'm." Caleb left the livery and started his search for the Marshal. He went to the General Store first. Billy watched him and when he went inside the store, Billy ran to the saloon to tell the Marshal. Sean was setting at his regular table drinking coffee when Billy came in.

"Marshal, there's a man just got inta town and said that was his brothers that got killed here a while back," cried Billy. "He was lookin' fer you. I didn't tell him where you was."

"Thanks Billy, I appreciate you tellin' me," said Sean. "Now you better go back to the livery and stay inside. Might be some trouble, might not." Billy did as instructed. It wasn't five minutes later when Caleb walked into the saloon. He saw the badge on Sean and went straight to him. Sean could see that he had a pistol on his right hip.

Sean spoke first. "You gotta be one a them Crandall boys," said Sean. "Been expecting you. We was told there was two of you."

"There was four of us when we left," said Caleb. "I'm Caleb and my brother Jacob got killed by some Dog Soldiers on the way here, and my brother Aaron took an arrow in the leg and died from blood poisonin'. Gideon run off a few days ago. Now I want ta know how my three brothers got killed here."

"First thing yer gonna do is take off that gun belt," said Sean. "I'll tell you the whole story when I see that gun belt layin' in the table."

"What if I don't take it off?" said Caleb.

"I will shoot you dead," answered Sean. "Now would you please take off that gun belt. I really don't wanna kill you today or any day for that matter."

"I hear that you are very fast and can most likely kill me, and I reckon you will if I don't take it off," said Caleb. "I'll go ahead and take it off, but once we get done talkin', I'm puttin' it back on. Whatever happens will hafta happen." Caleb took off his gun belt and put it on the table.

"First off Caleb, I got a telegram from your sister Ruth," started Sean. "You Pa is dead. Some doctor said his heart gave out. Got the telegram not long ago." Caleb sat down at the table, put his head on his arms and cried like a baby for a few minutes. He finally regained his composure.

"Even if my Pa is dead, I still gotta find out how my brothers got killed," said Caleb.

"Well here's what happened," began Sean. "That man they killed was my father-in-law. He was here havin' a visit. He was goin' out the door of this saloon gettin' ready ta leave when your three brothers saw him. They were out in the street not fifty feet from him. All three of'em cut loose with shotguns and killed him. I ran outside and shot two of'em. One of'em took off on his horse and Jeb, that's my dog, run him down and knocked him off his horse. His neck broke when he fell. One a the ones I shot was still alive, but just barely. He was the one called Joseph. Before he died he asked me to send that telegram to yer Pa sayin' they got killed but they killed yer brother's killer. Later on, I got a telegram from yer Ma sayin' that four of ya were comin' here ta find out how them three got killed. Now you know all there is."

"My Pa said I was to kill my brothers' killers and their friends and their families," said Caleb.

"Sounds like yer Pa wasn't right in the head," said Sean. "He musta thought he was God Almighty. So what'r you gonna do Caleb?"

"If I try to kill you, I know you'll kill me," said Caleb. "I'm not scared a dyin', but if I gotta die, it should make sense. My brother Gideon was right. I need to do what I wanna do. Our Pa ran our life and we was never allowed to think for ourself. Bout time I started doin' that. You just keep that pistol and gun belt Marshal. I won't be needin' it. I got me a good rifle on my saddle if I have any trouble goin' back home. I'll be leavin' now. Do ya reckon that boy at the livery would let me buy one a them pups. I sure could use some company goin' home."

"He might just give ya one," said Sean. "His folks won't allow him to keep a pack a dogs."

"Marshal, I wanna thank you for your kindness," said Caleb. "Now I'll go see about that pup." Caleb went to the livery and when he left town, there was a big pup on the saddle with him. "I'm gonna call you Mose," Caleb said to the pup.

As Caleb was leaving town, Michael arrived at the saloon. "Who was that fella leavin' town with the dog?" asked Michael.

"That was one a the Crandall boys," answered Sean. "Sit down and I'll tell you all about the Crandalls."

"Should I get us a bottle or do you want some more coffee?" asked Michael.

"Coffee'll be fine," said Sean. Michael went to the kitchen and came back with a full pot and filled their cups. "I'll git started now. Braddock was at Sand Creek and he killed a couple a soldier boys. Someone seen him ridin' off, and somehow they found out who he was. One a the boys he killed had eight more brothers and a Pa that was a bible thumpin' hell fire and brimstone preacher. He started sendin' his boys out ta kill Braddock. Braddock killed one in the mountains and then three more came here. They killed Braddock and I killed two of them. Jeb knocked one off a horse and broke his neck. The old man sent the last four here ta find out what happened to them three. Two were killed by some Dog soldiers, and one run off. That fella that just left here was the last one. His Pa died while they was on the way here. I got a telegram from his sister. Anyway, he decided he would start thinkin' fer himself. He knew I would kill'em if I had to. His Pa musta had a tight reign on them boys. Hope things work out for'm. That pup'll be some good company for'm."

CHAPTER SEVEN

The same day that Jug and Lolita left for Texas, Cookie came back to town. He was in good spirits and it appeared that he was very glad to meet Barbara and have her in the kitchen with him. Together they made some fantastic meals. There was so much new construction going on now. New hotels and saloons were being built. More shops were being built too. Abilene was going to have it's first newspaper. It seemed that every one of the men who were doing the construction work were eating their meals at "Maggie's Place."

Maggie had sent some telegrams and now she had four more girls. Maggie hired them on a trial basis to make sure they would work out. They were all beautiful, and the men loved them. Michael's piano had arrived, and they put it in one of the front corners. Betty helped behind the bar and Michael banged away on the piano. Maggie even sang once in a while. Whenever Maggie went up by the piano to sing, there was total silence in the place. Maggie was actually a very good singer. Sean was impressed. Of course he always said that it didn't matter if she could sing or not. She was so gorgeous that all eyes would be on her anyway. Things were quiet and business was booming. All was well until a tele-gram arrived from Judge Simmons. It went as follows:

Federal Marshal Sean O'Rourke
Abilene

Town Marshal and one deputy murdered in Kansas City<< stop >> new town marshal appointed << stop >> no cooperation between town marshal and county sheriff <<stop>> believe widespread corruption there from all persons in public office<< stop>> go there and clean up town

Federal Judge David Simmons
St. Louis

It was late afternoon when Sean had received the telegram and he decided to wait until dinner time to give the bad news to Maggie. Sean had Michael, Betty, and Jon join Maggie and him for dinner. They had just finished another good meal from Barbara and Cookie when Sean gave them the news. "I got a tele-gram today from the Judge," Sean began. "Been some trouble in Kansas City. Town Marshal and a deputy been murdered. The Judge thinks most of the public officials are corrupt. I gotta go up there and clean things up. I would like for Jon to go with me, and Michael to stay here."

"Are you sure you don't want me to go along?" asked Michael.

"I'd love for you to go too Michael," said Sean. "But things are really growing here, and I need someone to be here. You're a good man, Michael. You can handle everything. If things would get to where me and Jon were in trouble, I'd send for you. If somethin' did come up that you and the girls couldn't handle, Jason will help."

"I guess it's been quiet for too long," said Maggie. "I've been getting used to you being with me every day. I'll miss that, but I know who and what you are. You'll get it cleaned up, then you and Jon'll be back. I just hope it doesn't take too long."

"You and me both Maggie," said Sean. "I'll have a hard time sleepin' every night we're not together. Now let's have us a few drinks and then Jon and me'll get ourselves ready to leave in the mornin'. We'll be takin' the mornin' stage and we'll take our horses with us. Jon, I want you to take that Sharps that I got for Braddock. Take that and yer Henry and yer pistols and plenty of ammunition."

"We won't get killed fer lack a shootin' back, will we?" said Jon.

"No we won't," replied Sean. "I'll be takin' my Sharps, a Winchester, the ten gauge, and two pistols. Plenty of ammunition too. We'll be ready for anything."

After they finished their drinks, Sean took Maggie by the hand and was leading her upstairs to their room. As they were going past the kitchen, Sean looked in and Cookie was standing right next to Barbara and Sean could see that Cookie had his hand on Barbara's backside. "I told you them two would get together," Sean said to Maggie. "Ole Cookie had his hand on her backside when we walked past the kitchen."

"I'm glad for them," said Maggie. "Now let's get upstairs and you can put your hands on my backside." Sean did not need any encouragement.

~~~~

The next morning after an early breakfast, Sean and Jon finished their packing and had their horses ready to go. The stage left on time, and Maggie had a tear in her eye when she kissed Sean goodbye. Martha came to see Jon off too. Dog went with them. There were only three passengers total, so some of the time, Dog rode inside the stage. The other passenger didn't mind. He and Dog became good friends on the trip.

Several days later, the stage pulled into Kansas City. Sean and Jon went straight to the hotel where they had stayed after getting Anderson. There were some different people there this time, but nothing was said about the dog. They unloaded their gear and then boarded their horses at the closest livery.

"Let's get back to that hotel and git somethin' ta eat," said Sean. "As I recall, they got good food there."

"Sounds good," said Jon. "I'm plenty hungry myself."

They went back to the hotel and took at table at the saloon. The table was where they could see everything in the place and the front door, and no one could get around them without being seen. The same man who had waited on them before came over and got them some drinks. "I remember you from a while back," the man said. "You're that Federal Marshal and this man is a deputy a yours. I wish you men were here a while back. Somethins goin' on in this place and in this town too. Bad things been happening."

"When you get a chance, come back over and tell us some a what's been goin' on," said Sean.

~ ~ ~ ~

Just as the man walked away, a nasty voice came from behind the bar. "The dog can stay, but the breed's leavin'. I don't serve no breeds in my place."

"This man's a Federal Deputy and he stays here," said Sean. "Now you keep yer mouth to yerself before I put a dent in yer head." The man reached down behind the bar and pulled up a sawed off double barreled shotgun and pointed it at Sean.

"The breed goes," said the man.

"You even touch the hammers on that shotgun and I'll put a bullet between yer eyes," said Sean. "Now put that thing away before I hafta kill you." The man didn't heed what Sean said, and Sean saw his thumb move toward the hammers. Before he could get the shotgun cocked, he was falling backwards with a bloody hole between his eyes. The back of his head came apart, and pieces of skull and brains went all over the big mirror behind the bar as it was breaking. "Anybody else got anything to say about my deputy?" asked Sean. There was total silence in the place.

The man who had waited on Sean and Jon came over to their table. "That son of a bitch will not be missed," he said. "I know he stole this place from the previous owner, but nothin' was proved."

"How about you or someone go get the Town Marshal," Sean said to the man.

"I'll go get him," said the man. "But you watch yourself. I think that man and his deputies are a pack a murderers and thieves. The Mayor a this town is a damn thief, and the Judge is as crooked as they come."

"Go ahead and get'm over here," said Sean. "We can handle anything they got." After the man left, Sean had a few words with Jon. "Let's be ready for anything," said Sean. "Have your pistols ready and fully loaded."

"I'll be ready," said Jon. "I got me a feelin' that we're gonna have some trouble with them fellas."

About five minutes later, the Town Marshal arrived. He was a middle aged man, tall and slender. He had a Colt revolver on his right hip. There were three deputies with him. They all had Colts. The Marshal walked right to Seans's table, and the three deputies spread out. "None a you men better get behind me," said Sean. "You stay right where I can see you." The deputies did as instructed.

"I give the orders in this town" said the Marshal. "Now just who in the hell'r you, and how come you killed that man?"

"I'm Federal Marshal O'Rourke and this man is my deputy," Sean began. "That idiot pulled a shotgun on me and I killed'em." Sean and Jon both stood now.

"I heard a you," said the Town Marshal. "In this town we don't care if yer a federal man'r not. As I said before, I give the orders here. Now why did that fella pull a shotgun on you?"

"He didn't want my deputy being here," said Sean.

"Well anyone can see he's a breed," said the Marshal. "If he don't want breeds in here that's his business. That man you just killed was my brother-in-law. You're under arrest."

"Which one a you fellas wanna die first?" asked Sean. "One a you go ahead and try to pull a pistol so I can kill you and get it over with." The Town Marshal had two deputies on his right and one on the left. Nothing happened for what seemed like five minutes, then the deputy on the left and the one the far right made their move. Before they had cleared their holsters, both men lay dead on the floor. Sean had killed one and Jon had killed the other. The Town Marshal and his remaining deputy did not move one bit. Sean took his pistol and stuck in about an inch from the

Town Marshal's head. "You and your deputy will reach down and drop you gun belts. Then you will empty all your pockets and then undress down to your drawers."

"I'm not goin' down to my drawers for no man," said the Town Marshal. As soon as the words came out of his mouth, Jon took his pistol and cracked the Marshal on the side of his head. He hit the floor hard.

"You want some a this too?" Jon said to the deputy. "Now git it done." The deputy undressed and helped the town marshal undress.

Sean called to the bartender. "Come over here mister," Sean said. "You know how to use this thing?" Sean handed one of the deputy's pistols to him.

"I know how to use that thing," he answered. "I fought in the war."

"Well you're a Federal Deputy now," Sean said. "We'll be takin' these two to jail and lockin'em up. Your're gonna stand guard on'em. After we get'em in jail, you shoot anyone that tries to get'em out. Is that all right with you?"

"That's all right with me," said the bartender. "Maybe they'll try to escape and I can shoot'em. By the way, name's Cutright, Alex Cutright."

"Good to know ya Alex," said Sean. "I'm Sean O'Rourke and that pistol whippin' deputy is Jon O'Brien. Now you and me will get these two to jail, and Jon'll stay here and keep an eye on things till I get back. Deputy, you can carry that boss a yers. Now git movin'."

The jail was two blocks from the hotel. Sean found the cell keys and they put the Marshal in one cell and the deputy in another. "I'm goin' back to the hotel now Alex," said Sean. "Anybody tries to get them two out, you kill'em. Sean and Alex had taken all the gun belts with them to the jail. "You got plenty a fire power here," said Sean. "We should be back here shortly."

It was still quiet when Sean got back to the hotel. Another man was behind the bar now. "Do you work here?" Sean asked him.

"No, I needed another drink and no one was here to get it so I got it myself," the man said. "While I was back here, I went ahead and got drinks for the other boys."

"Do you live in this town?" Sean asked the man.

"Been here for bout ten years now," he answered. "I'm a clerk at the Post Office."

"Is this town fulla crooks and such?" asked Sean.

"Bout a month before the Marshal and Deputy was killed, things started goin' on," the man said. "Some thugs were goin' around tryin' to get a lot of the businesses to sell out. Most of'em didn't at first, then people started gettin' beat up and things. Then the Marshal and Deputy got killed. Then we got a new Mayor and a new Judge and a new Town Marshal. They're all a pack a thieves. There's too many of'em for us to stand up to. I think the telegraph operator is on their payroll too. We tried to get word out about things, but nothing was gettin' out. Somehow, someone got word to that Federal Judge in St. Louis. We been waitin' for somethin' ta happen. That somethin' is you, isn't it?"

"Yes it is," said Sean. "I'll get things cleaned up here one way or another. So if your Mayor is a crook, how did he get to be Mayor? That's an elected position."

"We had us an election, but it was rigged," the clerk said. "I don't know of one person who voted for that son of a bitch, but they said he won the election. Then he appointed that new Marshal. We never seen him here before. Then that Judge and all them other gunmen showed up. Every business in town is either run by them crooks or they get a big percentage of the profits. Anybody don't pay usually has some sort a accident. You see what we're up against."

"I see," said Sean. "I'll get things figured out. There's a County Sheriff isn't there?"

"We got one," the clerk said. "He used to be a good man till them crooks came to town. They got some kinda agreement. He don't mess with stuff in town, and the Marshal don't mess with stuff outta town. I heard they threatened his family too."

"Where's he at now?" asked Sean.

"There was some trouble in some small place east a here, and he went there with his two deputies," said the clerk. "I think someone got killed. His office is over in the same building as the Mayor. We'll get these bodies over to the undertaker."

Just as the second body was out the saloon door, several shots rang out. They were coming from the direction of the jail. Jon and Sean took off at a dead run. As they got closer to the jail, they could see five men firing into the Marshal office. Sean and Jon took aim and began firing at the five men. Two of them fell, but three of them got away. The two that fell were dead. Sean and Jon went to the jail. Alex was sitting at a desk and bleeding from his right shoulder and his left side. The Town Marshal and the deputy were dead in their cells.

"I told'em that if they didn't stop shootin', I would kill the Marshal and the deputy," Alex said. "I didn't hafta shoot'em. Them other fellas shots hit'em. Maybe they killed'em so they couldn't talk."

"We gotta get you a doctor," said Sean. "We need to keep a good man like you alive."

"His office is a half block down on the left," said Alex. "He's got a sign up. Name's Doc Walton. He used to come runnin' whenever there was some shootin', but here lately there's been so much that he just waits till someone comes and gets him. He's a good doctor."

Jon went after the doctor and was back in a few minutes. "Just what the hell happened to you Alex?" asked Doc. "Are you a gunmen now?"

"No Doc, just helpin' out these Federal boys," answered Alex.

"Well you just lie still while I get this bleedin' stopped, then we'll get you over to my office," said Doc. Jon and Sean carried Alex over to Doc's office. "You're lucky Alex," said Doc. "Both bullets went straight through and didn't take much with'em. You'll heal up good. Now just who are you two and why are you gettin' my people shot up?"

"I'm Federal Marshal O'Rourke and this is my Deputy Jon O'Brien," said Sean. "We got sent here to clean up this town."

"Well it sure as hell needs some cleanin," said Doc. "Don't suppose you can get it done without gettin' me more business can you?"

"That'll depend on whoever the boss is here," said Sean. "If he wants to die, I'll help'em out."

"Well I'm not sure who the boss is," said Doc. "Could be the Judge or could be the Mayor. They're both crooks. I figure they got a bigger boss somewhere else. I don't think they're smart enough to handle things around here. The hired help'r just some cheap gunmen and they got a bunch of'em. Hope you got plenty of ammunition."

"We got plenty a that," said Sean. "Is there some men in this town we can trust? When we start lockin' fellas up, we're gonna need some help."

"I'll get you some good men," said Doc. "That man that works at the Post Office is a good man."

"I already met him," said Sean. "I'll go see'm shortly."

"Well if you know him, he's the one that can get you some good men," said Doc.

~~~~

Sean and Jon went back to the hotel. The man from the Post Office was still behind the bar.

"What's the price of a drink now?" asked Sean.

"On the house, that bastard's been overchargin' us ever since he stole the place," he answered. "My name is Roger Talbert. Join us in a drink if you would."

"I surely would," said Sean. Roger poured Sean and Jon a drink and then proposed a toast.

"Here's ta gettin' rid a that scum," toasted Roger. Everyone in the place repeated the words.

"I'm glad you all feel that way," said Sean. "I'll be needin' a little help before too long."

"What would you have us do?" asked Roger.

"We're gonna start arrestin' some people here shortly and we'll need some men to help stand guard at the jail," said Sean. "Course if they don't want arrested, we'll kill'em if we hafta. Or I s'pose they could get outta town. I'd rather they didn't do that cause they might decide ta come back."

"What happened to Alex?" asked Roger.

"He got himself shot," said Sean. "He'll be all right. That Marshal and Deputy got killed while five men were firin' up the jail."

"Well that's two more sons a bitches we don't hafta worry about," said Roger. "Me and the boys'll give you a hand. Just say when. Now you need to know that the Judge and Mayor both have a couple of gunmen with them all the time. I guess they're kinda like body guards. You wanna be careful when you go after them. Let's go now out now and I'll show you where they both live and where their offices are."

Roger showed Sean and Jon where the municipal offices were. The building was at the east end of town. It was a big two story building and set there by itself. The closest building to it was a dress shop that was at least two hundred feet from it. There was no building directly across the street from it. It was evident that the Judge and the Mayor were there because there were several men around the place. They stayed a block back so they wouldn't be seen. Roger then showed them where the Judge and the Mayor lived. It didn't look like anyone was home at either place. Roger knew that both men were married, but they also spent a lot of time at a local brothel. After they studied the place a bit, they went back to the hotel.

"I don't think they'll do anything tonight," said Sean. "You men go on home when you're ready. Me and Jon'll take turns sleepin' and we'll come up with a plan in the mornin'. Is there any food in that kitchen? Me and Jon never did git ta eat." Roger ran back to the kitchen and came back with two plates of some stew. Sean and Jon ate their fill then Sean took first watch.

~~~~

Nothing happened during the night. Right after daylight, Roger and the other men started showing up. "We're here and we're ready to help," said Roger. "All of us boys were in the war so we know how ta shoot. We don't have a lotta guns, but what we got will get the job done."

"That's good," said Sean. "Things could get bloody. Now is there anybody else in town that can do telegraphy?"

"I believe we got someone," said Roger. "Ole Fred lives in a shack down by the tracks. He tells everone that he was a telegrapher for General Grant. He lost a leg at Petersburg."

"We'll need to see if he'll work for us," said Sean. "If he will, we'll get rid a that other fella. Someone'll need to be with Fred too standin' guard. I'll give that person my ten gauge if he don't have his own weapon. Now is there a newspaper in town?"

"We used to have two of'em," answered Roger. "Them crooks took one over and put the other one outta business. Tom Tucker run that paper and he's right here with us."

"Well Tom, is your equipment still operational, and if it is, how long would it take you to get up and printing?" asked Sean.

"I could be printin' in a day," answered Tom. "Just keep them crooks away, and I'll print whatever you want."

"Well when you start printin', you're gonna have a headline that says the local citizenry will be takin' back the town," started Sean. "Then you can say that all crooks will be prosecuted to the fullest extent a the law, up to and including hangin'. Have a big story about it. Now I want two a you boys to go with Tom and help him get started. Get your guns, and if anybody tries to stop you or gets in the way, shoot them. Don't hesitate. If you do, they'll probably kill you. Tom, you make a buncha copies and let me know when they're ready. We'll pass'em out all over town.

Now Jon and me and one other fella'r goin' to the telegraph office. We'll be back shortly."

~~~~

When they got to the telegraph office, the operator was sitting at his desk drinking coffee. "You're out of a job now," said Sean. "You got three choices. I can kill you right now. You can leave town right now, or you can go to jail. Make up your mind real quick like."

"I work for Western Union," the man said. "I don't know who you think you are but you can't fire me."

"You work for that buncha crooks, not Western Union," said Sean as he stuck a pistol in the man's face. "Now make up yer mind."

"I'll be leavin' right away," said the clerk as he ran out of the office.

"Don't even think about trying ta tell that Mayor or that Judge about this," yelled Sean. "We got people watchin', and if you go near them, we'll shoot you dead." The operator ran into a boarding house and came out in a few minutes with a small suitcase. He ran to the livery and was seen riding out of town a few minutes later at a full gallop. "Now we'll pay a visit to that other newspaper in town," said Sean.

When they got to the newspaper office, Sean sent Jon around to watch the back and he and the other man went in the front door. A man of about thirty was there setting some type. Sean could see that he was wearing a shoulder holster under his jacket. "What can I help you gentlemen with?" the man asked as he turned to face them.

"The first thing you can do is to remove that pistol from under your coat," said Sean.

"And what if I don't?" asked the man.

"I'll shoot you dead," said Sean.

"You can try," said the man. "Just who are you anyway?"

"Name's O'Rourke, Federal Marshal Sean O'Rourke," answered Sean.

"I have heard of you," the man said. "I hear you are the best there is with both rifle and pistol. I suppose you could probably kill me, but I don't think you would. Shooting a newspaper man would cause a big stink."

"I wouldn't mind the smell, now do like I said," said Sean. The man still didn't remove his pistol. He asked Sean if he could light up a cigar and before Sean could answer, he was reaching into his right coat pocket. Sean was not fooled one bit. When the man's hand started out of his pocket, Sean drew a pistol and fired. The man was thrown backwards with a hole in his chest. There was a small pistol in his right hand. When the shot was fired, Sean could hear someone running toward the back of the building. He heard a door open, then he heard a thump. He went back to see what had happened. Jon was standing next to a man laying on the ground.

"I hit'em with my pistol," said Jon. "Who is he anyway?"

"Don't know," said Sean. "He ran out the back door after I shot that fella up front. That pistol a yers is gonna get bent one a these days if yer not careful."

"I s'pose I coulda shot'm, but his way we can question him went he comes to," said Jon. "Maybe he'll be useful, maybe he won't."

"Well wake'm up, and let's get back to the hotel," said Sean. When they went out in the street to head back to the hotel, they could see plenty of activity down toward to municipal offices. It looked like the building was surrounded by several men. "Jon, I want you to go to the telegraph office and stay there till I get back to you," said Sean. "I'll take this fella with me. If anybody gives you any trouble, you know what to do."

When Sean got back to the hotel, Ole Fred was already there and ready to go. "I haven't touched a key since Petersburg, but it's not somethin' ya ever ferget," said Fred. "I'm ready."

"Thanks Fred, glad yer with us," said Sean. "Now one a you fellas go with Fred to the telegraph office. Jon is there. Tell'm to come on back here. You that's goin' with Fred, have ya got a weapon?"

"I got a spencer rifle, and it's been used some," said the man. "I'll shoot anyone that don't have proper business there."

"Good man," said Sean. "Now when Jon gets back, I want to go around ta every business in town and have a talk with'em. I'll need ta know who works fer them crooks and who don't."

"I'll be goin' with ya Marshal," said Roger. "I pretty much know who's in with'em and who isn't."

"All right Roger, let's go," said Sean. "The rest a you men stay here, but say alert. Them crooks haven't tried nothin' yet but they're not gonna just sit around and let us take over. Could be some shootin' any time now."

~~~~

Sean and Jon and Roger went to a General Store first. "This one here is run by them crooks," said Roger. "I don't think they'll be any trouble though."

Sean walked straight up to the counter. A middle aged man was there with a woman, probably his wife. "Name's Federal Marshal O'Rourke," Sean began. "Is this your place or do them crooks own it?"

"I don't know what you mean by crooks," said the man. "The Mayor owns this place, and I run it for him."

"Is he a relative a yours or somethin'?" asked Sean.

"No, I needed a job and he gave me one," said the man. "You're not going to hurt us are you?"

"I'm not gonna hurt you," said Sean. "You sound like you could be an honest man. Maybe you don't know that your boss is a crook and probably a murderer. If you do know and I find out, I will probably kill you. Do you understand?"

"I swear to you Marshal. We only work here," the man cried. "I keep my nose out of everyone else's business."

"Well that's good," said Sean. "Sooner or later there's gonna be a lotta shootin' in this town and we'll feel more comfortable knowing that you keep your nose out of everyone's business. Tell you what. After we kill your boss, which we are gonna do one way or the other, you can be the owner of this place. Does that sound all right to you?"

"I wouldn't mind being the owner," the man said. "He doesn't pay us hardly enough to live on anyway."

"I got one more thing ta say," said Sean. "If anyone comes here lookin' ta buy some ammunition and you know they work for the Mayor, you tell'em yer out of everything until the next shipment comes in."

"That won't be a problem." he said. "We are already out of .44 shells, and there's only a little black powder left. I never did carry any Spencer shells. Not much call for them."

"That's good," said Sean. "Them fellas might try ta get rough with ya if they don't believe ya. Be careful."

"There's another General Store at the other end of town," said Roger. "They don't work fer them crooks, but they pay'em a percentage."

"We'll talk to'em after we go to some a these other places," said Sean.

"I can tell you right now that every saloon in this town is owned by the Mayor, all five of'em," said Roger. "The men he has runnin' the places are a rough bunch. They treat their girls bad too."

"We'll fix that," said Sean. "I don't stand for mistreatin' women. Let's go over to that livery."

"I'm not sure bout this place," said Roger. "There's another livery in town too, and I'm not sure bout it either."

"We'll find out shortly," said Sean. When they entered the barn of the livery, a short middle aged man was getting some hay for some of the horses that were in some stalls.

"What can I do fer you?" he asked Sean and Roger.

"You can tell me if this is your place or not," said Sean.

"And just why do you need ta know that, and who the hell are you?" he asked.

"I'm Federal Marshal O'Rourke," answered Sean. "And you're gonna tell me if this is your place or if you work for that buncha crooks."

"This is my place," the livery man said. "Them crooks take twenty percent from me. If I don't pay, they say this place'll burn pretty good."

"Well we're takin' this town back," said Sean. "Could be a lotta shootin' soon. We could use your help."

"I got a Henry rifle here that some fella had on his saddle a while back," said the livery man. "He got himself stuck with a knife one night, and no one ever claimed his stuff. I know how ta use it."

"We'll let you know when we need you," said Sean. "In the meantime, if they come around collectin', you go ahead and pay'em just like nothin' was goin' on. We'll get your money back sooner or later."

Sean and Jon and Roger visited every business in town except the saloons and the banks. All of the other businesses were in the same boat as the livery owner. They were all paying off the crooks.

"I think it's time we visited the banks," said Sean. "I have money in that one bank. It'd be nice ta know if they was tied in with these crooks or not. If they aren't, I bet them crooks got some money in here anyway."

The President of the bank was still the same man who had opened the account for Bob Wallace. He remembered Sean from when he stopped in and withdrew some money after they had gotten Anderson. "It's good to see you Marshal O'Rourke," Mr. Brown said. "How can I be of service to you today?"

"I don't mean to question your integrity," Sean began. "I'm sure you know that a buncha crooks'r runnin' this town now. I need ta know if they got their hooks into you."

"I can understand your thinking," Mr. Brown said. "The Mayor and the Judge both have personal accounts here. They are very small accounts, and I think they just do that for show. Maybe they think that if they do some banking, some people will think they are legitimate business men or honest. I would say that the Mayor has a safe of his own. It should be full of money from what

I hear. Now I can vouch for the other bank in town. The President is a good family friend. I trust him."

"That's good and I'm glad you're not involved," said Sean. "We're gonna take the town back before too long. When you hear a lotta shootin', stay low."

"I always carry a small pistol on me," said Mr. Brown. "If the need arises, I can help."

"I thank you," said Sean. "Now I gotta go see a man about a newspaper."

~~~~

They went back to the hotel and questioned the man who had run out the back door of the newspaper office. "I just worked for that man," he said. "Everybody knows they're all crooks but a man's gotta eat."

"If that's true, when the shootin' starts, you can help us or get outta the way," said Sean.

"I believe I'll get outta the way," the man said. "Can I go now?"

"You can go," said Sean. "But don't be tellin' anybody about this." The man never said a word as he was leaving. Sean went over to Tom's place to see how the paper was coming along.

"I'll have enough copies for the whole dern town before dark," Tom said.

"Good, we'll get'em passed out in the mornin'," said Sean. "Now I'm goin' to the telegraph office to see if anythin's goin' on." Just as Sean got there, Fred was finishing a message. It was for the Mayor. Fred handed it to Sean. It went as follows:

Mayor Hanson
Kansas City

Did you get men sent after O'Rourke's woman<< stop>>
She must be taken

The Judge

Sean read the telegram. "Where did this come from and who
is this Judge?" Sean asked Fred.

"That's one thing about a telegram," said Fred. "You can't tell
where it come from and I don't know nothin' bout no Judge. I bet
he's the big boss though."

"I'd say you're right," said Sean. "Now I gotta get a telegram
to Abilene right now. Here goes:

Maggie O'Rourke
Abilene

Men coming to take you <<stop>> Don't know when
they started<< stop >> Could be in Abilene now Stay
armed<< stop>> tell Michael<<stop>> keep Jeb with you
at all times << stop>> be back soon as possible

Sean
Kansas City

"Put somethin' with that to tell the operator to get that to
Maggie darn quick and I'll be waitin' for a reply," said Sean. Sean
was furious now, but he couldn't do anything for her now other

than warn her. "Why do these sons a bitches gotta be messin' with my woman," Sean said to himself. "Any of'em left alive after this is gonna get hung."

A half hour later, a telegram came for Sean. It went as follows:

Marshal O'Rourke
Kansas City

Got your message<< stop>> Am well armed<< stop>> Michael well armed<< stop >> Betty and Tom armed <<stop >> Cookie armed << stop >> Jeb with me Get it done and get back to me

Maggie O'Rourke
Abilene

Sean went back to the hotel. "All right boys, in the mornin' we'll pass out them papers to the whole town," said Sean. "Who'll volunteer to take some down to the Mayor's office?"

"I know," said Roger. "We'll get one a the Mayor's saloon girls to take'em. They won't shoot her."

"You got one in mind?" asked Sean.

"Yes I do," answered Roger. "That Sally over at the Boar's Head can be a real bitch. She works for that bunch but she don't like'em. She'll do it. I'll slip over ta her place tonight and tell her what's up."

"I want all you men to go home and get some rest and be back here at daylight," said Sean. "Be ready for anything when you get here."

~~~~

All the men left and then Jon just stood there looking down the street for a few minutes. "Just why in the hell haven't they done anything yet?" asked Jon.

"I'll tell ya why," said Sean. "Cause they sent some men to Abilene ta take Maggie, and they're waitin' ta hear back. They're hopin' they got her and I'll leave after I find out."

"How do you know that?" asked Jon.

"Cause there was a telegram to the Mayor from someone called the Judge asking if my woman had been took yet," answered Sean. "I sent a telegram to Maggie tellin' her what's goin' on. She got the message and got back ta me. Everybody back home is armed, even Tom and Cookie."

"I'd say that nobody's gonna get Maggie then," said Jon. "I'd say someone's gonna get themselves shot ta pieces."

"Yep, and maybe Jeb'll rip out someone's throat again," added Sean.

That's right," said Jon. "Ole Jeb did rip out that man's throat back on the cattle drive."

CHAPTER EIGHT

The day that Maggie received the telegram from Sean, business at the saloon was very good as it had been ever since all the new construction had started. There were so many new faces in town it was hard to keep an eye on anyone. Several of Maggie's dresses had big pockets on each side and tonight she wore a green dress and several slips. There was a Colt revolver in each pocket. Jeb never left her side no matter where she went. Michael wore his Colt and there was a double barreled ten gauge against the wall beside the piano. Betty had her .32 in a dress pocket. Tom had a revolver on his left hip in plain sight for all to see. Cookie had a Colt revolver hidden under his apron. There was a double barreled shotgun at each end of the bar as always.

That night the place was packed clear full. As full as the place was, it still became totally quiet when Maggie went to the piano to sing. Finally about midnight some of the patrons started to leave. By 1am there were only about ten people left in the place. Of these ten people, no one looked suspicious or anything. Maggie announced that everyone could get one more drink, then she was closing the place for the night.

After the last customer was out the door and the working girls and Tom and Cookie and Barbara were gone, she closed up the place. "Well nothing happened tonight," Maggie said to Michael . "Let's hope tomorrow is the same."

"Me and Betty aren't goin' anywhere till you're safe in bed," said Michael. "This night isn't over yet. We'll be right here till you get up them stairs and into bed."

"Well I'm taking Jeb out the back door so he can do his necessaries and then I'll go straight to bed," said Maggie.

"We'll be right here waitin' on you," said Michael.

Maggie and Jeb went out the back door. Maggie left the door open so she could be heard by Michael if anything happened. She stood in the shadows away from the light of the open door. She also put her hands in her dress pockets. When she did, she also very lightly cocked the hammers on the pistols. Jeb went somewhere in the shadows to do his business. She thought she heard a board creak and she turned her head just slightly to look to her left. When she did, someone grabbed her from behind. Then another man stepped out of the shadows. Maggie could see that this man had a pistol in his right hand. The man holding her did not have a pistol in either hand but Maggie could feel that he had one in his belt. Maggie could also see that the pistol in the man's hand did not have its hammer cocked.

"Don't say one word or scream or anything or we'll kill you," said the man with the pistol. In the darkness, Maggie could make out the right foot of the man holding her. She squeezed the trigger of the pistol in her right dress pocket and the man let out a deafening scream. Before the other man could do anything, Jeb had him by his right wrist. Jeb dragged him to the ground and shook fiercely. The man's hand came off his arm and was in Jeb's mouth. The hand was still clenching the pistol. Jeb let go of the hand and got the man by the throat. The man didn't scream for long.

When Maggie fired the pistol in her pocket, her dress caught on fire. She rushed into the bathhouse and put out the fire with some water that was in the barrels. When she came back outside, the man she had shot in the foot was still screaming in pain. She calmly walked over to him and shot him through the head.

When Michael heard the first shot, he told Betty to watch the front door and then went to see what had happened. As he neared the back door, Betty yelled to him that she had heard some people running down the sidewalk out front. Michael went back towards the front door. As he neared it, several shots rang out and bullet holes were ripped into the front door. In the moonlight as Betty looked out a front window, she could see a man out front in the shadows. He had a pistol in his left hand. He had not noticed Betty. Betty took out her .32 and took careful aim. She fired through the window and the man was struck in the throat. Michael heard him fall. When that man fell, Michael could hear another man running down the sidewalk away from the saloon. Michael opened the door, spotted the man in the moonlight and took careful aim and fired. The bullet struck the man in the back of the head, killing him instantly. Betty ran out the door to check on the man she had shot. He wasn't dead but he would be very shortly. He tried to get some words out but never did. Then Michael and Betty ran out back to check on Maggie.

When they got out back, Maggie was sitting on the sidewalk with Jeb beside her. She was hugging Jeb and telling him that he was a wonderful dog. They saw the man's hand that had been removed from his arm and it was still holding the pistol. Then they saw that his throat had been ripped out.

"That Jeb sure is some dog," said Michael. "I'm glad he's on our side." Michael saw the other man's foot and he knew what had happened. "Did you burn your leg?" he asked Maggie.

"No, but I ruined a perfectly good dress and some slips," answered Maggie. "I heard that shooting out front. How many more of them were there?"

"There's two out front, both dead," said Betty. "I hope that this is the end of this business."

"I surely hope so too," said Maggie. "I'll send a telegram to Sean in the morning and tell him what happened. I hope things are well on his end."

Jason from the leather goods was awakened by the shooting and came over to see what had happened. "Just some more bad people tryin' to take Maggie to get at Sean," Michael told him. "There's two here in front and two more out back. I'll be needin' your help to get'em off the street. We'll get'em to the barber shop in the mornin'. That barber won't like this. He's been pretty busy lately just cuttin' hair and such. He'll be glad when we do get a regular undertaker in town."

Jason helped Michael move the bodies and then Michael went through their pockets. There was nothing that could identify any of them and there was fifty dollars total between all of them in their pockets. "I guess I'll sell their guns tomorrow and later if we find they had horses, we'll sell them too," said Michael. "The buryin' fund'll get a little more money."

"What's the buryin' fund?" Jason asked Michael.

"Anytime young Sean kills someone, he checks them for money, then sells all their guns and horses ," answered Michael.

"The money is used to get them buried and anything left goes to the buryin' fund. That way if the next man doesn't have any money or a horse or guns, we can use that money to get'm buried."

"Sounds like a good thing," said Jason. "Well I'm goin' back to sleep now. I'll give you a hand gettin' them bodies moved in the morning."

Maggie was still out back hugging Jeb. After maybe another five minutes, they went up to Maggie's room.

~~~~

The next morning, all the men returned to Sean's hotel. Tom Tucker was there with a good stack of newspapers. "I want you men to spread out and get a paper to all the businesses and anyone you see," said Sean. "Try not to get into a shootin' match. Roger, you get that woman over here and we'll have her take some over to the Mayor and the Judge."

"I'll be right back," said Roger as he went out the door. He was back in about fifteen minutes. Sally was with him but she was having a hard time waking up.

"Can't I get some coffee before I do whatever it is you want me to do?" Sally asked. Sean brought her a cup and filled it for her. "Hey, you're a good lookin' man," said Sally. "You must be that Marshal all the fuss is about. I might do you for free."

"Thanks Sally," said Sean. "I appreciate the thought. Now what we want you to do is take some a these newspapers over to the Mayor and Judge. They're over at the Municipal building. We figure they won't shoot you. Them and all their men been holed up there all night."

~~~~

"No they wouldn't shoot me," said Sally. "I make too much money for'em. They also like all them free ones they get."

"So you give them free ones all the time?" Sean asked.

"It's not just me," said Sally. "They make all us girls in town give them and all their hired men free ones."

"What happens if one of you don't wanna do free ones?" asked Sean.

"We usually get beat up and they take our money," said Sally. "We even had a couple girls come up missin' here a while back. No one knows if they run off or somethin' worse."

"Well we hope to make things better for you around here, Sally," said Sean. "Now as soon as you finish your coffee, would you take some a these papers over to the Municipal building?"

"Sure, I'll take'em over there," said Sally. "Now don't go gettin' yourself shot. I think I could wear you out."

"Thanks for the thought," said Sean. "After you get those papers dropped off, find yourself some good cover and stay there. Could be some shootin' shortly." Just as Sally walked out the door with the papers, one of the men brought a telegram to Sean. It was from Maggie.

Federal Marshal O'Rourke
Kansas City

Four men tried to take me last night<< stop>> they are dead<< stop>> no one here hurt

Maggie O'Rourke
Abilene

Sean was overjoyed when he read the telegram. "That takes a load off my mind," Sean said to Jon. "Now I can concentrate on the situation here."

"The men got all them papers delivered," said Jon. "What'll we do now?"

"We're gonna wait about an hour, and then we'll pay a visit to every place that's owned by these crooks," said Sean. "We'll tell'em we're gonna take over the town, and if they get in our way, we'll kill'em. I'm hopin' they stay out of it. You and me and Roger and me are gonna do the visitin'. When we go, I want you other men to stay right here. Stay alert."

When the hour was up, the three men started making their visits. The only businesses that gave Sean a hard time were the saloons. At the Boar's Head, Jon had to pistol whip the man who ran the place when he came after them with an axe handle. They tied him up and told the bartender they'd be back for him shortly. "I will beat the hell outta anyone who makes a move to let this man loose," said Sean. "Don't try me."

There was no more pistol whipping or any shots fired at the other saloons, but the person who ran each place was taken and put in jail along with the man Jon had pistol whipped. "You got no right to do this," one of them said as they were put in the jail. "We'll have your hide fer this."

Sean looked at Roger. "Do you know these fellas?" Sean asked.

"Sure, I know'em," answered Roger. "They're a bunch a scum. They mistreat their women. They water down the liquor and then overcharge for it. Them or their bosses run off the previous owners. I say we hang'em. No one knows if the previous owners were killed or just run off. I figure they was killed. No one's heard from'em. They were good men too. I knew each one of'em personally."

"We'll probably never find out what really happened," said Sean. "I'd say you're most likely right about them bein' killed. This bunch don't want no witnesses around. So how many men you think they got over there at the Municipal building?"

"Before any of'em got shot, they had fifteen men total and that's includin' the Marshal and his three deputies," said Roger. "They should only have nine men left."

"Well there's eight of us," said Sean. "I'll be going over to that building and askin' them if they read the paper and what they think they might do. I need a man to guard the jail."

"I'll get a good man in the jail," said Roger. "I'll tell'em if anyone comes in he don't recognize or anything, he should start shootin'."

The man was placed in the jail and Sean made his way to the Municipal building. He instructed Jon to keep the others at the hotel, but come running if shooting broke out. Sean worked his way to the dress shop which was the closest building to the Municipal building. He peered around a corner and hollered. "Did you boys get a chance ta read today's paper?" he yelled. As soon as he finished, several shots were fired. "I guess that means you read it," yelled Sean. "Oh, and by the way, this message is for you Mayor. Them four men you sent after my woman are dead." There was no reply. "Well you boys make up your mind," said Sean. "We're gonna get you outta there one way or the other. We might just burn you out. Now you think on that for a while." More shots rang out but Sean wasn't hit. He worked his way back to the hotel.

When the first shots were fired, Jon and the men had started toward the Municipal building but when Jon had seen what was happening, he had everyone return to the hotel.

"What're we gonna do now?" asked Jon.

"I'm gonna get my Sharps and get a good spot and see if I can pick off some a them," said Sean. "You take your Sharps and do the same. Maybe if we get some of'em, the others'll give up easier. You work your way back behind the building. I'll stay to the front. Take your time. The rest a you men just stay here but stay ready. We got them saloon bosses in jail, but there could be some a their help that want to get involved."

Both men got their rifles and worked their way to a good firing position. Sean got up on a roof of a general store and was around three hundred yards from the building. Jon found a good spot around two hundred yards to the back of the building. He had a small grove of trees for cover. Sean also had his spy glass with him. There were six windows on the front of the building, and there was a man at each window. Each man was armed with a repeating rifle.

The man at the window on the top left was exposing almost half of his body. Sean took careful aim and fired. He saw the man fall backwards. After that shot, Sean could only see the tops of the heads of the other men. When a man went running out the back door, Jon squeezed off a shot and the man was thrown to the ground. Jon reloaded just in time. Another man started out the back door. Jon fired but missed. The man ran back into the building. After a half hour, the men in the front windows started getting careless again. The man in the lower left window exposed his upper half. Sean took aim and fired. The man was knocked to the floor. Another man jumped out of a side window and made a run for some horses that were tied close to the dress shop. Jon spotted him. He waited until the man was mounted on the horse before he fired. The man was thrown sideways off the horse. Sean could not see anyone in any of the windows now. He figured they were hugging the floor or went somewhere else. He decided to go ahead and take a few more shots. He would shoot all around the other windows. If anyone was there, the big Sharps slug would easily go through the wall and get them. Sean fired eight more shots. He figured Jon would be wondering what the hell was going on. Sean didn't know it at the time, but two more men were killed when he fired the eight shots. Sean made his way back to the hotel.

"I'm gonna work my way over to Jon and tell'em what I got planned now," said Sean. "I'll tell you boys when I get back. Roger, you come with me. The two men made their way out to Jon's position.

"So how many did you get back here?" asked Sean.

"I killed two, but missed one," said Jon. "He ran back inside."

"Well I want you and Roger to stay out here and cover the back," said Sean. "I killed two at least. I was hoping to get more when I fired off them eight shots. I was hoping they might be just right next to a window and I shot around the windows hoping to hit some more of'em."

"Yep, that Sharps slug'll go right through a wall with no trouble," said Jon.

"All right now, I'll be goin' back to the hotel now," said Sean. "Me and the rest a the men'r gonna take some positions and then just open up on'em. We might fire off a hundred rounds. That should really shake'em up. When we open up, you two get anyone tryin' ta make a run for it."

Sean made his way back to the hotel and gave the men their instructions. "When we start firin', you men keep firin' till I tell you to stop," Sean began. "Don't get careless and expose yourself too much. They'll be shootin' back at us. Now let's get movin'."

When the men were in position, Sean opened up with his Winchester. The other men opened up too. There was some firing coming from the Municipal building, but the more Sean and the men fired, the less of it there was. Two men tried to make a break out the back door but Jon and Roger cut them down. Sean gave the word to quit firing. A white flag was being waved from one of the downstairs windows. "I better see some guns thrown out them windows or we'll open up again," yelled Sean. Three pistols were thrown out the windows. "I better see more guns than that," yelled Sean.

"There's only three of us left," yelled someone from inside the building. "There's just me and the Mayor and the Judge and I'm hit. I need me a doctor."

"You all come on out and get your hands behind your heads if you can get them there," said Sean. The wounded man came out the door first followed by the Judge and then the Mayor.

"I never killed nobody," cried the wounded man. "It was that Marshal and his gunmen Deputies. They got their orders from these two here, now I need me a doctor and I need'm now."

Sean sent someone after Doc Walton and another man to go behind the building to tell Jon and Roger that it was over for now. Doc Walton came and examined the wounded man. None of the men with Sean had been hit and all the other men in the building except the Mayor and the Judge had been killed.

"Get this man to my office," said Doc. "I doubt if I can save him but I'll try." Sean had two of the men carry the wounded man to the Doc's office.

"Now you two'r goin' to jail," said Sean. "Please try to run so I can shoot you." The Judge and the Mayor never said a word. There were five different cells in the jail. All of the saloon men were together in one cell. Sean put the Mayor and the Judge in separate cells.

The man who Jon had pistol whipped spoke. "Just why in the hell do them two get separate cells and all five a us are crammed in here?" he asked. "We never done nothin' too bad. It was them two and that Marshal a theirs."

"So you're sayin' that them two ordered all the bad things that went on in this town," said Sean.

"That's just what I'm a sayin'," the man said. "I'm not goin' to jail or get hung fer them sons a bitches."

"So you're sayin' that if we had a trial for these two, you would testify against them." said Sean.

"I would I reckon these other fellas would too," he said. "Am I right boys?" The other four said yes.

~~~~

"I'll be lettin' you outta jail now," said Sean. "We'll be havin' a town meetin' this evenin' and I'll expect all a you ta be there. If you're not, we'll be comin' after you."

"We'll be there Marshal. What time's the meetin'?" the man asked.

"Seven o'clock sounds good to me," said Sean. "That'll give the townspeople plenty a time ta eat supper and such and be there." The five men left.

"So we're havin' a town meetin'," said Roger. "Guess I better get the word around town so folks'll know."

"Hey Roger, is there an honest lawyer in town?" asked Sean. "I want some legal advice."

"Yep, we got one but he quit practicin' when them crooks came ta town," said Roger. "He lives just outside a town and been tryin' ta be a farmer. I'll get'm for you. I'll get all the men to put the word out about the meetin'."

"Tell that lawyer ta meet me at the hotel," said Sean. "If I'm not there, tell'em to stay there and I'll be along. I gotta go send a telegram now." When Sean got to the telegraph office, Fred was there and ready.

"My finger's itchin' ta go Marshal," said Fred. "Where we goin' today?"

"This is goin' to St. Louis to my boss," said Sean. "Now here we go."

Federal Judge David Simmons
St. Louis

Several gunmen killed in Kansas City<< stop >> Mayor and Judge corrupt and in custody << stop>> town Marshal and deputies corrupt and killed<< stop>> want to have trial for Mayor and Judge<< stop>> have a lawyer here<< stop >> can you appoint him as a Judge<< stop>> will charge Mayor and Judge with murder rape and extortion

O'Rourke

"Get that sent Fred, and put somethin' with it so it'll get to the Judge quick and I'll be gettin' a reply," said Sean. "Get that reply to me soon as it comes in." Sean went back to the hotel, and he and Jon sat down to a good meal. Roger and the other men were taking turns watching the prisoners. When they had just finished their food, a tall thin younger man came to their table and introduced himself.

"Gentleman, my name is Lawrence Todd," he started. "I understand that you are looking for some legal advice." He extended his hand, and they all shook.

"I am Federal Marshal Sean O'Rourke, and this is my Deputy Jon O'Brien," Sean began. "We were sent here to clean up this town by my boss, Judge David Simmons. I don't really want advice. What I want is a Judge. I'm waitin' to hear back from Judge Simmons to see if he can temporarily appoint you as Judge so we can have a trial for those two crooks we have in jail now. Would you take the job if we can do that?"

"Yes I would," said Lawrence. "If the Judge cannot appoint me, I believe that the citizens of the county and town can elect me to a Judgeship. I have no idea how that other man got to be a Judge here. I'm sure it was illegal."

"That's good news about an election," said Sean. "There's gonna be a town meeting at 7pm today. Please be there and we'll tell the townspeople what we intend to do."

"I'll be there," said Lawrence. "When we have the trial, who's going to be the prosecuting attorney?"

"We don't have one," answered Sean. "So I'll try it. If I do something wrong, I expect you to tell me."

"I will and I'm sure the Judge will too," said Lawrence. "I expect that he'll be defending himself and the Mayor. I'm going back and tell my wife everything. I will see you at the meeting."

~~~~

A half hour later, a telegram arrived from Judge Simmons. It went as follows:

Federal Marshal O'Rourke
Kansas City

I can temporarily appoint a Judge or the community can elect him to a Judgeship<< stop>> my advice is to get him elected<< stop>>good work

Judge David Simmons
Federal Court House
St. Louis

There was a huge turnout for the town meeting. The saloon men were there too. Sean started the meeting. "In case some of you don't know who I am, my name is Federal Marshal Sean O'Rourke," started Sean. "My Deputy, Jon O'Brien and I were sent here to clean up this town. We did that today. We have the Mayor and the Judge in jail. His Marshal, Deputies, and their gunmen are dead except for one who is in the Doc's office. Doc doesn't think he can save him. Anyway, we took your town back for you, and now you need to take charge of it. Lawrence Todd had agreed to become your Judge if you elect him. If you do not want to elect him, I will get him temporarily appointed so we can have a trial for the Mayor and the Judge. They will be charged with murder, rape, and extortion. You also need to have yourselves an election and get yourself a new Mayor, and he can get you an honest Town Marshal. So I'm gonna ask everyone right now. If you're in favor of Lawrence Todd for Judge, raise your right hand."

Every right hand at the meeting went into the air. "I guess it's unanimous," said Sean. "Now you people figure out when you're going to get things done. We'll be havin' that trial maybe as early as day after tomorrow if the new Judge doesn't object."

"No I do not object," said Lawrence. "Our country was founded on several principles. One of them was that every accused person has the right to a speedy trial. Let's you and I go over to the jail and tell the accused what we're doing."

When they entered the jail, both prisoners were asleep on their cots. Sean grabbed a metal coffee cup and banged it on the bars. "Wake up you two," said Sean. "I got someone here to meet you. Gentlemen, and I say that lightly, this is the new Judge. His name is Lawrence Todd."

"Gentlemen, I have just been elected to a Judgeship for this community," Lawrence began. "You are being charged with murder, rape, and extortion. I am assuming that since you are a Judge, you will be defending the both of you. Am I correct in assuming that?"

"Yes you are," answered the Judge.

"That's good," responded Lawrence. "Your trial will commence the day after tomorrow at 9am. If you need to get witnesses lined up, notify the Marshal and he will bring them to you so you can have a chance to talk with them." Then he and Sean stepped away from the cells. "We'll get a jury selected tomorrow morning," said Lawrence. "We'll do every thing in the Municipal building. There's a fine courtroom there. I'll see you tomorrow."

~~~~

Sean headed back to the hotel. Jon was at a table having a drink. "Guess who just got back in town," said Jon.

"I give up," answered Sean. "Who is it?"

"The County Sheriff, that's who," said Jon. "Good timin', huh. That's him over at the other end of the bar. By the way, Doc stopped in and said that fella from the shootout died."

"Too bad about that man," said Sean. "Maybe we coulda got more information outta him. I believe I'll go over and talk to that Sheriff." Sean walked over to him. "Excuse me Sheriff," Sean said. "I'm Federal Marshal O'Rourke. In case you haven't heard, there's been some shootin'. Several men'r dead, and the Mayor and that Judge is in jail."

"I heard all about it," said the Sheriff. "Bout time them crooks got what they deserved."

"How come you put up with them?" asked Sean. "You're a lawman."

"There was more a them than there was a me," said the Sheriff. "We had an agreement. I don't mess with the town, and they don't mess with anything outta town. I had a family ta look out for. I sent'em back east when all this started. Name's Jessie, Jessie Thornton. I hear you're gonna have a trial day after tomorrow. I can testify agin them if ya need me."

"We'll use you if we need to," said Sean. "Did you get that killin' over east straightened out?"

"Weren't no killin' after all," said Jessie. "Some woman came up missin' after her husband threatened ta kill her. She was missin' fer a buncha days, and everybody figured she was dead. We searched all over and finally found her. She run off with another man. I got my deputies stayin' over there for a few days ta make sure that woman's husband don't kill somebody. Well nice meetin' you. I'm goin' go get some sleep. See you tomorrow."

Sean went back over to the table with Jon. "That story the Sheriff just told me sounds kinda made up," said Sean. "I wish we had time ta find out if it's true or not. I got a bad feelin' about him. Seems kinda strange that he's not here when we get here and gets back right after all the shootin'. It's gonna chew on me for a while. Anyway I'm goin' over to that saloon and talk to Sally about testifying at the trial. You go over to the jail and make sure the men are alert and takin' their shift. See you back here shortly." Sean went to the saloon and Jon went to the jail.

Sally was setting at a table with a potential customer when Sean walked in. "Sally, please excuse the interruption but I need a word with you," said Sean. "I'm sure this fine gentleman will not be offended as you will be back shortly." Sally was really impressed with the way Sean spoke to her.

"I have never had a man talk that way around me," said Sally. "I'm gonna hafta to give you a free one yet."

"As I said before, thank you for the thought," said Sean. "Now would you please step over to this other table for a few minutes?" Sally went to the other table. Sean pulled out a chair for her. "I need you to testify at the trial day after tomorrow. The Mayor and Judge are being charged with rape."

"Well who did they rape?" asked Sally.

"Anytime a woman is forced to have sex when she doesn't want to and with someone she doesn't want to, it's rape," stated Sean. "You told me that you and the girls were forced to give free ones to the Mayor and Judge and all their men. If you didn't want to do it, it's rape. If you feared for your life or were afraid they would beat you if you didn't, it's rape. Even if you didn't fight them off or you acted like you enjoyed it because you were afraid, it's rape. Do you understand?"

"There sure was a whole lotta rapin' goin' on," said Sally. "Sure, I'll testify. I'll get some more girls if ya need'em. Do ya think a jury'll believe a whore?"

"Whores are women and should be treated with respect," said Sean. "Any man don't when I'm around will get his head broke."

"How bout that free one right now Marshal?" asked Sally. "I think I could wear you out."

"You go take care of that fine gentleman who's over there waiting for you," said Sean. "It's been a pleasure talking with you. I will see you at the trial. Now if you'll excuse me." Sean left and Sally just sat there for a few minutes. No one had ever been that nice to her. She went back over to her potential customer.

~~~~

"You are a gentleman, aren't you?" Sally asked him. "You better be because I am a lady."

"I can assure you Sally that I will treat you with the utmost respect," he said.

"Let's go find out," said Sally as she took his arm and led him upstairs.

~~~~

When Sean got back to the hotel, Jon was at the same table. "Is everything all right over at the jail?" asked Sean. "Did they get the prisoners fed? Did they have any visitors?"

"As a matter a fact, both of'em had a visitor," answered Jon. "Their wives come ta see'em. I could tell right off that their wives won't miss them fellas one bit. There was some words spoke that ya don't usually hear comin' out of a woman's mouth. Them women aren't even gonna stay and go to the trial. Both of'em said they'd be leavin' in the mornin'."

"Sounds like them women knew their men were crooks," said Sean. "Let's get somethin' ta eat and then get some sleep. Gotta get a jury selected in the mornin'."

They ate their food and then Sean headed up to his room. Jon took Dog out to do his necessaries. When Dog was finished, they went up to Jon's room. Jon had just gotten in bed when there was a knock on the door. Dog didn't growl so Jon knew that it was Sean and he went to the door and let him in. "What's up?" Jon asked. "Are you still thinkin' about that Sheriff?"

"Yes I am," answered Sean. "He just doesn't set right with me. I think we better takes turns keepin' watch tonight. I'll go first. I'll wake you in a few hours."

"All right," said Jon. "Wake me when it's my turn."

~~~~

Everything was quiet. Sean made rounds all around town and stopped by the jail several times. The prisoners were sound asleep and the man on watch was wide awake. Sean talked with him for a good while. "Just where does that Sheriff live?" Sean asked him.

"He has a room in one a the boardin' houses in town," he said. "He used to rent a house in town but when he sent his woman back east, he went to the boardin' house."

"Did his wife get sent east or did she leave him?" Sean asked.

"I don't really know," the man said. "Everbody just figured he was sendin' her back east. She was the quiet type. Always kept to herself. There weren't no kids."

"Which boardin' house does he stay in?" asked Sean.

"It's the one two buildins' this side of that hotel where you're stayin," said the man. "His room is on the second floor on the left corner."

"Nice talkin' to ya," said Sean. "Now keep alert. Never know what might happen." On the way back to the hotel, Sean looked up and saw the Sheriff setting in a chair in his room and reading a newspaper. Sean then went to Jon's room and woke him up for his watch. "That Sheriff lives in that boardin' house just down from us here and his room is on the second floor on the left corner. I saw him there readin' a newspaper when I came back from the jail. Keep an eye on that place when you make your rounds."

"Me'n Dog'll keep an eye on things," said Jon. "I'll get you if somethin' happens."

Sean went to his room and almost immediately fell asleep, and Jon and Dog went to work. The first thing Jon did was see if the Sheriff was still in his room. He was. Jon went to the jail after that and then started making his rounds. There was a fight going on at the Boar's Head. Some fella was getting the hell beat out of him by some well dressed man. Jon could hear the nice dressed man speaking. "I told you that Sally was a lady and should be treated as such," he said. "You will apologize or I will thrash you some more."

"She's just a damn whore," the other man said. The nice dressed man started punching him again. Jon decided that he had been amused enough and continued his rounds. When he got back to the boarding house a half hour later, the light was out in the Sheriff's room. Jon didn't think too much of it and headed to the jail. When he went in, there was blood all over the desk and the two prisoners were gone. Jon almost tripped over the man who had been on watch. He had been almost gutted with a knife. Jon ran back to the hotel and woke up Sean. "Someone killed the guard and let out the prisoners," cried Jon. "I couldn't see if that Sheriff was still in his room or not."

"I'll bet he's not," said Sean as he threw on some clothes and grabbed his weapons. "Let's get to the jail. I bet Dog can track which way they went." When they got to the jail, Dog got right on the scent and took off at a run. "He's headed right to the Municipal building. I bet when we get there, we'll find an empty safe and they'll be gone."

As they got to the building they slowed down. "Go slow now," said Sean. "They could be waitin' for us." Just as Sean finished talking, several shots were fired from behind the building and they could hear a couple of horses running away. They eased their way around back. The Mayor and the Judge were laying there dead. "I bet that Sheriff didn't want to share," said Sean. "Let's go inside. I bet we find a big open safe." Sean was right. There was a big safe and the door was wide open. It was empty.

"I wonder how much money he took," said Jon.

"I wouldn't know but it's got to be a lot," said Sean. "Let's get our horses and gear. We'll leave word with Roger. He can tell Lawrence what's goin' on. We'll get him tracked. He won't be expectin' anyone to come after him till daylight. With Dog here, we'll get'em."

"Do you think he might double back and catch a train?" asked Jon.

"He could do that," answered Sean. "But he knows that we could telegraph ahead and have some law waitin' for him. I figure he knows where he's goin'. Maybe he's had this all planned out. I figure he's the real boss in town. Maybe he's got extra horses waitin'. We'll take us some extra horses too."

Sean and Jon were on the trail in no time. Dog led the way. Sean could tell by the tracks that the Sheriff was overconfident and not moving very fast. "We'll be almost on him by daylight," said Sean. About an hour and a half later, they came upon a lone horse. It was still wet with sweat. "He changed horses not long ago," said Sean. "He must have more horses if he changed so soon. If he stays at this pace, it'll be light enough to shoot when we come upon him."

They spotted the Sheriff just as it got light enough to see. There was a small thicket of trees just ahead of the Sheriff. "He's probably got horses in there somewhere," said Sean. "I gotta stop him before he gets there. If he makes it, we might lose him."

"He's gotta be a half mile away," said Jon. "I know you're good, but that's a far piece."

"I know," Sean said as he stopped his horse and dismounted. He pulled the Sharps from the scabbard and got down on the ground in the prone position. "I hate to do this," said Sean. "But I'm gonna kill his horse. You go ahead and get Dog runnin' after'em so he can hold him till we get there."

Jon sent Dog after the sheriff while Sean took aim. Finally the Sharps bellowed. Not quite two or three seconds later, the

Sheriff's horse went down and the Sheriff went flying. Dog was on him before he regained his senses. When he got his senses back and saw Dog growling and just daring him to move, he reached for his pistol. When he did, Dog got him by the throat but did not bite. If the Sheriff moved any at all, Dog clamped a little harder each time. Finally the Sheriff got the idea and kept still. Dog held him until Sean and Jon got there and removed the Sheriff's gunbelt. Then Jon told Dog to let him go.

"I wouldn't upset my dog," Jon said. "He likes raw meat."

"There's over $200,000 in them saddle bags," said the Sheriff. "I'll split it with you if you let me go."

"I'm sure you would," said Sean. "That's not gonna happen. We'll be takin' you back. We're gonna have a trial and you're gonna get hung."

"You got no proof on nothin'," said the Sheriff.

"You killed that man standin' guard at the jail," said Sean. "You're probably the boss in town too. I bet you planned this whole thing so you could kill the Mayor and the Judge and not hafta share that money. You most likely give the orders to kill the Marshal and his Deputy. You weren't seein' bout trouble over east. You were gettin' everything ready so you could make your getaway. You knew we was comin' and gonna clean up the town. Where's your Deputies? I bet you killed them too."

"You can't prove a damn thing in court," said the Sheriff. "I won't get convicted in a court of law."

"You know Sheriff," Sean said. "You're most likely right. I think we'll hang you in them trees over there." Sean tied the Sheriff's hands behind his back and made him walk over to the small grove of trees. When they got to the grove, they could see two more horses tied in a small rope corral. "I'll pick out a tree and then get a horse," said Sean.

"You can't be doin' this," said the Sheriff. "Yer a Federal Marshal. You can't be doin' this."

"Don't be tellin' me what a lawman can't do," Sean said as he slung the Sheriff up on the horse. "You got anything to say before we send you to hell."

"My boss won't like you doin' this," said the Sheriff. "He'll be sendin' guns after you and he can afford the best."

"Well he didn't get the best when he hired you," said Sean as he swatted the horse's rump.

"Are we gonna tell Lawrence that we hung the Sheriff?" asked Jon.

"No we won't. He's probably into that due process stuff even for scum like this," answered Sean. "We'll just tell'em that we had to kill'em. We'll bury'm here. We got us some good dogs don't we? They're the only good thing anybody ever got from them Hawks. Let's get somethin' ta eat. Then we'll bury this scum and then head back."

~~~~

A half day later, Sean and Jon rode back into town. The whole town heard what had happened and was waiting when they returned. Lawrence was the first to greet them. "I'm assuming that you got him." said Lawrence.

"Yep, we got'em," said Sean. "We had to kill'em. There was no other way. We buried him out there instead of haulin' his body back here. There's over $200,000 of your town's money in these saddle bags here. I reckon it's from extortion and everything they did. We didn't find out what happened to the Sheriff's Deputies. I hope you all can handle everything now. I'm ready to head home."

We'll be fine," started Lawrence. "We'll be having some elections. We'll get us a new Mayor and a new Town Marshal and some Deputies. We'll elect us a new County Sheriff too. We sure want to thank you for coming to help us."

"I hope you never need me again under these circumstances," said Sean. "Now Jon and me'r gonna get somethin' ta eat. We'll be catchin' the next stage headin' south. I gotta go send some telegrams. Jon you go get us some food ordered. I'll be along shortly.

Fred was at the telegraph office and ready to go. "I'm ready Marshal," he said. 'My finger's gettin' that itch again."

Sean telegrams went as follows:

Judge David Simmons
Federal Court House
St. Louis

Job done<< stop >> all corrupt officials dead << stop>>
heading home

O'Rourke
Kansas City

Maggie O'Rourke
Abilene

Job done<< stop >> leaving on next stage<< stop>> have
missed you a lot

Sean

CHAPTER NINE

When Sean and Jon arrived back in Abilene, almost everyone from the saloon was there to greet them. Maggie ran to Sean and they hugged and kissed for a good while. Then she gave Jon a big hug and thanked him for making sure nothing happened to her man. Martha was there too and she was all over Jon after Maggie got done with him. Michael gave Sean and Jon both a big hug and shook their hands firmly. Betty gave Sean and Jon both a big hug and kissed them on the cheek. Tom was there with his wife and Cookie and Barbara were there holding hands like some little school kids. Jeb and Dog rolled around and played like a couple of small pups.

"It's good to have friends like all a you," said Sean. "I truly mean that. Now if you'll excuse us, Maggie and I will be busy for a good while." They ran up to their room like a newlywed couple and were not seen till late that day. Martha grabbed Jon and no one saw them till the next morning.

As they were laying in bed and holding each other, Sean asked Maggie to tell him about what had happened in his absence. She began by telling him about the four men who tried to take her that night. "We had just closed the place and everyone had gone home except Michael and Betty," Maggie began. "I was going to take Jeb out back to do his necessaries, and Michael insisted that he and Betty would not leave until I was safely in bed. They stayed up front at a table waiting for me. When I went out back with Jeb, I left the door open so Michael could hear me if anything happened. Jeb took off to take care of his business, and then I thought I heard something. When I turned to look, someone grabbed me from behind. Then another man came out of the shadows to my front. He had a pistol in his right hand. He told me not to try anything or they would kill me. I had a pistol in both of my dress pockets and I had cocked the hammers when I first went out the door. With my right hand, I pulled the trigger on the pistol and shot the man holding me in his right foot. He let go of me and started screaming in pain. Before the other man could do anything, Jeb had ahold of his right wrist and bit the man's hand clear off. Then he got the man by the throat and killed him. My dress caught on fire when I fired the pistol, so I went into the bath house and put the fire out with some water from the barrels. The man who had grabbed me was still screaming when I came back out, and I shot him through the head. When all this was going on, two more men were out front. Betty shot one through the window, and Michael killed the other one as he was trying to run away."

`"Damn. Maggie, I don't figure I'll ever hafta worry about you takin' care a yourself," said Sean. "Anybody that messes with you is gonna end up dead or worse. So you say ole Jeb took that man's hand clear off."

"Yes he did," exclaimed Maggie. "His hand was still holding the pistol when it came off. I would never believe something like that if someone had told me. We have us some wonderful dog."

"Yes we do," replied Sean. "Ole Dog did somethin' I never seen before either when we was after that Sheriff. Dog had him by the throat but didn't kill him. If the Sheriff tried to move, Dog just clamped down a little harder. He just held him there till Jon and me got there. I was tellin' Jon that them dogs are the only good things that anybody ever got from them Hawks."

"I'll have to agree with that," said Maggie. "Now other than that Sheriff, how was the rest of your trip?"

"Every official in that town was corrupt," started Sean. "The Mayor, the Judge, the Town Marshal and all his Deputies were all corrupt. They had killed the original Marshal and a Deputy and were extorting all the businesses in town. That is, the ones they didn't take over. The ones that were extorted were forced to pay a huge percentage of their profits. We didn't find out till a little later that the County Sheriff was actually the head man there. Anyway, we ended up killin'em all. They had several gunmen workin' for 'em. We killed them too. They got a new Judge now and are gonna have some elections and get some new officials. I almost got to play lawyer."

~~~~

"Just why would you be playing lawyer?" asked Maggie.

"Well, we had the Mayor and Judge in jail and was gonna have a trial," started Sean. "We had a new Judge then and we was gonna try them for murder, rape, and extortion. I was gonna be the prosecuting attorney. I had my witnesses all lined up. Anyway, before we could have the trial, the Sheriff killed the guard at the jail and let out the Mayor and Judge. Then he killed the Mayor and Judge and took off with a buncha money. We caught him."

"So when you caught him, you didn't bring him back for trial, did you?" asked Maggie.

"No we didn't," answered Sean. "We knew he was guilty as hell but couldn't prove a thing so we hung'em. We just told the Judge that we had to kill'em. We didn't say how."

"I can just see you in a court of law," said Maggie. "The first time somebody objected to something you said or did, all hell would probably break loose."

"You're most likely right," said Sean. "But I did have some good witnesses. Sally was a working girl there and she told me that all the officials and all their gunmen forced them to give them free ones. If they didn't, they would be beaten or worse. I told her that anytime a person is forced to have sex whether they resist or not, it is rape. Even if they act like they like it, but do not want to do it, it is still rape. She agreed to testify for me."

"Maybe you should have been a lawyer," said Maggie. "Not too many people care about working girls. I'm glad you did that."

"Sally was worried that no one would listen to a whore," said Sean. "I told her that she was still a lady and should be treated with kindness and respect."

"You're a good man Sean O'Rourke. There is none better," said Maggie.

"Thank you darlin'. Now I know we would have gotten them on the extortion charge too, but I don't know about the murder charge," said Sean. "No one saw anyone pull a trigger. Anyway, them two got what they deserved. I hope Lawrence, that's the new Judge, can get things goin' in the right direction. He's a good man."

"Speaking of good men, I need you again," said Maggie. A couple of hours later they were still holding each other.

"Maybe you're right," spoke Sean. "Maybe someday I should be a lawyer. It won't be long and everything will grow and they'll be courts, Judges, and lawyers all over the place. Every time I catch someone, someone'll want to have a trial to prove beyond a reasonable doubt and such. I hope that doesn't come too soon here. I'm not ready for that."

"I'm not ready for all that either," said Maggie. "If someone hurts us, we will do what we have been doing. Now let's get away from all this depressing talk. I think it's about time you and I took a belated honeymoon. What would you think about that?"

"I think that sounds like a great idea," answered Sean. "Any idea where you would like to go?"

"I don't need to travel all over the country," said Maggie. "I would be happy if we just went to St. Louis. It's a nice town with plenty to do. We might take a ride on a river boat. I'd like to see "The Palace" and I'm sure you wouldn't mind seeing Sam Draper again. I'd like to thank him for getting us that bathtub too."

"That's what we'll do then," said Sean. "We can go whenever you say. We'll hafta take the stage up to Kansas City and then catch a train to St. Louis. Won't take long at all."

"We'll be going in a few days then," said Maggie. "We'll make sure the saloon has all the supplies it needs. Michael will be able to handle things. Jon'll be here. Jeb and Dog will be here too. No one will mess with them after the things that just happened."

"So I remember seeing Cookie and Barbara holdin' hands when Jon and me got back to town," said Sean. "What's goin' on there?"

"They've been living together," said Maggie. "She moved in with Cookie about three days after you left for Kansas City. I think they want to get married but they wanted to wait till you got back. I'm pretty sure Cookie wants you to give the bride away."

"I'll do that gladly," said Sean. "We'll tell'em just to let us know when they're ready. Hey, just what is Cookie's real name anyway. I have never heard anyone call him by name."

"His real name is Donald Cook," said Maggie. "It's been so long since I've used his name. Anyway, Cookie is a good name for him to be called since he is a cook and his name is Cook. I never did ask if they would be going on a honeymoon. If they did, we would need to find another cook while they were gone."

"It'll work out darlin'," said Sean. "Now let's get dressed and get somethin' ta eat. I need to get my strength back."

~~~~

They went downstairs and went to their regular table. Michael and Betty were already there having a meal. "I don't know what this is, but it sure eats good," said Michael. "I believe I'll have some more. Can I get some for anyone else?"

"Sean and I will take a plate," said Maggie.

"No more for me," said Betty. "This stuff is delicious, but I can't eat another bite. I wish I could make things like this."

"I would just bet that those two in there would love to show you," said Maggie. "You know they want to get married don't you."

"Everyone around here figures that," said Betty. "They've been all over each other like some young school kids. I'm glad they found each other."

"If they get married and decide to go on a honeymoon, we'll need to get us another cook while they're gone," said Maggie.

"I think I can handle that," said Betty. "I'm not fast at cooking, but I can get it done. It won't be as fancy as what them two do, but it'll be good. Michael can help me in the kitchen. If Jon's here, he can help Tom tend the bar. When the kitchen slows down, Michael can get on the piano again. Maybe one of the other girls wouldn't mind singing."

"That sounds great," said Maggie. "Sean and I will be taking our belated honeymoon in a few days too. Everything here will be in good hands. I think I'll go into the kitchen after I eat and ask them two when they intend to get married." They all finished their meals, and Maggie and Betty both went into the kitchen. Michael and Sean stayed at the table and got themselves a bottle of Irish Whiskey.

"So you two are wanting to get married, and you want Sean to give the bride away," said Maggie as she approached Barbara and Cookie.

"Yes, we want very much to get married, and it would be fitting for Sean to give me away since he is the one responsible for getting me here," said Barbara.

"He would be happy to do that," said Maggie. "Now when would you two like to have the ceremony?"

" The sooner the better," said Cookie. "I can't wait to give this woman my name."

"I'm sure that we can get Jason to do the ceremony whenever you want," said Maggie. "Now do you two plan to go on a honeymoon?"

"We do not want to inconvenience you here," said Barbara. "We can go on a honeymoon anytime."

"Betty has already said that she would do the cooking while you are gone," said Maggie. "I suggest that Cookie talk to Jason tomorrow morning and get a date set. Sean and I are leaving on our belated honeymoon in a few days. We can get you two married before we go. Do you want a big wedding or do you want just a few people to attend?"

"We'll just have an open wedding and anyone who wants or has the time can come," said Cookie. "Everyone in this town has been good to me. Barbara and I will even make our own feast."

"Have you got a dress for the wedding?" Maggie asked Barbara. "If you don't , I can help you with that."

"I've got a dress all picked out," answered Barbara. "Cookie really likes it because it fits me like a glove."

"That's good," said Maggie. "Now after you get with Jason, let us know so we can let everyone else know."

~~~~

Two days later, Barbara and Cookie were married. It was another big wedding as most of the town attended. Michael had a great time on the piano and there was a lot of dancing that day. Sean was getting better. The new couple decided that they would wait until fall to go on a honeymoon. Barbara had never been to a place where the leaves changed color during the fall so they decided to wait till then.

Maggie and Sean left on their honeymoon the day after the wedding. As they were getting ready, Michael reminded Sean of what had happened that night at "The Palace." "I'd keep a sharp eye out there when you're visiting Sam." said Michael. "I don't know why I'm tellin' you this. You always keep alert. It's just the way you are."

"Maggie and me will both be armed," said Sean. "We'll be takin' some rifles on the trip with us too. I figure to take the

Winchester and the Henry. The Sharps'll be here if you'd have a need for it. I figure sooner or later, someone'll try robbin' stagecoaches around here. I hear they been doin' it some over in Missouri. Hope that coach isn't haulin' anybody's payroll when we're on it."

"I don't think there would be any big amounts of money goin' that way," said Michael. "There could be on the stages headed this way. Anyway, you and Maggie can handle anything that would get in your way. What are gonna do about Jeb when you're gone?"

"I figured that you would look after him," said Sean. "He's a good dog to have around here if there's any trouble. Jeb and Dog can take care of about any trouble that could come up. If you let Jeb sleep at the foot a your bed, you'll never hafta worry about anyone comin' in after you."

"Me'n Betty will take good care of'em," said Michael. "I hope he doesn't hafta kill anyone while you're gone."

~~~~

Before leaving on their honeymoon, Sean sent a telegram to the Judge telling him that he was taking a belated honeymoon and would see him in St. Louis shortly.

The stage left on time. Maggie had a pistol in her right dress pocket and another one in her purse. Sean wore two pistols and the rifles were in the coach with them. He did not have his badge pinned on. It was in a pocket on his vest. There were two other passengers with them. They were a couple. The woman was possibly twenty five to thirty and looked like a school marm. The man looked like a traveling salesman and was maybe forty. Maggie and Sean had never seen either one of them before they met on the stage. They said they were going back east because her mother was ill.

When they stopped for the first change of horses, they picked up another passenger. He was just some young man catching a ride to the next station. Someone was supposed to meet him there and tell him about a job that was available. While the horses were being changed for the second time, the passengers were given a meal. An older man and his wife ran the place. She did the cooking and such, and he took care of the horses. The stage driver and the shotgun rider always liked to stop there because she always made the best stew.

Two hours after they left the station, the driver yelled out that there were four riders up ahead of them. "They got guns out and they're wavin' fer me ta stop," the driver said. "We're not stoppin'. You all get down back there. Could be some shootin'."

"There won't be any shooting if you tell that driver he better stop," said the woman who looked like a school marm as she produced a pistol that was in her purse and pointed it at Sean and Maggie. Sean and Maggie just gave the woman a cold stare and didn't say a word.

"I'd do as she says," said her companion. "She doesn't mind shootin' folks." He started reaching inside his jacket. Sean figured he was reaching for a pistol. Just about the time he was pulling out the pistol, the stage hit a big bump. When it did, Sean drew a pistol and killed the man. At the same time, Maggie reached across with her left hand and grabbed the woman's hand that was holding the pistol. With her right hand, she gave the woman a right cross and caught her right on the nose. Blood went everywhere. The woman was knocked unconscious.

The four men up ahead could see that the stage wasn't going to stop and opened fire. The shotgun rider was hit in his left side, but returned fire. When the stage came to where the four men were on the side of the road, Maggie and Sean opened up with their rifles. It was over quickly. The four men lay dead by the road. During the exchange of fire, the unconscious woman caught a bullet in her chest and was killed. When the firing ceased, the driver stopped the coach. "Everybody back there all right?" the driver asked. "We'll be stoppin' fer just a bit while we git ole Zeb patched up. He took one in the side. Went clean through."

"We got two dead ones in the coach," said Sean. "They was part a the gang. Anyway, they're dead."

"Well I'll be," said the driver. "That woman sure looked like a school marm ta me. Never woulda figured that fella fer a robber. Glad you two was with us. Nice shootin'. I wonder what they was after. We're just haulin' mail and you two."

"Maybe there was somethin' in that mail that was important to'em," said Sean. "I never seen any of'em before. I'll strap'em to their horses and we can tie'em on behind. Somebody'll hafta double up. Don't need any corpses in the coach. When you get ole Zeb patched up, he can ride inside with my wife and I'll ride shotgun the rest of the way."

"That's mighty nice a ya," said the driver. "I'm sure ole Zeb won't mind as how that wife a yers is about the most gorgeous woman I ever did see."

"Yes she is," said Sean as he grabbed Maggie and hugged her. "Not only can you shoot, but you're darn good with your fists. You knocked that woman clean out. You know that pistol a hers coulda went off and shot you."

"It could have," said Maggie. "But it didn't. When I grabbed it, I put my thumb under the hammer so it couldn't go off."

"That was quick thinkin'," replied Sean. "I got me the best when I got you."

~~~~

When they got to Kansas City, the first thing they did was take the dead bodies to the Town Marshal's office. Roger Talbert was sitting at the Marshal's desk. "You're not the new Town Marshal are you?" asked Sean.

"No, we been takin' turns lookin' after everything," said Roger. "We're havin' the elections next week. Alex is runnin' for Mayor and I'm runnin' for County Sheriff. That reminds me. We found them two Sheriff's Deputies right after you left. They was north a town dead, shot in the back. Some travelin' Preacher come across'em and come in town and told us where ta find'em." Maggie had been outside on the sidewalk looking around before she went into the office. "Oh my, I heard a you. All them stories I heard about you were not quite true," Roger said to Maggie. "You're better lookin' than what I heard."

"Roger, this is my wife Maggie," said Sean. "Maggie, this is Roger Talbert. He helped me and Jon when we were here."

"Thank you for helping my husband," said Maggie. "And thank you for your kindness. I heard you say that you were running for County sheriff. Good luck with that."

"Thank you, ma'am," said Roger. "Now I suppose you two will be wantin' a hotel room. Alex is runnin' the hotel where you been stayin'. He wants to buy it but he don't know who ta buy it from. You shot the previous owner and the owner before him come up missin'.

Anyway, he'll be glad ta see you. Now I'll find Lawrence and see what we should do about these bodies. What did they do anyway?"

"They tried to rob the stage," said Sean. "We don't know what they was after cause it was only haulin' us and the mail."

"Well I'll find Lawrence," said Roger. "I know he'll be glad ta see you. You know who else'll be glad ta see you. Sally will. I don't know what all you said to her, but she's got her own place now. She started it right after you left. She calls it "Sally's Gentleman Club." I haven't been, but I hear it's a nice place."

"I'm glad for her," said Sean. "Maybe Maggie and me'll stop in and see her for a bit. Now we'll be goin' to the hotel. You and the boys should stop over later and have a drink with us this evening."

~~~~

When Maggie and Sean arrived at the hotel, Alex was standing just inside the door. "Come on in Marshal," said Alex. "If you need a room, it's on the house. Anything you want here is on the house."

"That's mighty generous Alex," said Sean. "Alex Cutright, this is my wife Maggie. Maggie this is Alex."

"I'm pleased to meet you," said Maggie. "I hope your wounds are healing well."

"The pleasure is all mine and I am healing well," said Alex. "Pardon my sayin' Maggie, but you're what dreams are made of. It's an honor to meet such beauty."

"Thank you for your kindness," replied Maggie. "I think Sean and I should check into a room and then get something to eat. I know I'm hungry."

"I'll put you in the same room Sean had when he was here last time," said Alex. "I'll get your luggage if you want and get it up to the room. You two can go ahead and get a meal. We have a good cook here."

Sean and Maggie went ahead and went to the saloon for a meal while Alex took care of their luggage. They weren't seated for five minutes when Lawrence arrived. "Good of you to come back to our town," said Lawrence as he approached their table. "Things are going for the better here." He went to Sean and shook his hand. "This beautiful woman has got to be your wife Maggie," said Lawrence. "I am Lawrence Todd and I am so very pleased to meet you."

"I am Maggie, and I am also pleased to meet you," said Maggie. "I understand that you are the new Judge here, and you're getting things straightened out. I hope it goes well for you."

"It will Maggie," said Lawrence. "It'll be good to get some honest people running things for a change. Did your husband tell you he almost got to play lawyer?"

"Yes he did," answered Maggie. "He could probably be a very good lawyer. He can be very convincing at times."

"Maybe some day when he's not a lawman anymore, he could take the time and get educated on the law," said Lawrence.

"I won't be goin' to any fancy law school," said Sean. "I'd be in a fight every day about somethin'."

"You can be a lawyer without going to any fancy school," said Lawrence. "I hear Abe Lincoln schooled himself. They said he was a darn good lawyer before he got into politics. Anyway, I have no idea who those dead bodies are. None of them fit any description of anyone that's on any wanted posters we have in this town. Do you suppose they were after something that was in the mail?"

"That's what I'm guessin'," said Sean. "They weren't after us. I don't s'pose we'll find out."

"No we probably won't, at least right now," said Lawrence. "Tampering with the mail is against the law. Besides, if it came in on the stage with you, it's already been delivered."

"You might find Roger and see who got mail," said Sean. "He was at the Town Marshal's office when we first got to town, and then he probably went to the Post Office after he found you. Could be that the mail is just settin' there waitin' ta be sorted."

"I believe I'll go to the Post Office right now," said Lawrence. "If you'll excuse me."

~~~~

When Lawrence got to the Post Office, Roger had just gotten there and was starting to sort the mail. "Is there any mail there that's for someone you don't know?" asked Lawrence.

"No, but there's this big envelope thing that's addressed to our former Mayor," answered Roger. "I reckon since you're a Judge and he's dead, you can open it up and see what's inside."

"I will," said Lawrence. "There could be something important in there or something personal that should get to any surviving relatives." Lawrence opened the big envelope and was amazed. "This is full of blank bank drafts from some bank down in Texas," exclaimed Lawrence. "I wonder who sent them?"

"There weren't no return address on that thing," said Roger. "Just why would a person want all them blank bank drafts?"

"Because, my dear friend, they are worth more than money," said Lawrence. "A person can fill one of these out for whatever amount he wanted and just about any bank would cash it, especially if they know that this bank really exists, and they recognize a signature on the draft."

"So someone could go all over the country with these blank drafts and make out like a bandit," said Roger. "So we gotta figure out who sent them things here to the Mayor."

"Yes we do, but I wouldn't know where to start," said Lawrence. "I'll go back to the hotel and talk to Sean. Maybe he'd have an idea."

~~~~

When Lawrence got back to the hotel, Maggie and Sean were still at their table having an after dinner drink. "Looks like you got something on your mind Lawrence," said Sean. "Musta been somethin' in that mail, wasn't there?"

"Yes there was," answered Lawrence. "Someone sent a bunch of blank bank drafts to our former Mayor. They were from a bank in Texas. There was no return address on the envelope. Have you got any ideas how we can find out who sent them?"

"Well Anderson was in Texas when we killed him and some of his men," said Sean. "Could be that there was another person tied up with him that we didn't know about. We've had two or three a his men tell us that Anderson had a boss. Maybe he did. Maybe all this is tied together somehow. Maybe these outlaws are gettin' more refined. Maybe they're lookin' for easier ways ta make money. Not too many people get shot when they're cashin' a bank draft. If I was you, I'd go to all the banks in town and tell them not to cash any drafts from that bank down in Texas unless they know for sure that they're legitimate."

"You know something Maggie," said Lawrence. "Your husband is beginning to sound more like a lawyer all the time. I bet he never uses the word legitimate very often or even at all."

"That's true," said Maggie. "I can't remember that word ever coming out of his mouth."

"All right you two," said Sean. "Don't be hangin' up my shingle just yet. Now Maggie and I are goin' over and pay Sally a visit. You can come with us if you like."

"I believe I'll pass this time," said Lawrence. "I always liked Sally even though I never was a close acquaintance of hers. My wife wouldn't be too happy if I went there even though she trusts me. You two go along. When are you leaving town?"

"Our train leaves at nine in the morning," said Sean. "If I don't see you before we leave, it's been a pleasure working with you, and I hope everything works out all right. If you ever need me and you can't reach me in Abilene, get ahold of Judge Simmons in St. Louis, and he'll know where I am."

"Thank you Sean, and it was a great pleasure meeting you Maggie," said Lawrence. "I hope the rest of your trip is more peaceful. God's speed."

~~~~

Maggie and Sean left the hotel and went looking for Sally's place. It was easy to find. She had a really nice sign up for all to see. Maggie and Sean went in the front door. There was a big desk not far from the door and to the left was a small bar area. There were a few men in the bar and some women were with them. The men were well dressed, and the women wore nice clothes. A beautiful young dark haired woman was at the desk. "May I help you this evening?" she asked them.

"Yes you can young lady," said Sean. "I'm Marshal O'Rourke, and this is my wife Maggie. We've come to pay Sally a visit. Is she available?"

"I should have known who you were when you walked in," said the lady. "Sally said you were a gentleman and a looker. I'll go get her. She's in her office going over the books."

When Sally first saw Sean, she went right to him and gave him a kiss on the cheek. "Well what brings you to my place?" asked Sally. "I just bet that this is your wife. No wonder I couldn't have my way with you. Your wife is exceptionally beautiful."

"Sally, this is my wife Maggie. Maggie, this is Sally," said Sean. "I believe I told you about her."

"Yes you did," said Maggie. "I'm pleased to meet you. It looks like you have a very nice establishment here."

"Thank you Maggie," said Sally. "This husband of yours put these ideas in my head. He's a good man. He sure got this town out of a mess. Are you that red-headed woman that has that saloon in Abilene? A lot of the men who come here have seen you and are always asking if we have anyone with red hair and looks like you."

"I am that red-haired woman and my husband, his friend Michael, and I are partners in our saloon," said Maggie. Just then a man came in the front door. Sean recognized him. He was the man who was with Sally when Sean needed to talk to Sally about testifying at the trial. The man walked up to Sally and gave her a good kiss.

"Introduce me to your friends," he said. "I know that this man is the Marshal but I don't know him personally, and I've not met this woman."

"Franklin Towers, this is Marshal Sean O'Rourke and his wife Maggie. "Maggie and Sean, this is Franklin Towers, my fiance'."

"We are very pleased to meet you," said Maggie. "When's the happy day?" Sean shook Franklin's hand, and Maggie gave Sally a big hug.

"The wedding is tomorrow," answered Sally. "We would like it if you two could come. Since you are here, I would like it if Sean would give me away."

"I would be honored. What do you say Maggie?" said Sean. "Should we stay another day?"

"Sure we can," said Maggie. "We can catch the next train to St. Louis. Besides, St. Louis isn't going anywhere is it?"

~~~~

The wedding was at one of the local churches. A good portion of the male population attended. Some of them brought wives with them. Some did not. The reception was at "Sally's Gentleman Club." There was food, drinks, and dancing. There was a guitar player, a banjo player, and a fiddle player. Everyone had a great time. After a few hours, Sean and Maggie wished the new couple well and went back to their hotel. "Franklin seems like a nice man," said Maggie. "I hope things stay good for them."

"He seems like a gentleman," said Sean. "I know he won't allow anyone to mistreat or slander the women. When we were here, Jon saw Franklin beatin' the hell outta some man because he wasn't being nice to one of the girls."

"Sounds reasonable to me," said Maggie. "Now let's get back to our room. We've got some time before the next train leaves. Let's use it wisely." When they got to their room, Sean opened the door then picked up Maggie and carried her in. Three hours later, they were on the train to St. Louis.

"What would you like to do first?" Sean asked Maggie. "St. Louis is a big place."

"Why don't we see if we can take a ride on a river boat," said Maggie. "Maybe we can take one of those week long cruises or something like that. I hear they have some real nice boats for things like that."

"We'll see about that first thing," said Sean. "If there isn't any leaving when we get there, we can make arrangements to go when the next boat is ready. If we have to wait a few days, we'll get us a nice hotel room downtown. We'll visit Sam Draper and Judge Simmons. So when we do take this boat ride, which way would you like to go, north or south?"

"The direction doesn't matter," said Maggie. "As long as we can get a good cabin and the food is decent, I'll be happy."

When they got to St. Louis, they went straight to the docks. There was a boat that was leaving shortly. It was fully booked except for one cabin. It was what they called "The Honeymoon Suite." It was very expensive, but money was not an issue. A porter guided them to their cabin. Sean gave him a good tip. "You can have your meals brought to your room if you want," said the porter. "That's included in your bill. There's a rope beside your bed. It goes down to the kitchen. There's a bell at the other end. If you ring that bell, a waiter will come up and take your order and bring it to you when it's ready. There's a menu on the table there, and we have all kinds of liquid refreshment. My name is Albert. If you need me for anything, I won't be far away. Now I'll leave you two alone."

Maggie and Sean were amazed. This was a beautiful suite. The bed was bigger than any bed either of them had ever seen. There was a balcony where they could sit outside and watch the scenery. There was soft carpeting on the floor. There were huge closets too. There were several mirrors on the walls. One was on the wall closest to the bed. "So if we're in bed making love, we can look over and watch ourselves," said Sean. "That could be interesting. Let's find out." It must have been interesting because they both seemed to really enjoy the mirror. After they were finished, they both decided it was time for some food.

"Pick us out something from the menu, and I'll yank that rope," said Sean. Maggie made her decision and after Sean yanked the rope, it wasn't two full minutes before the waiter arrived. He took the order and told them it would be about forty five minutes.

"I can bring you something to drink if you'd like," he said.

"Bring us a bottle of some Irish Whiskey if you would please," said Maggie.

"Right away ma'am," said the waiter.

"We can set out on the balcony and sip some whiskey while we wait for our food," said Sean. "Let's try to imagine what it was like a hundred years ago and what it might be like a hundred years in the future."

"A hundred years ago won't be hard to imagine," said Maggie. "There wasn't much here. It was probably very beautiful and quiet. A hundred years in the future will be a little harder to imagine. There will be a heck of a lot of more people. There will be more industries. New things get invented every once in a while. No one ever thought there would be steam engines. Some day, someone will invent something that will take their place. You and I will be long gone when that happens."

"Things will change," said Sean. "They always have. We can hope they always change for the better."

~~~~

There was a knock at the door, and the waiter announced that he was there with their food. He set up everything at their table and was on his way. Sean gave him a tip as he was leaving. "What are we having?" Sean asked Maggie.

"It's some kind of goose," said Maggie. "I thought it sounded interesting. Let's find out." They both took a bite.

Sean spoke first. "You did good Maggie," said Sean. "This is really good. I hope all our meals are this good." Maggie agreed.

~~~~

On the third day, they were invited to have dinner with the ship's Captain. They dined in the main dining room, and the Captain had his own private table at one end. It was the fanciest dining room either of them had ever seen. The tables were all covered with the finest table cloths. The China was the finest, and the silverware was of the best quality. The porter showed them to the their seats and a waiter brought them a drink while they waited for the Captain. When the Captain entered the room, there was no doubt about who he was. He was a middle aged man, tall, medium build, and had a full mustache. His uniform was flawless. He walked straight to their table and introduced himself.

"I am Captain Horace Bennett," he began. "It is an extreme honor to meet the both of you." Then he took Maggie's hand and kissed it and then shook Sean's hand. "I feel like I already know you," the Captain said. "When I saw your name on the passenger list, I knew it was you. I'm sorry. I'm getting ahead of myself."

"So Captain, why is it you think you know me?" asked Sean.

"I was a gunboat Captain during the war and I was a good friend of General Sherman's," Horace said. "He talked about you many times. He always said he wished he had more men like you. I have also heard of your reputation as a lawman. We need more men who can do what you do. I was also very anxious to meet this beautiful wife of yours. What I have heard about her beauty is not true. Maggie you are more beautiful than words can say."

"Thank you for your compliments, Captain," replied Maggie. "Sean and I are very glad to meet you too, and we are very pleased with your boat. How did you become the Captain?"

"That was easy," answered Horace. "I am the Captain because I own this boat. I was actually the Captain on her before the war. When the war started, I was commissioned in the Navy. The owner of the boat died during the war, and when I found out, I offered to buy it from his family, and they agreed. We used to mostly haul freight. I decided to take a chance and turn her into a nice vessel that people would want to take cruises on. So far, we have been successful. If things change, we can always go back to hauling freight."

"Some people like to be pampered," said Maggie. "I know I do once in a while. We haven't been to the gaming room, but I suppose you make a lot of money there."

"Yes we do," said Horace. "That's actually where we make most of our money. We have only the top players. I have honest dealers, and we allow no nonsense. Anyone causing any kind of trouble is asked to debark. If they refuse, I force them at gunpoint if necessary. We have had a few incidents, but I have not had to shoot anyone yet. You two should visit the gaming room. Sometimes I really like to just watch the gamblers. Some of them are really good. I think you would enjoy it."

"Maybe we will," said Sean. "I enjoy poker myself, but it might be fun just to watch a good game."

"So Bill Sherman told me about the time you was about to brain that Quartermaster Captain," said Horace. "Would you have really done that?"

"I sure would've," said Sean. "If the General hadn't a showed up, I would have split that man's skull."

~~~~

"Well you sure impressed Bill," said Horace. "He told me about what happened down around Atlanta. Looks like you healed up well."

"Yes I did," replied Sean. "I still think the General was looking out for me because I spent the rest of the war healing up and then doing nothing. I resigned as soon as I heard Lee surrendered."

"I resigned my Commission when it was all over," said Horace. "I sure do like this boat more than those ironclads I was on. No one is shooting at me either. Maybe one day no one will be shooting at you either."

"We both hope for that," added Maggie. "Sean has reduced the number of outlaws in the short time he has been a lawman."

"I heard that Anderson was sent to Hell," said Horace. "I'm glad you got that son of a bitch. Pardon my English, Maggie."

"That man was a no good, dirty, rotten piece of scum and finally got sent to Hell where he belonged," said Maggie. "He was taking up space that was needed for a good person. I just hope that no one decides to pick up where he left off."

"You have yourself a very good woman, Sean," said Horace. "I think I'll stay on her good side."

"She is a very good woman," added Sean. "Now let's talk about pleasant things and enjoy a fine meal."

~~~~

While eating their meal, Sean and Horace spent most of the time talking about the war. They were both very glad it was over, but neither of them was sure it would help the way people thought. They both agreed that a good portion of the white race was prejudiced against anyone of any color other than white. This would take decades, maybe even centuries to change. When the meal was finally over, Maggie told them she was tired of war talk and such and suggested that they visit the gaming room.

"That's a good suggestion," said Horace. "I'm sure you'd like to see how it's decorated and laid out and such since you have your own place. It might give you some new ideas."

~~~~

When they got to the gaming room, Horace took them around and introduced them to the bartender and all the dealers. Maggie was impressed with everything. It had a very nice bar with the best glasses and mugs available. The furniture was of the best quality, and there were several impressive paintings on each wall. Several glass chandeliers hung from the ceiling. There were several card games going, and Sean became interested in watching one of them. Maggie went around and was looking at all the paintings. There was a very nice one right behind the bar. It was a naked woman on a white horse. The woman was beautiful and some of her long dark hair hung over her large full breasts but did not completely cover them. Maggie went to the bar and was asking the bartender if he knew anything about the artist who painted it.

"No Mrs. O'Rourke, I do not know anything about this painting," he said. "You should ask the Captain. I believe he picked out every painting here. If you'll please excuse me. I need to go the stock room and bring out some more spirits."

As Maggie was standing there looking at the painting, a young well dressed man approached her. "Excuse me ma'am," he began. "You are the most beautiful woman I have ever seen. Would you spend the night with me for $100?"

Maggie had a hard time controlling herself. She hesitated for a moment and regained her composure and turned slightly to face the man. Then she reached into her purse and pulled out a pistol and stuck it right into the man's privates. She slowly cocked the hammer. "In case you didn't hear that nice bartender address me, my name is Mrs. O'Rourke," Maggie began. "My husband is Federal Marshal Sean O'Rourke and he's standing over there watching that card game. If he had heard what you just said, you'd probably be dead by now. Now I think I'll call my husband over here."

"Please don't ma'am," he said. "I'm deeply sorry. I just assumed that since you were alone that you were a working girl."

"Well we'll see how my husband feels about this," said Maggie. "Sean darlin', I need you over here please." The man was beginning to shake now.

"Yes Maggie darlin', what is it?" Sean asked.

"This gentleman here assumed I was a working girl and offered me $100 to spend the night with him," said Maggie. "I told him that if you had heard him say that, he would probably be dead by now."

"That's right Maggie. He would be dead by now," said Sean. "What do you think we should do with him?"

"I believe he should take a swim darlin'," responded Maggie. "Mister, very slowly, empty your pockets and such and show us whether you are armed or not."

He emptied his pockets and then took off his jacket to show that he was not armed. Maggie kept her pistol in his privates the whole time. "Please don't do this," he pleaded. "I am terribly sorry. What more can I do or say?"

"You can walk over to that door there and jump off this boat yourself or be thrown off," said Sean. "Maybe this will teach you some manners. You can put your belongings back in your pockets."

"All right, all right, I'll do it myself," the man said as ran out the door and jumped into the water about fifteen feet below. Sean and Maggie watched him for a few minutes to make sure that he could swim and wasn't drowning.

"Let's get back inside now," said Maggie. "I've had enough amusement for a little while."

"I suppose I know what all that was about," said Horace as Maggie and Sean came back inside. "I'm sorry that happened. We do get a few working girls from time to time. I do not mind as most of them are well acquainted with some of my regular passengers."

"I just hope that young man made it to shore all right," replied Maggie. "He probably won't be a passenger on your boat for a while."

"Probably not," said Horace. "Now if you'll excuse me, I need to get back to work. I do hope you will enjoy the rest of your cruise."

~~~~

They did enjoy the rest of their cruise. They spent most of their time in their suite enjoying each other's company. They took the rest of their meals in their suite too. When it was over and time to debark, the Captain came down to see them off. "Thank you for choosing my boat," Horace said. "It was an honor and a privilege to meet both of you."

"Thank you for your kindness," said Maggie. "Sean and I just loved your boat. Maybe one day we will be back for another cruise."

"I'll look forward to that day," said Horace.

~~~~

Sean hired a buggy to take them downtown. They took a room at a nice hotel close to "The Palace." It was mid morning. "How about we get a late breakfast then go see the Judge?" said Sean. "Then we can look up Sam Draper."

"That'll be fine, darlin'," said Maggie. "I could use something to eat." There was a small eatery next to their hotel. Sean had eaten there before and he knew they had a good cook. Sean ordered himself steak, eggs, potatoes, and biscuits. Maggie had flapjacks and eggs. After they were done, they headed to the Federal Courthouse.

Judge Simmons was at his desk in his office when they walked in. "It's so good to see you again," said the Judge as he stood up and went to Sean to shake his hand. "And this has got to be Mrs. O'Rourke. I'm happy to meet you." He took her hand and kissed it. "Please take a seat," David said as he pulled a chair out from the desk for Maggie. "How has your trip been so far?" he asked.

"Well there was an attempted stage robbery before we got to Kansas City," started Sean. "We ended up killin' five men and a woman."

"What were they after?" asked the Judge.

"There was no money on the stage but after we got to Kansas City, we found out that someone had sent the former Mayor of Kansas City a buncha blank bank drafts from some bank in Texas," Sean began. "They had to been after them bank drafts. That new Judge down there, Lawrence Todd, is tryin' to find out."

"I'll see if I can find anything out about them too," said David. "So things got cleaned up down there?"

"I'm pretty sure things will be all right there now," said Sean. "They're havin' elections and gettin' some honest people in office."

"That's good," said David. "I have a feeling that something like what happened in Kansas City is trying to get started here in St. Louis. I have heard rumors about unidentified people going around and trying to extort money from some of the businesses. No one has ever seen these people before or they are afraid to speak up. I have heard that some of these people have tried to get Sam Draper to sell his place."

"Well Sam won't let that happen," said Sean. "The Town Marshal was a man named Mike Kiley. When I met him last year, he seemed like an honest man."

"He is an honest man," said David. "But St. Louis is a big place and he has a lot of deputies. I can't vouch for them."

"I'll see Sam later today and see what he says about this," said Sean.

"So Mrs. O'Rourke, how do you feel about your husband being a lawman?" asked David. "It is a very dangerous job."

"Sean was a lawman when I first met him," answered Maggie. "I knew what I was getting into from the start. I know that he can take care of just about anything. Now would you please call me Maggie?"

"Of course I will call you Maggie," replied David. "So how long will you two be in St. Louis?"

"We'll stay here for a week or so then head back to Abilene," answered Sean. "We already took a nice cruise on Horace Bennett's boat."

"I know Horace, and that boat of his is very nice," said David. "Now I hate to do this to you but I have to be in court in fifteen minutes. If I do not see you before you leave, enjoy your time here and have a safe trip back. Send me a telegram when you get back in case I need you for anything." Sean and David shook hands again and David kissed Maggie's hand again, and then the two of them went window shopping.

Maggie had not been to a big town for a while, and she enjoyed all the shops. Sean decided to go see his friend Walter Black at the gunsmith shop. Walter was there behind the counter at work as usual. "Hey Walter, how are you doin'?" said Sean as they entered his store.

"It's good to see you again Marshal," said Walter. "I know who this woman is. Mrs. O'Rourke, I am Walter Black, and I am pleased to meet you. I have done a lot of work for your husband."

"Please call me Maggie," Maggie said. "Yes, your work has certainly helped my husband. I have heard that you might move your business to Abilene."

"I was thinking that I might do that," said Walter. "St. Louis is getting too big for me. I know I need a lot of people for my business, but there's a point where it gets to be too many. Besides, I don't like what's going on around here."

~~~~

"Are you talking about some people trying to extort money from some of the businesses or buy them out?" asked Sean.

"That's what I'm talking about," said Walter. "Two fellas came in here not long ago. I never seen 'em before. Anyway, they said they was sellin' protection. Protection from what, I asked'em. Oh, fires and such, one of'em said. I pulled out a double barreled shotgun and stuck it in one of their faces and told them that they was the ones that needed some protection. I told them if they ever got near my place again, I would start shootin' and just tell the law that they was tryin' to rob me so I defended myself. Haven't seen'em since. "

"Well I hope they leave you alone," said Sean. "If you did come to Abilene, your business would really do good. Abilene should be a cow town by next spring. The railroad should have a line there by then and the cattle pens should be done. Them Texas boys'll be bringin' their herds up there to ship and when they get paid, they'll need to be spendin' that money they just made. There's already a lot of new places bein' built."

"Sounds invitin'," said Walter. "Maybe I will. I don't know if I can get the wife to move. She likes being close to our children.

Course they're grown up now. We're expectin' some grandkids before too long."

"I can understand that," said Sean. "Now we'll let you get back to work. We'll be in town for a week or so. If you need me for anything, we're at that hotel closest to "The Palace." You take care now."

"Let's do some more window shopping then let's go find Sam," said Maggie.

"Whatever you desire, darlin'," replied Sean. "We can get another meal before we see Sam if you'd like or we can get a meal at his place. All this window shoppin' is makin' me hungry."

"Just a few more places and then we can find Sam," said Maggie. "I need to see some dress shops and keep up with any new fashions that have come out."

"Darlin', you would look good in anything, or nothin' for that matter," said Sean.

"Maybe we should go try out our room," said Maggie. "We have plenty of time to shop."

"Sounds good, let's go," said Sean.

A couple of hours later, they made their way to "The Palace." When they went in the doors, a woman ran right to Sean, grabbed him, and started kissing him. It was Susie. Sean politely pushed her away. "Susie, I'd like you to meet my wife Maggie," said Sean. "Maggie, this is Susie."

"Sorry Maggie, I just couldn't help myself," said Susie. "Your husband has that affect on me."

"I understand," said Maggie. "He has that affect on me too. Why don't you show me around while Sean finds Sam."

"Sure thing," said Suzie. "Sam's in the back room doing the books and I'll show you the place and introduce you to the girls."

Maggie was really impressed with the place. Everything in the place was of the best quality. The girls were very beautiful, and they were very nice too. She knew that when Sean was here, he didn't spend his off hours alone. "You got yourself a good man," said Susie after she had shown Maggie everything and had introduced all the girls. "Maybe one day I'll find me a man as good as him."

"I hope that for every woman," said Maggie. "But he's one of a kind. Finding another one like him would take some hard looking."

"I'm young yet," said Susie. "I got plenty of time. This is a good place to work in the meantime. Sam's a great boss. You know your husband saved his life in here one night."

"I believe I heard all about that," said Maggie. "Sean has saved several lives since he's been a lawman. Now I think I'll find Sean and Sam."

When Sean found Sam, he was at his desk going over the books. When he saw Sean, he got up and ran over and gave him a hug and then shook his hand. "It is good to see you my friend," Sam said. "I have been hoping that we would see each other again. Your line of work can be hazardous to your health. I heard that you finally got Anderson. I hope he's in hell where he belongs."

"I hope so too, my friend," said Sean. "The place still looks great and the girls are still beautiful. Speaking of beautiful, I want you to meet my wife Maggie."

"Everyone around here has heard about the red-headed beauty," said Sam. "She must really love you to put up with your line of work."

"I do really love him," said Maggie as she entered his office. "There is not a better man to be found anywhere."

"You are more beautiful than I have heard Maggie," said Sam. "You don't mind if I call you Maggie, do you?"

"No Sam, that's my name," said Maggie. "I just love your place and your people are the best."

"I run a good business here," said Sam. "At times I think about what I could do to make it even better, but I can't come up with anything."

"I wouldn't know what you could do either," said Maggie. "Now Sean and I would like to thank you for finding us that bathtub. It is a truly wonderful piece of work."

"It is all handmade," said Sam. "I knew you would like it. Who wouldn't? Are you two hungry? If you are, let's go out and order some food. We have a very good cook here."

"That sounds good," said Sean. "I'll let Maggie decide what we'll eat today. She picked some good food on that boat."

"My cook can make anything on the menu most of the time," said Sam. "Sometimes later in the day, we run out of certain things. I strongly recommend the pheasant. I don't know what he does to it, but it is very good. There is no wild taste and it melts in your mouth."

"That will be fine with me," said Maggie. "How about you darlin'? Do you want the pheasant or would you rather have a steak?"

"I can get a steak about anytime, " said Sean. "I'll try the pheasant."

"I'll have the cook get started," said Sam. "Now if I remember right, you like a good bourbon. I'll get us a bottle and some glasses."

~~~~

As they were eating, they talked about anything and everything. When they were finished and sipping an after dinner drink, Sean asked Sam about what was going on in town. "I've heard that someone is trying extort money from businesses in town or trying to get them to sell," said Sean. "I've heard that they have tried to get you to sell."

"I don't know who runs them, but yes, I have been visited by some people who are trying to get me to sell," said Sam. "I have been polite with them and told them to be on their way. They have not been nasty or anything to me. They have visited me three times. I heard all about Kansas City. I sure hope nothing like that will happen here. St. Louis is a big place. Speaking of those people, the ones who visited me before just came in the door. Excuse me and I'll go see what they want this time."

Sam went to the two men and then they went to his office in the back. "I'll wait a few minutes, then I'm going back there and see if I can be of help," said Sean.

"Don't shoot anyone if you don't have to," said Maggie as Sean got up and headed to Sam's office. As Sean got closer to the office, he could tell that a struggle was in progress. When Sean opened the office door, Sam was on the floor struggling with one of the men. The other man had apparently been knocked out and was laying there unconscious. Sean stood in the doorway watching. Sam was on top of the man holding him down. The man now pulled a knife and was trying to stab Sam. Sam pulled a small revolver from his jacket and shot the man in the chest. He died instantly. When the shot was fired, the other man started to awaken. Sam was still on the man trying to regain his composure. He did not know that the other man was awake now and had pulled a pistol and was getting ready to shoot him. The man did not know that Sean was behind him. As the man raised the pistol to shoot Sam, Sean pulled a pistol and killed him. Maggie and several of Sam's people came running when they heard the shots. "Sean, Sam, are you all right?" cried Maggie as she came running into the office.

"We are," said Sean. "But them two are not. What happened here Sam?"

"Them two tried to get rough this time," answered Sam. "I hit one in the jaw and knocked him out and then got into it with the other one. You saved my life again Sean. I thank you. Now some-one go get Mike Kiley."

~~~~

Town Marshal Mike Kiley was there in no time. He had a young deputy with him. "Well Sam, what happened here?" asked Mike.

"These two are the ones who have been trying to get me to sell," answered Sam. "Today they tried to get rough. This one here pulled a knife on me and I shot him. That other one was gonna shoot me and Sean shot him."

"This one fella is shot in the back," said the deputy. "Why is he shot in the back?"

"That's easy to explain young fella," said Sean. He was gonna shoot Sam and he was facin' away from me. I didn't have time to ask him to turn around."

"I'll be takin' your gun Mister," said the deputy. "We'll be havin' an inquiry about this."

"You be quiet, pup," Mike said to his deputy. "This here man is Federal Marshal Sean O'Rourke, and he don't make a habit a shootin' men in the back."

"I don't care who he is," said the deputy. "A man's been shot in the back, and I'm takin' his gun."

"You try to take his gun and we'll be goin' to your funeral," said Mike. "Now you go get the undertaker and have him get these bodies outta here."

"I'm just about tired a takin' orders from you old man," said the deputy. "You're not fit to wear that badge anymore. Now I'm takin' his gun."

"I hired you and now I'm firin' you, pup," said Mike. "Gimme that badge before I take it from you." The deputy hesitated for just a moment, then went for his pistol. Mike was faster and the young deputy fell dead on the floor with a hole in his chest. "Stupid pup," said Mike. "I knew sooner or later he was gonna be bad news. He seemed like a nice boy when I first hired him. I better go tell his sweetheart what happened. Sam, sorry this happened on my watch. You be careful. These two probly got some friends."

"Mike's probly right," said Sean. "If I was you, I'd get some trustworthy men workin' for me. I'll help you find some if you'd like."

"Maybe I will," said Sam. "I don't need to be lookin' over my shoulder all the time. I need to find out who's behind all this. I believe I need a drink. Let's go back out front and I'll get us some bourbon." Sean and Maggie went to the table, and Sam went to the bar to get everything.

"This has been some honeymoon," said Maggie. "Do you suppose anything else will happen?"

"I sure hope not," said Sean. "I don't like things that distract me from you."

"You know just what to say, darlin'," said Maggie. "I bet that when word gets around that you are in town, the rest of our stay here will be a quiet one."

~~~~

Maggie was right. It was quiet for the rest of their stay. On the day that they left, Sam, David, Horace, and Mike came to see them off. They would take the train back to Kansas City and then take the stage to Abilene.

CHAPTER TEN

J esse Strong was born a free man. His grandfather had been born a slave, but was given his freedom by his master. His grandfather was a blacksmith on a big horse farm in central Kentucky. He did such a good job that his master gave him his freedom in his eighteenth year. He also promised his former master that he would stay and work there, and he would make sure his offspring learned all he knew. Jesse's father learned smithing, but he excelled at horse training. The horses raised at this farm were the best breeds and sold for the highest prices. When Jesse was just ten years old, he started working with the horses. In a few years, he could watch a horse for a few minutes and know what type of shoe was needed for that horse. By the time he was sixteen, he ran the blacksmith shop at the farm. Jesse's parents both died the next year. Jesse lived in a small, one room house behind the blacksmith shop. He could also read and write and knew his numbers.

There were several slaves on the farm, but the owner, a Mr. Bradley Cooper, did not treat them like slaves. There was a young woman who worked in the kitchen that Jesse thought was the most beautiful girl he had ever seen. She was dark skinned, but she was not a slave. She was Osage. Her name was Dawn Littletree. Her mother had worked for the Cooper family for years. Whenever Jesse had the time, he would slip over to see her. He could tell that she liked him too. Dawn was just sixteen years old. She decided that she would marry Jesse when she turned eighteen.

In 1860 when Jesse turned eighteen, he was a huge man. He stood six foot four inches and was well over two hundred and twenty five pounds. There was not an ounce of fat on his body. The muscles on his chest and in his arms were huge. He could not wear store bought clothes because they would always rip apart. During the warm months, he never wore a shirt while he was working. He just wore his pants and his leather apron. Dawn made him some shirts that he could wear during the cold part of the year.

Everything was going along just fine until the war came. Kentucky was a neutral state when the war started, but after the Confederates invaded, the state became mostly pro-union. There were still a lot of slave owners and pro-southern people in Kentucky. The Confederate Army needed horses so when they invaded, one of the first things they did was go to the Cooper Farm. Mr. Cooper did not want to sell his horses to the Confederate Army or to the Union Army either. The rebs ended up just taking every horse on the place except some of the old brood mares. They also took all the supplies from the blacksmith shop. Jesse was in the shop when some of the gray soldiers came. There was a loud mouthed Sergeant in charge of the men who were there to get the supplies. He was mounted on a big gray horse. "Boy, git over here and load up them supplies on this wagon," the Sergeant said to Jesse. "Did you hear me boy? I said git over here."

"I'm not your boy and you can load that stuff your damn self," said Jesse.

"Well looky here boys. We got us an uppity nigger," said the sergeant. "I think maybe we'll just hang him before we leave."

There were three other soldiers with the Sergeant. They had dismounted and tied their horses over by the main house. They seemed to be amused when the Sergeant talked about hanging Jesse. "Yep, let's hang that nigger," one of them said. Jesse didn't know for sure what he was going to do, but he knew he wasn't going to let them hang him. There was a piece of steel behind the forge that Jesse was using to make horse shoes. It was about three quarters of an inch wide, about a half inch thick, and four feet long. When the sergeant turned his head for just a moment, Jesse saw his chance. He grabbed the piece of steel, leaped up and slammed it into the Sergeant's skull. Then quickly he went after the other three soldiers. They had put their rifles in a corner while they were loading the supplies and scrambled to get to them when Jesse came after them. They never made it to their rifles. After Jesse crushed the skull of one of them, the other two tried to grab Jesse but Jesse was too strong for them. He freed himself of them and killed each one with a crushing blow to the head with the piece of steel. Then he pulled the pistol belt off the dead Sergeant and mounted his gray horse and took off for the closest woods. The other soldiers were so busy rounding up all the horses all over the farm that they had not seen what had happened. When the bodies of the dead soldiers were found, their Captain went into a rage. "We came here peaceably and this happens," the Captain said. "I will not tolerate this." Then he had his men take Mr. Cooper and hang him from an oak tree in front of the house.

No one came after Jesse because no one had seen him or seen what had happened. When the Confederate soldiers first arrived, Mr. Cooper had the women hide anywhere they thought would be safe. Dawn hid in a big closet that had two compartments. If a person did not know that it had two compartments, it was a good hiding place. The soldiers set everything on fire and when they left, they took all the slaves with them. They did not stay to watch everything burn so Dawn was able to escape without being burned.

It didn't take Jesse long to realize that he was not followed. He waited till dark and headed back to the farm. When he got there, Dawn was setting in front of the smoldering house crying. Jesse got off the horse and went to Dawn. He picked her up and hugged her. "We got to be movin' now," said Jesse. "We don't know if them rebs will come back or if there's more of them around. We'll be headin' north."

"We can't leave Mr. Cooper hanging," said Dawn. "I want you to cut him down."

"I'm sorry but I can't do that," said Jesse. "If I do that, they'll know someone was here and maybe track us down. We gotta leave him like that He don't feel no pain now anyway. Now let's get on this horse. That reb had a little food in his saddle bags so we'll be all right for a couple days. I got a little money on me too. I'll take care a us."

"I have some friends who live up in Ohio," said Dawn. "It's a little town called Lebanon. If we can get up there, I know they'll help us out."

"That's a long way off," said Jesse. "I'll get us there. We might be dodgin' rebs till we get outta Kentucky. I don't know how far north they are. You gotta promise me that if we see some rebs, you'll do what I say and be quiet when I say."

"I will," said Dawn. "I'm not ready to die just yet. Besides, you gotta marry me."

"We'll get married," said Jesse. "Let's get ourselves to Ohio first."

~~~~

Jesse and Dawn did not have any trouble getting up to the Ohio river. There were no Confederate soldiers that far north, at least where they went. When they ran out of food, they stopped at farms along the way and were helped. Jesse had to pay a man to get them across the river in his boat. He charged extra for the horse. They were just east of Cincinnati. Jesse still had some money, so he bought enough supplies to get them to Lebanon. They could get there in a few days.

The trip to Lebanon was uneventful. Several travelers on the road stared at them. They were probably not used to seeing a colored man and an Osage woman on a fine, big gray horse and the man wearing a pistol belt. When they arrived in Lebanon, Dawn knew exactly where to go. Her friend lived on the east end of town on a small farm. Her friend had married very young. Her parents were dead and when her husband died of influenza, she moved in with her grandparents. Her name was Carla Tompkins.

Carla was setting out on the front porch of the house when Dawn and Jesse arrived. Carla recognized Dawn right away and ran to her. "Oh my, is that you Dawn?" Carla exclaimed. "It is so very good to see you again. I have needed some company. Just why are you here now?"

"The rebs came and took all the horses at the farm, and they hanged Mr. Cooper," Dawn said. "This is my intended, Jesse Strong. He had to kill some of the rebs too."

"Well let's go in the house," said Carla. "I'll introduce you two to my grandparents."

"Are you sure they'll want to meet me?" asked Jesse. "A lotta white folks don't care for colored folks."

"My grandparents don't care what color you are Jesse," said Carla. "They're good people." Carla took them inside and introduced them to her grandparents. "Gramma and Grampa, this is my good friend Dawn Littletree, and this man is her intended, Jesse Strong."

"I bet you're a blacksmith," said her Grampa. "You didn't get those big arms any other way."

"Yes sir, I've been a blacksmith for a good while now," said Jesse. "My Pa taught me."

"Well I bet I know where you can find some work," said Grampa. "There's a fella in town and he's gettin' horses ready for the army. I hear they need people who can handle horses that aren't green broke yet. I can take you over there tomorrow if you want."

"That'd be just fine," said Jesse. "Are you sure they won't mind me bein' a colored man?"

"Last I heard, the horses don't care what color a man is," said Grampa. "I don't know for sure about the man. We don't get too many colored folks around here. I don't figure he'll care as long as you can help with them horses. Now let's get you two settled."

"Dawn can stay in my room with me," said Carla. "Jesse can stay in the spare room."

"This is so nice of you," said Dawn. "We'll earn our keep around here. We will not be a burden. I can do all the cooking if you want Mrs. Tompkins. I did most of it at the farm in Kentucky. Jesse can work in your garden too when he's not working horses."

"I can see right now that we will all get along just fine," said Gramma. "I'm so glad that you are here. I know that Carla has been in need of someone her own age for company for some time."

~~~~

That evening at dinner, Jesse was amazed. They all sat at the same table. After the meal, Jesse went out and worked in the garden till dark. That night, Carla told Dawn all about the short time she had with her husband. "We married when I was only fifteen and he was eighteen," said Carla. "We were only together for six months when he died of the influenza. I think I cried for two months. Then I got to thinking about what it would have been like if I had been with child. Having a child without a father would have been a bad thing. When I decided it was good that I wasn't going to have a baby, I quit crying. I still miss him, but then I realize that we were not together long enough to really get to know each other. So do you know Jesse well?"

"I've known Jesse almost my whole life," said Dawn. "I told him we would get married when I turn eighteen."

"Why do you want to wait till then?" asked Carla. "I don't understand."

"I'm not sure why either," said Dawn. "I just had it in my head to wait till then. I seen lotsa girls get married real young. Some of them looked pretty scared at the time. Anyway, maybe I won't wait till then. I got a feelin' this war is gonna be a long one. I figure Jesse will get himself in it sometime or another. I know they don't have colored soldiers, but Mr. Lincoln might change that."

"Let's quit this depressing talk and get some sleep," said Carla. "We have all kinds of time to get reacquainted."

~~~~

The next morning after breakfast, Grampa took Jesse to meet the man who was getting the horses for the army. He told Jesse that it wouldn't be a good idea for him to wear his pistol belt when they went to see his possible employer. The man's name was Chester Townsend. He was maybe forty years old, tall, medium build, dark hair, and had a clean shaven face. When Grampa and Jesse got to his place, he was standing beside a corral and barking out orders at a couple of men who were in the corral with the horses. There were at least thirty horses in the corral. "I told you idiots to get that bay, not that chestnut," he said. "Don't you fools know anything? I swear. My ten year old can do a better job than you two." Then he saw Grampa and Jesse approaching.

"Looks like you could sure use some good help," said Grampa. "I got just the man for you right here."

"So boy, you know horses?" asked Chester.

"First off, the name is Jesse, Jesse Strong, not boy," said Jesse. "And yes I know horses. I can break'em and train'em and get shoes on'em."

"Well Mr. Jesse Strong, go in there and get that bay," said Chester. "You get him gentled down and get some shoes on him, and I'll give you a job. You two get outta there and let this fella see what he can do."

The two men were not too happy about being put aside for a colored man. As Jesse was entering the corral and the two men were leaving, one of them said the wrong thing to Jesse. "I hope that sombitch stomps yer ass you stupid nigger," he said.

Jesse stopped in his tracks and faced the man. "Mr. Townsend told you to get outta here and you're gettin' outta here." Jesse picked up the man over his head and threw him out of the corral. Then he looked at the other man. "Do you need any help leavin'?" Jesse asked him. The man never said a word. He just ran out as fast as he could. He helped the other man get up, and then they both walked up to Chester and told him they were done and wanted paid for what they had already done.

"You haven't done spit yet," said Chester. "Here's a dollar for each a you. Now git." The two men left, and Jesse could hear them cursing as they left. "All right Mr. Strong, let's see what you can do," said Chester.

It didn't take long, and the bay was behaving like a well broke horse. He never bucked one time as Jesse rode him. He never fought Jesse one bit as he was getting his first shoes. Chester was amazed. "You got yourself a job," said Chester. "I'll give you a dollar for every horse you gentle and another fifty cents for gettin'em shod. Only one thing I want to warn you about. These horses are for the army. Sometimes the army isn't too fast when it comes to payin' up, but they won't get no horses till the money comes. Does that suit you?"

"Sure does," said Jesse. "I'll go ahead and get started if it it's all right with you."

"It's all right with me," said Chester. "Just keep me informed as to when you need your supplies. Don't wanna be runnin' outta steel, nails, and such."

~~~~

The first month, Jesse did thirty five horses for Mr. Townsend. He would have done more, but that's all he had. Jesse had no idea where Chester was getting his horses, but he always managed to get in at least thirty every month. Jesse didn't know what the army was paying Chester for the horses, but Jesse was making plenty of money. Some of the local trash in town also noticed that Mr. Townsend and Jesse were making plenty of money. One afternoon after the army had gotten about fifty horses, they decided it would be a good time to rob them. There were three of them. Two of them were the ones who were there when Jesse first came to Mr. Townsend's place. Jesse and Chester were both in the office when the three of them crashed in the door. The one that Jesse had thrown from the corral was carrying a pistol. The other two had knives. "We'll have that money," the one with the pistol said.

"Not likely," replied Chester. "Now you fools get the hell outta here before I get angry."

"Go ahead and shoot'em, shoot'em both," one of the others said. "We got time to get away."

Jesse was only about five feet from the one with the pistol. The man was holding the pistol low and when he raised it to fire at Chester, Jesse grabbed his gun arm and slammed it across his right knee. They could hear the bones in his arm snap. The pistol fired but no one was hit. The other two men came after Jesse with their knives. "Maybe you two better just scat before you get yourself killed," said Jesse. They ignored Jesse and started slashing at him. Chester was still at his desk. The two men were so busy trying to slash at Jesse that they didn't see him reach into his desk and pull out a pistol. Chester never said a word, but when the two men heard him cock the hammer, they turned to look at him. Chester shot both of them in the head. They were dead when they hit the floor. "It's a shame this other one's not dead," said Chester. "I better go get the Sheriff and tell him what went on. Jesse, you stay here and keep an eye on him. I wouldn't care if you had to shoot him while he was tryin' to get away."

"He won't be goin' no where," said Jesse. "If he even moves, I'll break some more a his bones."

Chester was back in no time with the Sheriff and a doctor. "I seen these three around town," he said. "I figured they was up to no good." Then he looked at Jesse. "So you broke that fella's arm. Damn, you must awful strong. Anyway, he got what he deserved."

The doctor looked at the man and put a splint on his arm. "We'll get you to the office so I can get them bones set proper," the doctor said. "Then the Sheriff has a nice room for you down at the jail."

After the Sheriff left with the doctor and the prisoner, Chester asked Jesse if he would like a drink. "I never had anything stronger to drink than coffee," said Jesse. "I don't know if I should start now. "

"I think you should at least give it a taste," said Chester. "One taste won't turn you into a ragin' drunk. I don't drink much myself. I've had this bottle of bourbon here for six months. It's still well over half full."

"I'll give it a taste," said Jesse. "Grampa Tompkins takes a taste now and again. Gramma don't mind."

"Them are sure nice folks for lettin' you and your woman stay there," said Chester. "Not too many folks would do that." Chester pulled out two glasses and poured them each a little taste. "Now just take a real small sip. Swallow it slowly and enjoy the taste and the warm feeling."

"It does give you a nice warm feelin'," said Jesse. "Can't say as I can figure what it tastes like, but it's kinda good. I reckon a man could get to enjoy this stuff."

"That's what you need to remember," said Chester. "You need to learn to enjoy it and not abuse it. It can ruin a man's life. Well I'm gonna get home now. I better tell the wife what happened here today before she hears it second hand. I'll see you tomorrow Jesse."

Jesse finished his whiskey and then headed home. He decided that he had better tell everyone what had happened so they wouldn't get it second hand. Dawn was a little upset at first, but it didn't last long.

~~~~

The war kept grinding on and Chester's business was booming. He had to hire another man to help Jesse keep up. Horses were getting killed almost as fast as men were. Almost everyone in town had a family member who had been killed or wounded. Jesse felt a little guilty because he could not join the fight, but in the spring of 1363, that changed. A colored regiment was being formed. It was the 54th Massachusetts. Dawn was eighteen now and wanted to get married, but Jesse told her that he was going to do his part, and they would get married as soon as he got back. She begged and pleaded with him not to go, but in the end she gave in and said she would be there when he came back.

~~~~

Very few of the men in the 54th could read or write or even knew their left from their right. Jesse was one of the few men who they considered to be educated. They made him a platoon Sergeant. He made friends with another platoon Sergeant in his company. His name was Jim O'Rourke. In their first skirmish, they handled their men well and were recommended for decoration by their officers. During the assault on Fort Wagner, each of them had over half of their platoon killed and both of them were wounded while trying to hold one of the walls of the fort. They helped each other to safety and avoided capture. After they had healed and were ready to return to duty, they heard that the cavalry needed men so both of them were in the cavalry for the rest of the war. They mustered out at the same time. Jim O'Rourke was heading west and Jesse was going back to Lebanon to get married.

While Jesse had been away at the war, Carla had met and fallen in love with a young Captain. He had been wounded at Gettysburg. He would walk with a limp for the rest of his life, but he was a kind gentle man and Carla loved him deeply. Gramma and Grampa died two weeks after Lee surrendered. When Carla and her intended got married, they were going to live in Carla's house. The young Captain had enough money to buy a house, but Carla convinced him to save his money and live in her house.

Dawn knew that Jesse had saved lots of money and she began looking for a place for them. She hoped to have a place all picked out for when he got home. Things did not go well when she was looking for places. There were a lot of empty houses and farms because so many men had been killed in the war, but no one wanted to sell to an Indian woman and a colored man. She didn't understand. Why did people act this way?

Jesse didn't get home till a few months after the war finally ended. When he arrived at the farm, Dawn ran to him and hugged and kissed him till she was out of breath. "I missed you Jesse," she said. "Let's get married as soon as we can."

"That's fine by me," said Jesse. "Where's Gramma and Grampa?"

"They died not long after Lee surrendered," said Dawn. "Carla's gonna get herself married too. Maybe we can get that preacher to marry us too." Carla came out of the house with her intended.

"Jesse Strong, this is Mathew Boyd," said Carla. "He was a Captain in the army and was wounded at Gettysburg. We are getting married soon."

"I'm pleased to meet you Captain," said Jesse. "Carla's gonna make you a good wife."

"Yes she will, and please don't call me Captain," said Mathew. "Those days are gone. I do not miss them."

"I don't miss them either," said Jesse. "So maybe next time you see that preacher of your's, you could ask him if he'd marry us too."

"I'll ask him right after next Sunday service," said Mathew. "I don't attend church, but he's been a friend to my family for years. I'm sure he would marry you."

~~~~

The next several days, Jesse and Dawn went looking for property. They finally found a small fifty acre farm. The house wasn't much more than a shack, but it was theirs. Carla gave them several pieces of furniture and most importantly, a bed. Chester

Townsend was still supplying horses for the army and had given Jesse his job back. They were not near as busy as before, but the army still needed horses. They still had troops down south and more and more troops were being sent west. Since they were not so busy with the horses, Jesse had plenty of time to work on the house and get a garden planted.

~~~~

Carla and Mathew had a small wedding at Carla's house. Only Mathew's parents and Dawn and Jesse attended. Dawn and Jesse were married right after Mathew kissed the bride. Mathew's parents did not stay for Dawn and Jesse's wedding. His father mumbled something about Indians and coloreds and left. Jesse didn't care. He wasn't marrying into that family anyway.

~~~~

Everything went well for several months, then when late fall came, Chester Townsend died. The local doctor had no idea why so he said that maybe his heart gave out. Chester had a son who was in his late teens and he decided he would run the business. He knew nothing about horses so he had a hard time. He always complained about prices and everyone he dealt with was getting disgusted with him. He also thought that Jesse was being overpaid. He cut Jesse's wages by half. Jesse had saved a good bit of money and decided it was time to quit. They got a good crop from the garden and the house was ready for winter. Next spring they would move on. Neither one of them knew where they would go, but Dawn wanted to go down to the Nations and see her father and her uncle John Littletree again.

~~~~

When spring finally came, they went to Cincinnati and got train tickets all the way to Kansas City. Most of the other passengers acted like they had never seen a colored man before; let alone a colored man with an Indian woman. After they had been traveling for a few hours, a man in a fancy suit came over to Jesse and Dawn and told them that they should be in the stock cars with the livestock. Very politely, Jesse grabbed the man by his shirt right at his chest and pulled his face right down to his. "Mister, you will get back over to your seat and leave us alone," said Jesse. "If you don't, I'll pick you up and snap you like a twig."

"We'll see about that," said the man.

It wasn't five minutes and the conductor showed up. "That man said you are causing trouble," the conductor said. "If that's true, I'll be putting you off at the next place we stop for water."

"That man's a liar," said Jesse. "Anybody gonna be put off this train gonna be him. He's not good enough to ride with the livestock."

"Well I don't want no trouble," said the conductor. "I don't know that man, and I don't know you. Who am I s'posed to believe? Please don't cause any trouble. I can only imagine what that man said to you. A lotsa folks hate colored folks. I don't know why. Scared of'em I guess or mebbe they think they're different or all colored men wanna rape their women. You don't look like some crazy rapist ta me. Is this woman your wife?"

"Yes she is," answered Jesse.

"Well if that man bothers you again, you let me know and I'll take care of him," said the conductor.

"I'll do that as long as he don't push too far," said Jesse. "And thank you for your kindness." The conductor gave Jesse a nod and headed to some of the other cars. As soon as he was out of sight, the man in the fancy suit went back over to Jesse and Dawn.

"Just what is this damn world comin' to now," he said to Jesse. "We got uppity niggers and Injuns ridin' in the same car with white folks. My Pa'd roll over in his grave if he saw this."

"You get yourself away from us or you might be joinin' your Pa," said Jesse.

"Are you threatenin' me you damn darky?" the man said. He started reaching for something in his jacket. Jesse was pretty sure it was a pistol. When he was certain that it was a pistol, he grabbed the man's arm before he could bring it up to fire. He slammed the man's arm into the side of the seat in front of them. Jesse heard the bones in the man's wrist snap. The man dropped the pistol and began cursing Jesse. Jesse hadn't heard words like that since he first joined the 54th. Enough was enough. His left hook caught the man's jaw and he was out like a light. None of the other passengers had said a word the whole time this was going on, but when the man was knocked out, several of them applauded. The conductor came back through the car.

"I thought I told you to let me know if that fella's causin' any more trouble," he said.

"I didn't have time to get you," said Jesse. "That fool pulled a pistol. There it is on the floor. He's got some broke bones in his wrist. Best get him some medical attention."

"He can get his own help," said the conductor. "He'll be leavin' us at the next water stop. Should be there in just a few minutes. Maybe he'll stay unconsciuous till then."

The man did stay unconscious even while they carried him off the train. He was still there on the ground as the train was pulling away. "Damn, just what did you hit that fella with?" the conductor asked Jesse. "I never seen anyone stay out that long."

"Just used my fist," said Jesse.

"Are you one a them bare knuckle fighters or somethin'?" asked the conductor.

"Nope, just a blacksmith," said Jesse. "Been a blacksmith most a my life."

"I bet them horses don't sass you none when you're workin' on'em, do they?" asked the conductor.

"If you're nice and gentle with a horse, they'll be that way with you," said Jesse. "Ever once in a while a crazy one'll come along. Once they figure out who's boss, they calm down. May take a while sometimes."

"Well anyway, if anyone else bothers you, let me know if you can," said the conductor. "Name's Luther."

"I'm Jesse and this is my wife Dawn," said Jesse. "And once again, thank you for your kindness."

The rest of the train ride was uneventful. When they got to Kansas City, they decided they would go ahead and get a wagon and horses instead of taking the stage to Abilene. Jesse bought a good wagon and found some good horses. The man at the livery tried to cheat a little on the price of the horses, but when he saw that Jesse wouldn't be fooled and knew what he was doing, he gave in to a reasonable price. They got their supplies from a general store and Jesse also purchased a shotgun and a Spencer rifle. He already had a pistol, but the other two weapons would come in handy out on the trail. They began their journey as soon as the wagon was loaded.

"Not much out here to look at," said Jesse when they got out on the open plains of Kansas. "I s'pose a fella could get lost our here kinda easy if he didn't know his way around."

"I just hope we don't run into no stampedin' buffalo," said Dawn. "I never seen none, but there's s'posed to thousands and thousands of'em out here on the plains."

"They're probly a little farther west," said Jesse. "Gettin' ta be too many folks in this part a the country now. We don't wanna see no buffalo anyway. If we see them, there might be some a your relatives with'em."

"My relatives are all down in the Nations," said Dawn. "They been on that reservation for a good while. But there's still lotsa tribes out here that won't go on a reservation. I don't know what they'd make a us."

"I'd say we got more to worry about from white folks than we do any Indians," said Jesse.

"Let's just hope for no trouble at all," replied Dawn. "Now let's see if we can make twenty miles today."

~~~~

The trip had been good. The weather was good and they hardly saw anyone. A stagecoach would pass them once in a while, but that was about all the people they saw. When they were about two days from Abilene, they came upon a group of five men. They had three wagons with them and they all carried Sharps rifles and wore pistols. They were camped just off the road the morning that Jesse drove his wagon past them. All five of the men were setting around a small fire and drinking coffee. They never said one word as Jesse drove his wagon past them. "Them must be buffalo hunters," Jesse said to Dawn after they were a ways down the road. "The wagons are for the hides and all them fellas got Sharps. Big gun like that'll drop a buffalo." Dawn never said a word.

These five men were all brothers. They were the Chaneys, Tom was the oldest. Then came Bill, Fred, Joe, and Bud. All five of them had been on the wrong side of the law at one time or another. The most recent lawlessness was the general store they robbed back in Missouri. The law was closing in on them for other crimes, and they decided to rob the store and get themselves a stake and go buffalo hunting for awhile. The law wouldn't be out in western Kansas looking for them. The store owner and his wife were killed during the robbery. All five of the brothers were involved and were identified by witnesses.

~~~~

After Jesse was down the road a little, the five men were yakking away. "Did you see that woman?" Fred said. "She was Injun, but she was a looker. I bet that nigger's her man."

"I always wanted me a Injun woman," Joe said. "I hear they like it real good."

"You can take my word for it," Bill said." I had me a squaw fer a year once and she wanted it more'n I did. Couldn't git no rest. Traded her off fer a horse."

"I say we foller them some and have our way with that squaw," said Fred.

"We come out here to hunt buffalo, not squaws," said Tom. "Now we're all brothers and I'm the oldest so I'm in charge. You boys shoulda had yerself some women before we headed out. We got no time fer that. Now pack up and let's git movin'. We need to get farther west before some bounty hunter or some lawman finds us. If ya git ta thinkin' bout women while we're out here, use yer hand."

"Hand hell, I'll be havin' that squaw before mornin'," Fred said to himself. After they got packed and was moving, Fred talked Bud into slipping away during the night and going after the squaw. As soon as the other three brothers went to sleep, they slipped away.

~~~~

Jesse and Dawn made their twenty miles and were camped for the night. After the long day, they were dead tired and slept like babies. There was a full moon that night so Fred and Bud didn't have any trouble finding Jesse's camp. "We'll tie the horses about fifty yards out and slip in there," Fred said. "I'll knock out that nigger and you grab the woman." Bud nodded his head yes.

Jesse and Dawn were sleeping beside the wagon tonight instead of in it as they usually did. Fred was standing looking down at Jesse when Jesse awoke. As he raised up, Fred cracked him on the head with his pistol knocking him out. The sound of the crack woke Dawn and when she saw Fred and Bud, she tried to scream. Bud put a hand over her mouth preventing her from screaming. Dawn struggled and kicked and Bud's hand slipped a little. When it did, Dawn opened her mouth and then bit down hard. Blood started flowing. Dawn had bitten off the little finger of Bud's left hand. Bud started cursing and swinging his fists. He caught Dawn with a right to the jaw, and she was knocked out. "Damn, little brother," said Fred. "She done took yer finger off. I reckon you can have her first. Better wrap yer hand up with somethin' and get that bleedin' stopped. I gotta go take a dump."

Bud ripped off a piece of Dawn's slip and wrapped his left hand. Then he dropped his pants and was getting on top of her when she came to. Before she could scream or anything, Bud hit her jaw with his right hand but she wasn't knocked out. She kept struggling and was able to get him off of her. Bud pulled up his pants and grabbed Dawn again and threw her down. Then he started kicking her in the ribs, and one of his kicks caught her left arm, and Bud thought he heard the bone in her arm snap. She lay there helpless while Bud tried to mount her. Fred must have went a good ways off to take his dump because he never said one word or heard any of the struggling.

Jesse was starting to come to now. When he finally regained consciousness, he saw Bud on top of Dawn and about to enter her. Jesse got to his feet as quickly as he could. There was an axe on the side of the wagon. He grabbed the axe and before Bud could react, Jesse brought the axe down on Bud's skull almost splitting his head in half. Blood went all over Dawn. He threw Bud off of Dawn and stood over him making sure he was dead. Fred was making his way back now and could see Jesse standing over Bud. Fred pulled his pistol and took a shot at Jesse but missed. Jesse hit the ground and crawled over to his bedroll where he had put his pistol. Fred took another shot but missed again. Jesse now had blood in his eyes from where Fred had hit him in the head. He couldn't see clearly and tried to wipe the blood from his eyes. He fired at Fred but missed. When Bud realized that Jesse was shooting back, he took off at a dead run. Jesse wiped his eyes again and took aim. Fred was almost to his horse when Jesse fired again. Fred was hit in his left side. He let out a groan, but mounted his horse and escaped.

Jesse now turned his attention to Dawn. He could tell that her left arm was broken, and she probably had some broken ribs. "I'll fix you up as best I can darlin'," said Jesse. "We got to get you to a doctor pretty quick. I can set that arm, but busted ribs need looked after by a doctor. We don't want no lungs gettin' punctured. I'll wrap you up as best I can and when we get movin', you'll be layin' in the wagon and I'll go as slow as we can."

"Do you reckon that man'll come back?" asked Dawn. "I recognized them two. They was with them other men we passed yesterday. What'll we do if they come back?"

"I'll kill'em," said Jesse. "If they don't come after us before we get to Abliene, I'm goin' after'em and I will kill'em. Nobody gonna do what they done to my woman and live."

"Maybe them other fellas got nothin' to do with what happened," said Dawn.

"Maybe not, I reckon we'll find out if they come after us," said Jesse. Jesse took care of Dawn as best he could, and they were soon moving. He traveled as slow as he could.

~~~~

The bullet that had struck Fred had passed through and not hit any vitals. Fred rode as hard as he could, and when he got back to camp, the other brothers were still asleep. He dismounted and went to each brother and shook them. "Get up boys. That damn nigger done kilt our baby brother," exclaimed Fred. "He split his head with an axe and he shot me. We gotta get that nigger and hang'em."

"So you talked our baby brother into goin' after that woman," said Tom. "Just couldn't do without. Now I gotta go kill this nigger fer killin' my baby brother. If you wasn't my brother, I'd be killin' you right now. Get mounted boys. Let's go get this over with."

The brothers took off at a gallop. When they reached where Jesse had camped, they could see that he had moved out not long ago. "He can't be far ahead," said Tom. "Can't go too fast in that wagon."

It wasn't long and they had Jesse's wagon in sight. "Bill, you and Fred get on his right side and me and Joe'll get on his left," said Tom. "Stay around two hunnerd yards out. I'll drop one a his horses so the wagon can't move and after you see that horse drop, you open up with them Sharps."

Jesse could now see the four men. "We got two riders on each side of us," he said to Dawn. "They're stayin' back aways. How you feelin' darlin'? I'm gonna hafta get these horses runnin'. Cry out if it hurts you too bad."

Jesse had just got the horses moving faster when Tom fired. The horse on the left side reared up and fell straight down. It struggled for a second, then died. The wagon had come to a quick halt. Jesse went back into the wagon and grabbed everything he could and put it on both sides of Dawn to protect her. Then he grabbed his Spencer rife and jumped out the back. As soon as he cleared the wagon, bullets were coming from both sides. Jesse could tell that these men were using their Sharps. Jesse got under the wagon and crawled to the front. Dirt was flying all over as bullets hit the ground close to him. Jesse then took his Spencer and killed the other horse that was hitched to his wagon. He crawled up between the dead horses and used them for cover. He figured that now they would be shooting at him, and there would be less of a chance of them hitting the wagon. Dawn now had a better chance of not getting hit. Jesse had plenty of ammunition but he didn't want to waste any. He fired a few rounds to make sure these men knew he had a repeating rifle and knew how to use it. One of the rounds he fired killed Joe's horse. Joe laid behind the dead horse for cover. Tom, Fred and Bill had no cover on the open plain and backed off to about four hundred yards. They all got down in the prone position and took turns firing at Jesse. Jesse's dead horses were hit several times. Joe stayed behind his dead horse and continued firing.

"How long we gonna keep this up?" Joe yelled to Tom.

"As long as it takes, boy," said Tom. "That nigger'll get nervy and get up and run or somethin'. That's when we get'em."

"He don't look nervy ta me," said Joe. "I bet he was one a them nigger soldiers. Bet he's been shot at lotsa times the way he's actin'. Looks ta me that he knows just what he's doin'. He was smart killin' his own horse fer cover. And he's got a repeater too. I bet he's got plenty a bullets fer it too. He can shoot. He kilt my horse."

"I'd say he was shootin' at you, not yer horse," said Tom. "That woman a his has gotta be hidin' in that wagon. If we don't hit him soon, we'll put a few rounds into that wagon and see how he acts."

~~~~

Sean and Maggie were on the last leg of their stagecoach ride from Kansas City to Abilene when they heard shooting. Sean and Maggie were the only passengers on the stage. Sean told the stage driver to slow down and take it easy as they got closer to the shooting. Sean could now see what was happening. He told the driver to go slow and go up to the wagon and the dead horses.

"Are you carzy?" the driver asked Sean. "I don't wanna go over there and get shot."

"Go over there or get off," said Sean. The driver cursed a bit but did as Sean ordered. When they were fifty yards from the wagon, he had the driver stop. "Maggie, you stay inside with the Henry and I'm goin' out there and see what this is all about," said Sean. Sean took the Winchester with him and he still had two pistols on him. When he got out of the stagecoach, the shooting stopped.

"I'm a Federal Marshal," Sean yelled for all to hear. "Whoever a you is in charge git down here and tell me what this is all about."

Joe yelled to Tom. "He's a lawman. We can't be talkin' ta him. He might be after us."

"He don't know who we are, and we're not gonna tell'em," said Tom. "We'll just go down there and tell him that this nigger kilt our baby brother and shot another one, and we're makin' things right. He probly hates niggers too." Tom and Joe worked their way to Sean. When Fred and Bill saw them moving in, they went too. When they got to Sean, Tom spoke first. "I'm Tom Blanton and all these boys'r my brothers," Tom said. "That nigger kilt our baby brother and shot Fred here, and we aim to make things right."

"I'll see about that," said Sean. "You and your brothers stay put while I talk to that fella. One false move and that woman in the stage'll put a bullet in your head. She's a dead shot with that Henry." The brothers looked over at the stage and saw Maggie with the Henry. Tom shook his head and mumbled to himself.

Sean walked over to Jesse. He was still down between the dead horses. "Them boys there say you killed their brother and shot another one. Is that true?" asked Sean.

"Yes, it is," answered Jesse. "Two a them boys tried to rape my wife. She's in the wagon beat up pretty bad. I split one of'ems head with an axe and shot another one. That one there that I shot got away and brought them others down on us."

Sean looked in the wagon and saw Dawn. She was beat up pretty good as Jesse had said. Then he walked over to Tom. When he did, he gave Maggie a look. She knew that he meant for her to be ready with the Henry. "Your brothers tried to rape that man's wife," said Sean. "Seems ta me your brother got what he deserved."

"I don't see it that way," said Tom. "We got no law in this part a the country that says it's agin the law to rape a squaw. Besides, she's with that damn nigger."

Sean pulled a pistol and had it pointed at Tom's face. "You and your brothers will drop them Sharps and unbuckle them pistol belts. Anybody make a wrong move and your momma won't be able to recognize your face."

"Yer a lawman," said Tom. "You wouldn't just shoot me like that. Don't be droppin' them rifles boys. He won't shoot." As soon as the last words came out of Tom's mouth, Sean's pistol fired and Tom's head exploded. When Fred saw what had happened, he tried to bring up his rifle to fire at Sean. Maggie put a bullet in his head. The other two brothers were shaking now but they dropped their rifles and pistol belts. Jesse came out from between the dead horses now.

"What's your name?" Sean asked Jesse.

"I'm Jesse Strong and that's my wife Dawn in the wagon," answered Jesse.

"Well Jesse, what do you want me to do with these two?" asked Sean. "I can hang'em for you if you want, or would you like to kill them yourself?"

"I'd like to kill'em myself," answered Jesse. "Nobody gonna mess with my woman or me and live ta tell about it. I'll get my pistol."

"How's this gonna be a fair fight with you here and that woman settin' there with that rifle pointed at us?" asked Bill.

"We won't interfere," said Sean. "You got our word."

Jesse came back with his pistol belt on. It was tied down. "Give'em back their pistols Marshal," said Jesse. "I'll take'em both at once." Jesse had the blood away from his eyes now.

"Are you sure you want'em both?" asked Sean.

"I can handle'em," said Jesse. "I was in the cavalry, and I'm pretty darn good with this pistol when I hafta be."

"All right then," Sean said as he gave the two brothers their pistol belts. "I'll step aside now."

Bill and Joe stood side by side, and Jesse was about twenty five yards from them. "You are one dead nigger," said Joe.

"Don't be tryin' ta talk me ta death," said Jesse. As soon as Jesse finished talking, Bill made a move for his pistol. Before he had his pistol pulled, Jesse had his pistol out, and Bill was thrown backwards with a hole in his chest. Before Bill hit the ground, a bullet struck Joe in the chest. Both men were dead when they hit the ground. Joe had not even touched his pistol when he was hit.

"I guess you do know how to use that pistol," said Sean. "Now we better get that wife a yours into town. We got us a good doctor there. Let's get her onto the stage. I'll send someone back to fetch your wagon and them fellas' horses. I'll put their guns in the back. We'll sell'em in town and you can have the money. Same with their horses. I'll check and see if them guys are on any posters or not. I just bet they're wanted for somethin' somewhere."

They got Dawn on the stage and were soon moving. Sean told the driver to take it easy. "Are you gonna send somebody back ta bury them fellas?" the driver asked Sean.

"Do you think they deserve buryin'?" Sean answered back. The driver shook his head no and muttered something to himself.

After they had been moving for a while, Sean asked Jesse about himself. "So Jesse Strong, where you from and how did you end up out here?" asked Sean.

"I'm from Kentucky," started Jesse. "I was a blacksmith at a big horse farm. I weren't no slave. My grandpappy was born a slave but was given his freedom when he was eighteen. He was a horse trainer on the farm, and my Pa was a horse trainer, and I was a blacksmith. I lived and worked on the farm. Mr. Cooper treated us good and paid us well. He did have some slaves though, but he didn't mistreat them. My wife Dawn lived there too and worked in the kitchen. Her momma had worked there before her. When the war started, the rebs came and took all our horses and hung Mr. Cooper. Four a them rebs thought they were gonna hang me, and I killed'em. I got away, and Dawn was hidin' in a closet in the house. They burned the place down but didn't stay around to watch, and she was able to get out without bein' burned. She had a friend up in Ohio, and we went up there. She helped us, and I got a job with a man who got horses ready for the army. Made some good money. When they started up the 54th Massachusetts, I joined up."

"So you were in the 54th," said Sean. "A good friend a mine from back in Tennessee was in the 54th. His name was Jim O'Rourke."

"Are you serious?" asked Jesse. "Me and Jim was best friends. We were both platoon sergeants in the same company. We both got shot up at Fort Wagner and helped each other keep from gettin' captured. We both joined the cavalry at the same time. I sure would like to see Jim again. Haven't seen him since we mustered out."

"Jim's dead," said Sean. "He came out west and was gonna go back in the army cause he said they was gonna form up a couple of colored cavalry regiments. He was a deputy of mine. He got killed by one of the Hawks. Jim was a good man. I miss him. We grew up together back in Tennessee. His family lived and worked on our farm."

"I sure do wish I coulda seen him," said Jesse.

"Well tell me why you're out here now," said Sean.

"I quit my job when the boss died, and his boy took over," said Jesse. "That boy was an idiot. Anyway, Dawn decided she wanted to go down to the Nations and see her relatives again. They're Osage."

"What's was your wife's last name?" asked Sean.

"Littletree," answered Jesse. "Her Pa and her uncle John are down there."

"John Littletree is a good friend of mine," said Sean. "Him and his village helped us in a big gun battle with the Anderson bunch. We got us some good people in common. Tell you what, if you ever need a job, I can always use another deputy. Things been quiet for a spell, but you never know. Maybe you can work for me while your wife heals up."

"I'll think on that," said Jesse. "I guess I wouldn't be the first colored deputy would I? I'll talk to Dawn about it when she starts healin' up some."

CHAPTER ELEVEN

When the stage pulled into Abilene, they took Dawn right to Doc Rawlins office. He was there lancing a boil on a man's butt. "Be right there soon as I put somethin' on this man's backside," Doc said. He finished with his boil patient and had them take Dawn to his examination table. "Whoever set this arm did a good job," Doc said. "Couldn't have done better myself. She's got five broken ribs but I'm pretty sure there's no danger to her lungs. Her jaw is slightly fractured but it should heal well. There a small piece of bone caught between two of her teeth. I have no idea where that came from."

"She bit off a man's little finger," said Jesse. "Must be some a his bone."

"She must be one tough woman," said Doc. "Most women couldn't handle a beating like this. She's gonna need a good bed to rest and sleep in. I don't wanna see her even out of a bed for a week. I'll give you something for her to take if the pain gets too strong. Now if you have a place to take her, you may leave now. Just let me know where it is, and I'll pay her a visit tomorrow."

"I'll have a place for them," said Maggie. "Now if you fine gentleman will help her, we'll get her straight to bed." The whole crew was at the saloon when they arrived there. They were all eager to hear about Maggie and Sean's honeymoon. Jeb was glad to see Maggie and Sean too.

Jon spoke first. "You'll be able to put them in the room out back," he said. "I've been staying with Martha lately. I cleaned the place just the other day."

Sean then spoke. "Everybody, this is Jesse Strong and his wife Dawn," Sean began. "Jesse was a friend of Jim O'Rourke, and now he's my friend." Jesse gave Sean a nod of appreciation as he and Maggie helped Dawn to the back room. "His wife is Dawn Littletree. John Littletree is her uncle," Sean added. "They will be staying here for a while so Dawn can heal. She's had a bad experience. Now could someone get me a nice glass of bourbon. I feel a little thirsty right now."

Michael went to the bar and then came back with some bourbon and several glasses. Sean sat at the regular table and was joined by Michael, Jon, and Betty. Maggie joined them after she got Dawn and Jesse settled in their room. "So how were things in our absence?" Sean asked Michael.

"Been pretty quiet," said Michael. "Business has been good with all the new businesses getting started. We almost had a couple of fights, but I escorted the gents outside and told them to fight out there. Another saloon opened up but our business hasn't dropped any. The railroad and the cattle pens should be ready by spring. So how was your trip?"

"How about we tell you tomorrow," said Sean. "It's been a long day. I wanna get somethin' ta eat and then soak in that tub for a few hours with this wife a mine."

"That sounds really good," added Maggie. "I really missed that big tub while we were gone."

~~~~

After a good meal, Sean went straight to the bath house and made sure there was plenty of water and started heating some up. Three hours later they finally made their way upstairs to their room. As they were lying in bed holding each other, Maggie looked into Sean's eyes. "We had us some honeymoon, didn't we darlin'," she said. "Most couples don't get to have a honeymoon like ours."

"No they don't," said Sean. "And you can't really say that all this happened cause I'm a lawman."

"That's right," replied Maggie. "We were just at those places at the time those things happened. Now give me a good kiss and let's get some sleep." An hour later, they finally went to sleep.

Maggie and Sean didn't come downstairs till almost 9am. Everyone was setting at their usual table drinking coffee. "We thought maybe you was dead," said Jon. "I never seen you sleep this late before. Not even when you was healin' up from bein' shot."

"Who said we were sleepin'," said Sean as he pulled out a chair for Maggie. "Now what's a fella gotta do to get some coffee and somethin' to eat around here?"

"I'll get you some coffee Sean darlin'," said Michael. "I'll get you some too Maggie. Now what should I tell Cookie you want for breakfast?"

"I'll have some ham and eggs," said Maggie.

"Sounds good," said Sean. "I'll have that too." Now I s'pose you all wanna hear about our honeymoon."

"That's why we're here," said Betty. "Curiosity is killing us."

"Well Maggie, you go ahead and get started," said Sean.

"We had plenty of excitement," Maggie began. "Some people tried to hold up our stage on the way to Kansas City. We had to kill them. One of them was a woman. She was on the stage with us and was hit by a bullet from her own gang. There was a man on the stage with her, and then there were four more ahead of us. Anyway, they're dead. There was no money on the stage but there was a bunch of blank bank drafts in the mail."

"You forgot to tell them that woman had a gun on you and when the stage hit a bump, you grabbed her gun and then punched her out," said Sean.

"And you shot the man with her as he was going for a pistol," added Maggie. "The four up ahead wanted the stage to stop, but the driver didn't, and we shot it out. They're dead. We're not."

"You're a good story teller," said Michael. "Please go on."

"When we got to St. Louis, we took a week long cruise on a very nice river boat," said Maggie. "We stayed in a honeymoon suite and had room service if we wanted it. One day in the gaming room, a young man made an insult to my honor, and he took a swim. The Captain of the boat was a good friend of General Sherman and had heard of Sean. He was a gunboat Captain during the war. Anyway, we had a wonderful time on the boat."

"So what did you do next?" asked Betty.

"We got a nice hotel downtown close to "The Palace," started Maggie. "We paid Judge Simmons a visit and shopped and we had a good visit with Sam Draper. I just love his place."

"Was there any trouble there?" Michael asked Sean.

"As a matter of fact, there was," answered Sean. "Some people who were trying to get Sam to sell his place got rough one day. Sam killed one of'em, and I killed the other. When the Town

Marshal arrived, his young deputy got stupid about me havin' to shoot that man in the back. The Marshal had to kill him."

"So you had to shoot him in the back," said Jon.

"Yes I did," answered Sean. "I was behind him and he didn't know I was there. He was about to shoot Sam in the back and I had no choice. The rest of the stay in St. Louis was good. Maggie you tell them about the stage ride from Kansas City to here."

"When we were on our last leg of the trip, we heard a lot of shooting," Maggie began. "We went slowly to the shooting. Four men were shooting at Jesse. The two horses that were hitched to his wagon were dead and he was down between them for cover. Dawn was inside the wagon. Sean got out and told them he was a Federal Marshal and told them to come in so he could find out what was going on. They wanted Jesse dead because he had killed their brother, but they didn't tell us that it was because he had tried to rape Dawn. Anyway, Sean had to kill one of'em, and I killed one. Jesse killed the other two in a gunfight. Sean let them have a shoot out. Sean had offered to hang them, but Jesse wanted to kill them himself. He took on two of them, and they're dead and here we are."

"You're honeymoon was a little more exciting than ours," said Michael.

"I offered Jesse a job as a deputy too," said Sean. "He'll talk it over with Dawn when she gets better. Now I need Jon and someone to go out and bring in Jesse's wagon and round up those horses we left out there. There was three left after all the shootin'. Should be able to use them to haul the wagon. I saw an undertaker sign up as we came into town yesterday. Send him out to get those bodies. I guess I'll let him get them buried. I can use the buryin' fund. Maybe they got some money on'em. "

"I'll take Dog and get young Billy from the livery to go with me," said Jon. "Dog'll find them horses."

"Michael, have we got any new posters since I was gone," said Sean. "I just bet them fellas was wanted for somethin' somewhere."

"There's a few over at the jail," answered Michael. "I looked at'em, but I didn't see any with descriptions of anyone I've heard of. There was one that had five brothers on it. I think they was the Chaneys. They robbed a general store in Missouri and killed the owner and his wife. They're worth $200 a piece."

"There was five of'em out there till Jesse killed one of'em," said Sean. "I'll be lookin' at that poster. I just bet that's them. Did it have their names on it?"

"Yes it did," answered Michael. "I remember seeing the name Tom. Can't remember any other ones."

"How about gettin' that poster for me?" Sean asked Michael. "I'll be talkin' to Jesse when you get back." Michael returned in just a few minutes. There were no drawings on the poster, but the description of the brothers fit the five dead brothers very well. "I'm pretty sure that those five men were the Chaney brothers," said Sean. "I'll be tellin' Jesse. He can have all the reward money."

"If he gets all that money, he won't want to be a deputy," said Michael. "He won't need to do any kind of work for a good while."

"That may be but I just bet that he's not that kind of man," replied Sean. "He knows right from wrong. I figure he's the kind of man that would want to help make this country a better place for honest folks no matter what color they are."

Sean went to the back room. Jesse was there looking after Dawn. "That Doc said she looks good," said Jesse as Sean entered the room. "He'll be back in three, four days and check on her again. We wanna thank you for all this."

"No need to thank us," said Sean. "You're my friend now and friends look after friends. Now I got some good news for you. Them five brothers were wanted by the law. You got $1000 bounty money comin'. I'll be sendin' a telegram and make sure you get the money."

"But I only killed three of'em," said Jesse. "You and Maggie killed the other two. Part a that money is yours."

"Maggie and me got plenty a money. We don't need it," said Sean. "Besides, you woulda killed'em if we weren't there anyway. It woulda taken you a little while, but you woulda got'em killed. I have no doubts."

"Glad you got some confidence in me," said Jesse. "I do believe I woulda kill'em sooner or later. They weren't too smart. They woulda slipped up sooner or later."

"So, Jesse Strong, would you be my deputy?" asked Sean. "I need good men and you are sure as hell a good man."

"I'll give it a try for a while and see how it goes," answered Jesse. "It'll be an honor to work with you." Then Jesse extended his hand to Sean and they shook.

"Consider yourself sworn in," said Sean. "I'll be back later today and I'll have a newer pistol for you. It'll be a conversion. No more cap and ball for you." Sean tipped his hat to Dawn and left.

As soon as he was out the door, Dawn spoke. "Are you sure you wanna be a lawman?" she asked Jesse. "Lotsa folks hate colored folks. They might really hate a colored lawman."

"They best be lookin' at my badge and not the color a my skin," said Jesse. "Just like them reb soldiers. They finally learned that a colored soldier could kill them just as dead as a white soldier. It'll be all right darlin'. I won't let nothin' bad happen. You seen how the Marshal was when them brothers wanted me dead. He don't mess around. He shot that man without hesitatin'. Maggie shot that other one in the head. If the other deputies are like the Marshal, I'll be in good company."

"I'll still worry about you," said Dawn. "Now can I get something to eat? I'm kinda hungry."

"I'll get you somethin' right now," said Jesse. When Jesse went to the kitchen to get the food, Sean was there talking to Cookie. Sean looked at Jesse.

"What did Dawn say after I left?" asked Sean. "I bet she said she was gonna worry about you."

"Yep, that 's just what she said," answered Jesse.

"That's to be expected," replied Sean. "Maggie worries about me all the time. I worry about her too. That's just the way it is. Just don't let the worry run things. Now get Dawn some food. This fine man here with the apron on is Cookie. That gorgeous woman there is his wife Barbara. Cookie and Barbara, this is Jesse Strong." They all shook hands. "His wife is Dawn," added Sean.

"I'm pleased to meet you folks," said Jesse.

"We're pleased to meet you too," said Cookie. "Any friend a Jim and Sean is a friend a ours. Hope you like our cookin'."

"Looks mighty good," said Jesse. "Eatin' like this will get Dawn healed up good real quick. Now if you'll excuse me."

~~~~

After Jesse left the kitchen, Sean stayed in the kitchen for a while and talked with Cookie and Barbara. "So how have you two been doin' now that business is pickin' up?" asked Sean. "We're not over workin' you, are we?"

"No, we're doin' fine," answered Cookie. "Barbara and me are a great team. We can keep up no problem. The way things have been, we can pretty much figure out how much of somethin' we need. The same people been comin' regular like. If we do get busier than we have been, we'll need to make sure we get more wood in. I reckon we'll see how it is when them Texas boys get here. I had an idea about that too if you don't mind me speakin' up."

"You know you can tell me anything Cookie," said Sean. "If you got an idea that's got to do when them Texas boys get here, I'm ready to listen."

"Well them boys will have money burnin' holes in their pockets and sooner or later they'll wanna do a lotta drinkin'," said Cookie. "They all carry guns. I think we should make them check their guns at the bar when they first come in. They can have'm back when they leave. Maybe they won't like that, but we can see how they react. Maybe we could try havin' people check their guns now and see what happens. Most folks here don't carry guns, but some do."

"Well there's no law against carryin' guns that I know of," said Sean. "But this is our place and we outta be able ta make our own laws inside this place. I think we'll give it a try. I'll talk with Maggie and Michael and see what they think. Enough a that. So are you two still plannin' on a honeymoon in the fall?"

"Yes we are," answered Barbara. "I still want to go where the tree leaves change color. I think that would be so beautiful."

"It surely is," replied Sean. "When you see the color of them maple leaves it can be breath takin' sometimes. So what are you two plannin' for dinner tonight?"

"Barbara's gonna whip up some Mexican stuff that I can't even pronounce," said Cookie. "I know it'll be good."

"I can't wait," said Sean. "I'm getting' hungry just thinkin' about it and I don't even know what it might be. I'll see you two later." Sean went out to the saloon and got Maggie and Michael and went to their regular table.

"What is it darlin'?" asked Maggie. "You got something on your mind?"

"I was just talkin' to Cookie, and he had an idea about what we should do when the Texas boys get here," said Sean. "It's a good idea, and I think we should try it before then, like maybe tomorrow."

"I bet I know what it is already," said Maggie. "We should have customers check their guns at the bar when they first get here. They can get them back when they leave."

"That's right," said Sean. "What do you think Michael?"

"I'm all for not gettin' shot," answered Michael. "When them boys get up here, sooner or later there will be some trouble. It would be better if it was not in here. I think we should try it. If some men wanna shoot each other we can make'em go outside and shoot each other."

"Let's start tomorrow," said Sean. "Someone can make us a big sign. We'll put it just inside the door so it can't be missed. Anybody don't want to oblige us will be asked to move on. Now I understand that some folks can't read. We'll hafta help'em out. Now who can make us a good sign?"

"Betty can do it," said Michael. "She can do fancy writin' and such. I'll have her get started now." Jon walked into the saloon just as Michael finished talking.

"I went through them fellas pockets out there and they had three hunnerd dollars between'em," Jon began. "We found the horses they was ridin' but we also found out that they had three

wagons too. We hitched up ta Jesse's wagon and one a theirs and
brought'em in with all the horses. Still two wagons out there. I'll
get them horses and wagons over to the livery and we can get
them other two wagons tomorrow."

"That money was probly from that general store they
robbed," said Sean. "We'll get them horses and wagons and their
guns sold and find out if that store owner had any kin. Then we
can send them the money. I gotta send a telegram to that place
anyway and let'em know that the Chaney's are dead and to send
the reward money here. I'll go do that now."

Sean went to the telegraph office and sent his message. He
told the operator to find him when an answer came back. After he
left there, he decided to have a look around town and check out
some of the new businesses. The first place he stopped at was the
newspaper office. There was a young man inside and a woman
with him. Sean went in and introduced himself. "I'm Sean
O'Rourke. So you're gonna be a newspaper man," said Sean.
"When do ya figure to be up and runnin'?"

"I'm Phil Downs and this is my wife Teresa," the man said.
"We hope to have our first issue out in a few days."

"Glad ta meet you," said Sean. "What'r you gonna write
about?"

"Anything and everything," said Phil. "We'll write about how
this town is growing and about the people in it. We'll put in
national news and such when we get it on the wire. We might
write about you Marshal. You're a well known man."

"I'd appreciate it if you didn't write too much about me," said
Sean. "I got too many people that don't like me already. Write
about that McCoy fella. He's the one that got the railroad to come
here. He's gonna be a rich man when them Texas herds start

comin' here next spring. So what will you charge folks for a paper?"

"Probably a nickel," said Phil.

"How are you gonna make enough money to stay in business if you only get a nickel a paper?" asked Sean.

"We will make money when people advertise in our paper," answered Phil. "That's where a newspaper makes money. It's not on the paper sales."

"Tell me how this advertisin' stuff works," said Sean.

"Well they tell me that you are a part owner of "Maggie's Place," started Phil. "Well say that you're going to have something going on special at a certain time and you want a lot of people to know. You tell us what you want the people to see, and we put it in the paper. We charge you for it, but the result is that you get more customers for whatever was special that you had us put in the paper. The paper makes money and you make money. You spend a little to get more back."

"I think I understand," said Sean. "If this town really grows and a lot of businesses advertise in your paper, everybody will make money."

"That's what it's all about," said Phil. "It'll take time, but I'm a patient man."

"Well good luck to you," said Sean. "I'll be lookin' forward to your first issue. Good evenin' to you."

The next place Sean went was the new saloon that had recently opened in town. It wasn't as nice as Maggie's Place, but it was all right. The bartender was surprised to see Sean in there. "Didn't expect to see you in here Mr. O'Rourke," he said. "Name's Frank Bowden. I'm runnin' this place for Bill Thompson. I reckon you know him."

"Yep I know Bill," said Sean. "He said he was gonna build some places down here, and he sure did. Which a them hotels is his?"

"Both of'em," answered Frank. "Now can I get you a drink. It's on the house. Bill said if you ever came in here you was to drink for free."

"I appreciate that," said Sean. "I'll have a free one today, but after today I'll pay just like any other customer. Got any good bourbon?"

"Sure do," answered Frank. "I hear that you like an Irish Whiskey once in a while too. I'm gonna try to keep a bottle or two here at all times. Bill has a fondness for it too."

Sean thanked Frank for the drink and stood at the bar looking around. There was a a couple of card games going on, and Sean saw three woman in the place. They were attractive. "This place'll do all right," Sean said to himself. "He'll need more girls come spring." Sean finished his drink and nodded a goodbye to Frank. Then Sean went to the leather goods store to see Jason. "How's our Justice of the Peace doin' lately?" Sean asked Jason.

"Been pretty busy workin' the leather," replied Jason. "Haven't done much Justice of the Peace'n. How've you been? I hear you had an exciting honeymoon."

"Yep we did," said Sean. "I sure hope things don't get excitin' here. Looks like your boy there has growed six inches since I saw him last."

"He's havin' what they call one a them growin' spurts," said Jason. "He out grows his clothes before he wears them out. His mother is good with a needle though. She lets things out till there's no more to let out."

"That's good. That means he's healthy," said Sean. "Pretty soon he'll be chasin' after any good lookin' young girl comes along."

"He's already got his eyes on one," said Jason.

"Is that so Greg? You been thinkin' bout girls already?" said Sean.

"I think it's about time," said Greg. "I'm already thirteen."

"Well make sure you treat girls nice and with respect," said Sean. "Make sure that you understand that they are not just here for a man's pleasure. You be good to a woman and I guarantee she'll be good to you. What am I doin'? I reckon your Pa has told you all this stuff."

"He has,' said Greg. "Ma has too."

"I reckon you'll turn out all right son," said Sean. "I'll be seein' you two later. Good seein' you again." Sean left and headed to another new business.

"That man is a good man isn't he Pa?" said Greg.

"Yes he is," said Jason. "He's a darn good man."

~~~~

Sean was just down the street from the leather goods store when the telegraph operator found him. It was about the Chaney brothers. The telegraph said that it was the store owner's family who had put up the reward for the Chaney's and to get with them, and they would settle up. Sean had the operator get out his pencil and start writing. "Tell them folks that the Chaneys had $300 on them and we will sell their horses, wagons, and guns," Sean started. "Anything over $1000 we will send back to them. If it's less, don't worry about it." The operator went back to his office and Sean decided to go back to Maggie's Place. He was feeling a little amorous, and he and Maggie were not seen for the rest of the day.

The next morning, Betty showed up with the new sign she had made. It was made of several boards that were tacked together. It was about three foot by four foot and painted white with black letters. The lettering was very fancy but very readable. It went as follows:

All firearms of any kind
will be checked at the bar.
No exceptions.
Any knife with a blade longer
Than four inches will also
Be checked at the bar

Any weapons will be returned
When leaving

Failure to comply will result
In permanent expulsion
From this establishment
or worse

The Management

"Damn, that's a mouthful," said Sean when he and Maggie came downstairs and saw the sign. "I didn't even think about knives but it's a good idea to include them. Well, what do you think Maggie? Are we ready to do this?"

"Yes we are. Let's put the sign right in front by the door so it can't be missed," said Maggie. "Betty, you did a great job with the sign. Thank you. The only problem I can think of now is that we will have some customers that can't read."

"Someone'll make sure they know what it says," said Michael. "I reckon we'll see how it goes in a few hours."

~~~~

Around noon, a lot of the workers who were helping build some of the new businesses came to the saloon for a meal. None of them carried any weapons and also thought that checking the weapons was a good idea. That evening, things were a little different. A few drifters came to the saloon and decided that they were not going to check their guns. Maggie convinced them that it would be better if they did. She had one of the shotguns from behind the bar pointed at them, and Jeb was right beside her. They apologized for their rudeness and checked their guns. When the drifters were done for the evening, Maggie handed them back their guns while Tom kept his hands on one of the shotguns. Jeb escorted them to the door. They left town without incident.

Five days later, two very hard looking men came into the saloon. No one had ever seen them in town before. As soon as they had read the sign, one of them announced, "I'll give my gun to anyone who's man enough to take it from me." Then the two men sat down at a table near the piano and yelled for someone to bring them a bottle and two glasses. Sean was setting at his regular table at the time. He checked the two pistols he was wearing to make sure they were fully loaded and walked to the two men's table. "You two will be leavin' now," Sean said to them. "You can leave on your own, or we can have you carried out. We got a new undertaker in town and he could use the business." Jeb came over to Sean's right side and sat down and started a low growl.

"Hey Chuck, this must be that famous gunman we heard so much about," the man who had made the announcement said. "I think we better just kill him now so he won't be so famous. So gunman, are you gonna give us a chance ta stand up or are you gonna make us draw settin' down?"

"You can go ahead and stand up," said Sean. "But if I see either a you makin' a wrong move before you get standin', this dog'll be on one a your throats so fast, you won't have time ta even think about tellin' your momma goodbye. The other one a you will have a bullet in his head."

"You sure can talk mister," Chuck said. "It'll be an honor for us to shut you up." Then the two of them slid their chairs back from their table and started to stand. As soon as they started to stand, both of them went for their pistols.

"Jeb," Sean said as he was pulling his pistol. As the bullet from Sean's pistol was striking Chuck's forehead, Jeb had the other man by the throat. It was over quickly. Neither man had even touched their pistol.

"Just who in the hell were those two?" cried Maggie. "I bet they were someone who came here for something besides a drink."

"I got no idea," said Sean. "I'll go through their pockets and see if I can find anything." Sean went through their pockets. Each man had close to a thousand dollars in big bills on him. Chuck had a wrinkled up piece of paper with a note on it. The note said, "Rest of money will be paid when job done. Contact me in St. Louis." There was no name or anything after that.

"Looks like someone's hired these two ta kill me," said Sean. "Someone in St. Louis wrote the note."

"Could be Anderson's boss," said Michael. "Remember that Anderson put up some money and that one fella told us Anderson's boss put up some more. Looks more and more like that son of a bitch did have a boss."

"Yes it does," added Maggie. "Sean darlin', why did you let Jeb kill that man when you could have done it yourself?"

"I saw the look in Jeb's eyes when he was beside me," said Sean. "I could tell that he wanted to make sure nothing happened to me, so I let him have one of'em. He sure is some dog isn't he darlin'?"

"He sure is," said Maggie. "Between you and Jeb, a woman couldn't ask for better looking after."

"Well we better get this place cleaned up," said Sean. "I'll take this money to the bank for the buryin' fund and see if the general store'll buy their guns. Michael, you get the undertaker and then find out if those two had any horses. If they did, get'em to the livery. Ask anyone you see if they'll take a look at these two. Maybe someone might know'em or know of'em."

When the undertaker got there, he took one look at the two dead men and said, "I know these two. I seen'em some time back at a saloon in Kansas City. They're the Whatley's. One of'em is Chuck and the other one is called Razor. They're hired killers. A fella I was with at the saloon told me that these two would kill anyone for a price."

"Why was that one fella called Razor?" asked Sean.

"They said he slit a couple men's throats with a straight razor," said the undertaker. "I heard that he had already shot'em but they weren't dead so he slit their throats."

"Sounds like a nice fella," said Sean. "Razor won't be slittin' any more throats. I wonder who hired him."

"I'd say it was someone with a lot a money," said the undertaker. "I heard these two didn't come cheap. Now my assistant and I will get these bodies out of here for you. Who's paying for this?"

"They are," answered Sean. "Charge whatever you think is fair." The undertaker shrugged his shoulders and then he and his assistant removed the bodies.

~~~~

That night after Maggie and Sean had made love, Sean could tell that Maggie was worried. "What is it darlin'?" Sean asked her. "Are you worried about men comin' after me for bounty money again?"

"Yes I am darlin'," Maggie answered. "Things have been quiet here for a little while, and now it's happening again."

"I understand Maggie," said Sean. "I worry too, but not for me. I worry for you and all my friends. Sooner or later, whoever's responsible for this will slip up, and I'll get'em, and he will pay up."

The next two weeks were very peaceful in town. The newspaper finally came out with its first issue. It was mostly about all the new businesses in town and what progress the railroad was making. A few of the places even advertised. Sean was impressed. Doc Rawlins had seen Dawn several times and said she was healing better than expected. She could now do just about whatever she wanted, but slowly and easily. Jesse was starting to think that being a deputy wasn't such a bad job because nothing had happened that needed the law's attention. That changed the third week. A telegram came from Judge Simmons. It went as follows:

Mashal O'Rourke
Abilene Kansas

Border gang terrorizing new settlers near Missouri Kansas border due east of Abilene << stop>> Name of gang unknown<< stop >> Take deputies and clean things up

Judge Simmons St. Louis

Sean had dinner with Michael, Jon, and Jesse that evening and told Jon and Jesse to be ready to move out in the morning. "Michael, I want you to stay here. I know that you will be able to handle anything that comes up. Jeb will stay here with Maggie, and Dog'll be with us," said Sean. "Maggie'll make sure Dawn is doin' good, and with Michael, Maggie and Betty, the place'll be in good hands. Jesse, you can pick out one a them horses we got from the Chaneys. We'll take a couple pack horses and some spare horses too. "

"Are you sure you don't need me with you?" asked Michael. "Maggie has proved more than once that she can handle things. And ole Jeb won't let nothin' happen to her."

"That's true my friend," said Sean. "But I will feel better havin' you here."

"I understand," replied Michael. "I'll make sure nothin' goes wrong."

~~~~

That night, Sean and Maggie had a nice long talk. "Now I want you to have Jeb with at all times," said Sean. "I mean all times. Don't let him outta your sight even for a minute."

"Maybe he'd like to take a bath with me," said Maggie.

"If that makes you both happy, that'll be all right with me," said Sean. "I want you to be careful now that we have everyone checking their guns and such. You just never know when someone might try somethin'. Have Betty keep a pistol on her too. Maybe Tom should have one at all times too. Tell Cookie and Barbara to keep one close in the kitchen."

"Darlin', you worry more than I do," said Maggie. "Sounds like you love me."

"Yes Maggie, I do love you," said Sean. "Sometimes I love you so much it hurts."

"You better make sure you get back to me then," said Maggie. "Cause we'll be having a new family member for you to love in about seven and a half months."

"What are you sayin' darlin'? asked Sean. "Are we havin' a baby?"

"Yes we are darlin'," answered Maggie.

"Are you sure. I mean it's early yet," said Sean. "How can you tell after only a month and a half?"

"Because, my love," said Maggie. "I have never ever been late for my time, not ever. I am one and a half months late now."

"That's wonderful," said Sean. "With your looks, we should have the most beautiful baby ever. C'mere darlin' and let me hold you some more."

"We can do more than hold," said Maggie. A good while later they fell asleep in each other's arms.

Early the next morning when Sean got up to leave, Maggie gave him a stern look. "Now don't be telling the men or anyone that we are expecting. I don't want anyone treating me any different. Sometimes people get funny when they know someone is with child."

"I won't say a word till you say it's all right or you're startin' to show," said Sean. "Now you just stay in bed as long as you want. I'll get myself somethin' ta eat and me and the boys'll be on our way." Then Sean gave her a good long goodbye kiss. "Jeb, you look out for Maggie while I'm gone," Sean said as he was leaving their room.

CHAPTER TWELVE

Sean made sure that Jon and Jesse were well supplied and then they hit the trail. They headed northeast. They would head that way till they came to the border. Then they would head south and go down almost to the "Nations". The first two days out they never saw a living soul. The third day they ran into a family of Quakers who said they were heading west to get some of that free land. Sean talked to them for a good while. "One thing you wanna keep in your mind when you go west for free land," said Sean. "Somebody out there already thinks that land is theirs."

"You mean the Indains?" the father of the family asked.

"Yep, that's what I mean," said Sean. "Most of'em don't take too kindly to folks settin' up on land they say has belonged to their people since the beginning of time."

"We're God lovin' folks, and we wouldn't harm anyone or take anything from anyone," the father said.

"Well they won't look at it that way," said Sean. "They are not farmers. They roam all that land following the game and such. People tillin' the soil would not be liked. They don't believe in the same God that you do anyway."

"God'll look after us," the man said. "Now we'll be on our way." Sean happened to notice a newspaper on the seat between the man and his wife. Something on the front page caught his attention.

"Can I trouble you for a minute and have a look at that newspaper?" asked Sean. "Where did you get it out here anyway?"

"I got it from a fella who was on a freight wagon and he got it from someone else," said the man. "I been readin' it a little bit at a time. Seems some Federal Judge was murdered up in St. Louis."

Sean took the paper from the man and read the headline. It went as follows:

Federal Court Judge and Wife Murdered

Federal Judge David Simmons and his wife were shot down by four unknown assailants last Sunday as they were walking home from Church. Judge Simmons was struck by not less than ten bullets. His wife Sandy was struck eight times. No suspects have been apprehended.

The story went on but Sean did not read any farther. He realized something. The Judge was murdered last Sunday. That was four days ago. That telegram he received came yesterday. Judge Simmons couldn't have sent that telegram. Sean gave the newspaper back to the man and then told the men. "Boys, the Judge has been murdered," Sean said. "He was killed before that telegram was sent. Someone else sent that telegram to get us away from Abilene. We gotta get back in a hurry. We got these extra horses. We're three days away. I intend to get there in a day and a half."

~~~~

They rode hard and kept changing horses and made it back to Abilene in a day and half. They came into town at a full gallop and rode straight to the saloon. Sean ran inside to see Maggie, Betty, and Michael were setting at their regular table having a meal. "What is it? What's going on? Why are you back already?" Maggie asked Sean when he went to their table.

"We found out Judge Simmons was murdered last Sunday," answered Sean. "He couldn't have sent that telegram to me. Someone sent it to get me outta town. We hurried back thinkin' the worst."

"Well it's been quiet here," said Michael. "We never heard anything about the Judge being murdered. How did you find out?"

"We ran into some Quaker who had a newspaper," said Sean. "Speakin' a newspapers, why didn't word get here about the Judge. We got a telegraph. That newspaper fella shoulda got the news or someone shoulda let me know about the Judge."

"Yes, someone should have," said Maggie. "That is unless they didn't want you to know."

"I'll be payin' a visit to the telegraph and the newspaper," said Sean. "Be back shortly."

Sean questioned the operator and he swore that nothing came in on the wire about the Judge being murdered. Phil at the newspaper didn't know anything either. Sean went back to the saloon. "Well they don't know anything," said Sean. "I bet they got someone here watchin' everything. There's a lotta new faces in town. They didn't expect us back that soon. They probly wanted us to get a good ways off so we wouldn't have a chance to get back quick in case someone rode after us for help."

"What are you thinking Sean?" Maggie asked.

"I think someone had that telegram sent to pull me away from here so they could get to you," answered Sean. "Tryin' to use you ta get ta me."

"Well we'll just have to make sure that doesn't happen," said Maggie. "Darlin', did it ever occur to you that maybe they drew you out of town so they could ambush you somewhere out there? There's a lot of places all over that anyone with the know how could set up a good ambush. You aren't the only person who can shoot a Sharps rifle."

"That's true Maggie," said Sean. "There were plenty of sharp-shooters during the war, and I do worry about you too much. You've proved more than once that you can take care of yourself. I reckon we'll just sit tight for a while."

Just when Sean finished talking, the telegraph operator showed up with a telegram for Sean. "This just came in," said the operator. "Seems they already got a replacement for that Judge that was killed. Fella by the name a Clarence Lucas. More news will be comin' in shortly. I thought you'd wanna know about this."

"Thanks. I'll be wantin' to see more when it comes in," said Sean.

"I'll be getting' back now," said the operator.

"Maggie, seems mighty odd to me that the Judge was killed four days ago and we never got word and now he's been replaced already and we're gettin' the word pretty quick," said Sean. "Does that seem strange ta you?"

"Yes it does darlin'," answered Maggie. "Things like that are never done quickly. I wonder who this Clarence Lucas is and how he got the job so quickly. A Federal Judge has to be appointed by the President of the United States. Something seems wrong."

"Maybe when more comes in on the telegraph we'll know somethin'," said Sean. "Let's get somethin' ta eat now. I'm hungry."

~~~~

Maggie and Sean had just finished their meal when Phil Downs came in. "Marshal, I thought you'd like to see the headline for to-day's paper," said Phil. "This just came in on the wire." The head-line and the story went as follows:

Federal Judge Clarence Lucas Vows to bring Murderers to Justice

Federal Judge Clarence Lucas has vowed that he will not rest until the killers of Judge David Simmons and his wife are brought to justice. No expense will be spared and no stone will be left unturned.

The story went on and on, but there was nothing about who Judge Lucas was or where he came from and how he got himself appointed so quickly.

~~~~

"Thanks for bringing that to me Phil," said Sean. "If you get any word about this new Judge, I'd be obliged if you'd get it to me."

"Of course I will," said Phil. "Does this mean you have a new boss Marshal?"

"Yes it does," answered Sean. "I reckon I'll find out soon enough if I wanna work for this fella or not. He might want things done different than David did."

"I'll be getting back now Marshal," said Phil. "Good seeing you Mrs. O'Rourke."

"You might be right Sean darlin'," said Maggie. "This new Judge might not want you hanging anyone and maybe he'll want criminals brought in alive."

"Well it won't hurt him to want," said Sean. "I'd sure like to know more about him."

~~~~

That evening, Sean had all his deputies and their women at their regular table for dinner. Dawn was there too as she was healing fast. "Well boys, we got us a new boss," Sean began. "Don't know a damn thing about him. Seems mighty peculiar ta me that he got this job so quick. I reckon I'll be hearin' from him soon. I'll let you boys know what I know when I know it. Now I wanna thank you all for bein' my friends. Now let's eat." No one said another word. They just tore into their food.

~~~~

The next morning while Sean and Maggie were drinking coffee at their regular table, the telegraph operator brought Sean a telegram. It went as follows.

Federal Marshal O'Rourke
Abilene Kansas

O'Rourke<< stop>> you and your deputies will report to
my office with all due haste for an investigation into
your activities for the last six months<< stop>> I repeat
with all due haste

Clarence Lucas
Federal Judge
St. Louis

"Well what do you think a this," said Sean. "An investigation
into our activities. Investigation for what. We been killin' outlaws.
I'll be damned if I'll be goin' anywhere for any investigation."

"Calm down darlin'," said Maggie. "Maybe he needs to talk to
you face to face."

"If he wants my face, he can come here and see it," said Sean.
"Dave Simmons had records of everything that's happened since I
been Marshal so there's no need for any investigation. Besides, I
can tell right now that I don't wanna see his face. I won't be goin'
to St. Louis."

"That's fine with me," said Maggie. "I want you here with me
anyway. You better tell the men about this."

"I'll wait and tell the men after I send my response back to
this new Judge," said Sean. "Maybe I'll get a response back real
quick. I'll go get it sent right now." Sean went straight to the telegraph office and sent the following telegram.

Federal Judge Clarence Lucas
St. Louis

NO

O'Rourke

Sean was surprised when a response came back before he even got back to the saloon. It went as follows.

Federal Marshal O'Rourke
Abilene Kansas

What do you mean no<< stop >>You have been ordered to report to my office and you will do so<< stop>>I have been appointed by the President and you will do what I say

Clarence Lucas
Federal Judge
St. Louis

Sean looked at the telegraph operator. "Send that son of a bitch back the same message I sent earlier," said Sean.

"You mean you want me to send "NO" again?" asked the operator.

"That's just what I mean," answered Sean. "I'll be at the saloon waitin' for the response." Sean made his way back to the saloon. Michael, Jon, and Jesse were setting at the regular table drinking coffee. "Well boys, that new Judge has ordered us to go to St. Louis for an investigation into our activities for the last six months," started Sean. "I told'em "NO". Then he sent back another one ordering us to go, and I said "NO" again. Can't wait to see what he says now. I reckon we might not be lawman shortly."

"You reckon that Judge'll fire us?" asked Jon.

"I don't know about you, but I'd say he'll probly fire me," said Sean. "Somethin's not right about this whole situation. I got a bad feelin' about this man."

"I can get by without bein' a lawman," said Jon. "I been shot enough times."

"That goes for me too," added Michael.

"Well Jesse, you didn't get to do too much lawmannin'," said Sean. "I know you woulda been a good one too."

"That's all right Sean," said Jesse. "You gimme that reward money so I won't hafta find any job for a long time, maybe never. I still got money from when we was in Lebanon too. Me and Dawn'll be just fine. I'll still be there if it ever happens that you need me."

Jesse had just finished talking when the telegraph operator came in with another telegram for Sean. It went as follows:

O'Rourke
Kansas City

You and your deputies are terminated<< stop>> turn in your badges

Clarence Lucas
Federal Judge
St. Louis

"Well boys, we're fired," said Sean. "Have you got a piece a paper?" Sean asked the operator. "I got a message for you ta send back." The operator gave Sean some paper and a pencil and Sean wrote the following.

Clarence Lucas
Federal Judge
St. Louis

If you want my badge come and get it you son of a bitch

O'Rourke

"Do you really want me to send this?" the operator asked Sean.

"I wouldn't a wrote it if I didn't want it sent," said Sean. "Now get it done."

Maggie came over to the table. "Well darlin', how are you and the Judge getting along?" she asked.

"Me and the boys got fired," answered Sean. "I told'em we wasn't goin' to St. Louis and he fired us. He said to turn in our badges. I told'em if he wanted 'em he could come and get'em."

"Is that all you said?" asked Maggie.

"No darlin'. I called him a son of a bitch too," said Sean.

"I figured you would have some nice words for him," said Maggie. "I have an idea now. Why don't we have a big party and celebrate you not being a lawman any more. How does that sound?"

"That sounds good darlin'," said Sean. "We can get Barbara and Cookie to fix up somethin' real good. Michael can play the piano and maybe we can get the blacksmith over here for his fiddle playin'. We can do some more dancin'. I think I keep gettin' better. Invite anyone you want. I know. We could close up the place and make it a private party."

"I'll talk to Barbara and Cookie right now," said Maggie. "I'm getting excited just thinking about it."

"Maggie darlin', you know that I'll be findin' out who killed the Judge, don't you?" said Sean.

"I know Sean," said Maggie. "You didn't need to say it. I know that you will find out. The Judge was not just your boss but he was also your friend. Friends take care of friends."

~~~~

Four days later they had their party. Almost all of the townspeople were there at one time or another. Sean had waltzed for the first time when he and Maggie were married. Now he could waltz like he had done it for years. Maggie was impressed. The party had started at noon that day and went on till almost daylight the next morning. Maggie and Sean spent the next several hours in the bathtub. They were awakened when the postal clerk was banging on the bath house door. "Wake up Marshal, wake up." he said. "I got a letter for you all the way from St. Louis. It's marked urgent and it's from a fella named Sam Draper."

"All right, all right, I'm comin'," said Sean. "And don't call me Marshal anymore. Name's Sean." Sean got out of the tub and went to the door stark naked. The clerk was a little startled to see Sean naked, but handed Sean the letter and left. Maggie was still asleep in the tub. "Wake up darlin'," said Sean. "Got a letter here from Sam and it's marked urgent. Looks like it got here pretty quick." Maggie stretched her arms a little and yawned.

"Well go ahead and read it darlin'," said Maggie. "I'm sure if Sam marked it urgent, it must be urgent." Sean opened the letter and started to read. It went as follows:

My good friend Sean.

I'm sure you know by now that David and his wife were murdered. Of course no one has been arrested yet. This new Judge seems to have been appointed very quickly. That seems very odd to me. No one here knows anything about this new Judge or has even heard of him. He goes around with four men at all times. He calls them his bodyguards. He tells everyone he doesn't want to be assassinated like David was. I know they are just gunmen. I have my suspicions, but can't prove anything. I would bet a year's wages that this man is behind all the corruption that has been going on. Not just here in St. Louis, but what happened in Kansas City. I wrote this letter because I do not trust the telegraph operator here. If this Judge is who I think he is, he will be sending men after you. He must know that you will want to find out who killed David. I hope this letter gets to you.

Be careful my friend.

Sam

"Well Maggie, Sam has his suspicions too about this new Judge," said Sean. "Maybe I won't hafta go lookin' for David's killers. Maybe they'll come for me."

"Well if men come here, it's to our advantage," said Maggie. "We know the territory here and maybe they don't. Maybe they'll come soon, and we can get this over with."

"Damn Maggie, you've turned into a good scrapper," said Sean. "I didn't quite expect to hear that from you."

"Well darlin', anyone messing with my man, me or my friends, is going to pay up," said Maggie.

"You're gettin' me worked up darlin'," said Sean.

"Well let's do something about that," said Maggie.

A couple of hours later, Maggie and Sean were dressed and setting at their table drinking coffee. Michael, Jon, and Jesse came over and joined them. "Boys, I got a letter from Sam Draper," Sean began. "Seems he has suspicions about this new Judge too." Michael was about to say something when Phil Downs came into the saloon.

"This just came in Marshal," said Phil. "I heard you were friends with this man so I figured you'd want to know."

"Well what is it?" asked Sean. "What's so important?"

"Sam Draper was found dead," said Phil. "There were six bullet holes in his back. He was found in his office. There were no witnesses and no suspects."

CHAPTER THIRTEEN

Clarence Lucas was born in Pittsburgh Pennsylvania in 1830. His father Randolf was a lawyer and his mother was the daughter of a Presbyterian minister. Religion and law were pounded into Clarence's head at an early age. His father was a very well known and made a very good living as a defense attorney. He was always on some high profile case. When Clarence was ten years old, he started going to the courtroom to see his father in action. There was one trial when Clarence was twelve years old that he would always remember. Some well known prominent citizen had killed another man. There were four witnesses to the crime but Clarence's father got the man acquitted. Right at that moment, Clarence knew that he would become a lawyer.

Clarence was an excellent student but what he really excelled at was school yard lawyer. Any time there was a fight during recess or after school, Clarence was right in the middle of it mediating and getting it settled. Several times when a teacher was going to whip a student for whatever reason, Clarence always spoke up in behalf of the student and convinced the teacher not to whip him or her.

Clarence attended Church every Sunday with his mother and father and always volunteered for anything that the Church was doing that needed help. He was very well liked by all the parishioners.

When the time came, Clarence went to Harvard. At the end of his first year, his mother died from pneumonia. Clarence was very upset by this but what really upset him was that his father didn't seem upset at all. When he questioned his father about this, his father just told him that everyone dies sooner or later, and it was her time. He would miss her deeply, but he wasn't going to sit around and grieve for months. Life must go on he said.

Clarence graduated from Harvard at the top of his class and received his law degree. He went back to Pittsburgh and went into business with his father. He won all of his cases for the first five years and became very popular. Very high profile cases started coming his way. He and Randolf were now considered equal partners. After five years, Randolf started letting Clarence take on most of the cases. It seemed that Randolf was never around when Clarence needed a bit of advice.

Clarence lived in his father's house. It was a huge house, and they had a cook and a housekeeper. Clarence always had the company of women but he had no intention of getting married until he considered himself very wealthy. He would stay with a woman for a while, but anytime one of them would push for matrimony, the relationship would end. He would frequent ladies of the evening from time to time when he did not have a steady woman on hand.

During his sixth year as a lawyer, Clarence lost a very big case. It was the first case he had ever lost and he was extremely upset because he thought Randolf should have given him some help.

They had a heated argument at home that evening. "I think I could have won that case if just maybe you would have given me a little help or advice," said Clarence. "Don't you want this firm to win it's cases?"

"Quit your whining," said Randolf. "You needed to lose a case sometime. Besides, the firm still made money. That's why we make clients give us a retainer. You cannot win every case, no matter what you do."

"Maybe we can't win every case but we still should have won this one," said Clarence. "Winning would have gotten us even more money."

"I'm going to tell you something now that just might make you despise me," Randolf began. "Look around you and tell me what you see. Everything in this house is of the best quality. We eat the best food. This house is big enough for a family of twelve. How do you think that we got all of this?"

"We got all this by you being a good lawyer and making good money," said Clarence.

"And how did I make good money?" asked Randolf.

"By winning big cases," answered Clarence.

"And how did I get the big cases in the first place?" asked Randolf.

"By first winning the small cases and getting a good reputation," answered Clarence.

"That sounds admirable son, but there are plenty of lawyers who are very good but never get that big break," said Randolf. "Just how do you think I got my big break?"

"Was it that case that I watched when you got that rich man acquitted of murder when there were four witnesses?" asked Clarence.

"That was it," said Randolf. "Now just how could I get a man acquitted of murder when four people saw him do it?"

"You are a very good lawyer father," answered Clarence. "You put reasonable doubt in the minds of the jury."

"No son, I did not," replied Randolf. "What I did was bribe a couple of jurors. The Judge was also on the rich man's payroll."

"Are you serious?" asked Clarence. "All these years I thought you were the greatest lawyer on this earth. I became a lawyer because of you. You should be in prison."

"I told you that you might end up despising me," said Randolf. "I'm still a good lawyer, but I go where the money is. I took the money route because of your mother. She always had to have the best of everything. She was always pushing. We put up a good front but we were tired of each other. We slept in the same bed all those years but there was nothing there. I've had a mistress ever since you were fourteen. She's a good woman and has made no demands on me. I'll understand if you want to leave the firm."

"Not only will I be leaving the firm, but I intend to become a prosecutor and then a judge," said Clarence. "I'll be moving out and you can have your mistress move in."

~~~~

It wasn't long and Clarence had become a prosecuting attorney. He had a very good reputation for being hard on crime, and he always went for the maximum penalties. When a Judgeship position opened up, Clarence was easily elected. He stayed honest for a long time but was soon overtaken by greed. He realized that as a judge with his good reputation for being hard on crime, he was beyond reproach. He became involved with political machines and money flowed freely. Clarence never knew that it was so easy to make money. When the war broke out, he decided that it would look good on his record if he was in uniform so he got himself commissioned in the Union Army. He was a Lieutenant Colonel but he was not a military lawyer. He got himself assigned as a Quartermaster. He knew that money could be made there if a man didn't get too greedy.

Being a Lt. Colonel, Clarence was always in charge of some supply depot somewhere. It did not take him long to realize that he had a lot of dishonest people who worked for him. He used this to his advantage and formed them into a tight knit organization. Supplies were always getting sent to the wrong place or lost or stolen or even blown up. All a man had to do was not get too greedy. He kept himself allied with his superior officers. Anything they needed, he got it for them. A lot of these officers were politicians and that would come in very handy after the war was over. Most of his organization was with the Army that was fighting in the west, but he also had people who were in the Army of the Potomac.

It was down in Missouri that Clarence's people first came into contact with George Anderson. Anderson's men were always ambushing supply trains. Men on both sides were getting killed. Clarence knew that Anderson was a crazy man, but he figured Anderson was still interested in making a buck. Clarence saw this as an opportunity. He had a Captain in his organization who was very good at talking anyone into anything. Clarence decided he would send this man, Captain Don Purdue, out with one of the supply trains in hope that they would be attacked by Anderson. Once attacked, he would surrender to Anderson and then talk Anderson into some profitable ventures. Anderson was not a regular Confederate soldier. He was a guerilla fighter and out for self profit. Purdue would sell the supplies to Anderson, and Anderson could resale them to the Confederacy or use them however he wanted. No one would be killed doing this. Just in case Anderson did not agree, Clarence had several extra wagons that were loaded with soldiers and not supplies. Anderson went along with Purdue's proposal when he found out about the soldiers in the wagons.

They couldn't always let Anderson's men have supplies without it looking like there had been a fight, so sometimes Purdue had his men shoot up some of the wagons. When there were new men with them that Purdue wasn't sure could be trusted, they were killed. This would make it look like there had been a fight. Of course the men killed were reported as "killed in action." Any man in Clarence's organization that ran his mouth too much always came up "killed in action." Thousands of men were dying regularly, so a few more wouldn't matter. The main thing was not to get too greedy. A wagon here and a wagon there would not arouse suspicion. Not only did Clarence have dealings with the guerillas, his organization made money selling supplies to civilians, regular Confederates, and even other units in the Union Army. Black Marketeering was very profitable. Clarence and Anderson both became very wealthy during the war, and no one in Clarence's organization was ever under suspicion.

When the war ended, Clarence used his influence and got his political allies to appoint him to a high court judgeship in Texas. He and Anderson would secretly stay in touch with each other. Anderson was still a crazy man and continued raiding and killing after the war, but whenever Clarence knew where there was a lot of money to be made, whether it was by cattle rustling or horse stealing, he would let Anderson know, and Anderson would give him a percentage.

When this new Marshal came along after the war, Clarence thought that maybe it was time for his organization to try to become somewhat legitimate. It was Clarence's idea for Anderson to take up ranching. Most of the men who were in Clarence's organization during the war stayed with him after the war was over. He had them get involved with businesses in towns all over several states. They would either buy the businesses or extort money from them. They would get their people in municipal offices so they could run things.

This new Marshal was doing too much damage and when Clarence heard that Anderson had put a bounty on O'Rourke's head, he added another $2000 to it. When Clarence found out that O'Rourke was a hard man to kill, and Anderson was dead, he knew that he needed to try a different approach. He stole some blank bank drafts from a bank in Texas and had them sent to one of his men, the Mayor of Kansas City. When the Marshal wiped out his men in Kansas City, Clarence hired the Whatleys to kill him. They had a good reputation for getting things done, but apparently it wasn't good enough. This was when he decided to have Judge Simmons killed and get himself appointed in his place. With all of his political friends, that would not be a problem. This would make him O'Rourke's boss. He would leave Texas and be in Missouri when everything happened.

Don Purdue was Clarence's right arm and would do anything for his boss. Clarence was never far from Don. Clarence had him hire the best gunmen he could find. They needed to be men who would not hesitate to shoot someone in the back. Clarence explained to him that this Marshal was not a man to be faced. When the time was right, Clarence had Purdue and his men kill Judge Simmons. Clarence was right. Getting himself appointed as Simmons replacement was not a problem. The telegraph operator was on Clarence's payroll so word of the Judge's murder did not get to Abilene right away. When it was discovered that Sam Draper had written a letter to the Marshal and it was too late for his men to get it back, Clarence had his men kill Sam. Clarence's men had been trying to get Sam to sell "The Palace" for some time. Now it would probably sell at public auction as none of Sam's relatives wanted to own the saloon, and Clarence's people would be the highest bidders.

~~~~

Clarence was not sure how Marshal O'Rourke would react when he received the telegram telling him and his deputies to report to him for investigations into their activities. At first he thought that O'Rourke, being a good law abiding man, would do as his boss requested. He soon found out that O'Rourke wanted no part of him. When the telegram came that said that if the judge wanted his badge, he could come and get it, and that he was a son of a bitch, Clarence knew that he had to rid himself of this man. Firing him would not make him go away. He called Purdue into his office. "I want O'Rourke dead," started Clarence. "I want the men who were his deputies dead. If they have women, I want them dead too. Do you understand me Don?"

"Consider it done," said Don. "I've heard about O'Rourke's woman. She'll be easy to spot."

"Do not underestimate this man," said Clarence. "There is no one better with a rifle or pistol. I hear he can kill a man with that Sharps of his at a thousand yards. They say that if you blink, you won't see his draw. He lived with the Cheyenne for some time. He can sneak up on anything and he can track. He's very good with his fists too. The men who rode with him are very good too. All the men who Anderson sent after O'Rourke were killed. I have even heard that his woman has killed a few men who tried to take her."

"The other ones that tried to get O'Rourke were fools," said Purdue. "They talked when they should have been shootin'. They probly could've shot him in the back but were too proud. I'm not. My men are not. O'Rourke will be dead. His men will be dead. Their women will be dead. I have ten men who will do what I say and when I say it. Two of them were sharpshooters during the war. The rest of them have killed several times already. They will not hesitate when the time comes."

"Well get everything you need and get going," said Clarence. "I want this done quickly. I still want two men here with me. I have been going around with body guards. It wouldn't look right if I quit having them so soon."

"I'll get you two good men," said Purdue. "Eleven of us will be leaving day after tomorrow. We'll take the train to Kansas City. Then we'll go by stage to Abilene. There is a daily stage out of Kansas City. We'll go on three different stages. Four of us will go the first day. Three will go the second day, and four will go the third. Once we all get to Abilene, I'll figure out the best way to get this done."

"Once you leave, don't contact me till the job is done," said Clarence. "When the job is done, send a telegram and just say "Done.""

CHAPTER FOURTEEN

"So they've killed Sam too," yelled Sean. "Sons a bitches. Somebody's gonna pay for this. When I find out for sure who's behind this, I'll send him to hell where he belongs."

"Will we be goin' to St. Louis?" asked Michael.

"St. Louis is a big place," answered Sean. "You and me have been there but Jon and Jesse are not that familiar with the place. We would be very outnumbered plus we are not sure who we're after. I believe we'll stay right here and see if they come after us. I know that will be hard since new faces are showin' up here almost every day. They could be here already just waitin' for the right time. I don't want any of you doing anything alone. Same goes for our women. Michael, if Betty needs to go shoppin', you go shoppin' too. Stay well armed. Jon, since you've been with Martha, make sure she knows how to handle a pistol and keeps one with her. Make sure she has it close, even when she's with customers. Keep Dog close too. Jesse, you make sure Dawn can handle a gun."

"We'll be ready for whatever comes," said Jon. "I just hope they come soon. I'm not that good at waitin'."

"Sean darlin', since you want us not to do anything alone, you're going with me to the bank right now," said Maggie. "Then I need a few things from the general store."

"Let's go," said Sean. "I can look around some while you're shoppin'."

~~~~

Maggie and Sean were half way to the bank when they saw a wagon coming into town. The man driving it looked familiar to Sean. "Hell, that's Walter Black," said Sean. "He musta decided to come here and set up his business." As the wagon got closer, Sean knew for sure that it was Walter. "So you decided to come here and make some money off them Texas boys," said Sean when the wagon got close to him.

"That's part of it," said Walter. "I just got tired of the big city. Didn't like the way things were goin'. Weren't makin' no money nohow. Nobody buyin' guns ceptin' gamblers and a few people thinkin' they were hunters. I'm ready for a change. Didn't tell no one we was leavin' ceptin' the kids. We just left. I heard about the Judge gettin' murdered. I was in Kansas City when that happened."

"So you didn't hear that Sam Draper was murdered too, did you?" asked Sean.

"No, I didn't know that," answered Walter. "Probly that bunch that was tryin' ta get'em ta sell."

"So where's all your stuff?" asked Sean.

"I hired a freighter to bring it here for me. Should be here in a day or two," said Walter. Me and the misses'll stay in this wagon till we get us a new shop built."

"If you 're tired a stayin' in that wagon, I can supply you with a free room for a spell," said Sean. "As long as you and the misses don't mind sleepin' in a saloon."

"We might just take you up on that for a night," said Walter. "I got somethin' I want you ta see. I Just know you'll like it."

"Well take your wagon over to the livery and c'mon back to the saloon," said Sean. "We'll get you fixed up with a room for the night." Maggie and Sean went on to the bank and then did their shopping at the general store. Walter and his wife were entering the saloon when Sean and Magggie got there.

"So how's this workin' for you?" asked Walter as he pointed to the sign for turning in weapons. "Had any trouble?"

"We had some at first," answered Sean. "But things been all right now for a while."

"It's a good idea," said Walter. "Don't know how them Texas boys'll take it."

"Well they'll abide by it or move on," said Sean. "We'll give'em help leavin' if they need it."

"I'll go ahead and show Mrs. Black the room," said Maggie. "You men can talk for a while." Maggie could tell that Mrs. Black was very tired and needed some rest. Mrs. Black was impressed when Maggie showed her the room. "This is nice," she said. "That's a big bed too. Walter'll like that. He says I crowd him some."

"Well you go ahead and get some rest," said Maggie. "It's hard to tell how long the men'll be talking." Maggie left the room, and Mrs. Black laid down on the bed and was asleep in no time.

~~~~

Sean took Walter to his regular table. "Would you like a drink?" asked Sean. "We got anything you could want."

"A beer sounds good," said Walter. Sean went too the bar to get the beer and a drink for himself. Michael was in the saloon and he came over and joined them.

"So Walter, are you settin' up shop here now?" asked Michael.

"Yes I am," answered Walter. "Time for a change. Now I got somethin' that I know you both'd like to see." Sean was comimg back to the table as Walter reached into a gunny sack and pulled out somethi:ng that was all wrapped up. Then he unwrapped it and set it on the table.

"Is that a toy cannon?" asked Michael.

"It may look like a toy, but I assure you it is not," answered Walter. Sear: just stared at if for a while. Then he spoke.

"That thing's got about a ten inch barrel and the bore looks about an inch," said Sean. "Someone did a real nice job on them wheels. If that thing'll really fire, some damage could be done."

"Well this thing'll really fire," said Walter. "I made the whole thing myself. I had a customer who was an artillery officer durin' the war and he asked me if I could make him a cannon. He wanted it for a decoration on his desk, but he also wanted to make sure it would shoot. When it was done, we took it out and tried it. I assure you, it works. We used 200 grains of powder and I made some balls for it. We shot some buckshot in it too. This thing can be deadly. Anyway, it wasn't too much trouble makin' the thing so I made a couple more."

"Well I'll take one of'em off your hands," said Sean. "It'll make a nice decoration on the other side of the bar. You know what else would go with this. A toy soldier standing beside it holdin' the ramrod. Let's go out somewhere tomorrow and try it out. Now have you figured out where your new shop is gonna be?"

"It's already being worked on," said Walter. "I was able to get ahold of some of the men who were building some of the new businesses in town and they jumped right on it for me. I got ahold of'em while I was still in St. Louis. Should be done before too long."

~~~~

The next morning after breakfast, Sean and Walter went out to try the cannon. Sean set up some boards that were supposed to represent a man sized target. Sean didn't care about the solid balls. He wanted to see what buckshot would do at about five yards. He loaded up twenty pieces of double 00 buck. Walter made a long fuse so they would not be too close. It let out a tremendous roar when it fired. The cannon rolled back about five feet and flipped over. The target was just torn to pieces. After the smoke cleared, Sean walked over to the target and then he looked back at the cannon. "Well being on that side's safer that this side," said Sean. "But I reckon if a fella got careless, he could get hurt there too."

"We could have gotten by with less powder," said Walter, "I just wanted to show you that it would handle that amount."

"It sure as hell did," said Sean. "This thing'd sure tear up a man if the need'd arise."

"Well let's hope you don't hafta use this on anyone," said Walter. "Now make sure you clean it good and let's get back. I wanna see how them boys are doin' on my new shop."

~~~~

Purdue made sure that his men were well supplied before they boarded the train in St. Louis. He had them all set in different places so it wouldn't look like they were all together. They had certain instructions to follow and if anyone did not abide by them, Purdue would kill them. When they got to Kansas City, they would break up into their groups. The first four going to Abilene would have a man in charge of them. He would make sure they would stay out of trouble and not draw any attention to them. He would buy the stage tickets so the others would not be seen too much. When they got to Abilene, they would separate and stay in different hotels and most important of all, they were to stay sober. The leader of the group would look around the town and find out where O'Rourke stayed and where his woman was. He would also see if he could find out who his former deputies were.

The leader of the first group was a man named Clem Darsey. He had ridden with Bloody Bill during the war and was no stranger to murder. The other three men were Wesley Hanks, Jeff Bowden, and Bo Billings. All three of these men had ridden with Bedford Forest and were expert pistol shots. All of these men had a weakness for women and liquor, but Bo had another weakness. He hated anyone of any color but white. He hated Chinese, Indians, Negroes, and anyone with red hair. No one ever knew why he hated red hair. Some people thought it had to do with the Irish, but no one knew for sure. Despite their weaknesses, these men were expert killers and could be trusted when the time came for killing.

The second group consisted of Fred Langley, the leader, Ted Barber, and Mike Allen. When they got to Abilene, it would be their job to find a place to camp west of town a few miles and get horses back to the last station stop where the stage changed

horses before going on to Abilene. The third group would be getting off there. The three men in this group had all ridden with
JEB Stuart and were also expert pistol shots. Ted Barber and Mike
Allen were not drinkers so Fred would not have to worry about
that. They did however, like the women.

Purdue was with the third group. His men were Sam
Alexander, Tom Horton, and George Samuels. Sam and Tom were
Union sharpshooters during the war. The were both deadly shots
with their Sharps rifles. Both men had telescopic sights mounted
on their rifles. Sam said that he had been in O'Rourke's unit at
one time. George had spent most of the war being a runner. He
would take messages from a Commanding General to units that
were engaged in combat. He was very good at this and got
through the whole war without being wounded one time. He too
was also an expert pistol shot. When this group arived at the last
station before Abilene, they would go with the second group to
the camp site and figure out the best plan of attack. If anyone
wondered or asked what they would be doing when they left the
station, they would say that they were buffalo hunters and other
men with wagons and supplies were coming later to meet them.
The first group would stay in town for four days and learn where
O'Rourke and his former deputies and their women were. After
four days, they would report to the campsite.

~~~~

When the train from St. Louis to Kansas City pulled into the depot, Lawrence Todd was there. A friend and his wife were coming
from back east for a visit. While he was waiting on his friend, he
thought he saw a face that fit a description that was on a wanted
poster. He shrugged it off and met his friend. As the day wore on,

he decided to check out the poster again. He excused himself and left his friend and wife to visit with his wife. When he read the poster, he was almost positive that the description fit the man he had seen perfectly. The name on the poster was Bo Billings. He strolled around town for a while to see if he could spot him. He was about to give up when he got close to the stage depot. Bo Billings and three other men were on the stage that was leaving. Lawrence went to the station master. "That is the stage to Abilene, isn't it?" asked Lawrence.

"Sure is," the station master answered. "Leavin' on time too."

Lawrence went straight to the telegraph office to send a telegram to Abilene. It went as follows:

Federal Marshal O'Rourke
Abilene Kansas

Bo Billings on stage to Abilene with three men << stop>>
not known if men are together << stop>> Billings wanted
for murder in three states

Lawrence Todd
Kansas City

The telegraph operator got the telegram to Sean quickly. Sean was at the saloon. He and the men were at the regular table drinking coffee at the time. "Well boys, some fella named Bo Billings'll be showin' up in town shortly," Sean began. "Lawrence Todd tells me that he's wanted for murder in three states. Three other men are on the stage too but Lawrence didn't know if they're together or not. If this is some fellas comin' here for us, we got some time to get ready for'em. It'll be a few days before that stage gets here. Don't nobody let their guard down though. Could be some of'em here already. If we do find out that these fellas are here after us, I'd sure like to take one of'em alive if possible. I figure I can make'm talk one way or another."

~~~~

The next few days, everyone stayed vigilant, but nothing happened. Finally the stage with the four men arrived in Abilene. Sean watched them as they got off the stage. He did not have a poster so he didn't kow which one was Bo Billings. Sean could see that all four were armed. The four of them went their separate ways. Two of them checked into one hotel and the other two checked into another. They all had separate rooms. Jon and Michael were with Sean and after the men had checked into their hotel, Sean had Jon hang out in the lobby of one hotel and Michael in the other. They all would keep an eye on these men.

After about an hour, Clem left his room and headed for Maggie's Place. Michael had been in the lobby of Clem's hotel, and he followed Clem back to the saloon. Clem did not notice that he was being followed. Michael went over by the piano. Clem was a little stunned to see the sign about checking weapons, but he unbuckled his gun belt and took it straight to the bar. Tom there. "I'll get it right back to you when you're ready to leave," said Tom. "Now what can I get for you?"

"I'll have me a beer," said Clem. Then he turned and saw the painting on the wall. "Oh my, that painting takes my breath away."

"Just wait till you see her in person," said Tom. "She looks even better than that."

"I don't see how she could," said Clem. Just then he spotted Maggie coming down the stairs. "Oh Lord," said Clem. "She makes a man hurt. Just how in the world could a woman look that good? Is that Maggie and is this her place?"

"Yep, that's her and this is her place," said Tom. "That fella over at that far table is her husband and that other fella by the piano is his best friend. Them three are partners in this saloon." Maggie was downstairs now and went behind the bar.

"Maggie, this fella here was impressed by your beauty," said Tom. "What's your name mister?"

"Clem, Clem Darsey," said Clem. "I am pleased to meet you Maggie. You are more beautiful than I have heard."

"Thank you for your kindness," said Maggie. "I hope you like our place. My girls will be here shortly if you need company."

"I'm all right for now," said Clem. "Maybe later this evening I'll come back."

"So what are you doing with yourself Clem?" asked Maggie.

"Just passin' through on my way to Texas," said Clem. "Probly go down there and get me a job pushin' cows around."

"Well good luck to you," said Maggie. "Now if you'll excuse me, I must go talk with my husband."

"So what did that man have to say?" Sean sked Maggie as she sat down beside him.

"Said his name was Clem Darsey and he's just passing through on his way to Texas," answered Maggie. "He's figuring on getting a job pushing cows."

"Thanks darlin', we'll keep an eye on him," said Sean.

Clem finished his beer, and Tom returned his gunbelt. Clem left and went back to his hotel, but he didn't go to his room. He went to Bo's room. Bo was napping on the bed. Clem woke him up. "What do you want?" mumbled Bo. "I was havin' me a good dream. I just scalped me a buncha redsticks and was havin' me a squaw before I bashed her brains in."

"Sounds like a dream I don't wanna have," said Clem. "I know where O'Rourke is. That's gotta be him over at the saloon called "Maggie's Place." There was a big fella there too by the piano. I bet that fella was one a his deputies. They was both armed. I met that red haired woman too. Damn she's a looker. I'm not gonna like killin' her."

"Don't you worry yerself about that," said Bo. "I'll get her killed. You know I hate red hair anyhow. So you say she's a real looker?"

"Yep she is," said Clem. "I never knew that some woman could look that good."

"Well I just gotta see her myself then," said Bo.

"Don't be doin' nothin' stupid over there," said Clem. "They make you check your guns when you go in there."

"Mebbe they do and mebbe they don't," said Bo as he was putting on his gun belt. He also had a bowie knife that he wore on his left side. "I wanna get me a look at this red haired bitch before I gotta kill her."

"You just remember what I said," said Clem. "Don't be doin' nothin' stupid." Bo just shrugged and left the room and headed to Maggie's Place. Clem headed over to the other hotel where Wesley and Jeff were staying. Wesley and Jeff were coming down the stairs from their rooms when Clem entered the lobby of the hotel. Jon was sitting in the lobby reading a newspaper. Dog was with him. "Let's go outside where we can talk," Clem said to Wesley and Jeff. The three men went out into the street. Jon stayed in the hotel lobby. He could see the three men through a window on the door.

"That crazy Bo is headed to that saloon over there," Clem said to the two men. "I hope he don't get crazy and do somethin' stupid. That red haired woman is over there, and red hair makes Bo crazy. O'Rourke's in there too and another man who was mebbe a deputy a his."

"Mebbe you shoulda kept Bo from goin' over there," said Jeff. "He could mess up this whole thing."

"The only way a man can stop Bo from doin' somethin' is ta kill'em or knock'em out," said Clem. "Bo is crazy, but he's a good killer. If he'd go in there and get crazy, mebbe he'd take care of everything for us."

"O'Rourke's s'posed to be purty good with his pistols," said Wesley. "I doubt Bo could take'm."

"Well mebbe O'Rourke'll mess up and give Bo his back." said Clem. "But somehow I doubt that'll happen. Men like O'Rourke don't mess up. That's why they're still breathin'."

~~~~

Inside the saloon, Michael and Tom had just gone out the back door and were going to the freight office to bring over a wagon load of whiskey. Maggie had gone back upstairs for something and Sean had just taken Jeb out back so he could do his necessaries. Jesse was at their regular table and Sean had asked him to keep an eye on things till he got back in a few minutes.

When Bo got to the front doors of the saloon, he stopped momentarily and looked inside. Then he pulled his pistol and held it down on his right side and walked through the doors. When

Jesse saw him, he could not tell that Bo was holding his pistol as he was on Bo's left side. "You'll hafta check your gun at the bar," Jesse said.

Bo turned to see this very big colored man looking at him. "Damn, yer a big buck," said Bo. "Let's see what color yer blood is." Bo then raised his pistol and fired at Jesse. The bullet caught him in the right shoulder and threw him backwards. When he hit the floor, his pistol fell out of his holster. He didn't move. When Maggie heard the shot she came out of her room and started running down the stairs. When Bo saw her, he never said a word. He turned his pistol to her and started shooting. When Maggie saw the pistol aiming at her, she ducked as the first shot was fired. It missed, but Maggie slipped and started rolling down the stairs. Bo fired again and missed. Jesse was up now but he couldn't find his pistol. He went straight at Bo. Bo saw him coming and turned the pistol on him and pulled the trigger but the pistol misfired. He cocked the hammer and tried again. It misfired again. About that time, Sean came running back into the saloon.

"What the hell's goin' on?" yelled Sean. "Where's Maggie and you been hit Jesse?"

"Maggie fell down the stairs there," said Jesse. "You take care a her. I'll take care a this white trash."

"I can shoot'em right now," said Sean.

"No, you look after Maggie. She's maybe hurt bad," said Jesse. "This white trash's not goin' nowhere."

Sean got to Maggie. She had been unconscious and was just coming to. She looked up at Sean, and then looked down. "Oh darlin', I'm bleeding down there," said Maggie. "Get me to bed, then get Doc Rawlins." Sean gently picked her up and took her to their room.

"Now I'm gonna break you in half," Jesse said to Bo as he went for him. Just as he got close, Bo pulled his bowie knife with his right hand.

"I'm gonna carve you up boy," said Bo. "We gonna see what color yer insides are." Bo slashed at Jesse and the tip of the knife caught Jesse across the chest as he jumped back to avoid the knife. Jesse looked own at his chest and saw the blood from the slash. His gunshot wound was not bleeding much. Jesse tore off his shirts and wrapped it around his left arm.

"We're done dancin' now," said Jesse. "You got any prayers you better say'em now cause you're gonna be dead."

"We'll quit dancin' when I'm ready ta quit dancin'," said Bo. "After I gut ya, I'm gonna scalp ya. I never scalped me a buck this big before." Bo made another slash at Jesse. Jesse blocked the slash with his left arm. Bo tried to drag the edge of the knife so the blade would cut through Jesse's shirt. Before he had dragged the knife very much, Jesse grabbed Bo's right arm with his right hand. Jesse was in great pain from the gunshot wound, but with his great strength, he forced Bo down to his knees. Bo swung away with his left arm and was punching Jesse in his right side, but the blows had no effects on Jesse. Jesse pulled the knife from Bo's hand with his left hand and raised the knife well up above his head. Then he brought the knife straight down and into the top of Bo's head. The force was so great that the knife went in up to the hilt and the tip of the blade was sticking out below his chin.

"Sean had just come out of their room to get Doc Rawlins when he saw Jesse slam the bowie knife into Bo's head. "I'd say this one's dead," said Sean. "You sit yourself down Jesse and get somethin' over that wound. I'll be back with Doc shortly."

~~~~

When Bo fired his first shot, the three men in the street pulled their pistols and headed toward the saloon. When Jon heard the shot and saw them pull their pistols, he and Dog went into the street after them. "You three best drop them pistols," said Jon. "Or I can kill you right now if you want."

"You can't get all three of us," said Clem. "You might get one us of before we get you."

"Well I'll get one a you for sure and Dog'll get one," said Jon. "Make up your mind. Dog is gettin' edgy. He just loves rippin' out a man's throat."

Michael and Tom had heard the shooting and came running back. They saw Jon and the three men in the street. "Need any help Jon?" Michael asked Jon as they approached from Jon's right side. Michael and Tom both had their pistols drawn.

"I'm all right," answered Jon. "But these fellas can't make up their minds if they're ready to die or not." Jeff started to raise his pistol. "Dog," Jon said and Dog was on him. "Don't kill'em." Dog had Jeff by his gun arm. The pistol fired one time as Dog drug Jeff to the ground. The bullet struck the ground next to Michael. "I'd let go a that pistol if I was you," said Jon. "Sometimes I can't control what Dog does. He's not used to grabbin' folks by the arm. He really likes throats." Jeff finally let go of the pistol. He lay there screaming in pain. Dog stood over him growling just daring him to move.

Sean was in front of the saloon now and had his pistol aimed at Clem. Jeb was with him. "Go ahead and drop them pistols boys," said Clem. "We got no chance now."

"One a you boys get some rope and tie up these fellas," said Sean. "I gotta get Doc." Doc had been out of town on a call and was returning when he heard the shots. He hurried back. He had just stopped his buggy at his office when Sean arrived.

"Doc, we need you. Maggie's hurt, and we got a wounded man," said Sean. They both ran back to the saloon. Doc took a quick look at Jesse and saw that the bleeding had stopped and the bullet had passed through.

"He'll be all right," said Doc. "Now take me to Maggie."

When Doc saw Maggie, he could see that she had not been shot but was bruised up some. Then he saw the blood down below. "How far along were you Maggie?" Doc asked.

"Only about a month and a half," answered Maggie. "Can you tell anything? Have I lost the baby?"

"I'm sorry Maggie, but you have lost your baby," said Doc. "I'll get this bleeding stopped and get you cleaned up. You are a young strong woman. You weren't far along. You'll be all right in no time. You should be able to have as many children as you want before long." Maggie and Sean both cried a little but then held the tears back. "Nobody knew you were pregnant did they?" asked Doc.

"No, we weren't gonna say anything till she started showing," said Sean. Jeb knew something was wrong, and he laid at the foot of the bed with a mournful look on his face.

Doc got Maggie cleaned up and then told her again that she was young and would be all right in no time. "I'll go have a look at Jesse now. I'll check on you tomorrow," said Doc as he was leaving the room. Maggie and Sean cried a little more when Doc left the room.

Jesse's wound was not serious. The bullet had passed through but did chip a few bones. Doc was able to pick out the bone chips. "You're a lucky man Jesse," said Doc. "You'll have some pain for awhile since some bones got chipped but you're young and strong and you'll heal fast. That knife cut is only a scatch. Yes sir, you are very strong." Doc said that as he looked over and saw Bo's body with the bowie knife in his skull. "I reckon you're the one that put that knife in that man's head."

"Yep, I done it," said Jesse. "He needed to die, and I helped'm out."

"Well you take it easy now and I'll check on you in a few days," said Doc. "If you get to having too much pain, come see me and I'll get you something."

"Thanks Doc," said Jesse. "How's Maggie?"

"I best let Maggie and Sean tell you," answered Doc. "She is gonna be all right though. Now I better go look at that other fella. I hear Dog had ahold of'em."

Dawn had been in their room the whole time all this was happening. Jesse had always told her that if she heard any shooting or a ruckus, she was to stay put. She did as she was instructed. Finally she decided that she had waited long enough after the shooting had stopped and went into the saloon. Jesse was sitting at the regular table all bandaged up and had no shirt on. "So you got another shirt ruined," said Dawn as she leaned down and hugged Jesse.

"Not so hard now," said Jesse. "It hurts a little, and I'm glad you got a little humor in you about this."

"Well it wouldn't do any good to get crazy and cry all over the place," said Dawn. "We been through some things and I'm learnin' that whatever happens, you'll take care of us. Now let's get you to bed. Tomorrow I'll be startin' to make you a new shirt. They went to their room, and Dawn pulled off Jesse boots and put him to bed. Now you get some rest. I'll see if Maggie needs anything."

"Maggie's bein' looked after," said Jesse. "How bout you gettin' down here with me?"

"You just been shot," said Dawn. "Did gettin' shot make you crazy?"

"I been shot before durin' the war," said Jesse. "It didn't make me crazy then, and I'm not crazy now. I just want my woman."

"Well all right, but you let me do the workin'," said Dawn as she undressed and slipped into bed with him.

~~~~

Maggie and Sean cried a little more and they held each other for a while. "You get some rest now darlin'," said Sean. "I'll be goin't ta see them three men now."

"Don't kill'em all just yet darlin'," said Maggie. "See if you can get at least one of them to talk. We want to know if any more are coming."

"I'll take care of things darlin'," said Sean. "You go ahead and rest."

~~~~

Doc patched up the man who Dog had grabbed. "You'll heal mister, but you may not have the use of that arm for a good while," said Doc. "Could be some bad damage, tendons and such."

"Probly won't need my arm anyway," said Jeff. "I figure I'll be gettin' myself shot shortly." Doc never said a word. He just packed up his bag and went back to his office.

~~~~

The three men were tied up now and were in the saloon. They were also tied to the chairs that they were sitting on. Sean went downstairs and approached Clem. "I figure you're in charge a this bunch," said Sean. "Are you gonna tell me anything, or am I gonna hafta force it outta you?"

"You'll get nothin' outta any of us," said Clem.

"We'll see," said Sean. "Jon, you go get some good ropes and our horses. Bring three extra horses. Michael, I'll be wantin' you to stay here while Jon and me are out with these fellas. Get the undertaker to get that body outta here."

~~~~

Jon returned with all the horses and the ropes. The three men were untied from the chairs and put up on the three extra horses. The horses were tied together, and Jon had them tied to his horse. "Where you takin' us?" asked Clem.

"Out to find a good tree," said Sean as he mounted.

CHAPTER FIFTEEN

They headed west out of town. They passed the old Hawk place. Sean had not been there since it had been burned. A couple of miles later they came to a small stream. There were some likely looking trees on both sides of the stream. "I'll find the best tree," Sean said. "Hold'em here. If anyone gets feisty, shoot'em in the leg or somethin'." Sean was gone only for a few minutes. "I got a good one just over there a ways. Let's go." When they got to the tree, Sean took one of the ropes and made a good noose. Then he placed it around Wesley's neck, and then threw it up over a big limb and tied it off on the trunk.

"You can't be doin' this," said Wesley. "You're no lawman any more. We didn't have no trial or nothin'."

"Anybody got anything they wanna tell me?" asked Sean. The three men remained silent. Sean slapped the horse on the rump, and Wesley was hanged. "Must notta got that noose in a good spot," said Sean. "He musta kicked for five minutes. Now has anybody got anything to say ta me?" Clem and Jeff were silent. Sean got another rope and made a noose. Then he placed the noose around Jeff's neck and then threw it over the same tree limb and tied it off on the trunk. "Anybody got anything to say now?" asked Sean.

"You go ta hell O'Rourke," said Jeff.

"You first," said Sean as he slapped the horse's rump. After Jeff had quit kicking, Jon handed Sean another rope. "We won't need this," said Sean. "I got somethin' real special in mind for Clem here."

"What do you mean special?" asked Clem.

"Well I don't know if you heard or not, but I spent a good while with the Cheyenne," said Sean. "I reckon you heard that they got all kinds a ways ta kill a fella real slow like. Most folks beg ta be killed before it's over."

Clem's faced turned a strange color on the way back to town. After a few minutes he spoke. "Are you just gonna leave them boys back there hangin' like that?" he asked.

"They won't be goin' anywhere," said Sean. "We'll get'em down sometime."

~~~~

When they got back to town, Sean took Clem into the saloon, and Jon took the horses to the livery. Michael was there. "I see two of'em aren't with us anymore," said Michael. "Why's this one still alive?"

"I got somethin' special for him," answered Sean. "Now would you go find Walter for me? Tell him I need a couple of fuses for my new toy. One short one and one that'll last maybe a half hour."

"What toy is that?" asked Clem.

"You'll see soon enough," said Sean. "Now while were waitin', you should be thinkin' about things you wanna tell me if you want ta live."

"Why should I tell you anything?" asked Clem. "You're gonna kill me no matter what I say."

"I'll tell you somethin' mister," started Sean. "I'm a man a my word and if I say that I won't kill you if you tell me what I need ta know, then I mean it."

"Bull shit," said Clem.

"Suit yourself," said Sean. "If I was you I'd be thinkin' bout all the things I was gonna miss when I was dead. Have you got a family? Maybe you got a momma somewheres that'll miss that face a yours. Will you miss women? Will anybody else miss you? You sit there and think a while."

~~~~

Michael returned a half hour later with the two fuses. "Walter asked me what you were up to," said Michael. "I told him you were just playing with your new toy." Jon was back from the livery now.

"Jon, you get my toy," said Sean. "There's powder and buck-shot behind the bar. Grab it too. Michael, I want you to stay here while Jon and me go out and give Clem here a demonstration." Jon got everything and Sean grabbed Clem and they went out the back door. Sean grabbed a few boards and took them with them. They got out just past the edge of town, and Sean found a good spot to set up for the demonstration. He set up the boards and loaded the cannon with the buckshot. He placed the cannon about five yards from the boards. He made sure Clem and Jon were in a safe position and then lit the fuse. The cannon roared, and the boards were torn to bits. The cannon flipped over a few times and finally came to a stop. After the smoke cleared, Sean looked at Clem. "I wanted you ta see what this thing can do," said Sean.

"So what. You hang me or shoot me with that thing," said Clem. "I'll be just as dead."

"So you got nothin' ta say yet?" Sean asked.

"Hell no," answered Clem. "I'm dead no matter what. I'll not tell you a thing."

"We'll see," said Sean. "Now let's get back to the saloon."

~~~~

When they got to the saloon, Michael told Sean that several people were running around trying to find out what the explosion was. "I told'em you were just playing with your new toy and not to be worried."

"That's good Michael. Now we're gonna get down to business," said Sean. "Clear everything away from that back wall over there and close the front doors and put out a closed sign. Say we'll be back in an hour on the sign." Michael and Jon moved several tables, and then Michael hung up a closed sign and put a note on it that said they would be back in an hour. "Now take Clem here and set him on the floor with his back against the wall," said Sean. "I'll need me a board maybe four ta five foot long and a bit a rope." Jon went out back and returned with the board and some rope. "Now take that board and spread his legs apart and tie that board so he can't get his legs back together," said Sean.

"Just what the hell'r you doin'?" said Clem. "If yer gonna kill me, then kill me and git it over with."

"Don't rush me," said Sean. "You'll be dead soon enough if you don't talk." Then Sean slowly loaded the cannon again and made sure that Clem watched him. It was loaded with bucksot. When it was loaded, Sean sat it on the floor between Clem's legs and lowered the barrel so it was right on Clem's privates. Then he placed the long fuse on the cannon. Clem was beginning to shake now.

"You didn't learn this from no Cheyenne," said Clem.

"No I didn't," said Sean. "I just said that ta get you thinkin'. Now I'm gonna tell you how this is gonna work," Sean began. "This fuse is s'posed to be a half hour long. I'm gonna start askin' you questions and if you don't answer or say what I want to hear, I'm gonna light the fuse. I'll be askin' more questions when that fuse is lit. Whenever you answer a question after the fuse is lit, I'll stop the fuse. Then I'll ask more questions and if I don't get a good answer, I'll light the fuse again. We'll go on till you say what I want to hear or the cannon goes off. Now I give you my word. If you tell me what I want to know, I will not kill you. These men will not kill you. If the cannon goes off and you survive, we will not kill you. Now do you understand?"

"Go to hell O'Rourke," shouted Clem. "Ask away."

"All right, here we go," said Sean. "Have you got a mother?"

"Course I got a mother," answered Clem. "What the hell kinda question is that?"

"Fine answer," said Sean. "Where does she live?"

"None a yer damn business," answered Clem. Sean immediately lit the fuse.

"Just wait a minute," cried Clem. "She lives in Lexington Kentucky." Sean put out the fuse.

"Have you got any brothers or sisters and is your Pa alive?" asked Sean.

"Pa's dead and I got a sister," answered Clem.

"Where does she live?" asked Sean.

"I don't know," cried Clem. Sean lit the fuse again.

"Wait, wait, wait," cried Clem. "She's in San Francisco. She's married to some banker." Sean stopped the fuse.

"Have you got a girl somewhere?" asked Sean.

"No I don't," answered Clem. Sean lit the fuse again. "I said I don't and I don't. I got my favorite whores but I got no regular girl." Sean stopped the fuse again.

"Where are these whores?" asked Sean.

"Some'r in St. Louis and some'r in Kansas City," answered Clem.

"You're doin' fine now," said Sean. "Now let's get serious. What did you do in the war?"

"I was in the Army of Northern Virginia," Clem answered. Sean lit the fuse again.

"All right, all right, I rode with Bloody Bill," said Clem. Sean stopped the fuse again.

"Did you know George Anderson?" asked Sean.

"I knew'm," answered Clem. "Anybody that rode with Bloody Bill knew Anderson or of him."

"Did you ride with Anderson after the war?" asked Sean.

"I thought about it, but when I heard about some Marshal killin' a lotta his men, I changed my mind."

"That was a good answer," said Sean. "Now who was Anderson's boss?"

"I don't know nothin' bout Anderson havin' no boss," answered Clem. "Men like Anderson don't have bosses." Sean lit the fuse again. Clem started crying. "I mean it mister. I don't know nothin' bout no boss. Mebbe one a them other fellas knew. I don't." Sean did not stop the fuse. Two minutes rolled by. "Mebbe Purdue knows ," cried Clem.

"Who's Purdue?" asked Sean. The fuse was still lit. Another minute went by before Clem answered.

"He's my boss," answered Clem. Sean stopped the fuse.

"Now we're gettin' somewhere," said Sean. "How bout a drink. Michael, get Clem a drink. Bring me one too. Hell, bring the bottle. Michael came back with the bottle and Sean poured himself and Clem a drink. Sean held the glass while Clem drank. "That was good," said Sean. "Let's have another." Sean poured again and again helped Clem take his drink. "Now we'll get back with the questions," said Sean. "Was that fella with the bowie knife in his skull Bo Billings?"

"Yes, that was him," answered Clem.

"Good answer. Now who is this Purdue fella and where did he come from?" asked Sean.

"I heard he was a Captain in the Union Army and did a lotta profiteering from supplies and such," said Clem.

"Darn good answer," said Sean. "Have another drink." Sean poured the drink and held it so Clem could get it drunk. "Hell, have another one," said Sean and he poured another one for Clem and helped him with it.

"You're tryin' ta get me drunk," said Clem. "Well no matter; if I gotta die, I might as well die happy."

"In that case you might as well have another drink," said Sean as he poured Clem another drink. "Now back to the questions. How many more men are coming here?"

"I can't tell you that," said Clem. "Purdue'll kill me." Sean lit the fuse again. "Stop, stop, stop," cried Clem. "Gimme another drink and I'll tell you. Just stop that fuse."

"The fuse stops when I hear an answer," answered Sean.

"Seven more are comin'," said Clem. Sean stopped the fuse and got Clem another drink. Clem gulped down the drink.

"When will they be here?" asked Sean.

Clem was starting to slur his words a bit but he got out the answer. "Three of'em'll be here on the next stage," answered Clem. "The other four will be on the next stage after that but are not coming into town just yet."

"And why is that?" asked Sean.

"Lemme think a bit," said Clem. Sean lit the fuse again. "Now just hold on there. I know the answer," cried Clem. "I just gotta get it out. Sure could use another drink." The fuse stayed lit. "I got it, I got it," yelled Clem. "They're gettin' off the stage at the last station where they change horses before comin' into Abilene." Sean stopped the fuse.

"Have another drink," said Sean as he poured it for Clem.

"Maybe you should back off the drinks a little," said Michael. "He might pass out on you."

"He'll be all right," said Sean as he helped Clem with the glass.

"Now tell me the rest of it," said Sean.

Clem mumbled a few words and then told the rest of what he knew. "I was in charge of the first group, and we was to find all a you. When the second bunch got here, I was to tell them what all I knew, and then they would find a campsite a few miles west of town and then get horses back to the last group at the station. Then they'd go to the campsite. My group was gonna be here four days then head out to the campsite. Purdue was gonna come up with the best plan of attack. He's got some sharpshooters with him. One of'em said he was in your unit one time during the war. Now how's 'bout another drink?"

"One more question and you can have all the whiskey you want," said Sean. "Now who's Purdue's boss?"

Clem was really slurring his words now and Michael thought for sure he was going to pass out. Clem mumbled and mumbled and finally came up with the answer. "Lucas," he exclaimed, "now gimme my whiskey." Clem gulped down the drink and then slumped over.

Sean looked down at the cannon. "You know, I don't think that fuse would have lasted a half hour," said Sean. "Well at least we got our answers. Now I gotta figure out how we'll handle things. Get Clem up and get him over to the jail. We'll take turns watchin' him. Jon you take first watch and then I'll spell you. Michael, get the place opened back up. Anybody asks why we was closed, just tell'em we had to clean up a few things." Then Sean went upstairs to check on Maggie. She was awake.

"So how did it go darlin'?" asked Maggie. "Did you learn anything?"

"I know everything now," said Sean. "We hung two of'em and after a while, the last one was very cooperative."

"So what are we up against?" asked Maggie.

"There was eleven of'em all told," started Sean. "The first four were s'posed to find us and the layout here. The second bunch would come in the next day which is tomorrow and see what the first bunch found out. Then they would make a campsite west of town and then get horses back to the fourth group when they got off the stage at the last station before Abilene. Then they would all meet at the campsite and the boss would figure out the best way to get us all killed."

"Is that Judge their boss?" asked Maggie.

"Yes he is," answered Sean. "After I get his men killed, I'll figure out a way to get him killed."

"Why don't you use his own man to do it darlin'," he wouldn't suspect that.

"That's a good idea darlin'," said Sean. "I'll think about all this. Now how are you doin'?"

"I'm done crying now," answered Maggie. "We're young, and I'll be all right. We can have all the children we want later. We have plenty of time."

"I love you Maggie," said Sean.

"I love you too Sean," said Maggie. Sean bent down and kissed her and then pulled off his boots and took off his pistols and laid down beside her. He fell asleep in no time.

~~~~

Michael rounded up everyone and had the saloon back open for business as usual in no time. A few customers noticed the blood on the floor in a couple of places but they never said a word. He did not play the piano as he knew Sean and Maggie were sleeping.

Sean awoke in a couple of hours. While he had been sleeping, he had also been thinking about how to handle the situation. Maggie was still asleep. He kissed her on the cheek and slipped out of bed and put on his boots. He put on his pistols and came downstairs. He went to the regular table and asked Betty if she would bring him something to eat. She returned with some food shortly. When she handed the plate to Sean, he asked her to set with him for a few minutes. "We lost the baby," said Sean holding his tears back. "We didn't want anyone to know until she was showing or it was totally obvious."

Betty got a blank stare on her face and then started crying. After a few minutes, she got control of herself. "You kill them sons a bitches," said Betty. "I'll help you if you need me."

"Thanks Betty. You can help me by makin' sure Maggie does what Doc says till she's better," said Sean. "She might think she needs to be out here all the time and such before she's ready."

"I'll take care of her," said Betty. "I am so sorry Sean. I am so sorry."

"Doc says she'll heal good and things'll be all right later," said Sean. "Now would you get Michael over here. I got an idea."

Michael was there in a few minutes. "That second bunch is s'posed ta be here on the next stage," said Sean. "I'm gonna have Clem meet them and tell them all he knows and then that bunch'll leave and make their campsite and meet up with that last bunch. We should be able to find their campsite and maybe we can set up a good ambush for them."

"Do you think that Clem'll do this?" asked Michael. "You can't trust a man like him."

"The only thing a man like Clem trusts is money," said Sean. "I'm gonna offer him $2000 to kill Judge Lucas. He'll do it for the money, but also I'll tell him that if he don't, I'm gonna find his momma and kill her. I know where his sister is too."

"You think he'll believe that?" asked Michael.

"I think he will," answered Sean. "He watched me hang his men and when I tell him that these men caused the death of my unborn child, he'll know I mean it."

"Oh Lord, I didn't know about Maggie," said Michael. "What can I say. I am deeply saddened by this. Is Maggie all right?"

"Doc says she will be fine in no time," said Sean. "She wasn't far along. We weren't gonna say anything till she was showin' or it was obvious. We'll both be fine, but I will get my revenge. Lucas is goin' ta hell where he belongs. His men are goin' with him. Now I'm goin' over to the jail and tell Jon what I have planned. Then me and Clem'll have a nice talk if I can get him awake."

Sean went to the jail and told Jon his plan. Jon thought it was a good idea. I'll leave Dog here with you," said Jon as he was leaving. "I reckon Jeb's over with Maggie now. Is she all right?"

"We lost the baby," said Sean. "We didn't tell anyone about it. She wasn't far along. She'll be all right according to Doc."

"I am so sorry," said Jon. "We gotta kill these sons a bitches."

"We will," said Sean. "We will. Now would you go get them bodies we left out there? This next bunch is s'posed ta find a camp site west a town. Where we hung them boys would be a good spot for'em. If I was lookin' for a camp site, I would use that spot. If I'd known that they was gonna be campin' to the west, I wouldn't've left them bodies out there. Strap'em to some horses and try to cover up any sign as best you can. Tell the undertaker he'll have some more business."

As Jon was about out the door, the undertaker showed up. "They said I could find you here Mr. O'Rourke," the undertaker said. "I didn't think I should bury that man with that knife stuck in his head. I couldn't pull it out so I had to saw his skull open some more. Here's the knife. I thought it might belong to you or one of your men."

"That was nice of you to do that," said Sean. "But that is not our knife. It was his."

"Oh well, someone might make good use of it anyway," said the undertaker. "I'll be going now."

"I'll have two more customers for you in a short while," said Sean. "Jon there'll be bringin'em to you. I'll get you paid."

"Will there be any more customers in the near future?" the undertaker asked.

"If I was you, I'd figure on seven more in about three days," said Sean.

"Business is business," said the undertaker. "I'll take it wherever I can get it." Then he handed Sean the bowie knife and left.

"Seems that man's got a profitable business," said Jon. "I'll be leavin' now. Be back shortly."

~~~~

After Jon left, Sean cold see that Clem was still out of it, and he decided he needed some coffee. "Dog, you keep an eye on things here," said Sean. "Don't let nobody through that door that you don't know." Sean walked back to the saloon and got some coffee.

"Everything all right?" Michael asked him.

"Yep, just needed some coffee," said Sean. "I'll be goin' back to the jail now. If you see Jason, tell'em I need to talk to him for a few minutes."

"I will," said Michael. Sean went back to the jail.

He finished his coffee and leaned back in the chair and put his feet up on the desk. He thought he heard Clem stirring. "You awake in there Clem?" asked Sean. "I'll get you some coffee if you want."

"I could use some," mumbled Clem.

"Well sit tight, and I'll be right back with some," said Sean. Sean was right back with the coffee as he had said.

"How you feelin' Clem?" Sean asked.

"Like I drank a little too much," Clem answered. "You got me drunk didn't you?"

"I furnished the whiskey. You did the drinkin'," said Sean.

"You gonna kill me now?" asked Clem.

"I told you I was a man a my word, and I said I wasn't gonna kill you if you answered my questions," said Sean. "You did that so I'm not gonna kill you, but you're gonna do some things for me."

"What makes you think I'll do what you want?" asked Clem.

"I'll tell you why there Clem," Sean began. "I sent a telegram to some friends a mine in Kentucky. They know where your momma is. If they don't hear from me in a couple a days, your momma will be with the angels."

"So you'd have my momma killed," said Clem.

"Without battin' an eye," said Sean. " That Bo fella caused the death of my unborn child. You fellas came here ta kill us. I'll be sendin' that bunch a yours ta hell where they belong."

"You said I had to do some things for you. What are they?" asked Clem.

"When that next bunch gets here on the stage, you're gonna meet with their leader out in the street and tell him you know all they need to know," Sean began. "Then you're gonna help'm git his horses, and then he's gonna get out there and find that camp site and git them horses to Purdue. Tell'em you'll be out in three more days. We'll have ten guns on you, and we'll blow you to hell if anything looks funny. You'll be carryin' your pistol but it won't be loaded."

"What if he wants to get somethin' ta eat or a drink while he's here?" asked Clem.

"Him and his boys can get a meal but no drinkin'," said Sean. "If he asks where your other boys are, you tell'em they're at their hotel room, and you gave'em orders to stay there till this second bunch left."

"I reckon I can do that and not get killed," said Clem. "Now what else is there?"

"Well you're a man who likes easy money," said Sean. "That's why you been doin' what you do. I got a proposition for you and if you don't do it, it'll be like the other thing. Your momma dies."

"Well what is it?" asked Clem.

"You're gonna kill Judge Lucas for me," said Sean. "I'll give you $2000 to do it when we're done with Purdue. I'll give you half when you leave here and you'll get the other half when it's done."

"I s'pose if I take off with the $1000 and not do the job, you'll kill my momma," said Clem.

"You s'pose right there Clem," said Sean.

"Maybe I don't love my momma a thousand dollars worth," said Clem.

"I believe you do," said Sean. "If you did take off and not do the job, besides your momma dyin', I'll hunt you down and kill you. I'm very good at that. I'll get your sister too."

"I reckon I'll do what you want," said Clem. "Now can a fella get somethin' ta eat here?"

"Dog, keep an eye on things. I'll be back shortly," said Sean.

~~~~

When Sean left the jail and headed to the saloon, he saw Jason and went to talk with him.

"Jason, I'll be needin' a little help in a couple days or so," said Sean.

"Sure Sean, anything, what do you need?" asked Jason.

"I'll have a man in jail and I'll need someone to keep an eye on him while me and the boys are out after some no goods," said

Sean. "Could be an over night thing. You'll need ta keep'em fed
and such. You'll need ta be armed and anybody tries ta get in that
jail that you don't know, you give'em a warnin' and then shoot'em
if you hafta. I don't think that'd happen cause I don't think any
of'em are in town yet, but I want you ta be careful. Keep your son
away from the jail. Don't let your wife come over there either. Tell
you what I'll do. I'll borrow Billy's dogs, and they can be there with
you. Sam and Susie are good dogs. Talk nice to'em and they'll take
care a you."

"Just get me when you're ready for me Sean," said Jason.
"That man in the jail won't be goin' anywhere while I'm on watch."

"Thanks Jason," said Sean. "I'll see you in a couple a days."
Then Sean went to the saloon and got a plate of food for Clem and
some more coffee.

"This is some good stuff," said Clem as he was wolfing down
the food. "Someone's a damn good cook."

"Yes they are. Now you finish up and just lay back and relax,"
said Sean. I got a chamber pot here if you need it. You won't be
goin' out to no outhouse. We'll get that pot dumped in the
mornin'. I'll get you out a little while before that stage gets here so
you can move a little and get stretched out. You can spend the
night dreamin' about how you can spend $2000."

Clem never said one word after he finished his meal. He set
the plate and the spoon under the bars and went over to the cot
and laid down. He was asleep in no time. Michael came over when
it was his time to relieve Sean. "Nothin' goin' on," said Sean. "He's
asleep now and he's gonna do what we want. He's got a chamber
pot in there, and he's been fed so he don't need nothin'. See you
in a few hours."

Jon was already back and had delivered the bodies to the undertaker. "I cleaned up the sign as best I could," Jon told Sean. "Nobody but a full blooded Indian would be able to tell if someone had been out there. Not some reservation Indian either."

"That's good," said Sean. "Ole Clem's gonna do what we want. Now all we gotta do is wait on that next stage."

"Now how'd you get Clem to go along with you?" asked Jon.

"I told'em I know where his momma is, and I'll have her killed if he don't," said Sean. "He's also gonna kill Lucas for us."

"Now why would he do that?" asked Jon.

"Same reason," answered Sean. "He thinks I'll kill his momma if he don't. Plus I offered him $2000 to do it."

"Money can be a persuader," said Jon. "What'r you gonna do with that bowie knife?"

"I figured I'd give it to Jesse if he wants it," answered Sean.

"Well if he don't want it, I'll take it," said Jon. "That's a good lookin' knife, and that Bo fella took care of it looks like. That undertaker didn't scratch it one bit when he sawed ole Bo's head to get it out."

"All right, it's yours if Jesse doesn't want it," said Sean. "Now I believe I'll check on Maggie."

~~~~

Maggie was awake and anxious to know what Sean had figured out. "Have you got a good plan darlin'?" asked Maggie.

"I do darlin'," answered Sean. "If everything goes as planned, there won't be no gunplay tomorrow. Clem'll tell that second group what they want to hear and they'll get outta town. Then they'll meet up with their boss. I just need ta find their campsite and ambush'em either there or as they head ta town."

"So how many of them will there be?" asked Maggie.

"Only seven," Sean answered. "We'll get'em killed. Between me , Michael, and Jon, we'll have no problem. Dog'll be with us too. Jeb'll be with you and Jesse'll be here too."

"You know darlin'," said Maggie. "I think one of the reasons you are so good at what you do is that you are so confident in yourself. There are seven of them and three of you, and you are positive that you will get it done. Most men would worry a good bit about the odds."

"Maggie darlin', I am confident. I always have been confident when it comes to just about everything," said Sean. "If a man's got no confidence, he won't be long for this world. Now how are you feelin'? Do you need anything? Are you having any pain? Can I get you something ta eat or drink?"

"I'd like some food and some hot tea," said Maggie.

"All right, I'll get it for you," said Sean. "I can't remember you ever drinkin' much tea though."

"I just got the urge for some," said Maggie. "I haven't had any for a good while so I thought I'd have some."

""I'll be back shortly," said Sean. "Jeb, you stay right here."

Sean went to the kitchen and got a plate of food for Maggie. Cookie looked at him a little funny when he asked for some tea and he had to look around and make sure they had some, but they did. "Go ahead and take the plate to Maggie," said Cookie. "I'll run the tea up to her when it's done."

"Much obliged," said Sean. Sean took the plate to Maggie and she ate like she hadn't eaten for a while. Cookie made it up with the tea before she had finished the meal.

"Sorry the tea took so long Maggie," said Cookie. "I didn't want to leave too many tea leaves in it for you."

"Thanks Cookie, you're always the gentleman," said Maggie.

Maggie finished her food, and then Sean went downstairs and had himself a meal. He and Michael had a drink of whiskey afterwards. Jesse came over to the table and had a drink too. "Well boys, we'll let ole Clem outta jail a couple hours before the stage is due. I'll give'em his gun to wear but it won't be loaded of course. I'll have'm go out in the street when the stage gets here and meet the leader of that second group. We'll be all round'em where we can't be seen, and if anything don't look right, we'll kill'em. I told'em that second group could get a meal if they wanted, but no drinkin'. Then they git their horses and go find that campsite and then go get Purdue. Me'r Jon'll find the campsite and get back here and tell the rest. Then I'll figure out the best way ta get'em killed. I'll let Jon know everything when I spell him at the jail after a bit."

"Your plan sounds good," said Michael. "Now if ole Clem doesn't cross us, it'll be all right."

"Clem won't cross us," said Sean. "He likes money better'n he likes them other fellas. You can bet on that."

"Jesse, that undertaker cut that bowie knife outta that man's head cause he didn't think he should bury'm with it stuck there," said Sean. "He give it ta me. Do you want it?"

"No, I don't need no knife that big," said Jesse. "I think Jon wants it. Give it ta him."

"That's what I'll do," said Sean.

~~~~

Sean gave the knife to Jon and relieved him at the jail and filled him in on everything. Everything was quiet that night. The next morning after all the men had their breakfast, Sean got Clem out of jail and let him go over to the saloon to eat. Then he let him walk around a bit to get loosened up. About a half hour before the stage was due, Sean gave Clem his gun belt to wear and explained everything to him again. "Now I'll go over this one more time," said Sean. "When that stage gets here, you will stay in the street and meet the leader of this next group. You will tell him that you know everything they need to know, and then you'll help him get his horses. If he wants ta get a meal for him and his men while they're here, that's all right, but absolutely no drinkin'. We'll be all around you. Anything looks the least bit funny, you and that other fella will be dead. Won't be no hesitatin'. We'll just open up. They'll be ten of us watchin'. Do you understand?"

"I'll do my part," said Clem.

~~~~

Sean had Jon on the roof of the General Store and Michael was on the roof of the stage depot. Jesse was in the saloon, and Sean was sitting in a chair in front of the newspaper office. Sean didn't have ten men watching, but Clem didn't know that. Clem was in front of the saloon waiting. When the stage pulled into town, Clem went out into the street toward to stage depot. When the stage stopped, five people got off. First was an older woman and then an older man, probably her husband. Then Fred, Ted, and Mike got off. Fred saw Clem in the street and went over to him. Ted and Mike stayed back. "Everything all right?" Fred asked Clem as he got closer.

"Everything's all right. I know everything we need ta know," answered Clem. "We can get them horses now, and you can be on your way."

"Me'n the boys'd like ta get somethin' ta eat while we're here," said Fred. "What's a good place?"

"That saloon over there's the best eatin' in town," said Clem. "But no drinkin' and they make you check your guns when you go in there."

"Are you serious?" asked Fred. "I never did hear nothin' about no place makin'a man check his guns. We'll see who checks guns and who don't."

"I'm tellin' you right now that if you go in there, you'll check your gun," said Clem. "We don't want no trouble. Do you hear me?"

"Yeh, sure I hear you," said Fred. Then he motioned for the other two to come over and they headed to the saloon.

Jesse had heard most of the conversation, and he told Tom and Betty to be ready for some trouble. Clem came through the door first and took his gun belt off and laid it on the bar and then took a seat at a table. The other three stopped at the sign and just stood there looking around. Fred went over and sat down next to Clem. The other two followed and sat down. Tom and Betty both slid their shotguns up over the bar and pointed them at the table. "Hey mister, you that checked your gun," said Tom. "You best get away from that table. We don't wanna shoot you by mistake." Clem got up and moved to the bar out of the field of fire. Tom and Betty both cocked the hammers on their shotguns. Jesse had his pistol out and pointed it at Fred as he cocked the hammer.

"I'm gonna ask you one time real nice like to lay your gun belts up on the bar," said Tom. "If you do as I ask, We won't shoot you. Now would you fellas please lay your gun belts on the bar?"

"I reckon we will," said Fred. "I never argue with a scatter gun when it's pointed at me. Give'em up boys." One at a time, the three of them laid their gun belts on the bar and then went back to the table. "I hope your food is good," said Fred. "I wouldn't a wanted ta get shot if the food was bad."

"We got the best food in town mister," said Tom. "They're fixin' pork chops and taters and beans today. Got fresh baked bread too."

"Well serve it up," said Fred. "All a us'll have a plate."

"Now what's this bout no drinkin'," said Fred. "Nothin' wrong with me gettin' a drink."

"There'll be no drinkin', period," said Clem. "When Purdue says you can have a drink, then you can have a drink."

"I reckon I'll just have some coffee then," said Fred. "They'll be plenty a time for drinkin' and some whorin' when this job's done."

~~~~

They all ate their meal and drank their coffee without any more bad words or trouble. When they were finished, Fred even told Tom to tell the cook that this was the best meal he had eaten since he left home. Tom returned their gun belts and the four of them went to the livery and got the horses. Fred didn't ask Clem once where his men were. The three men left town heading west and once they were out of sight, Sean got Clem and put him back in jail. Clem didn't object or complain.

~~~~

Sean and his men met back at the saloon. "Jon, I want you to track them three and find their campsite," said Sean. "They will probably head for the stage station tomorrow to meet Purdue. They'll probably leave one man at camp when they go. Make sure you're not spotted. Maybe you can take the one they leave. That'll be one less for us later."

"You forget sometimes that I'm half Cherokee," said Jon. "They won't see me."

"I would bet a hundred dollars that they'll be campin' where we hung them boys ," said Sean. "That'll really work out good for us. Jesse, how bout you watchin' the jail for a while? Ole Clem just got fed, and he's got a chamber pot, and we put a bucket a water in there for'em. He won't need nothin'. Dog'll be with you too. Anybody shows up you're not sure about, give'em a warnin', then shoot'em. I'll spell you later. Let Dawn know what you're doin' and tell her ta stay away from that jail."

Clem was sound asleep when Jesse got to the jail. Jesse found an old newspaper to read and made himself comfortable. Dog looked content.

Jon took off tracking the three men. Sean was right. The campsite the three men picked was right where Sean had hanged the others. They set in for the night and the the next morning at daylight, they had their breakfast and two of them headed for the stage station. When they were out of sight, Jon circled around the lone man and tied his horse in the trees along the stream just a little west of the man. Jon slipped up on the man with no problems. Ted was sitting by the fire sipping coffee when Jon cracked him on the head with the handle of the bowie knife. While he was unconscious, Jon threw him across his horse and tied him to it. He put out the fire and then led Ted's horse to where his horse was tied. Then he led both horses into the stream so there wouldn't be any tracks. He rubbed out the tracks from both horses and his boot prints. Then he mounted his horse and led the other horse and stayed in the stream for another mile before heading back to town. When they were a couple of miles from town, Ted came to. "Just who in the hell are you?" Ted started yelling.

After a few minutes, Jon stopped and dismounted. He went to Ted's horse and stood there staring at Ted. Ted was tied with his belly down and ropes went under the horse's belly tying his hands and arms to his feet and legs. Sean grabbed Ted by the hair and raised up his head so Ted could see him. "I'm one of the men you were sent here to kill you son of a bitch," said Jon. Jon didn't let Ted say one word. He pulled out the bowie knife and cut Ted's throat clear down to the bone. Blood went everywhere. Jon mounted and went on in to town. He took Ted to the undertaker and then reported to Sean.

"Well Sean, you were right," started Jon. "They camped right where you said they would. Two of'em took off this mornin' for the station, and I got the other one for us. He's at the undertaker right now."

"Good work Jon," said Sean. "So they'll be back at the camp-site later tomorrow. We got plenty a time ta figure things out. Now I'll go see Clem for a while. I got a question for him." Sean headed to the jail. On the way there, he ran into Jason. "I'll be needin' you tomorrow mornin'," said Sean. "We'll be after them no goods and if all goes well, we'll be back before dark or early the next mornin'. I doubt you'll have any trouble in town, but remember what I said. Keep your boy and wife away from that jail and don't let nobody in that you don't know or aren't sure of."

"I'll do my best for you Sean," said Jason. "I'll be ready."

~~~~

Sean left Jason and went to the jail house. Jesse was at the desk and Clem was laying on his cot but he wasn't asleep. "I got one more question for you Clem," said Sean.

"Yeh, what is it now?" asked Clem.

"I need ta know what Purdue looks like," said Sean. "I wanna know for sure which one he is when I kill'm."

CHAPTER SIXTEEN

"Purdue'll be easy for you to spot," said Clem. "He's a big man, mebbe six foot three, medium build, dark hair and mustache, and always wears a big brown hat. He's a lot taller than them others. He fancies himself a gunmen but I never seen'm draw on nobody. I seen'm shoot people but only in the back or when they weren't 'spectin' it."

"Did he shoot Judge Simmons?" asked Sean.

"Yep, he did," answered Clem. "I seen'm put a couple in his wife too. He was there when Sam Draper got kilt too."

"You helped kill both of'em, didn't you?" asked Sean.

"Yep I did," answered Clem. "I felt bad bout'em killin' that woman, but that's what we was paid for. I never put no slugs into her. Purdue always told us if we didn't do as he said, he would kill us. He must notta noticed that I didn't put no slugs inta that woman or I'd be dead. I heard he had his own men killed durin' the war if they wouldn't go along with his doins'."

"Sounds like you picked yourself a good boss," said Sean. "We'll be goin' out ta kill Purdue and them others in the mornin'. I'll have a different man watchin' the place. He'll kill you if you try anything or if anybody else does. If somethin' happens ta him, I'll kill you and your mother and your sister."

"You'll have no trouble from me," said Clem. "I intend ta stay right here and sleep the whole time."

"That's good," said Sean. "Jesse, I'll be over at the saloon talkin' with Jon and Michael. Someone'll spell you after a while."

~~~~

Sean went over to the saloon and had a meeting with Jon and Michael at their regular table. "We'll be leavin' at daylight," started Sean. "I wanna be out there well before they get get there. Both a you take your Sharps and your repeatin' rifles and your pistols and plenty a ammunition. We'll get out there to the west away from where they'll be. That way they won't see no fresh tracks. They'll probly get there a little before dark and wonder where the hell that one fella is, but it'll be too late to do much lookin'. They'll keep a man on watch all night. I figure ta steal their horses and take out the man on watch. Dog'll be with us. Come daylight, we'll pick some good spots and when they all get up and give us some good targets, we'll open up with our Sharps. Maybe we'll get lucky and get three of'em with our first three shots. Clem said a couple a them boys was sharpshooters durin' the war. One of'em was s'posed to even be in my unit at some time. If them boys was sharpshooters, they'll know what they're doin'. Once you shoot, you better move. They'll spot your smoke easy out there. Soon as we can, we'll move in on'em. We might hafta do a lotta crawlin'. There's a lotta open ground even down by the stream and around them trees."

"Do you want any of'em taken alive?" asked Michael.

"I want'em dead," answered Sean. "Any of'em left alive when this is over is gonna be hung. I would like ta look Purdue in the eyes when I kill'm, but as long as he ends up dead, it don't matter."

"We'll get'em killed," added Jon.

"I'm gonna go over to the livery and talk to young Billy," said Sean. "I wanna borrow his dogs tomorrow. I want'em ta be in the jail with Jason. I'll see you boys later."

~~~~

Sean went over to the livery. Billy was there with Susie moving some horses around. "That dog sure knows what she's doin'," Sean said to Billy. "Where's Sam today?"

"My uncle borrowed him so he could breed him with his dog," answered Billy. "He'll be back home in a few days."

"Well I'd like ta borrow Susie for tomorrow if you don't mind," said Sean. "I got a prisoner in the jail and Jason's watchin' him for me. I'd feel more comfortable if Susie was with'm."

"Sure that'll be all right," said Billy. "She knows Jason pretty good, and she'll help'm keep an eye on things."

"I'll be gettin' her at daylight," said Sean. "If things go well, she'll be back before dark or early the next mornin'. See you in the mornin'." Then Sean went over to Jason's store and told him he'd need him at daylight, and Susie would be with him.

~~~~

When Sean got back to the saloon, he was surprised to see Maggie setting at their table. "What're you doin' outta bed darlin'?" Sean asked her. "Did Doc say you could be up and about?"

"I feel fine," said Maggie. "I'm tired of doing nothing but laying around. I won't do anything that'll hurt me. Thanks for your concern. Now let's get something to eat."

Sean went to the kitchen and came back with their food. "What would you like to drink now darlin'?" asked Sean. "They got fresh coffee on and Cookie says he'll get you some tea if you want."

"Coffee'll be fine," said Maggie. Sean brought them some coffee, and while they were eating, he told Maggie what was in store for tomorrow.

"You keep Jeb with you at all times when I'm gone," said Sean. "And keep a pistol on or near you too."

"I'll be fine while you're gone darlin'," said Maggie. "Jeb'll be with me, and Jesse and Tom and Cookie'll be here. Betty can shoot too. We'll all be worried about you men. I'll be hoping that when this is over, that'll be the end of it. Now I have a question for you darlin'. Once that Judge is dead and a new Judge is appointed, will you go back to being a lawman again? That is, if they ask you."

"I've thought about that too, and I don't know if I would or not," said Sean. "It's kinda nice not being a lawman at times, but I'm not a lawman now and I'm doin' just what a lawman would be doin'. I reckon I'll make up my mind once it happens."

"Well you are a darn good lawman, and it won't bother me any if you go back to being one," said Maggie. "I'll do my worrying as usual. If you weren't a lawman, there'd still be some old enemy around. You've got a reputation with those pistols of yours. Sooner or later, somebody'll want to know if they're better than you or not. Now let's talk about something else. How's the progress on Walter's shop coming?"

"He'll be up and runnin' in no time," said Sean. "There's gonna be so many new places around here I won't be able to remember who's who. The railroad is gettin' closer, and they keep workin' on the cattle pens. It'll be interestin' when the first drive gets here. I hope we see Jug come spring or summer. I bet he's doin' good if the Comanche haven't bothered'm."

"Lolita's a good woman too," said Maggie. "Jug did good when he got her."

~~~~

That night, Maggie and Sean stayed wrapped in each other's arms the whole night. About an hour before daylight, Sean got up and dressed to leave. Maggie woke up, and he bent down to kiss her. "I love you Maggie," said Sean. "I'll be back before dark or the next mornin'. Jeb, don't leave Maggie's side." Then he went downstairs and grabbed some coffee and a biscuit and rounded up his supplies. He went to Billy's and got Susie and took her over to the jail where Jason was waiting. "You two already know each other," said Sean. "Now remember what I said Jason. Keep your son and wife away from the jail. Anybody shows up that you don't know or aren't sure of, give'em a warnin' then shoot'em if you hafta. If Clem here gives you any trouble, kill'em. I hope ta be back before dark."

"I'll take care of things here Sean," said Jason. "You just be careful out there."

"We will Jason," said Sean as he was leaving. Sean went back to the saloon and Jon, Dog, and Michael were out front with all the horses and ready to go. "Looks like you boys are ready," said Sean. "Let's get movin'."

~~~~

It didn't take long to get to where they were going. There was a high rise on their side of the steam, and they stopped to come up with a plan. "They'll come in from the east," said Sean. "We'll stay to the west so they won't see any fresh tracks. We can keep the horses down behind this rise or we can tie'em in the trees a few hundred yards from where they'll be. We can wait up here and see what they do. Then we'll figure out where to put ourselves for in the mornin'. Should be some good moon tonight."

"Let's just leave the horses behind the rise," said Jon. "I'll take'em down to the steam shortly for a drink so they won't be thristy and then bring'em back and hobble'em loose and let'em graze. Dog'll make sure they don't wander off. Then we'll tie'em good for the night."

~~~~

When Jon took the horses for water, Sean got out his spyglass and looked around. The rise they were on was about five hundred yards from the tree where Sean had hung the other men. From this rise, Sean could see for almost a mile to the east and west. He could also see several hundred yards on the other side of the stream. He spotted some down trees that would be good spots for the men. They were maybe three hundred yards from the hanging tree. One was upstream and one was downstream. He would place Michael at one spot and Jon at the other. Sean would stay on the rise so he could see everything.

Jon returned with the horses and then hobbled them loosely behind the rise so they could graze. Now all they had to do was wait. After a while they had a meal, but no cooking fire. They just had a biscuit and some jerky. Finally about an hour before dark, Sean could see the six riders approaching. They were a little down wind of the riders and they could be heard talking as they approached their campsite. "Just where in the hell are you," they could hear one of them yelling. "Ted, Ted, where are you?" he kept yelling. Then they all dismounted, pulled their pistols and started looking around.

"I don't see no tracks or no sign at all," yelled Fred. "His horse woulda left some tracks. You don't s'pose some Injuns got'm do ya?"

"I don't figure any Injuns are this far east," said one of the others. "But mebbe they don't know that they aren't s'posd ta be here."

Then the big man in the group spoke. Sean could tell that this was Purdue, but he couldn't hear what he was saying as he wasn't yelling. "Could be some renegades done this, but I got me a feelin' that O'Rourke's around. He spent some time with the Cheyenne and one a his deputies was half Cherokee," said Purdue. "It's too late to do any trackin' tonight so we'll look in the mornin'. I want them horses tied good and a man on guard. Take two hour shifts and no smokin'."

"Can we have a fire and cook some supper?" asked Fred.

"May as well," answered Purdue. "Chances are that whoever done this knows we're here anyway. Might as well have some hot food."

Sean watched through the spyglass as the men finished their meal and then bedded down. Their horses were tied in the trees not far from them and one man stood guard. "We'll go ahead and get a little sleep ourselves," said Sean. "In about four hours, Jon can slip down there with Dog and get their horses and take out the guard if he can. Then when they wake up at daylight, you two will be behind them down trees and I'll be up here. It would be nice if they was all standin' up at the same time so we can get us a good shot. If you do get a good shot, take it. And remember to shoot and move."

The four hours rolled by and the men were awake. Jon and Dog slipped down to the campsite. Apparently the guard decided to ignore Pudue's orders and he lit up a cigar. Jon spotted him easily and made his stalk. The man had no idea that Jon was there when Jon split his skull open with the butt of his Sharps. Then for good measure, Jon slit his throat with the bowie knife. Then he decided to scalp him so maybe they would think that Indians had done it. The others were snoring away when Jon and Dog left with their horses.

When Jon got back to Sean, Sean took one look at what Jon had in his hand and knew that Jon had scalped the man. "That was probly a good move," said Sean. "Scalpin' makes most folks a little edgy. There's only five of'em now. Odds are gettin' better. Now you and Michael get to your spots. Got a good while till daylight but if one of'em would wake up before then, we might get us a shot since we got some good moon ." Michael and Jon went to their positions. Dog stayed with the horses.

No one in the camp stirred till daylight. Fred had gotten up and was relieving himself when he noticed that the horses were gone and no one was on guard. He ran around and woke up the others. "The horses is gone, and I didn't see Mike no where," said Fred. They were all looking around when Purdue spotted Mike.

"That fool couldn't do without a cigar for a while," said Purdue. "See what it cost him." Just as Purdue was bending over to pick up the cigar and show the men, a shot was heard and a bullet zipped by. Sean had taken aim on Purdue and just as he had squeezed the trigger, Purdue bent down to pick up the cigar. Purdue would have been a dead man if it weren't for that cigar. The men scrambled for their weapons as shots from Jon and Michael came in. No one was hit.

Sean reloaded the Sharps and waited for a good target. He spotted one of the men taking aim with a Sharps. Sean could see the telescopic sight on the Sharps. It looked like he was sighting in on Michael. Sean didn't have a good shot at him as he was mostly behind a tree, but he fired anyway. He heard the man let out a yell when the bullet struck his rifle. The bullet hit the rear sight of the rifle and ricocheted up and tore the telescopic sight off the rifle. Sean could hear the man cussing. The man threw the rifle down, pulled his pistol, and stayed low. Sean could only see the man's legs from the knee down, but he sighted in and fired. The man screamed as the bullet crushed his left knee.

Jon spotted the other sharpshooter and took aim. He saw the dirt fly next to the man's head and knew that he had missed. He moved to his left and found a good position behind another tree. The sharpshooter had seen Jon and was taking aim when a bullet from Michael's Sharps tore into his neck. Sean decided it was time to switch from the Sharps to the Winchester. He took the Winchester and worked his way closer, firing as he went. At about a hundred yards he started firing into the camp as fast as he could. When Michael and Jon realized what Sean was doing, they switched to their repeaters and did the same. As Sean was reloading, he could hear someone from the camp yelling. "That's enough. Quit shootin'," he yelled. "We had enough."

Sean and the men quit firing. Sean waited a few minutes and then yelled. "I wanna see all a you standin' with no guns on you and your hands on your head," he yelled. "Michael, Jon, you cover'em, and I'll ease down that way. If one of'em even twitches, send'em ta hell." There were only three men standing when Sean got closer. One of them was Purdue and Fred was another one.. Sean didn't know the other standing man or the other two who had been hit. The man who had been shot through the neck was dead, and the one that Sean had shot through the knee was bleeding terribly. Sean looked down at him.

"Don't you recognize me Captain," the wounded man said. "I was in your unit right before you became Sherman's aide."

"You look a little familiar," said Sean. "Just what in the hell'r you doin' with this bunch? Didn't you get enough killin' durin' the war."

"I got to where I was numb to it," the man said. "I figured I might as well get paid doin' it."

"Well if you don't bleed to death in the next few minutes, I'm gonna hang you," said Sean. "Michael, you and Jon tie up them others. This big fella here is Purdue. We'll save him for last." While the others were being tied up, the man who had been shot through the knee, bled to death. Sean tied Purdue to a tree while the other two were being thrown up on horses to be hanged. Sean made nooses on two ropes and threw them up over the same limb that he used for the others and tied them off at the trunk. He placed the nooses around their necks. "You fellas got any last words before I send you ta hell?" asked Sean.

"We'll see you in hell," one of them said.

"I already been," said Sean as he slapped the horses on the rump.

"Purdue, I'm gonna ask you some questions before I kill you," said Sean.

"So what makes you think I'll talk to you?" said Purdue.

"I think you're the kinda man who likes ta hear himself talk," said Sean. "Now I wanna know. Was Lucas Anderson's boss?"

"Hell no, he wasn't," answered Purdue. "Anderson never took no orders from nobody. Him and Lucas just worked together."

"Did you enjoy killin' Sam Draper and the Judge?" asked Sean.

"It was just a job," answered Purdue. "I got paid, and I did it."

"Are you ready ta die?" asked Sean.

"Course not, nobody is," said Purdue.

"I hear you fancy yourself a gunmen," said Sean. "Is that true?"

"I'm damn good with a pistol," said Purdue. "There's nobody alive now that can say otherwise."

"That's true," said Sean. "Men who were shot in the back and men who were shot in the front and not expectin' it are not here ta speak up."

"Let me loose, and we'll see," said Purdue.

Sean checked both of his pistols to make sure they were fully loaded. Then he handed one of them to Jon and had him place it on the ground about twenty feet from him. The other pistol he put back in his right holster. "Michael, you untie Purdue and stand aside," said Sean. Michael untied Purdue and stepped aside. "Purdue, you go over and pick up that pistol and hold it down to your side. I will not shoot while you do this. Whenever you're ready, you try to shoot me." Purdue hesitated for a moment and then went over and picked up the pistol. His eyes never left Sean the whole time. "That's good," said Sean. "I want you lookin' in my eyes when I kill you."

Purdue never said a word. He just stared into Sean's eyes. He tried to raise the pistol to fire but before it was halfway up, Sean had put three holes in his chest. Purdue was thrown flat on his back but somehow he was not dead yet. The pistol was still in his hand, but he couldn't raise it. Sean walked over to him and looked into his eyes. "This is for my unborn child you son of a bitch," Sean said as he put a bullet into Purdue's forehead. "Lucas'll be joinin' you shortly."

No one said anything for what seemed like five minutes, then Michael spoke. "Sean darlin', I have seen you shoot so many times, and I know I have said this before, but I believe that you are getting faster," said Michael.

Sean never said a word. He took the pistol from Purdue's hand and put it back in his holster. Then Sean let down the hanged men and rounded up the horses. Then he spoke. "I must be gettin' soft," said Sean. "Used ta be I'd leave these fellas out here for the buzzards and the coyotes. Now I'm takin' em to the undertaker."

"Well Sean, he's gotta make a livin'," said Jon. "He probly gets tired a waitin' on someone ta die."

"Well check their pockets and belongins', and we'll sell their guns and horses as usual," said Sean. "Let's get back. I miss that woman a mine."

~~~~

When they got back to town, they went to the undertaker first and dropped off the bodies. Then they stopped at the saloon and unloaded their gear. Maggie was downstairs and came out to meet them. Betty and Martha was there too. "I missed you darlin'," said Sean as he went to Maggie and kissed her.

"I missed you too darlin'," said Maggie. "Did you send them to hell?"

"Yes we did darlin'," answered Sean. "Now I'll go tell Clem that his boss is dead." Sean went to the jail and Jon and Michael took the horses to the livery. Jason had seen them as they came into town and was standing in front of the jail. "Didn't have any trouble did you?" asked Sean.

"Not one bit," answered Jason. "Clem there slept almost the whole time. He just woke up."

Sean went into the jail and went to Clem's cell. "You boss is dead," said Sean. "He's in hell where he belongs. Tomorrow you'll be on the stage to Kansas City. You'll be in here till the stage is ready to go. Now I'm gonna go spend some time with my wife. Jason, would you stay here till I get someone to relieve you?"

"No problem. I can stay as long as I'm needed," said Jason. "Susie don't mind either."

Sean went back to the saloon and got himself a drink. Maggie sat with him. "Darlin', how'd you like to soak in that tub a yours for a while?" asked Sean. "I think that'd be nice."

"Finish your drink and let's go," said Maggie.

"Finish it hell. I'll take it with me. Let's go," said Sean.

Sean got a fire going and the water was heated in no time. "Doc says we can't be doing it just yet," said Maggie. "But it will feel good to have your body against mine. I have missed you terribly."

"I wasn't gone that long this time and I missed a you a bunch too darlin'," said Sean. "I love you Maggie."

"I love you too Sean darlin'," said Maggie.

A couple of hours later, they were dressed and eating a meal. Then they went to bed. They both slept the whole night through. Sean woke first about an hour after daylight and then remembered that he had to get Clem on the stage. "You stay in bed Maggie," said Sean. "I gotta go get Clem on the stage, then I'll be back and we can get some breakfast." Sean got dressed, put on his pistols and then kissed Maggie goodbye.

Sean went to the bank first and got the money for Clem and then he went to the jail. "All right Clem, I'm lettin' you out now," Sean said. "Stage leaves in a half hour. I'll take you to the saloon and you can have some coffee and a biscuit. Here's $1000." Clem's eyes lit up when he saw the money. It was in big bills. He rolled it up and put it in a pocket. Here's your gun belt too. Put it on. There's no bullets. With $1000 you can get all the bullets you want somewheres else."

They went to the saloon and Clem had his coffee and a biscuit. The stage was ready when they walked out the door of the saloon. "Now I expect ta hear somethin' about that Judge being killed in the next three weeks," said Sean. "If I don't, you know what'll happen. If I hear that you run your mouth to anyone about this, you know what'll happen. If anything that's not s'posed ta happen, goodbye momma and sister. Now git on that stage." Clem never said a word as he got on the stage.

Sean walked back in to the saloon. Michael and Jon were there drinking coffee. "So you think he'll do it?" asked Jon.

"I do," answered Sean. "I think he really thinks I'll really kill his momma and sister. Now what's for breakfast today?" Sean went to the kitchen and told Cookie to get something ready for Maggie and him, and then he went upstairs to get Maggie.

~~~~

Two weeks went by and everything was quiet in town. Jesse was healing fast and had told Sean that when he was healed, he and Dawn would be going to the Nations to visit her kin. The only excitement that happened in town was one night when some drunk kept calling Jesse boy. Jesse had asked him nicely to stop, but the man persisted. Jesse put a few bumps on the man's head.

One morning the next week, Sean and Maggie were at their table having breakfast when Phil Downs ran into the saloon. Mr. O'Rourke, I have a headline and a story that I think you should see before the edition comes out. You'll be the first one in town to read it."

"All right, hand it here," said Sean. The healine went as follows:

Second Federal Judge Murdered

Federal Judge Clarence Lucas was murdered in his office by an unknown assailant. The assailant was killed in the exchange of gunfire between himelf and Lucas's two body guards. It appears that Judge Lucas was shot first, two times in the head and died immediately. Both body guards were killed. One died at the scene and the other died an hour later on the operating table. He was never able to speak. It is believed that the assailant was a hired killer because he had a very large sum of money in his possession at the time of his death.

Sean thanked Phil for the news but didn't say another word till Phil was out the doors. "Well the son of a bitch got it done," said Sean. "Now we'll see what happens."

"Yes, now we'll see," said Maggie.

Here ends The Sean O'Rourke Series, Book 3, *O'Rourke's Revenge*. Continue reading for a preview of The Sean O'Rourke Series, Book 4, *O'Rourke's Law or no Law at All*.

The Sean O'Rourke Series

Book 4

O'Rourke's Law or No Law at All

by

Michael E. Cook

CHAPTER ONE

Another month and a half rolled by and according to Doc Rawlins, Maggie was as good as new. Maggie and Sean were spending a lot of their time together and everyone expected her to announce sometime soon that she was with child. Jesse had healed well, and he and Dawn were on their way down to "The Nations" to visit her father and uncle. Jesse assured Sean that he would always be there for him if the need arose. Jon was still with Martha but nothing was ever mentioned about the two of them doing anything permanent. Cookie and Barbara still acted like they were newlyweds and Michael and Betty were not seen from time to time. Construction continued for the new businesses and the railroad got closer.

It was now the summer of 1866 and the warmer weather seemed to slow everyone down some. That is everyone except some of the Southern Cheyenne. Several raids had been done in western Kansas and several people had been killed. Black Kettle did not want to fight with anyone, but he couldn't control the "Dog Soldiers." Every treaty that the Cheyenne had signed up to this point had been broken, and some of his young men were tired of it. More and more white settlers were screaming for protection by the Army. Two colored cavalry regiments, the 9th and 10th were formed. Many white folks did not believe the colored troops could handle the job. Those white folks were proved wrong many times over the years.

George Custer was offered the rank of full Colonel if he would take command of one of the newly formed colored cavalry regiments, but he did not want to command colored troops. Instead, he went to the newly formed 7th Cavalry at Ft. Riley Kansas as a Lt. Colonel. Sean was never in the Army of the Potomac, but he had heard of Custer's reputation. Custer was not afraid to lead his men in a charge, and although his units always had high casualty rates, Sean knew that Custer's recklessness helped end the war. Sean also knew that the tactics of a regular army would not work against the Cheyenne or any tribe for that matter. The people of Abilene were not worried about the raids yet because they were happening farther to the west for now.

Another month rolled by and it was still quiet in Abilene. Sean and Maggie were having breakfast one morning at their regular table when a telegram came for Sean. The operator came running into the saloon all excited and yelling for Sean. "Marshal, Marshal, this here's an important telegram," he cried. "You'll be surprised when you see who it's from."

"All right, calm down there fella," said Sean. "Don't be callin' me Marshal anymore. Name's Sean. Now gimme that telegram." The operator stood there waiting for Sean's reaction. The telegram went as follows:

Sean O'Rourke
Abilene Kansas

O'Rourke<<stop>>with   Seventh   Cavalry   Fort   Riley Kansas<<stop>>understand you lived with Cheyenne several years<<stop>>would like to employ you as Chief Scout for campaigns against Cheyenne Arapaho and Sioux

George A. Custer
Fort Riley Kansas

"Well what do you think a that darlin'?" Sean asked Maggie. "The boy General wants me to scout for'm against my old friends."

"What do you mean by boy General?" asked Maggie. "I heard he was just a Lt. Colonel."

"He is a Lt. Colonel now but they called him the boy General during the war," answered Sean. "He was the youngest Brevet General during the war. I heard he was only 22 or 23 at the time. He made Brevet Major General near the end of the war."

"What is a Brevet General?" asked Maggie.

"Well during the war, some men get temporarily promoted to higher ranks," said Sean. "They're needed durin' the war, but when it's over the army downsizes and all them Generals aren't needed. They made Custer go back ta bein' a Captain when the war was over. I think he was a Captain when they made him a Brevet General. I'd say it really hurt his pride. I heard he's a real ambitious man. I even heard that he wants ta be President of these United States someday. Couldn't give me that job."

"So what are you going to tell Mr. Custer?" asked Maggie. The operator was still there waiting for Sean' response.

"That's easy. Just send Custer a big "NO", said Sean.

"Are you sure this is what you want me to send?" asked the operator. "Custer's a famous man. He might not take kindly to you being that blunt."

"You let me worry about what Custer might think and send what I told you," said Sean. The operator mumbled something to himself and left.

After a few minutes, Maggie could see that Sean was doing some thinking. "What is it darlin'?" asked Maggie. "You're not worried about Custer. You're worried about the Cheyenne aren't you?"

"Yes I am," answered Sean. "If I was Black Kettle I'd probly fight and get all my people killed. There's too many white folks and more comin' west all the time. The Cheyenne and all the tribes are gonna end up gettin' brushed aside. Their way a life is gonna be over soon and nothin' I can do'll change that. The buffalo herds'll get wiped out, and farmers and cattle ranchers'll take the land. Sooner or later the tribes'r gonna end up on some reservation dependin' on hand outs from white folks who don't wanna give'em hand outs. You mark my word. One day they'll even take the reservations away from'em."

"There's an awful lot of buffalo out there," said Maggie. "Do you really think white folks can kill that many of them?"

"They'll kill'em for hides and once they understand that the buffalo is the main food source for the plains tribes, they'll kill'em to help starve the tribes," said Sean. "This'll happen darlin'. Not right away, but we'll see it happen before we have any grandkids."

"So you're expecting some grandkids someday," said Maggie. "We can't have any grandkids without kids first so maybe we better go work on that."

"Sounds good Maggie," said Sean. "I'd rather be in the throws of passion with you than thinkin' about what I was thinkin'."

"Throws of passion," said Maggie. "I've never heard you say that before. It sounded good. Let's get to that throwing."

~~~~

"I don't know about you but I think we did some pretty good throwin'," said Sean when they were finished. "I know it's early, but I feel like soakin' in that tub with you."

"Sounds good darlin'," said Maggie. "Let's go."

~~~~

After they had been soaking for a good while, Maggie could tell that Sean still had something important on his mind. "I can tell by just being here with you that you have something on your mind," said Maggie. "Tell me about it. Maybe I can help ease your mind if there's something that's troubling you."

"It's not really troubling me," responded Sean. "I just been thinkin'. It's been some time since Lucas got himself killed and and we haven't heard one thing about him gettin' replaced. When Lucas got the job real quick, we thought it was odd. Now it's been all this time and that seems odd too."

"Well darlin', it could be that no one will take that job right now," said Maggie. "Two Federal Judges killed so close together like that. Maybe anybody they have in mind is going to investigate and try to find out what actually happened and why. We have no idea how many people knew that Lucas was a crook. Anyone who did know probably won't say anything because they might be incriminated too."

"You could be right darlin'. No one'll say anything," said Sean. "I would expect some sort of investigation if I was gonna take a job where two men ahead a me got themself killed. All this thinkin' is makin' me hungry. Let's get dressed and see what Cookie and Barbara got goin' today. Whatever it is, I know it'll be good."

~~~~

Sean was right. The food was good. Cookie had made some venison cooked slow with onions and mashed potatoes and gravy and some greens. Barbara had added some spices and gave it a little bit of a kick. There was even apple pie for dessert. Sean and Maggie ate their fill. It was Saturday and there was always a huge crowd on Saturday. The place would start filling up early afternoon and stay full till the wee hours of the morning. Cookie and Barbara always had everything ready and were ready for the crowd.

About two hours before dark, three men that Sean had never seen before came into the saloon. With all the new things going on in town, new faces didn't bother Sean, but there was something about these three. When they entered the saloon, they stood at the sign that said to give your weapons to the bartender. The three of them stood there talking among themselves until Michael approached them. "Do you men need any help reading the sign?" Michael asked them.

"We don't need no help," one of them said. "We just never been no place that made you give up yer guns."

"That goes for knives too," said Michael. "Now if you're comin' in, please take your hardware over to the bar. If not, please remove yourself from this establishment."

"Damn, he said please," the one who had spoken earlier said. "Since he said please, I reckon we'll give'em up. Let's take'em to the bar boys. I'm getting' thirsty." The three of them took off their gun belts and handed them to Tom.

"You'll get these back whenever you're ready to leave," said Tom. "Now what'll you have? There's a table over there. Have a seat if you want and I'll bring it to you."

"Give us some rye whiskey and three glasses. Name's Carl," the man said. "We'll be over at that table."

"Comin' right up," said Tom. Carl paid for the bottle and the three men sat there quietly and sipped their whiskey. Michael went over to Sean.

"Let's keep an eye on those three," Sean said to Michael. "I just got me a feelin' about them. They're not slammin' down their whiskey so it looks ta me like they wanna stay sober for a spell."

"Well they turned in their weapons without too much fuss," said Michael. "I'll stay over by the piano and keep an eye on them. If I see Jon before you do, I'll tell him too."

"They did turn in their gun belts but they could still have some weapons tucked away," said Sean. "We don't frisk anyone who comes in here. We rely on people's honesty. Trouble is, not everyone is honest." Maggie was still there with Sean. "Darlin', you make sure Jeb doesn't leave your side and make sure you're armed," said Sean.

"I'm always armed," said Maggie. "The only time I don't have a pistol on me is when you and I are making love or in the tub. Then there is always a pistol close by. You know I keep a pistol right beside my side of the bed."

"I know that," said Sean. "Sorry I seem edgy. I just got me a feelin' about them three fellas. Hope it's nothin'."

"Me too darlin'," said Maggie. "Sure would hate to have any trouble in here tonight with this big crowd."

~~~~

A couple of hours rolled by and the three men were still drinking from the same bottle. A very well dressed middle aged man sporting a fancy cane now entered the saloon. Sean could tell that the three men's eyes never left that man. The man walked up to the bar where Tom was waiting. "I do not carry any weapons," said the man. "My name is Robert Sharpton. Could I get a glass of some Irish Whiskey?"

"You surely can Mr. Sharpton," answered Tom. "We always try to keep some Irish Whiskey on hand. Our owners fancy it."

"And who might the owners be?" asked Robert.

"Well you see that big Irishman over at the piano and that red headed beauty with that handsome dark haired man at that table over there," said Tom as he pointed towards Sean's table. "Well this place belongs to the three of them."

"Is that painting on that wall over there the same woman at that table?" asked Robert.

"Yes it is," answered Tom. "That's Maggie and the place is named after her."

"She's uncommonly beautiful," said Robert. "I'll make it a point to meet her while I'm in here this evening."

"That won't be a problem," said Tom. "Maggie always goes around and mingles with the customers. Excuse me Robert. Got another customer."

When Tom went to wait on the other customer, Carl left his table and came up behind Robert. Robert could tell that something sharp and pointed was against his back. "You and me are gonna turn around and walk outta this place like everything is all right," Carl whispered to Robert.

Sean could see that Carl had come up behind Robert, but he couldn't tell exactly what was happening. The other two men that were with Carl were up now and heading for the door but they still kept their eyes on Carl and Robert. Michael and Sean saw the two men moving. Michael was closer so he went to the door to stop the two men.

Robert had no intention of going with Carl and he moved a little away from him, turned, and without saying a word, he cracked Carl on the head with his cane. Carl went down and when he did, a knife fell from his hand. When the other two men saw Carl go down, they both pulled small pistols that they had hidden in their boots and pointed them at Robert. Before they could get their hammers cocked, they were both falling backwards with holes in their chests. Sean stood there with the smoking pistol in his hand. Carl was up now and was reaching for something that was stuffed in his pants. Michael saw him reaching for something and didn't hesitate. His bullet passed through Carl's chest and struck next to the mirror behind the bar. Carl hit the floor dead. Sean checked to make sure all three of them were dead.

"Are you all right mister?" Sean asked Robert. "Seems those three wanted to do you harm."

"I'd say you were right," said Robert. "I have no idea who those men were and why they would want to harm me. My name is Robert Sharpton and you must be Sean O'Rourke. I have heard about you and your reputation. I see what I have heard is true. I thank you for saving my life."

"Glad to be of service," said Sean. "We don't like it when bad things happen in our place. So you say you have no idea who those men were and why they would want to harm you."

"That's mostly true," said Robert. "I'd like to have some words with you when you have the time, but first I'd like to meet that wife of yours. She's uncommonly beautiful."

"Maggie, this gentleman would like to meet you," Sean said as he waved for Maggie to join them. "Maggie, this is Robert Sharpton. Robert, this is Maggie." Robert took Maggie's hand and kissed it.

"I am so pleased to finally meet you," said Robert. "I have heard about you for a long time and what they say about you is not quite true. You are more beautiful than I have heard."

"Thank you for your kindness," said Maggie. "I am glad that you are not hurt."

"That big Irishman over there that shot this one fella is Michael O'Connor," said Sean. Michael walked over to Robert and extended his hand. They shook.

"I'll get some help and we'll get these bodies out of here," said Michael. Jon walked in and walked over to Sean to see what had happened.

"I just took Dog out to do his necessaries, and I come back in and there's three dead men in here," said Jon. "What did I miss?"

"Jon, this well dressed fella is Robert Sharpton and Robert, this is Jon O'Brien," said Sean. Jon and Robert shook hands. "These three were tryin' ta do harm ta Robert here. They're dead and he's not."

"Well all right," said Jon. "I'll help get these bodies outta here. Don't shoot anyone else while I'm gone."

Jon and Michael drug the bodies outside and then they had some more men help take the bodies over to the undertaker. The undertaker apparently was asleep in the back of his shop so they just laid the bodies on his back porch. They went through the dead men's pockets and found nothing that would identify them. They did have $500 between all three of them. "That's a good bit a money ta be carryin' around," said Michael. "I reckon sooner or later we'll find out what they were up to."

"Maybe they was hired ta kill that Robert fella," said Jon. "Maybe he's somebody important or rich or somethin' and someone wanted'm dead."

"Well let's tell young Sean about the money and such," said Michael. "The buryin' fund's gonna make some more money looks like. These three probly had horses too."

When Jon and Michael got back to the saloon, Robert and Sean were sitting at Sean's regular table enjoying some Irish Whiskey. Michael and Jon went over and joined them. "Those three had $500 on them all told and there was nothin' that would identify them," Michael said. "We'll find out tomorrow if they had horses or not."

"What will you do with that money?" asked Robert.

"It'll go into the bank with the buryin' fund," said Sean.

"What's the buryin' fund?" asked Robert.

"Well sometime back I started it," Sean began. "Whenever we kill an outlaw, we take whatever money was on him, sell his horse and guns, get'm buried, and then put what's left in the buryin' fund. If the next outlaw killed don't have any money or anything, we use the fund to get'm buried."

"That sounds reasonable," said Robert. "Most folks would keep all that money."

"I don't need it," said Sean. "What with this place and reward money and money made from a cattle drive, I would probly never hafta work another day in my life if I didn't wanna. Last reward money we got, I give to Jesse Strong. He's not here now. He was a deputy for a short while. Just a short while back he took his wife down to "The Nations" ta visit her relatives. Jesse is a colored man and his wife is Osage."

"I don't care what color a man is," said Robert. "If he worked for you, he must be a good man."

"He sure as hell is," said Sean. "And he is about the strongest man I ever did see. He took a bowie knife and rammed it into the top of a man's skull and the tip was stickin' out below the man's chin."

"Damn, I just bet that he was a blacksmith too," said Robert.

"Yep, he was," said Sean. "He worked on a big horse farm in Kentucky before the war. He was in the 54th durin' the war too. Ended up in the cavalry, and he can shoot too. He killed two men in a gunfight not long ago. Anyway, let's get this place livened up some. Michael, how bout playin' somethin' fast on your piano. Maybe someone'll get up and dance."

"I'll see if I can get anyone movin'," said Michael. Michael went back to his piano and started playing. Jon grabbed Martha and started dancing. Then a few other men grabbed some girls and joined in.

"Now Robert, you said somethin' earlier about it being mostly true that you had no idea why them three fellas would want to harm you," said Sean. "Now just what did you mean by mostly true?"

"Mr. O'Rourke, you and I need to have a very private conversation," began Robert. "What say we meet here for breakfast. It is just too crowded in here now and our conversation must be private."

"That's fine by me," said Sean. "Now I'm concerned for your safety tonight. Do you have a hotel room?"

"No I do not," said Robert. "I got onto town late and I wanted to come right here first."

"Well I have a room for you out back," said Sean. "I'll have Jon's dog stay with you. That's Dog over there watchin' Jon dance. I can assure you that with Dog in your room, no one will get in there and live to tell about it."

"So that dog is named Dog," said Robert. "What's the name of the other dog that goes everywhere Maggie goes?"

"That's Jeb," said Sean. "He's me and Maggie's dog. We got him and Dog from the Hawks. They was usin'em as cow dogs. The Hawks won't need'em anymore. Ole Jeg and Dog have both ripped out some men's throats. Jeb here bit a man's hand clean off. You won't hafta worry bout Dog. I'll get you two introduced. Be nice ta Dog and he'll be nice ta you."

When the song was finished, Jon and Dog came back over to the table. "Jon, I'd like ta borrow Dog here ta spend the night with Robert." said Sean. "He's stayin' in your old room out back."

"In that case I better introduce Dog to Robert," said Jon. "Dog, this here is Robert. You'll be in his room tonight. Don't let nobody else in there unless you know'em."

"Did Dog understand what you just said to him?" asked Robert.

"Yes he did," said Jon. "Won't nobody get in your room that you don't want in there." Robert reached over and petted Dog.

They made friends right off. "Dog just did his necessaries so he'll be good for the whole night," said Jon. "Whenever yer ready ta turn in, just tell'em ta c'mon and he'll go with you."

~ ~ ~ ~

Robert finished his drink and told Sean that he would see him for breakfast. Dog went with him and slept at the foot of the bed. Nothing happened during the night.. Robert woke up right after daylight and Dog was standing beside the bed staring at him. "I suppose you need to go out for a minute," said Robert. "All right, you go on out and I'll be out in a minute." When Robert came out the door to go to the saloon, Dog was there waiting for him. He and Dog went to the saloon together. Sean, Jon, and Michael were at their table drinking coffee.

"I guess you had a good sleep," said Sean. "Dog looks like he had one too. Have some coffee. Breakfast'll be ready shortly." Robert joined them at the table and Michael got Robert some coffee.

"I did sleep good last night," said Robert. "Haven't slept that good for a long time. Now I suppose you want to know why I need a private conversation with you."

"It's been on my mind some," said Sean. "And if you haven't figured it out yet, these two men were my deputies so anything you say here will be considered private."

"I figured that these two were your deputies," said Robert. "I'll get right to the point. I am here of my own free will to investigate the killings of the two Federal Judges. Now before we on, can we go ahead and eat breakfast? I haven't eaten since yesterday afternoon and I'm famished. I didn't feel like eating last night with everything that had happened."

Cookie brought them all out some ham and eggs and fresh coffee. Not a word was spoken while they ate. Then Michael spoke.

"Why did you say that you were here of your own free will?" asked Michael.

"I have been selected as the new Federal Judge. No investigation has been ordered so I'm doing one myself," said Robert. "I have heard rumors about Lucas and I would like to know if they are correct or not."

"Well I don't know what you've heard," said Sean. "Lucas was a thief and a murderer. He had Dave Simmons killed so he could be my boss. I have no idea how a man like that got to be a judge in the first place."

"Well let's go back to Dave Simmons," said Robert. "When did you first meet him and how did you become his Marshal?"

"It was durin' the war," started Sean. "I had killed some deserters who had murdered a civilian family. They was raping a dead woman when I killed'em. I was takin' their bodies back to the Commanding General when I met Dave. He was a General's aide. He musta been impressed with what I'd done. He found out all about me. He said he was a Federal Judge and asked me ta be a Marshal after the war."

"The way you were talking, It sounded to me like you knew that family that was killed," said Robert.

"I knew'em," said Sean. "I was raised in that part a Tennessee. That woman they raped was gonna be my wife after the war. We was childhood sweethearts and got back together when we was fightin' over that way."

"Sorry for your loss," said Robert. "Please continue."

"Well I took the Marshal's job," started Sean. "Spent a lotta time killin' the Hawks and the Anderson bunch. Found out they worked together some. Ever once in a while, one a them outlaws would tell us that Anderson had a boss. There was several attempts on my life this whole time. Anderson had put $2000 on my head and we heard that his boss put up another $2000. After we got Anderson killed, things slowed down some. Then we got sent to Kansas City. Every public official in that town was corrupt. We knew there was a bigger boss somewhere. One day we got a telegram from the Judge tellin' us that some border gang was causin' trouble over east and when we were on the trail, we found out that Dave had been killed. I figured it couldn't have been Dave who sent that telegram so we got back to town. Nothin' was goin' on. Then my friend Sam Draper got killed. Then we got a telegram from a Judge in Kansas City tellin' us that a Bo Billings was headed our way and there were three other men on the stage with him. Bo was wanted for murder in three states."

"So what happened next?" asked Robert.

"Well we found out them four was together and was part of a group of eleven killers who were comin' here ta kill all a us." said Sean. "We found out about the other ones and who their boss was, and we got'em killed. We also found out that Lucas was their boss."

"I'll not ask how you managed to find all this out," said Robert. "So do you have any idea who might have killed Lucas?"

"I'd say one a his own men did it," said Sean. "If he was a big a crook as they say. Maybe one a his men decided he wanted a bigger share of the action. Maybe Lucas didn't wanna share anymore and the man killed'em. I don't know. Just guessin'. We heard he was doin' a lotta black market stuff durin' the war. We heard he even had his own men killed. Maybe someone finally got even with'm."

"I have hear rumors about his war time experiences too," said Robert. "If any of it is true, then Lucas did have some friends in high places and probably still does. Maybe those three men who you killed yesterday work for such men."

"So you think it's possible that those three men were after you because you might know somethin' about Lucas, and who worked for him and who got him appointed?" asked Sean.

"It's possible," said Robert. "A man would have to know some powerful people to get himself appointed as a Federal Judge. Those powerful people would have the President's ear."

"So are you worried that if you take the job you'll get killed too?" asked Sean.

"No, I'm not worried about getting killed," said Robert. "I was in the war too. I commanded an infantry battalion most of the war. Got shot up a couple of times. My wife died right after the surrender so I'm not worried about making some woman a widow. All I really want to know is what I'm up against. I hate corruption, especially when the corruption is by men who were placed in positions of trust by their fellow citizens. I intend to make it my personal duty to clean up any corruption that I find."

"Good luck with that," said Sean. "I imagine that some places were just a terrible mess after the war. Some politicians want revenge for the war and others just want us all to be brothers again. I think we been lucky out here so far. Haven't even heard anyone around here call someone a carpetbagger."

"Let's move on to some other things," said Robert. "I know Judge Simmons told you to hang George Anderson when you caught him, but did you hang any other men without being told?"

"Yes I did," answered Sean. "I hung some a the Hawks and that Sheriff in Kansas City. I also hung some a that bunch that was sent here ta kill us by Lucas."

"And you feel that you had the authority to hang them?" asked Robert.

"Weren't nobody else around to do it," said Sean. "They was all guilty a murder and it needed done. I did it. You got a problem with that?"

"I could be removed from the bench for what I'm going to say," said Robert. "If you will become my Marshal, I will want you to do just what you've been doing. One day we will have more law and more courts and such but right now we don't. For the time being, we need a quick and firm hand. When I accept my appointment next week, will you be my Marshal?"

"I have thought about this for a good while," said Sean. "Maggie will go along with whatever I do. She knows that even if I weren't a lawman, there would always be trouble from an old enemy. Yes sir Robert, I'll be your Marshal," said Sean. "I can't speak for Michael and Jon though."

"I reckon we've gone this far with you Sean darlin'," said Michael. "I reckon we'll go the rest of the way."

"I reckon we will," said Jon.

"I want to thank you men," said Robert. "After I'm sworn in I'll send a telegram. When you get that telegram, consider yourself sworn in again. Now let's have some Irish Whiskey and have a toast. I know it's early in the day yet, but a toast seems appropriate."

"Michael and me been doin' a special toast ever since the war," said Sean. "I think you'll like it." The glasses were filled and each man raised his glass. "Here's to not getting killed," toasted Sean.

"Here's to not getting killed," all of them repeated.

"That's a good toast," said Robert. "Now I'll be leaving on the next stage. I look forward to working with all of you. We'll have O'Rourke's law or no law at all."

Books by Michael E. Cook

The Sean O'Rourke Series

Book 1: A Killer For The Common Good

Book 2: A Killer For The Common Good—LAWMAN

Coming soon

Book 4: O'Rourke's Law or No Law at All

Available in paperback and eBook formats
at Internet retailers everywhere.

ABOUT THE AUTHOR

This is Michael E. Cook's third book of "The Sean O'Rourke Series. Book 1 took us through our young hero's early life in Tennessee, his life with the Cheyenne, the Civil War, and his beginnings as a lawman. In Book 2, our hero develops his skills as a lawman. We are now up to early 1866, and Michael continues the series hoping to bring you as a reader, right into the action. The era of the great cattle drives, the buffalo hunters, and the Plain's Indian Wars are about to start and our hero is right in the middle of it. The scars left from the war will not heal for a long time to come. The country is growing fast and the law cannot keep up. It will soon also be the era of the outlaw. The few lawman that there are must be dedicated hard men. The action can be fast and intense. Michael invites you to come along for the ride.

Contact the author at mailto:cookorourkeseries@gmail.com

www.ingramcontent.com/pod-product-compliance
Lightning Source LLC
Chambersburg PA
CBHW021942170626
46808CB00001B/3